TANGLED WEBS

A Novel of the Underdark

Elaine Cunningham

TANGLED WEBS

First Printing: April 1996
Printed in the United States of America.
Library of Congress Catalog Card Number: 95-62378

9 8 7 6 5 4 3 2 1

ISBN: 0-7869-0516-6
8557XXX1501

TSR, Inc.
201 Sheridan Springs Road
Lake Geneva, WI 53147
U.S.A.

TSR Ltd.
120 Church End, Cherry Hinton
Cambridge CB1 3LB
United Kingdom

FORGOTTEN REALMS

FANTASY ADVENTURE

**Books by
Elaine Cunningham**

Daughter of the Drow

Elfshadow

Elfsong

Silver Shadows
(Summer 1996)

ACKNOWLEDGMENTS

Thanks to editors Brian Thomsen, for his patience and good humor, and Marlys Heeszel, for carefully picking up the stray pieces of the story and dusting in all its corners. To game designer and sage Steven Schend, for Waterdeep, for shared obsessions, and for sending me care packages of gaming accessories and other much-needed background information. To Bob Salvatore, for his good-natured support of this project, for his generosity with both time and advice, and for the wonderful storytelling that drew me in to the FORGOTTEN REALMS in the first place. To Jim Lowder, who mid-wifed the characters way back when and who continued to encourage me long after he was obligated to do so. And to Bill, Andrew, and Sean, who will always be the reasons why.

DEDICATION

Fortunate indeed are those who can point to a remarkable teacher who made a real difference in their lives. I have been blessed with three. One of these is Jim Lowder, the extraordinarily supportive editor who worked with me on both *Elfshadow* and *Elfsong*, and whose influence will stay with me for as long as I continue to write. From time to time I still hear his phantom voice at my shoulder when I'm at the computer, envision his snide (okay, "incisive") comments written in red all over my manuscript margins. Strange though it might sound, this is a *good* thing.

For demanding more, for teaching me to edit myself, and for being there still as a friend when the solitude gets deafening and when I wonder why I ever thought I could write in the first place, this book is dedicated to Jim Lowder—with the condition that he puts away that damned red pencil when he reads it!

Thanks, Jim.

Chapter 1
SKULLPORT

ar below the streets of Waterdeep, in a cavern buried beneath the bottom of the sea, lay the hidden city that legend and rumor had named Skullport. Most of those who came here sought to trade in goods that were banned in civilized ports, and the dregs of a hundred warring races did business in an atmosphere of knife-edged danger. Yet beneath the streets of Skullport were even deeper realms, places that the most intrepid merchants strove to avoid. In one particularly noisome labyrinth—a series of winding tunnels and despoiled crypts—a dungeon had been fashioned for those who disturbed the tenuous balance of the city.

Once the burial place of a long-vanished tribe of dwarves, over the centuries these catacombs had become home to other, more dangerous creatures. From time to time, treasure hunters came seeking an undiscovered dwarven cache; most of these seekers remained as piles of moldering bones, giving powerful testament to the traps and monsters that lingered in the dank stone passages.

It was a forbidding place, even to a drow accustomed to walking the endless tunnels of the Underdark. Magical elven boots muted the sound of her footsteps, and a glittering *piwafwi* cloaked her with invisibility, yet Liriel Baenre kept keenly alert for possible dangers. To speed her way, she carried foremost in her thoughts the remembered face of the man imprisoned in this, the worst of Skullport's dungeons.

Slender as a human girl-child and seemingly not much older, the young drow appeared delicate to the point of fragility. Her black-satin skin gave her the look of living sculpture, an image that was enhanced by the supple, tightly fitted black leathers and ebony-hued chain mail she wore. She was beautiful in the fey manner of elvenkind, with fine, sharp features and a cloud of thick white hair as glossy as moonlight on new snow. Hers was a mobile face that

1

could be one moment impish, the next coldly beautiful, dominated by a pair of large, almond-shaped eyes the color of Rashemaar amber. These eyes spoke of a restless intelligence and an ever-ready supply of mischief. By all appearances, the drow girl hardly seemed capable of storming this deeply buried stronghold. And yet, that was precisely what she intended to do.

Liriel moved easily through the utter darkness of the tunnel. The gloom presented no problem, for the eyes of a drow could detect subtle heat patterns in the rock and the air currents. The eyes of a drow *wizard* were even more sensitive; in the tunnel ahead, Liriel perceived the faint, bluish aura—visible only to those who had inherent magical talent and assiduous training—that warned of magic at work.

The drow crept cautiously closer. The eerie glow curtained off the tunnel like a luminous sheet, but since it was a magical aura visible only to wizards, it cast no illumination upon the scene around it. Liriel debated for a moment whether to risk creating a true light and decided it might be wise to view the trap through the eyes of those who had created it. That it *was* a trap, she did not doubt for a moment.

As easily as thought, Liriel conjured a globe of faerie fire. The magical light bobbed in the air beside her, floating here and there in response to her unspoken directions and bathing the grim scene in faint white light.

Bones littered the tunnel on both sides of the telltale blue aura, tumbled haphazardly together with abandoned weapons and gear. The tunnel's floor and walls had been splashed repeatedly with gore, and the stone was caked with the dull, dark red of long-dried blood. Whatever the trap was, it had certainly proven effective.

Liriel's gaze fell upon a shallow, much-dented bronze bowl embossed with finely wrought designs and lined with ivory. It seemed strangely out of place among the grisly remains and the practical tools scattered around her feet, and the curious drow crouched to examine it. As she picked it up, the "lining" fell out—it was not ivory but bone, and too thick to be anything but the skull of a dwarf.

The drow settled back on her heels to examine this discovery. Something had sliced neatly through the dwarf's head, cutting through helm and bone so cleanly that the edges of both were as smooth as if they'd been ground and polished by a master gem-cutter. This told her much about the dwarf's death.

Liriel kicked through the scattered debris until she found a heavy thigh bone that had once belonged to a good-sized ogre. As she expected, the bone was severed near the upper joint, at just about the spot where a dwarf's head would reach if the two treasure-hunting fools had stood side by side. The drow rummaged through the pile, selecting similarly cut bones from the remains of several different races, and then laid them out beside each other. In moments she had a fairly precise idea of the trap's danger—and its limitations.

Liriel took up the ogre's leg bone once again. Keeping her hand well away from the magical danger zone, she thrust one end of the bone into the glowing aura. From either side of the tunnel wall, discs of gleaming blue whirled out from the solid rock. The spinning blades met, crossed, and disappeared back into the stone.

The drow regarded the bone in her hand. The tip had been sheared off, so quickly that she hadn't even felt the impact, so silently that the only telltale sound was the muffled clatter as the bone shard fell to the blood-encrusted rock.

Not bad, Liriel acknowledged silently, but too predictable. A drow wizard would have enspelled the blades for random attack, so that each strike would come from a different place. Or perhaps such a provision *had* been made to deal with those who might figure out the first attack and try to slip in under the trigger area.

Liriel picked up two more long bones, one in each hand, and held the first into the glowing aura. Again the blue discs sped from the tunnel walls. The moment they crossed paths through the first bone, Liriel thrust the second one down low. The blades continued undeterred along their course and disappeared into the rock. The second bone did not trigger the magical trap at all.

Too easy! Her lips twisted into a smile that mingled triumph with contempt. A drow would have expected a second intrusion—and a third!—and would have ensured that the blades could reverse their paths instantly to meet any challenge.

Now that she saw her way clear, Liriel triggered the trap one last time. The moment the circular blades met and crossed, she dove under their path and rolled through the portal to safety.

In Skullport and environs, however, "safety" was a relative term. As Liriel rose to her feet, she glimpsed a flicker of reflected light on the wall of the tunnel ahead. Something was approaching from a side passage. Instantly she summoned the innate drow magic of levitation and, still invisible, floated up to the tunnel ceiling some

3

twelve feet off the floor. She flattened herself against the damp stone to wait and observe.

A wisp of luminous smoke rounded the sharp bend, then recoiled as if surprised to find itself in an empty corridor. After a moment's pause the smoke came on, flowing around the corner until there was enough to form a small, glowing cloud. The luminous mass writhed and twisted, finally settling into a hideous, vaguely human shape. As Liriel watched, horror-struck, the wraithlike cloud solidified into decaying flesh. The undead thing looked this way and that, its red eyes gleaming in the darkness.

Liriel had never seen a ghoul, but she recognized the creature for what it was. Once human, it had been twisted into a mindless but cunning beast that fed on carrion. Somehow it had sensed that the magical trap had been triggered, and it had come to feed. This would account for the clean-picked bones that littered the tunnel. It did not, however, explain the ghoul's ability to take on a wraithlike form.

The ghoul shuffled around the passage, sniffing audibly and pawing the air with filthy, clawed hands. Liriel noted that it narrowly skirted the magical trap, showing a perception that only a gifted wizard could have possessed. As she studied the creature's movements, the drow realized that it was retracing her steps. It was following the invisible path left by her innate dark-elven magic. But *how?*

She thought fast. Without doubt, the undead creature had once been a wizard, probably talented enough to have prepared for an afterlife as a lich. If his plans had been altered by attacking ghouls, he might somehow have managed to combine the two transformations. If that were so, it meant the ravenous creature below her was armed with a lich's magic and a ghoul's terrible cunning.

Her own command of magic was formidable, but Liriel knew better than to fight this mindless, undead thing. In a spell battle, strategy was as important as power. Accustomed as she was to the multilayered intrigues of her people, she could not outthink a being that acted solely on hunger and instinct.

At that moment the ghoul looked upward, turning its red eyes fully upon Liriel's face. A long, serpentine tongue flicked out in anticipation, rasping audibly as it passed over the creature's fangs. The drow shuddered, though she was certain the ghoul could not actually *see* her. Her invisibility granted her little comfort, though, when the lich-ghoul's clawed fingers began moving jerkily through the gestures of some long-unused spell.

Liriel seized the leather thong that hung around her neck and gave it a sharp tug. Up from its hiding place beneath her tunic flew a small obsidian disk engraved with the holy symbol of Lloth, the Spider Queen, the dark goddess of the drow.

The girl clutched the sacred device and quickly debated her next move. Even a minor priestess could turn aside an attack by undead creatures, but Liriel had attended the clerical school for only a very short time and was accounted a rank novice. On the other hand, she was a princess of House Baenre—the most powerful clan in mighty Menzoberranzan—and she had left her homeland armed with the favor of Lloth and the captured magic of the Underdark. But Liriel had traveled far since then, in ways that could not be measured in miles alone. She found herself inexplicably hesitant to call upon the deity of her foremothers.

Then the lich-ghoul's lips began to move, spewing graveyard dust and foul spittle as it chanted soundless words of power. An unseen force closed around Liriel like a giant hand, pulling her down toward the waiting creature with a yank so sharp and sudden that her head was snapped painfully back and her arms thrown open wide. Her *piwafwi* flapped open, disclosing her to the undead creature. But Liriel managed to keep her grip on the sacred symbol, and with a drow's lightning-fast reflexes, she thrust it into the ghoul's upturned, slavering face.

"In the name of Lloth, I turn you," she said simply.

It was enough. Crackling black energy burst from the symbol and sent the undead thing reeling back. For a moment the ghoul huddled against the far wall, cowering before the revealed power of the drow goddess. Then its hideous body dissolved into smoke, and the wisps scattered and fled like a flock of startled birds.

Liriel heaved a ragged sigh and floated the rest of the way down to the tunnel floor. But her relief was mixed with vague, nagging misgivings. She had reason to know that Lloth was capricious and cruel. Fortunately, the ghoul did not bother to inquire into the goddess's character. Power was power, and Liriel was alive because she had dared to wield it. There was a certain basic practicality to this reasoning that quieted the drow's uneasiness and sped her steps. She once again drew her *piwafwi* close about her and glided silently down the tunnel, making her way unerringly toward the dungeons.

The drow girl had explored Skullport for several days now and had learned many of the city's secrets. She had reveled in Skullport's lawless freedom, its endless chaotic possibilities. But Liriel was young, and certain that her destiny lay across a vast sea on an island known as Ruathym. She was impatient to get on with it.

Her ears caught the echoes of a distant song, a rollicking tune sung with enormous gusto but little discernible talent. Liriel followed the voice, tracing the intricate path the sound took through winding passages and reverberating stone as effortlessly as a surface-dweller might follow a tree's shadow to its source.

Before long she came to a small, dank cave that in eons past had served as a crypt. Now a prison cell, the cave was secured by iron bars as thick as Liriel's wrist and a massive door that was chained and locked not once, but three times. The small stone chamber was cold, and lit by a single, sputtering torch that gave off more foul-smelling smoke than light. A few deep shelves, long emptied of bones and treasure, had been chiseled into one stone wall. On the opposite side of the cave was a plank bed, suspended from the wall by two rusted chains. And sprawled upon the bed was the singer, who kept time to his music by tossing bits of moldy bread to the creatures that scuttled about the floor of the cell.

The prisoner did not seem at all downcast by his grim surroundings. He was a giant of a man, deep-chested and broad of shoulder, with a face bronzed by the sun and wind, and bright blue eyes nearly lost in a maze of laugh lines. The man's braided hair, vast mustache, and long beard were all of the same sun-bleached hue, a color so pale that it almost hid the streaks of gray. This was Hrolf of Ruathym, better known as Hrolf the Unruly, a genial ship's captain with a taste for recreational mayhem. Liriel had learned that this rowdy pastime had gotten him barred from many civilized ports and had landed him—not for the first time—in Skullport's dungeons.

She reached into her pack and took out a statuette she'd purchased in a backstreet market: a roughly carved, rather comic rendition of a Northman skald with a horned helm, a bulbous nose, and a moon-shaped belly. It was not an impressive work of art, but some wizard with a sense of whimsy had imbued it with an especially powerful magic mouth spell, one that would capture any song and play it back, over and over, for nearly an hour. Liriel figured that an hour should just about do it. As she triggered the statue's magic, the wooden bard stirred to life in her hands. His tiny, bewhiskered face screwed up into an expression of intense concentration as he absorbed the lustily sung ditty.

6

"When you meet with the lads of the *Elfmaid,* my friend,
You would rather face Umberlee's wrath.
Hand over a measure of all of your treasure,
Or swim in a saltwater bath!"

"Come ashore with the lads of the *Elfmaid,* my friend.
We're awash on an ocean of ale!
Some taverns to plunder, some guards to sunder,
And then, a short rest in the jail!"

Liriel winced. Dark elves did not include ballads among their numerous art forms, but since leaving Menzoberranzan she'd heard many good songs. This was not one of them.

Even so, her slender black fingers flew as she shaped the spell that would lock the music into the statue's memory. The cost of a magic mouth spell was a small thing compared to the worth of the man imprisoned within the crypt. Hrolf was reputed to be one of the finest captains to sail the Sword Coast. He was also the only captain Liriel could find who was willing to take on a drow passenger.

With the song safely stored inside the wooden skald, Liriel silently removed her *piwafwi* and stepped into the circle of torchlight. She cleared her throat to get the singer's attention.

Hrolf the Unruly looked up, startled into silence by the sudden interruption. Liriel propped her fists on her hips and tapped her foot in a pantomime of impatience.

"So. When do we set sail?" she demanded.

A broad grin split the man's face, lifting the corners of his mustache and giving him a boyish appearance that belied his graying beard and braids. "Well, chop me up and use me for squid bait! It's the black lass herself!" he roared happily.

"A little louder, please," Liriel requested with acidic sarcasm as she cast quick glances up and down the corridors. "There might be two or three people up in Waterdeep who didn't hear you."

Hrolf hauled himself to his feet and walked stiff-legged over to the door of his cell. "It's glad I am to see you again, lass, but you shouldn't ha' come," he said in a softer tone. "Just a day or two more, and they'll be setting me free."

The drow sniffed derisively and bent down to examine the locks on the cell door. "Sure, if by freedom you mean a couple of years of enforced labor. It'll take you at least that long to work off the damage done to that tavern."

"Gull splat!" he said heartily, dismissing this dire prediction with a wave of one enormous hand. "The penalty for tavern brawls is never more than a few days' stay in this sow's bowels of a dungeon."

"The Skulls decided to change the law in your honor," Liriel responded, referring to the trio of disembodied skulls that appeared randomly in Skullport to pass sentence on miscreants. "The idea of waiting around for years doesn't appeal to me. I'd rather fight our way from here to the docks and have done."

"Not a bit of it," Hrolf insisted. "Laws are all good and well—fighting's better, of course—but *bribes,* now! That's the way for a sensible man to do business! And no place better'n Skullport for it, so don't you worry yourself. The *Elfmaid* came to port fully loaded. A bundle of ermine skins and a few bolts of fine Moonshae linen should serve."

Liriel cocked an eyebrow. "Did I mention that your ship and cargo have been impounded?"

That was true, as far as it went, and as much truth as the drow wanted him to hear. Although it appeared Hrolf's freedom was not for sale, Liriel had already managed to buy free the ship and the crew. She thought it better to let Hrolf think otherwise. By all accounts, the captain took his ship's well-being more seriously than his own.

"Took the *Elfmaid,* did they?" The captain pondered this development, chewing his mustache reflectively. "Well then, that's different. Fighting it is!"

The drow nodded her agreement. She quickly cast a cantrip, a minor spell that would reveal any magic placed upon the locks. When no telltale glow appeared, Liriel took a small bundle from her bag and carefully removed the wraps that padded a small glass vial. With infinite care she unstoppered the vial and poured a single drop of black liquid onto each of the chains and locks.

A faint hiss filled the air, and the locks sagged and melted as the distilled venom of a black dragon ate through the metal. It was a pricey solution, but it was quick and quiet, and Liriel had no real need to practice thrift. Just days earlier, she had led a raid on a rival drow stronghold and claimed a share of the massive treasure hoard buried there. Her share would take her to Ruathym in style, with enough left over to hide a cache or two for future use. Yet there was a strange tightness in Liriel's throat as she remembered the battle and the friends who had fallen there. One of those friends, although gravely wounded, had survived and was awaiting her even now on

8

Hrolf's ship. Just thinking of Fyodor, and his own great need to reach Ruathym, heightened her impatience.

Motioning for Hrolf to stand back, she kicked open the door, keeping a careful distance from the still-melting chains. Dragon venom could eat through boot leather—not to mention flesh and bone—as easily as it dissolved metal.

The captain watched, intrigued, as Liriel set the enspelled statue on the bed and triggered its song. His face lit up with pride as his own song poured forth from the little figure.

"That'll keep 'em away for a bit," he observed with a touch of wry humor. Obviously, Liriel concluded, the man held a realistic view of his musical talents.

Hrolf turned to regard the drow with obvious respect. "I was glad enough to offer you passage on the strength of your smile, but to be getting a ship's wizard in the bargain! With your magic, lass, we're as good as a-sail. May Umberlee take me if I'm not getting better at picking my friends!" he concluded happily.

Liriel cast a startled glance at the man's bluff, cheerful face. His easy claim of friendship struck her as odd. She'd met him only once, shortly before he'd begun the spectacular brawl that landed him in this predicament. He seemed a companionable sort, and she was glad to have found passage with an able captain who could also fight like a bee-stung bear. But friendship was still new to her and not something to be taken lightly. For a moment she envied these short-lived humans, who seemed to come to it so easily.

"We're still a long way from the ship," Liriel reminded the man. She stripped off the extra swordbelt she carried and handed it to him. He buckled it on without a word and then drew the sword, regarding its keen edge with pleasure. After a few practice swings to get the feel of the blade and to awaken muscles stiff from disuse, he followed the drow out into the tunnel.

The way was lit by an occasional torch thrust into a wall bracket, so Hrolf was able to walk with assurance, if not silence. The drow set a slow, steady pace, trying to minimize the noise of Hrolf's heavy footsteps. She could fight well when necessary, but she knew the wisdom of avoiding trouble. So far, despite the encounter with the magic-wielding ghoul, breaching the dungeon's defenses had seemed almost too easy. But then, no one expected anyone to try to sneak *in*. Liriel suspected that getting out would be another matter entirely.

A faint sound caught her ear. From a nearby passage came the

9

reverberating tread of many boots and the guttural speech of goblinkin. She pushed Hrolf into an alcove and shielded them both with her sheltering *piwafwi*. To her relief, Hrolf the Unruly did not protest this precaution or leap out roaring to engage the goblins in battle. The captain and the drow waited for many moments, then watched silently as the guards marched past in sharp formation.

They were squat, muscular creatures—goblin hybrids of some sort—broad as dwarves and haphazardly garbed in ill-fitting, cast-off leather armor. Obviously overfed and underpaid, the guards nevertheless carried a daunting assortment of well-honed weapons. All told, there were twelve of them, enough to give pause even to the dark-elven and the unruly.

The goblin patrol halted in the tunnel ahead, gibbering among themselves and shouldering off the packs they carried. Liriel muttered a curse.

"What're they doing?" Hrolf asked, his voice just above a whisper.

"Taking a break," she responded in kind. Whispering caused the voice to carry too far, and Liriel was frequently amazed that few humans seemed to realize this. Dark elves whispered when they *intended* to be heard—the audible equivalent of a knowing smile.

"They're blocking the tunnel," the drow added grimly, "and we don't have time to wait them out."

The captain pondered this for a moment, and then patted the short sword strapped to Liriel's hip. "I've heard tell that a drow can take a dozen goblins, easy."

The girl shrugged. She could handle a sword well enough and throw knives with deadly precision, but her skills were slanted more toward magic than mayhem. "Some drow can. I'm not one of them."

"Ah, but do yonder goblins *know* that?"

The drow snapped a look back at the captain, surprised that a human had offered such a devious—yet simple—solution. They shared a quick, companionable grin, and she accepted his plan with a nod.

Hrolf patted her shoulder, then drew his sword. "Go, lass. If the ugly little bastards don't spook, I'll be right behind you."

Against reason, despite the suspicious nature bred and ingrained in her by her treacherous kindred, Liriel believed him.

She pulled her sword and walked, silent and invisible, into the circle of goblins. Then, tossing back her *piwafwi*, she dropped into a menacing crouch and presented her blade.

"Hi, boys," she purred in the goblin tongue. "Want to play?"

The sudden appearance of a battle-ready drow in their midst stole whatever courage the creatures possessed. The goblins squeaked in terror and fled, leaving their packs and many of their weapons behind in their panic.

Hrolf strode to the drow's side, grinning broadly. "Well done! D'you think, though, that they'll be back—bringing friends?"

"Not a chance," Liriel said flatly. "They're guards, and they ran. If they admit that, they're as good as dead." The drow knelt and began to rifle through the abandoned packs, while Hrolf devoted himself to selecting a few promising weapons for his own use. Liriel's search yielded up several large, well-rusted keys. She smiled and brandished them at Hrolf.

The captain nodded happily, recognizing the significance of this find. He'd been dragged down to this dungeon through a succession of gates. The keys would speed their escape, though each gate was also guarded by magical traps and at least one species of ugly, well-armed creatures. Neither prospect worried Hrolf. Unlike most of his people, he held magic in high regard, and he'd seen enough of this elf maid's talents to entrust that aspect of the escape to her. As for the other—well, he had a sword now, didn't he?

* * * * *

Fyodor of Rashemen leaned against the rail of the ship, gazing out over the noise and confusion that was Skullport. Merchants, sailors, and dockhands milled about the rotting wooden docks, busying themselves with a dizzying variety of wares. Flocks of *wykeen,* a kind of sea bat indigenous to the underground port, wheeled and screeched overhead. The black water lapped at the ship with a restless rhythm that echoed the pulse of the far-distant seas. Yet there was no moon to order the tides, no sky at all but a soaring vault of solid stone.

This teeming underground city, so different from the villages of his distant homeland, astounded Fyodor. Most amazing to him was the peace that existed between ancient enemies, all in the name of trade. Dwarves tossed crated cargo to orcs; humans hired themselves out to beholders; svirfneblin bartered with illithids. It was just as well, this unnatural harmony. A nearby fight—any fight— could set him off on a deadly battle frenzy.

Fyodor was a berserker, one of the famed warriors of

Rashemen, a champion among the protectors of his homeland. Unlike his brothers, however, he could not control the rages or bring them on at will. When the Witches who ruled his land had come to fear that his wild battle-rages might endanger those about him, they sent him on a quest to recover a stolen artifact, an amulet known as the Windwalker. Its magic was ancient and mysterious, but the Witches thought it might be used to contain the young warrior's magical curse. Thus Fyodor's only hope for controlling his battle rages, and ending his exile from his homeland, lay in the amulet—and in the magic of the drow girl who carried it.

His search for the Windwalker had taken him from snow-swept Rashemen into the depths of the Underdark, where he'd met the beautiful young wizard. Liriel had been first an enemy, then a rival, and finally a partner and friend. Fyodor had followed the drow across half of Faerûn and would gladly travel with her to Ruathym— and not just for the magic she wielded.

The young man's eyes, blue as a winter sky, anxiously scanned the crowded streets. Liriel had arranged passage on this ship for them both and had promised to meet him here. She was late. He could imagine far too many things that might have detained her.

"Troubles?"

The laconic question jarred Fyodor from his grim thoughts. He turned to face the ship's mate, a ruddy, red-bearded man much his own size and build. Nearly six feet tall and heavily muscled, the sailor had the look of a Rashemi. Fair-skinned and blue-eyed, he had a certain familiar directness of gaze and an open countenance defined by broad planes and strong features. The sailor's resemblance to Fyodor's own kin did not surprise the young man, for they no doubt had ancestors in common. The ancient Northmen who'd settled the island of Ruathym had also traveled far east to Fyodor's Rashemen.

"Just wondering when we'd be off, Master . . ."

"Ibn," the first mate supplied. "Just Ibn. We sail with the captain."

Fyodor waited, hoping the man would elaborate. But Ibn merely pulled a pipe from his sash and pressed some aromatic leaves into the bowl. A passing sailor supplied flint and stone, and soon Ibn was puffing away with stolid contentment.

The young warrior sighed and then subsided. Clearly, he could do nothing but wait. Except for his concern over Liriel's delay, the waiting had not been unpleasant. The sights beyond the dock could have occupied him for hours, and the ship itself was well worth contemplating. The *Elfmaid* was an odd combination of old and new: her long, graceful form was reminiscent of the ancient dragonships, and she was clinker-built of strong, light wood. Yet the hull was deep enough to provide an area belowdecks for storage of goods and some cramped sleeping quarters. Castles—small, raised platforms—had been added both fore and aft, and both were hung about with the brightly painted shields of the warrior-bred crew. With its enormous square sail and row of oars, the ship promised to be both fast and maneuverable in any number of situations. Its most remarkable feature, however, was the figurehead that rose proudly over the lancelike bowsprit: a carved, ten-foot image of an elf maid. More lavishly endowed and garishly painted than any elf who'd ever drawn breath, the figurehead gave the ship her name as well as a playful, rakish air that Fyodor found rather appealing.

The young man also felt at home among the crew. They seemed to accept him as one of their own, even while showing him immense deference. Fyodor thought he knew the reason for that. He had heard that in Ruathym, warriors were afforded great honor and high rank. It would not be unlike Liriel to mention his berserker talents in an attempt to gain passage on a Ruathen ship. Fyodor did not object to this; it was better that the crew was forewarned. Since the Time of the Walking Gods, when magic had gone awry and his battle frenzies became as capricious as the wind, he had taken every precaution he could to avoid bringing harm to those around him.

The first mate took his pipe from his mouth and pointed with it. "Captain's coming," he observed. "Got company, as usual."

Fyodor looked in the direction Ibn had indicated. A huge, fair-haired man sprinted toward the ship, swinging a beefy fist back and forth before him like a scythe as he cleared a path through the crowd. Despite his size and his short, bandy legs, the captain set an incredibly fast pace. Behind him was Liriel, running full out, her slender limbs pumping and her white hair streaming back. Behind *her* roiled a swarm of knife-wielding kobolds.

"Step lively, my lads!" roared the captain as he swatted a bemused mongrelman out of his way.

His crew took this development stoically, going about their business with an ease and speed that bespoke frequent practice. Ibn cut the ropes securing the ship to the dock and then seized the rudder; the other men took their places at the oars. To Fyodor's surprise, the *Elfmaid* shot away from the dock, well beyond the reach of the

13

captain and his drow companion.

Before Fyodor could react to this apparent desertion, the captain skidded to a halt. As Liriel ran past, the enormous man seized the back of her swordbelt with one hand, jerking her to an abrupt stop. With his free hand he gathered up a handful of her tangled hair and chain mail vest. Lifting the drow easily off her feet, the captain hauled her back for the toss. As Fyodor watched, slack-mouthed, the man heaved Liriel up and toward the ship.

The captain's strength, combined with Liriel's dark-elven powers of levitation, sent the drow into impromptu flight. Hands outstretched before her, she hurtled toward the *Elfmaid* like a dark arrow, her eyes wide with wild delight.

Fyodor caught the drow's wrists and immediately began swinging her around and around to defuse the force of their collision and to help slow her flight. With each circle, the drow lost a bit of momentum but none of her obvious enjoyment. The moment her boots touched the deck, however, Liriel tore free of Fyodor and ran over to clutch the railing.

"Hrolf!" she called out, her face twisted with dismay.

A startled moment passed before Fyodor realized that the word was a name, not a signal that the drow was about to become seasick. Liriel gazed at the dock where the captain had last stood. In his place a swarm of angry kobolds danced and hooted, growing rapidly smaller as the ship pulled away.

Wishing to ease her distress, Fyodor strode to Liriel's side and pointed down into the dark water. Below them, swimming for the ship with strong, steady strokes, was the captain. "He dove in right after he set you aflight," he explained.

Liriel nodded, and her lips curved in a smile of relief. Then, in one of the abrupt changes of mood that Fyodor had come to know so well, she lifted her chin to an imperious angle and turned a lance-sharp glare upon the first mate.

"What do you mean by this delay? Get the captain aboard at once!"

Ibn recoiled as if he'd been stabbed, but he was accustomed to following orders, and the drow female gave them with the force and conviction of a war chieftain. Before the mate realized what he was about, he'd already set the rudder and tossed a coiled rope over the rail.

The coil unfurled as it flew, and Ibn's aim was true. Hrolf seized the knotted end and began to pull himself hand over hand toward the ship. In moments he scrambled over the rail to stand, dripping and triumphant, on his own deck.

"Good lad, Ibn," he said heartily, slapping the mate on the back with a force that nearly sent the man sprawling. "The water gates lie ahead; be ready to raise her."

But the mate had other things on his mind. "What do we want with *her?*" he said bluntly, tossing a dark glare and a curt nod at the drow.

Hrolf flung back one dripping braid and faced down the red-bearded sailor. "This is Liriel, a princess in her own land and a wizard worth any ten I've seen this mooncycle!" he announced in a voice loud enough to reach every man on the ship. "She's also a paying passenger. See to it you treat her with proper respect, or answer to me. And know this: the man who lays a hand on her loses it."

A moment of stunned silence met the captain's words.

"But she's an elf," protested one of the men, voicing a typical Northman's distrust of the fey folk.

"She's a drow!" added another fearfully, for the dark elves' vile reputation was known in a hundred lands.

"She's a *she.*"

This last observation, voiced in dire tones, apparently summed up the crew's protests. The men nodded and muttered among themselves, many of them forming signs of warding.

"Oh, stow your nonsense with the rest of the cargo!" Hrolf roared, suddenly out of patience. "All my days I've heard that a female aboard meant ill luck, but never have I seen a sign of it! Has yon lass caused us a moment's trouble?" he demanded, pointing to the enormous figurehead.

"Not a bit of it; the elf maid brings good fortune," one of the crew ventured thoughtfully.

"That she does," the captain stated, and his voice rang out, as powerful and persuasive as that of a master thespian. "Never has a storm taken us unaware; never have creatures of the sea decided to make of us a midday meal! And what of the men who claimed the elf maid would bring us to grief? How many of those men sleep in Umberlee's arms, and our time not yet come?"

The uniformly angry expressions on the Northmen's faces wavered, fading to puzzlement or indecision. Hrolf, who apparently knew his men well, waited for the planted idea to take root. "I say it's high time the *Elfmaid* was honored by one of her own," he stated. "Besides, who but the black lass has the magic needed to take us up

15

through the gates? With half of Skullport on my heels, d'you suppose the Keepers will send us through without question and blow us kisses to speed our way?"

There was no arguing with Hrolf's logic, and the crew knew it. The Keepers were hired mages who raised ships though magical locks leading from the underground port to the Sea Caves—an impassable and rock-strewn inlet south of Waterdeep—and from there to the open seas. These magical portals had been established centuries earlier by Halaster, a mighty wizard who'd left his insane stamp on nearly every corridor of the Undermountain, and to this day the gates were the only way to move ships to and from Skullport. Without the permission of the Keepers—or the aid of a powerful wizard—the *Elfmaid* would never sail beyond this subterranean bay. The crew could like it or not, but the drow female offered them their only chance of escape.

Liriel, however, was concerned with a more immediate problem. Three small ships, loaded with fighters, were being rowed with deadly determination for the *Elfmaid*. They gained steadily on the larger ship; battle seemed inevitable.

Fear, an emotion so new to Liriel that she had no name to give it, rose like bile in her throat. She was never one to recoil from a fight, but she knew that if Fyodor joined this battle, the dark waters would soon be warmed with blood. The drow could not permit this.

She spun to face Hrolf. The rowdy captain had already taken note of the approaching threat, and his eyes glinted with anticipation. "Show me a place belowdecks where I might go," she demanded. "Fyodor will come with me and stand guard, for I cannot be interrupted while spellcasting."

Hrolf's eyes dropped to Fyodor's dark sword, and a flicker of disappointment crossed his bewhiskered face.

"Do as we discussed, and all will be well!" Liriel added in a tone that did not invite or allow discussion.

Hrolf yielded with a sigh and a shrug. "Well then, lad, here are your orders: Let no man through the hatch until our wizard gives you leave."

Fyodor nodded, hearing what the captain said, and what he implied. Hrolf was in command of this ship, and under ordinary circumstances a berserker would follow a commander's orders to the death. The captain knew this and had phrased his words accordingly. Fyodor hoped, as he followed Liriel down a short ladder into the darkness of the hold, that he would be able to do as Hrolf commanded.

The captain paused before dropping the hatch. "Good luck to you, lass. And you, lad—see that you take good care of her." He gave Fyodor a shrewd once-over and then a wink. "But then, I don't have to be telling you *that,* now do I?"

Hrolf dropped the hatch with a thud, and then came the grating sound of something heavy being dragged over to obscure the opening. Angry voices drew nearer, and Liriel and Fyodor heard the sharp *ping!* of loosed arrows. Above all rang Hrolf's voice, shouting gleeful battle instructions to his men.

"I can't concentrate with all that going on," Liriel grumbled. "Come closer—sit down here beside me. I'm going to cast a sphere of silence. You don't need to hear the battle—just watch the hatch and kill anything that tries to get close to me."

Fyodor smothered a smile as he settled down on the wooden floor beside his friend. The drow's brusque manner did not fool him for a moment. If pressed, she'd claim she was merely being practical; her pride in her dark-elven ways was too strong for her to admit to sentiment. Practical, she certainly was. Fyodor did not yet know the crew well enough to discern defender from invader, and in the throes of battle frenzy he would fight until he died, or until no one stood to oppose him. Still, he could not resist the temptation to let Liriel know he saw her well-meaning sham for what it was.

"If I am to keep watch, I would do better with a light," Fyodor said mildly.

Instantly the soft glow of faerie fire lit the room. Liriel cast him a sidelong, suspicious look, but if she perceived his gentle teasing she gave no indication. Getting down to business, she opened a small spellbook and then took from her spell bag the items she would need for the casting.

It was a difficult spell, one of the most advanced in the book of gate spells given her by her father, the mighty archmage of Menzoberranzan. It was also one of the most unusual, allowing a person or entity to journey piggyback through an established gate along with the rightful traveler. Liriel only hoped that a ship and its entire crew could be considered an entity.

She began the deep concentration that such powerful magic demanded. Her body began to sway, and her gesturing hands pulled power from the weave of magic and bound it to her will. Yet she remained intensely aware of the battle above—for despite her words, the magical silence she cast encompassed only Fyodor—and she listened for Hrolf's signal. When the spell was cast, she sat immobile, her hands cupped around a sphere of summoned power as she waited for the precise moment to set it free. Finally the signal came: the quick pattern of stomps and pauses that she and Hrolf had prearranged. Another ship had entered the magic locks; it was time for the *Elfmaid* to join it.

The young wizard flung her hands high, releasing the contained magic. All at once the world shifted weirdly.

Liriel was swept up in the rush and roar of falling water and the whirling colors of a rainbow gone mad. Her physical form seemed to melt away as her mind took on the chaos and complexity of a crowded room. The drow felt, individually and all at once, the thoughts and fears of every person on this ship and on the other ship as well. At that moment she knew every person's name and could have said what each was doing. The multifaceted clarity lasted but a heartbeat before the many minds united in a single emotion: terror. This melting of barriers, this sudden and unfathomable sharing, was beyond anything that most of them had imagined possible.

Then, just as suddenly as it had begun, the spell was over. Liriel opened her eyes and was relieved to find herself and her surroundings whole—not joined board and sinew with the other ship and its crew. That was the risk in such a spell, even if there was but one wizard following another. Her father had warned her with stories of wizards who had been permanently conjoined by this spell, only to go mad in the attempt to share one body between two minds.

Liriel reached out a single finger to break the sphere of silence that protected her friend, much as a child might pop a soap bubble. "It's over," she said, and a quick, eager smile lit her face. "Let's go see the stars!"

Fyodor returned her smile with a heartfelt one of his own. He, too, had missed that sight during their sojourn in the tunnels surrounding Skullport. Still feeling somewhat dazed by the magical transport, he shouldered open the trapdoor and crawled up onto the deck.

Beneath a brilliant night sky, the men of the *Elfmaid* stood staring at the equally stunned faces of the crew of the ship that floated beside them, its rail near enough to touch.

Hrolf was the first to shake off the spell, bellowing at his crew to drop weapons and man the oars. Fyodor took his place at an oar, and soon the ship had pulled well away from its host. When it became clear that the other ship had no inclination to pursue, Hrolf set the sail and released the oarsmen to their rest.

Fyodor strode across the deck toward the place where Liriel stood alone in rapt contemplation of the stars. He found it oddly reassuring that someone who had spent nearly her entire life below ground could have a soul-deep love for the sky and its many lights and colors. In moments like this, Fyodor could believe that he and the beautiful drow were not so very different after all.

Not far from Liriel stood the captain and mate, deep in discussion. Fyodor did not intend to listen, but Hrolf's voice carried in the still night air like the call of a hunting horn.

"Well then, that's one more port that won't be glad of us for some time to come! Looks like we'll be adding Skullport to the list," said Hrolf.

"Looks like," the mate agreed.

"But it was a stay to remember and a good fight to end it with!"

"That it was. Lost the cargo, though."

The captain winked. "Never you mind. We'll make up the difference on the way home, and more besides!"

Fyodor stopped in his tracks, stunned and enlightened. He quickly recovered his wits and hurried over to Liriel. Seizing her by the arm, he drew her well away from the scheming sailors.

"There's something you must know," he said in a low, urgent voice. "I fear that this is a pirate ship!"

The drow stared up at him, her amber eyes full of genuine puzzlement. "Yes," she said slowly.

He fell back a step, incredulous. Liriel already *knew,* and it mattered not! Though why he should be surprised, he did not know. The drow girl was not lacking in character. She had proven to be a fiercely loyal friend and possessed a fledgling sense of honor. Yet she was utterly practical, as amoral as a wild snowcat. There was little in her experience that equipped her to fathom Fyodor's stricter code of honor.

"Liriel, these men are thieves!" he said, trying to make her understand.

The drow huffed, then threw up her hands in exasperation. "Well, what in the Nine Hells did you expect? Just for a moment, Fyodor, *think.* Don't you suppose it might be a little difficult for a drow to book passage with a shipload of paladins? Out of Skullport, no less?"

Fyodor was silent for a long moment, absorbing the truth of his friend's words and struggling to find a balance between honor and necessity.

"Well?" Liriel demanded, her fists on her hips and one snowy eyebrow lifted in challenge.

The young warrior smiled, but ruefully. "It would seem, little raven, that this sea voyage will be more interesting than I'd expected," he said, deliberately using his pet name for her to help defuse her ready temper.

Liriel relaxed at once and slipped one arm through his. "That's the problem with humans," she said as they strolled companionably across the starlit deck. "You never expect half the things you should expect. One step, two steps ahead, and you think you're done!"

"And the problem with drow," Fyodor teased her in return, "is that you can never stop thinking. With you it is always the head, and never the heart."

But the girl shook her head, and her golden eyes were bright as they looked up into the endless, starlit sky. "There are those who think, and those who dream," she said softly, repeating one of Fyodor's favorite maxims. "But I, for one, refuse to choose between the two!"

Chapter 2
A GATHERING STORM

t was early spring, and the northern seas were chill and inhospitable. Huge chunks of floating ice made navigation treacherous. Pods of whales swam northward, returning to the cold waters of their summer home and providing an additional hazard to ships. Other, more dangerous creatures were also on the move. The Northlands' brutal winters forced them to find shelter in the depths of the sea. Now, with the coming of spring, these creatures stirred from their torpor and sought the surface, and food. Some of these monsters had never been seen by a man who lived to tell of them, but they left behind evidence of their ability to crush ships and devour entire crews.

The coastal waters north of Luskan, known as the Sea of Moving Ice, were particularly dangerous, and Caladorn Cassalanter had been hard pressed to find a ship that would venture so far. Finally he'd booked a place aboard the *Cutter*, a sturdy merchant cog that traveled north every year during this season, when sea lions gave birth on the rocky islands and large ice floes. Harvesting the pups was grim business, but the silky white pelts brought a fine price from the decadent nobles of Waterdeep. And with piracy on the rise, even at this uncertain time of year, the ship's captain had willingly accepted Caladorn's offer of a strong arm and a keen blade to help protect the valuable cargo.

Caladorn's family was among the richest of Waterdeep's nobility, but the young man had set aside name, rank, and privilege to earn his own way. Despite his best intentions and the rough garments he wore, he stood out among the crew. Broad-shouldered and tall, he wore his weapons well and moved with the measured grace of a seasoned fighter. There was a natural, unconscious pride to his bearing and a certainty of purpose in his eyes that belied his claim of being a bored young nobleman out for adventure. For Caladorn was one of the secret Lords of Waterdeep. Troubling rumors, rumbles of some pending conflict, had been filtering south for some time. Caladorn sailed north to find answers.

The sun had newly risen, and the young Lord stood first watch in the crow's nest. It was not an enviable position. Heavy mist hung, like a shroud, over the water, drenching his cloak and clinging to his dark red hair in salt-scented icicles. But all thought of discomfort vanished as his eyes settled on the apparition taking shape before him.

A ship slowly emerged from the mist, floating toward them like a vast and silent ghost. Her sails hung in tatters, but the port flag— the bright silk banner that claimed Waterdeep as her home— snapped and fluttered in the chill wind.

Caladorn shouted an alert and climbed nimbly down the rope webbing to the deck. Most of the crew had gathered near the port side, weapons at hand. Caladorn shouldered his way over to Captain Farlow, a stout, black-bearded former mercenary. Rumor had it that in battle Farlow slaughtered his enemies as coldly and efficiently as he dispatched seal pups. At the moment, Caladorn was glad of the captain's fierce reputation.

"What do you make of it?" he asked, nodding at the apparently deserted ship. "Stripped by pirates?"

Farlow shook his head. "Not any that sail these waters. No Northman would leave a good ship adrift—they hanker after ships like most men crave cold ale and warm women. And look to the deck," he added, pointing. "Rows of barrels, neat as you please. Pirates would've torn the place apart and stolen anything worth taking."

"What took the crew, then?" demanded one of the hunters. "Plague?"

"Not likely, at this time of year," Caladorn said. It was not unusual for far-traveling ships to pick up some deadly illness along with their intended cargo, but that was a hazard peculiar to summer. "The ship can't have been adrift that long. Unmanned, it couldn't have survived the winter amid these ice floes. And see the port flag? It would be torn to ribbons by this wind in a matter of days. Hours, perhaps."

The captain shot a quick look at the young nobleman. "A trap, then?"

"It is possible," he admitted, understanding the path Farlow's thoughts had taken. A Waterdhavian ship, appearing in the known route of a merchant vessel laden with expensive pelts? And the ghost ship was a caravel, one of the fast and sturdy vessels for which Waterdeep's shipyards were justly famed. Several similar ships had been lost at sea over the last few seasons. Not odd, considering the dangers of a seagoing life and the whims of Umberlee, the unpredictable goddess of the sea. Not odd at all, until one considered the fact that two of these ships had recently reappeared in southern ports, flying Ruathen colors.

Caladorn did not doubt that this vessel had also fallen to the Northmen raiders. But that, he suspected, was not the entire story. He had fought beside—and against—men of Ruathym, and he knew them to be proud and fierce warriors. They would fling the stolen ship into battle, not use it for ambush. Yet it certainly appeared that the caravel had been left there for them to find. Not a trap, he reasoned, but a message.

"I'm going aboard," Caladorn said abruptly. "Keep the *Cutter* back a safe distance, if you will. All I ask is the use of one of the rowboats, and that you stand by to await my findings. Be this piracy or plague, word of the ship's fate needs to reach the city."

The captain gave a curt nod. Like all men of the sea, he knew that every lost ship was sought by dozens of longing eyes. Those who had the misfortune to love a missing sailor would never stop searching the watery horizon with mingled hope and dread. When the waiting stretched out into years and love became an undead thing, even bad news was preferable to none at all.

"You—Narth and Darlson. Lower the skiff. The rest of you, stand steady to fight or sail, on my order," Farlow commanded.

Maneuvering the tiny craft through the choppy seas took longer than Caladorn expected, but at length he stood on the deck of the abandoned caravel. He quickly searched it from hold to aft castle but found no crew, either alive or dead. Nor was there any sign of a recent battle. Finally, desperate for clues, he decided to examine what was left of the cargo.

With the flat of his dagger, he pried the wooden lid off the first of the barrels. A ripe, salty smell emerged—the familiar scent of pickling broth used to preserve the spring herring catch. Yet floating in the brine were long, lank strands, the green of kelp, but of a strangely familiar texture.

Caladorn pushed back his sleeves and plunged both hands into the brine, getting a good grip on the coarse green stuff. He hauled sharply upward, expecting to pull a clump of the peculiar seaweed from the brine. To his horror, he found himself looking into the open, sightless eyes of a female sea elf.

Even in death she was beautiful, her delicate features and the intricate mottled pattern of her skin perfectly preserved by the brine. Caladorn was of no mind to notice this fact. His hands shook as he lowered the elf gently back into her macabre coffin. After giving himself a long moment to compose his wits and settle his innards, he opened the rest of the barrels, some dozen in all. All of them were stuffed with pickled sea elves.

The young Lord's thoughts whirled as he tried to sort out the meaning of this atrocity. It was no secret that the Northmen held little love for elves. This was as true of the tundra barbarians as it was of the seafaring folk of Luskan, Ruathym, and the northern Moonshaes. But who would do such a thing, and for what reason? And why would they leave the dead sea elves for a Waterdhavian ship to find?

Many possible suggestions came to mind, each more dire than the last. There had been reports of recent attacks on sea-elf communities. Perhaps this was a plea for help; perhaps the elves themselves had left their slain comrades behind after a battle, hoping to send a grim message to Waterdeep that they dared not take in person. After all, a port flag flown so far from home was a well-recognized distress signal. But Caladorn rejected this notion almost as soon as the thought formed. It seemed unlikely that the proud elves would subject any of their kindred to such an indignity.

Perhaps some faction within the Northmen had declared war upon the sea elves, possibly in a dispute over fishing rights or, more likely, just for the sport of it. The Northmen gloried in feats of arms—many of them venerated Tempus, god of battle—and they had been deprived of warfare for an uncomfortably long time. Several years earlier, Waterdeep and her allied cities had enforced a peace between the warring kindred of Ruathym and Luskan. Since then, piracy had risen sharply, and raids on small coastal villages had become commonplace. Life was easier, Caladorn thought grimly, when the Northmen fought among themselves and left others alone.

He carefully replaced the lids and began the process of loading the barrels aboard the *Cutter*. There was no question in his mind that the bodies must be taken to Waterdeep. Caladorn knew elves were reticent to disturb those who had moved past this life, but perhaps a cleric at the elven pantheon temple would be willing to seek out the spirit of one of these slain elves. And if no priest would yield to reason, Caladorn would find one who could be persuaded at the point of a sword.

Let the other Lords worry about diplomacy. This puzzle involved his beloved city, and he resolved to have the answer, at whatever cost.

* * * * *

Rethnor stamped the snow from his boots as he strode into the council chamber. It was a simple room, constructed according to the Northmen taste with an intricate webbing of exposed wooden beams and furnished with a massive pine table and five unpadded chairs. The only concessions to comfort were the fire blazing in the fieldstone hearth that lined one full wall and the presence of a serving girl who would bring ale or mead upon command. Rethnor thrust his fur hat into her hands and took his place at the table where the other High Captains of Luskan awaited him.

There were five Captains, men whose task it was to rule the city and oversee its trade and its ambitions. Luskan was a strong and prosperous port, controlling much of the valuable trade of the northern lands. Silver from the mines of Mirabar, timber taken from the edges of the vast Lurkwood forest, scrimshaw from Ten Towns, dwarf-crafted weapons—all passed through the customs of Luskan and went out upon her ships. Yet no man seated in this room was content with Luskan's riches, or her boundaries.

"Your report, Rethnor?" demanded Taerl, who currently presided as First High Captain. The five of them took turns as leader of the council, conceding the role to another with the coming of the new moon and low tides. It was ancient custom, and it served well to keep five ambitious men from battling each other for ascendancy.

"We are making progress in the conquest of Ruathym," he began.

"Progress?" Suljack, a distant cousin of Rethnor's and ever a competitor, spat out the word as if it were a bit of spoiled meat. "Have we become so soft that even our words are weak things? *Victory*," he proclaimed, pounding the table for emphasis. "That is the concern of warriors."

Rethnor leaned back in his chair and hooked his thumbs nonchalantly in the broad strap of his swordbelt. He was the best swordsman in the room, and they all knew it. From his position of strength, he could propose subtle strategies that would be scorned and spurned if they'd come from the lips of a lesser warrior.

"Ruathym is weak and growing weaker," he said in an even voice. "So far this has been accomplished without attracting the attention of Waterdeep and the so-called Lords' Alliance. If we continue this course, we can conquer the island in one sudden, brutal attack. Waterdeep and her minions will be less likely to object if presented with an accomplished fact, but a prolonged war would surely draw the attention of the meddlesome southerners."

"What of it? I do not fear Waterdeep!" growled Suljack.

"Nor do I," Rethnor retorted. "But need I remind you, Cousin, that Waterdeep forced an end to our last war with Ruathym? Although we were close to conquest, we lost all!"

"There is honor in honest battle," persisted Suljack.

"There is no honor in a stupid refusal to learn from the past!" Rethnor thundered, past patience with his fellow Captain. His cold gaze settled upon Suljack, daring him to make the challenge personal. The other man turned away, subsiding into sullen silence.

"I hate the decadent southern cowards as much as any of you," put in Baram, the oldest member of their group and the most conciliatory. "But I hate still more the thought of becoming like them. We are warriors, Rethnor. Subtlety is not our keenest weapon, and I would not like to see it become the one most often wielded."

"It is but one weapon among many," Rethnor said. "Our fleets, our warriors—their time will come. We cannot conquer Ruathym or rule the seas without them. When the moment is right, we will strike."

"And how are we to know when this strange fruit is ripe?" asked Taerl.

"I will tell you," Rethnor said simply. "I have placed spies in the seas surrounding Ruathym and on the island itself."

"They are worthy of trust?" put in Kurth, a dour and suspicious man with a temper as black as his beard.

"I have *ensured* their loyalty."

A moment's silence fell over the group. Rethnor's voice was so cold, his face so hard, that the other men could not help but wonder what price he'd exacted, what grim methods he'd employed.

At length the First High Captain cleared his throat and agreed, with a curt nod, to Rethnor's plan. "We will prepare for this attack and await your word. Suljack and Kurth, you will see to converting merchant ships for battle. Baram, begin to muster warriors in preparation for the invasion." He turned to Rethnor. "All other details we leave to you. You are the only one among us who enjoys intrigue as much as battle."

The distaste in Taerl's voice was not lost on Rethnor. "One weapon among many," he repeated, placing one hand on the grip of his oft-used broadsword. "My blade is thirsty; the wait will be no longer than it must."

Truth rang clear in Rethnor's words, and the wolfish grin on his face spoke plainly of his lust for battle. The other men nodded their approval and their relief. Rethnor might have strange new notions, but he was a Northman first and foremost.

* * * * *

Shakti Hunzrin moved through the corridors of House Hunzrin, ignoring the guards and servants that glided through the dark halls. Like most of Menzoberranzan's drow, they were as silent and delicate as shadows that had magically found substance. Shakti, however, was solid, with a tread that tested the stone floor and a girth that almost equaled that of a human.

Her talents, too, were different from those of most drow. Shakti was a canny manager, and at no time in the city's history were such skills needed as badly as now. In the aftermath of war, the chaos that was Menzoberranzan teetered on the edge of catastrophe. Food supplies had dwindled; trade had fallen off. Most noble families kept mushroom groves within the walls of their compounds—safe from the threat of poisoning by a rival clan—but the common folk went hungry more often than not. Shakti had addressed that problem, working hard to restore the rothe herd and revive the neglected fields. She also made sure it was known whose doing this was. The common folk of Menzoberranzan didn't care which eight backsides warmed the thrones of the Ruling Council. They did care that their young ones were fed, that there was a market for their crafts. Slowly, steadily, Shakti was building a power base of a different kind, one that dealt in the everyday needs of most of the city's drow.

Yet she was not blind to the fact that power currently resided in the hands of the matriarchy, and that nearly every priestess in Menzoberranzan was consumed with the ambition to rise to the head of her clan and to improve the rank and station of her house. It was no accident that Shakti's older sister, the heir to House Hunzrin, had fallen ill with a rare wasting disease.

Shakti intended to play the game, but she would not lose sight of her larger goals, her broader vistas.

27

Elaine Cunningham

The young priestess entered her private room, taking care to lock the door and ward it against prying eyes. When her haven was secure she sighed with relief, then raised her hands to massage her aching temples. Shakti often had headaches—the result of straining her eyes to make sense of the blur that was her world. Nearsighted from birth, she had gone to great lengths to keep her affliction secret. The constant struggle to keep from squinting gave her a pop-eyed, frantic appearance. Clerical spells might have improved her vision, but no drow dared admit to physical defect.

Yet when her blurred gaze fell upon her most prized possessions—the snake-headed whip that proclaimed her rank as high priestess of Lloth and a scrying bowl that had been the gift of Vhaeraun, the drow god of thievery—a bold thought occurred to her. If the gods were willing to grant such gifts as she already possessed, why couldn't she petition them directly for healing? What better symbol could there be for her farsighted ambition?

For it was Shakti's goal to restore the drow to their original vision of glory. According to the Directives of Lloth, the drow must first dominate the Underdark and from there expand to eradicate the lesser races of elves. The drow god Vhaeraun encouraged the dark elves to establish a presence on the surface immediately. As a dual priestess of Lloth and Vhaeraun, Shakti saw life through a broader perspective than most of the city's drow imagined possible. Why shouldn't her eyesight keep pace with her vision?

Action followed quickly upon thought. Shakti fell prostrate to the floor, earnestly petitioning the drow goddess and god.

In quick response came a white-hot blaze of pain as healing magic flowed into the priestess—far too much of it. Even in this, the rival deities competed.

Shakti's body contorted, her head reared up as the waves of power coursed through her. Shrieking in agony, the priestess clutched at the nearest object—the gilt base of her mirror. Her reflected eyes stared back at her, wide and frantic and fiery red.

In some corner of Shakti's mind that the pain could not reach, a bubble of childlike wonder began to form. Reflected in the mirror was a room outlined in detail such as the young drow had never seen, had never imagined possible. The titles on the books lining her shelves, the intricate detail on the carved gargoyles that decorated the mantel, the sheen of dust on the study desk—I really must have the house servant flogged for such neglect, she noted absently—were all sharply, gloriously visible. Lloth and Vhaeraun had granted her request.

Shakti's last scream of anguish lifted into a peal of triumphant laughter.

Much later, the drow priestess came to herself. She sat up gingerly and found the pain had disappeared, leaving behind an unnatural contentment that bordered on euphoria. It was enough for her just to look and to *see*.

But the moment passed quickly, and the focus of Shakti's newly sharp vision tunneled inward upon her goals. She had found a cure for her myopia—a sure omen that nearsightedness was not an immutable sentence. It had been so with her, and so it would be for Menzoberranzan.

She would play by the rules—she would become Matron Mother of her house and she would see her clan advance in rank—and then she would use that power to lift the eyes of Menzoberranzan's drow from their constant, incestuous warfare, to turn their focus from this single cavern to the wider world. Broader vistas, new possibilities. There were many ways to accomplish this, and Shakti planned to explore them all.

The priestess warded her chamber with still more privacy spells and set her personal guard—a pair of drow-shaped stone golems—to watch the door. Golems were perfect guardians, incapable of thought or treachery. When all was secure, she placed the scrying bowl on a table, carefully filled it from a flask of still-warm blood, and ringed it with candles.

Briefly, Shakti thought of the last image she had received from the scrying bowl through the eyes of the dying wizard Nisstyre: the beautiful face and taunting words of Liriel Baenre. In outwitting the drow male, the thrice-bedamned princess had once again bested Shakti.

With newfound discipline, Shakti thrust aside the familiar hatred and envy that thoughts of Liriel always evoked in her, and she focused her mind on the steps that must be taken before vengeance could be hers.

Liriel possessed a human artifact that enabled her to take drow magic to the surface. Retrieving this artifact was an important part of Shakti's overall plan. Her ally Nisstyre had come close, but the curse of the drow—a quick rage and a burning desire for revenge—had overcome Shakti and had resulted in the loss of both ally and amulet. She would not make that mistake again.

Calmly, she considered her course. At that last encounter, the

Baenre princess had been in an underground port city, doing battle with Nisstyre and his fellow merchants of the Dragon's Hoard—all followers of Vhaeraun. Though their leader had been slain, Shakti planned to reestablish ties with the band, for they were valuable in bringing both information and merchandise from the surface lands. But to find her slippery rival, Shakti sought a more direct route and a more powerful ally than drow merchants.

Bold steps. A broader vision. That was what was needed.

Cupping the scrying bowl with her hands, Shakti began to chant a spell that would open a window to another plane. Not the Abyss—the drow's first choice for power and allies—for much about her work had to be kept secret from the priestesshood of Lloth, and Abyssal denizens were notorious for treachery. Nor did they hold sway in the places where Liriel now stood. No, Shakti sought another, lesser-known place: the elemental plane of water.

Drow were adept at traveling the lower planes, but they had little to do with the elemental planes. Yet, Shakti reasoned, if Liriel sought the vast waters of the surface world, what better place could Shakti look for an ally? She had learned to do so at considerable cost, for the hideous Abyssal creature that had shown her the path to the plane of water had enacted a grim pledge from the drow priestess. Shakti quickly thrust that thought aside. It was her darkest secret, one she did not care to contemplate until forced to do so.

The priestess stared deep into the bowl, watching as the blood darkened to ebony and the surface took on a glossy sheen. Then all color vanished, and the bowl seemed full of a wraithlike mist.

Shakti deepened her concentration and *thought* herself into the mist. There was a sudden tug, a moment of intense confusion, and then she was surrounded by swirling fog. A large eel with iridescent scales floated past her with an undulating, swimming motion. Momentary panic threatened to claim the drow as the realization of her success took hold. Shakti gripped her wits and reminded herself that she was not plane walking. She had merely sent her spirit to the elemental plane, leaving her physical form in the implacable care of the golems. Nothing here—not the strange water, not the denizens who inhabited it—could harm her. So she began to walk through the alien landscape, marveling at the twin sensations of heaviness of movement and weightlessness of body, amazed that the water flowed through her as easily as if it were air.

For the first time, Shakti thought she understood why Liriel Baenre might have desired to explore the surface worlds. This foreign plane showed her amazing things, and her new eyes drank in every strange detail.

On the far edge of the watery landscape was a strange sight: a cloud of bubbles, roiling and seething. It was a being of some sort, though unlike anything Shakti had ever seen or imagined. Although formless, it was not without intelligence or ambition. The traveling spirit of the drow perceived the being's emotional storm—an overwhelming sense of discontent, frustration, and rage—and turned to follow it to its source.

The drow was reassured to know that even here there were beings who were disillusioned, eager to break from their traditional ties. They were like loose threads, seeking a new and orderly pattern they had not yet defined. Shakti was more than willing to provide them with one. She had vision enough to spare and could easily weave any number of loose threads into her growing web of power.

* * * * *

The light of a waxing moon shimmered on the surface of the water as the little craft slipped away from the coast of Ruathym. It was a clear, cold spring night, and in the frigid skies each star burned with stark clarity. Hooded and cloaked against the chill, a single sailor settled down among piles of wet, bulging sacks—a strange cargo, and one that could destroy many a Ruathen in the days to come.

The oars dipped quietly into the water, taking the boat out past the shallows where the people of Ruathym went to swim and to gather clams during low tide. From time to time, the traitor cast a furtive glance up at the stars, which seemed to burn down like so many accusing eyes.

Yet the boat moved forward steadily, each stroke of the oars scattering the reflected moonlight like broken dreams. From time to time, the quiet rhythm was interrupted as the rower paused to drop into the waters seed that would bear a bitter fruit.

The night was old before the sacks were empty, and the moon had sunk low behind the forested hills of Ruathym. The lone sailor quickened the rhythm of the oars, for there was one task yet remaining. Tonight, death must come to the quiet village, and the spirit of a potential hero must take its place in the mead halls of Tempus, god of battle. It would not be a place of honor. The man's death would not be a glorious passage, bravely won, but a bitter gift

31

from the hand of a friend. It was this, more than the murder itself, that formed the deepest betrayal.

With a crunch of pebbles, the boat struck the shore. Moving quickly, the assassin pulled the craft onto dry land and secured it in its accustomed place. The port village of Ruathym lay sleeping—even the fisherfolk were still abed. But soon the people would begin to stir, and a cloaked figure would seem suspect. So the assassin tossed back the cowl and walked openly down the streets that led to the cottage of the young war leader. If any saw, none would question.

And so, in the quiet before dawn, death came in a single, quick stroke. One stroke—that was all it took to steal the glory of one Ruathen and slay the honor of another. The assassin knew the single flash of the knife would send many others to Tempus's mead hall as well, for the loss of this leader would weigh heavily in the scales of fortune, fortune that would turn against Ruathym in the war that was soon to come.

The assassin slipped out into the streets, marveling that the villagers could sleep, unknowing. Or perhaps they did know, these folk who from childhood could read the changing moods of sea and sky. Perhaps they tossed fearfully in their sleep, dreaming of a coming storm despite the clear skies and fair winds.

Chapter 3

THE OPEN SEA

single glass-covered portal, not much wider than the palm of Liriel's hand, admitted a narrow stream of light into Hrolf's cabin. The drow sat cross-legged on the cot, her books scattered about her. The dim light, softened by the setting sun to a rosy glow, did little to banish the claustrophobic gloom of the tiny space, but it was more than enough illumination to meet the needs of a drow wizard.

At last she closed her spellbook and stretched, working out the stiffness caused by several hours of study. She rose and padded over to the portal to watch the fading sunset colors and wait for her time under the stars.

Liriel had grown accustomed to the brightness of the surface lands, but daylight at sea was another matter. The endless vista of sea and sky was a brilliant, blinding shade of blue. Even on cloudy days the glare from the silver water pained her eyes. And the relentless sun that baked the humans' skin to a weathered brown had set hers painfully aflame after but one day at sea. None but Liriel could see the burn on her ebony skin—to her heat-sensitive eyes, her face and arms shone like molten steel—until the blisters rose the next day. A penitent Hrolf, aghast at his own lack of forethought, had insisted that the drow take his cabin as her own. So Liriel hid herself away during the lengthening days of spring to sleep and to study her spells, and each day she added to the Windwalker's store of power.

The young wizard fingered the golden amulet that hung over her heart. The Windwalker was a simple thing, a small sheathed dagger of ancient make suspended from a chain of gold. Simple, but it held enormous power. It was her link with her drow heritage and her hope for the future.

The amulet had been crafted long ago by magic-users who took their strength from natural sites of power and from the place spirits that once were common in the northern lands. It could store such powers, temporarily, so that a magic-wielder could leave the place of power for a time.

Liriel had reasoned that the innate magic of the Underdark drow, which dissipated in the light of the sun, was a form of place magic. She had adapted spells and rituals that stored her magical drow heritage—and her dark-elven wizardry—in the amulet.

The drow waited until the last rays of sunlight had vanished; then she carefully twisted the amulet's tiny hilt. Instantly the cabin was flooded with eerie blue light—invisible to the heat-blind—that pulsed with the strange radiation magic of the Underdark. Quickly, as she did every night with the coming of darkness, Liriel performed the rituals that stored her newly learned spells in the amulet.

The Windwalker did not accept and retain all of Liriel's spells, but held enough to indicate a seemingly endless capacity. No wonder Kharza-kzad, her former tutor, had told her half the drow of Menzoberranzan would cheerfully kill to possess such power. Yet it saddened Liriel that the power she most wished to master—the ability for Fyodor to control his berserker rages—remained stubbornly beyond reach.

When her day's work was finished, Liriel snatched up a book of Ruathen lore and made her way up to the deck. It promised to be another clear night, with an endless sky and stars beyond counting. Most of the crew had been released from their labors. A group of them sprawled comfortably on deck, spooning up seafood stew and listening as Fyodor spun a tale from his homeland. The young man was a natural storyteller, and the sailors were caught up in the rhythm of the tale and the rich cadences of Fyodor's resonant bass voice. The story was one Liriel had heard before, one that described a battle between Rashemen's warriors and the Red Wizards that ruled neighboring Thay. The sailors met each mention of the wizards with hisses and dark murmurs and cheered the exploits of the Rashemi berserkers. Fyodor paused in his storytelling long enough to meet Liriel's amused gaze with a sober nod.

The drow caught his meaning well enough. Most Ruathen distrusted wizardly magic. The daring escape from Skullport had left the crew shaken and in awe of the elven wizard, and most of them gave her a wide berth.

"You're out and about late this evening," observed a tentative voice behind her.

Liriel turned to face Bjorn, the youngest member of Hrolf's

crew. The lad had a mere tuft of yellow beard and gangly limbs too thin for strength and too long for grace. But Bjorn could read the winds and sense the coming weather with an almost magical precision. This gift earned him a solid place aboard any ship. Nor was it his only gift. When not about his work, the lad whittled wood into clever little statues and painted them in the bright colors loved by the Northmen. At the moment Bjorn was seated on the deck, packing up the pots and flasks that held his paints.

The drow stooped to examine his latest work. It was a wall plaque depicting a single ship upon a storm-tossed seascape. A beautiful, wild-eyed goddess emerged from the crest of a crashing wave, her hand outstretched—perhaps to steady the faltering vessel, perhaps to crush it.

"Umberlee?" Liriel asked.

"Yes. The Lady of the Waves," Bjorn said reverently, but he made a sign of warding as he spoke of the goddess.

Liriel understood his reaction completely. She'd heard enough about the capricious Umberlee to recognize that particular brand of devotion. Fear *and* worship—Lloth inspired and demanded both, as well. The drow nodded and copied Bjorn's gesture, which seemed to puzzle the young artist.

"Is Umberlee your goddess?" he asked.

Liriel shrugged. "No, but dry her off and paint her black, and you'd hardly notice the difference."

The lad's eyes bulged, and he repeated the warding sign as if to stave off the result of such blasphemy. Eager to change the subject, he reached for a steaming bowl and handed it to the drow. "You were late this evening. I saved you some soup, knowing there'd be none later."

Surprised and grateful, Liriel took the bowl and settled down on deck beside the boy. He picked up his own supper, and they ate in silence. Still, it was the most companionable moment she'd spent with anyone other than Fyodor or Hrolf since coming aboard. Most of the twenty-odd crewmembers dealt with Liriel's presence by ignoring it.

Most, but not all. From the corner of her eye, the drow noted that Ibn was watching her again. There was something about the burly, red-bearded sailor that seemed disturbingly familiar to Liriel. Where most of the Ruathen approached life with a bluff, straightforward manner, Ibn seemed to think far more than he spoke. His few words gave away little, his eyes still less. More complicated than his mates, Ibn occasionally reminded Liriel of a drow. Which was to say, he was trouble.

Liriel pondered the matter as she finished off the salt-laden chowder. The first mate was plotting something; in Liriel's mind, that was a given. She could wait for him to play out his hand, or she could confront him in an open and forthright manner. She'd learned the latter approach often befuddled dark elves, who fully expected their plots to be met with equally convoluted counterstrategies. The response this tactic invariably elicited—a moment of veiled surprise, followed by a frantic effort to ferret out the layers of conspiracy that surely must be hidden under the seemingly simple approach—amused her. How, she wondered, would Ibn respond to a direct challenge?

At length, Liriel decided to take the man's measure. She bid Bjorn a good night and made her way over to the red-bearded sailor.

"Speak your mind and have done," she demanded.

The mate seemed not at all disconcerted by her blunt words. He took the pipe from his mouth and tapped the ashes into the sea.

"Every hand aboard shares the work. I don't see you doing aught but sleeping away the days and staring into books by night," he said scornfully, nodding toward the lore book tucked under the drow's arm.

Liriel's chin lifted. "Might I remind you that I am a paying passenger? If you feel the need to assign me a role, you may consider me ship's wizard."

"Wizard!" Ibn leaned over the rail and spat to demonstrate his contempt. "There's things that need doing, but magic ain't one of them. Harreldson's been cooking. Waste of a good sailor."

The drow's eyes widened with disbelief. This man expected her to take the part of a scullery servant? "In my family's household only slaves prepare food," she said coldly. "*Male* slaves, at that. What you suggest is absurd."

Ibn folded his arms. "Not so, if you plan to eat. I have command during the night hours. On my watch you'll help with the provisions or you'll go without."

Liriel gritted her teeth as she held the man's implacable gaze, and she entertained herself with fantasies involving traditional drow methods of retaliation. Artistic dismemberment was a favorite indulgence. Slow-working poisons added a piquant ambiance. Giant scorpions played a significant role.

The gist of her musings must have shown on her face, for when she suddenly whirled and seized a harpoon from the weapon rack, Ibn backpedaled fast and dove for cover behind a barrel of salted fish.

Nor was he the only one to think ill of her intentions. A strong hand seized the drow's wrist and spun her about.

"What are you thinking, little raven?" demanded Fyodor.

Liriel let out a hiss of exasperation and jerked her hand free. "I'm *thinking* of fishing! According to that idiot behind the barrel, I'm expected to help with provisions. I assume it's either that or cook!"

"Ah." A glint of humor appeared in the young warrior's eyes, and he turned to Ibn's hiding place. "I have traveled with her for many days, my friend. In this you may trust me: it would be the wiser course to let her *gather* the food."

The sailor picked himself up, all the while glaring with undisguised hatred at the drow. Liriel blew him a kiss and then strode to the rail, harpoon in hand. She kicked off her boots and quickly peeled off her clothes, for they would only hamper her in the water. All she needed was the Windwalker, her amulet of Lloth, and a few of the daggers and knives strategically bound with thin leather straps to her forearms and calves.

From the corner of her eye, Liriel saw Fyodor's frown and the warning glance he sent toward the other men on board. Hrolf had forbidden the men to touch her; Fyodor's grim stare commanded them to avert their eyes.

The drow's exasperation increased fourfold. She had yet to accustom herself to human notions of modesty. Drow had a keen appreciation for beauty—including that of the body—and had few taboos about nudity. The main reason they wore clothing at all was because it offered protection from attack and hiding places for weapons!

Ignoring her too-fastidious friend, Liriel climbed the railing. She tossed the harpoon into the water and dove in cleanly after it.

The icy shock stopped her heart. One beat lost, then the rhythm picked up again, thundering in Liriel's ears as she struggled to move her benumbed limbs. The drow was accustomed to the waters of the Underdark, which came from melting ice in lands far above her homeland, but this was *cold*. She knew she could not remain in these waters for long. Getting down to business, she broke the surface, grabbed the floating harpoon and a lungful of air, and dove deep.

Starlight filtered through the water, turning the sea into a silvery, dreamlike world. It was beautiful, but Liriel knew better than to linger. In moments the drow marked her prey, a large fish favored by the pirates for the pink flesh that tasted equally good raw, cooked, or smoked. She lifted the harpoon to her shoulder and hurled. The barbed weapon flashed through the water, trailing a length of thin rope behind it and taking the fish through the gills. Liriel immediately swam for the surface, the rope's end in hand. As she rose toward the boat, she noted that there were several strange markings carved on its underside—curving patterns oddly reminiscent of drow script.

Calling upon her levitation magic, she shot out of the water and floated lightly up to the railing where Fyodor awaited, grim and watchful. He'd taken off his cloak and had it ready for her. With a nod of thanks, she took the warm garment and handed him the rope. The fish was at least half her weight, and she could hardly be expected to haul it up herself.

As she wrapped herself in the cloak, Liriel noticed that Ibn was looking past her out to sea. His face was unreadable, but an air of malevolent satisfaction rose from him like a miasma. Liriel knew with certainty that this time Ibn would not speak his mind if asked.

Well enough—there were other ways of getting answers to her questions.

Beneath the cover of Fyodor's cloak, the drow's hand crept up to her symbol of Lloth. Her fingers closed around the obsidian disk, and she silently cast a mind-reading spell, one of the first lessons taught to novice priestesses. From Ibn's thoughts she took a single word—shark—and several quick images: a triangular fin slicing through the water like a small gray sail; rapacious jaws lined with rows of sharp teeth; a small, dark-skinned body torn past recognition.

So. This shark was a hunter, a dangerous one, and if Ibn had his way, she would be its prey. Again, well enough—she was forewarned.

Angry now, Liriel strode over to the weapon rack and selected another harpoon, this one larger and heavier than the first.

"Going down again?" Ibn asked casually as he refilled his pipe.

From the corner of her eye, the drow gave him a long, measuring gaze. No sign of his intent showed on his face, and not once did his eyes shift toward the place where he'd spotted the shark. Liriel noted this with a touch of perverse admiration. She had grown up in

Menzoberranzan and had survived many such games, but few were the drow who could play them better than this red-bearded human.

At that moment Fyodor pulled the fish over the rail. It dropped to the deck, still thrashing weakly and splashing icy water upon the boots of the men who'd gathered to watch the peculiar scene.

"I'm going back in for another fish," Liriel announced. Taking full advantage of the audience, she turned to face Fyodor and then dropped his cloak to the deck. "I'm afraid I've gotten your cloak all wet. Would you mind getting me a warm blanket? I think there's one somewhere in Hrolf's cabin. Ibn will haul up the next fish for me. . . . Won't you?" she asked, turning to the first mate.

Ibn did not respond, though Fyodor gave her a narrowed, suspicious look. She returned it with a smile. Of course the warrior knew she was up to something, but he had to choose between staying to question her, or doing something about her disconcerting nudity. With a deep sigh, Fyodor chose the latter and disappeared into the hold.

Liriel tied the loose end of the harpoon's rope to a winch and attached a float to the line. The rope was not all that long, but she didn't think she'd have to go very far to find the shark. She'd taken the first fish not far from the ship. If this shark was like any of the other predators she knew, it would be drawn by the scent of blood.

The drow plunged in again, dreamily imagining the look on Ibn's face when he hauled up her catch and came face-to-fang with this shark of his.

Liriel swam quickly toward the site of her first kill, taking a slightly different path downward. She was more at home in the water than were most drow, but she knew she was out of her element and kept careful watch. The image she'd taken from Ibn's mind—the sight of her own mangled body—was still vivid.

The drow's only warning was a flash of silver on the outermost edge of her vision. Instantly she whirled, the harpoon on her shoulder and ready to throw.

To her shock, Liriel found herself facing not a shark, but a young male elf—the first nondrow elf she had ever encountered.

The faerie elf was every bit as strange and alien a creature as she'd been taught to believe. His short-cropped hair was green, and his skin was mottled with a silvery green pattern that seemed to waver with the movement of the water. There were gills, like those of a fish, on his neck, and delicate webbing between the fingers of the hand that gripped a ready spear. He was no taller than Liriel, but he was well made and he held his weapon with the air of one who knew its use. Yet he did not strike. He merely stared at the drow with openmouthed astonishment.

Liriel was equally dumbfounded. Oh, she knew that some elves lived in water, and she wasn't particularly surprised to encounter one. What amazed her was that he did not attack.

From her earliest days Liriel had heard tales of the bitter enmity all the fair races of elves held for the drow. Defeated and forced underground many hundreds of years ago, the drow could expect nothing but cruel death at the hands of the faerie elves. Why then the hesitation in this one's hands and the curiosity in his eyes?

A sleek gray form sliced through the water toward the distracted sea elf. Liriel shook off the moment of immobilizing shock and hurled her harpoon. The weapon tore past the elf, less than a handbreadth from his mottled face.

The water directly behind him exploded into a churning mass. The harpooned shark struggled and thrashed, but moved inexorably upward as Ibn hauled on the line.

Although Liriel would have dearly loved to witness the mate's surprise, she had another problem to consider. A second sea elf, this one with long hair plaited into kelplike strands, swam to his comrade's aid. The elves flanked her, spears poised for attack.

Clutching the Windwalker, Liriel called upon her innate drow magic to conjure a globe of darkness. Black water instantly enveloped all three elves. The drow used the impenetrable darkness—and the moment of surprise—to make her escape. With the speed and agility for which drow were famed, she twisted in the water and darted to one side. Not quick enough. A sharp tug jerked her head painfully back as a spear tore through the strands of her floating hair.

Liriel's first impulse was to kill both of the sea folk. Indeed, a dagger was in her hand before the thought had fully formed. But the first male elf, the curious one, had not attacked. Of that Liriel was certain. He did not look like one who would throw and miss. And she had been virtually unarmed, unable to turn aside a thrown spear. Fyodor would not have attacked under those circumstances either. There was something in the elf's eyes that reminded Liriel of her friend's steadfast honor.

The drow found that she had no desire to finish the battle. Her lungs burned with the need for air. She swam toward the starlight, keeping careful distance from the still-struggling shark, and leaving the sea elves to their own domain.

Aboard the *Elfmaid*, all was going exactly as she'd hoped. Ibn was at the winch, cranking furiously. He glanced up when Liriel climbed over the rail, but his face gave away nothing of surprise or disappointment.

Suddenly, the drow felt weary of intrigue. She accepted the blanket Fyodor offered her and then strode over to the first mate. Pulling a dagger from her leg strap, she quickly slashed the rope that tethered the wounded shark to the ship.

"Don't waste your time," she said in response to Ibn's incredulous stare. "I don't mind killing a shark, but I don't think I'd care to eat one. The thing reminds me a little too much of some people I know."

Her remark caused a passing Hrolf to pull up sharply. "Sharks? Now you're hunting sharks, lass?" He looked the shivering drow up and down. "And in these waters! A strong man could die of the cold. Why did none of you warn her?" he bellowed, looking to his mate for an answer.

Liriel brushed aside the question. "Hrolf, I'm afraid the ship might be under attack. I saw two faerie elves, water-breathing males. There might be more."

"Sea folk? Here?" the captain asked with obvious surprise.

The drow nodded. "We fought."

"You fool female!" Ibn exploded. He bore down on Liriel, shaking a clenched fist. "You've bought us trouble, that's sure."

Hrolf waved the man into silence. "Did you hurt them, lass?"

"She did not."

The words were spoken by a new voice, definitely male but high in pitch and soft as the wind. There was no sign of the speaker, but Hrolf's face lit up.

"Xzorsh!" the captain cried happily. It was an odd word—a click followed by a sibilant *zzorshhh*—but it flowed off Hrolf's tongue with familiar ease. The captain snatched up a rope ladder and draped it over the side of the ship. "Come aboard, lad, and welcome you are!"

Liriel's eyes widened as the green-haired sea elf climbed aboard. She knew Hrolf to be a rogue, but could he be on good terms with one of the wicked sea faerie? Obviously so. The stranger bowed low to the captain, his webbed hands spread palms-up before him as if to indicate he was unarmed.

"I come with a warning, Captain Hrolf," the elf said in grave, melodious tones. "There is a disturbance in the lower seas. The

41

deep dwellers are rising, forcing lesser predators into bold and desperate attacks. Did you not see the sharks?"

"Some of us did," Liriel said, tossing a quick, arch glance at the first mate.

"I know you sea folk aren't fond of sharks," Hrolf commented, "but they're no threat to the ship. And the creatures from the depths come near the surface every spring."

"Not all do," Xzorsh said soberly. "No vurgen has been seen near this area in my lifetime, yet since the last new moon I myself have seen three."

Hrolf stroked his beard thoughtfully. "That is odd," he admitted at last. "Vurgens are rare."

"Well, I've certainly done my part," Liriel put in dryly.

Her remark surprised a bawdy chuckle from Hrolf, but his face abruptly sobered as he returned to the matter at hand. "Giant gulper eels, lass," the captain explained, "big enough to swallow a man whole and mean enough to bash small ships to driftwood with their spiked tails. Vurgens are bad business—make no mistake about that—but they're worse omens. Seems as if they come up only when they're chased by something even bigger."

"That is my fear," Xzorsh agreed. "Sittl has gone ahead to warn the sea folk community nearby."

"Sittl." Liriel folded her arms and glared at the sea elf. "That would be the male who tried to skewer me, I suppose."

"Don't take it personal, lass," Hrolf advised cheerfully. "The sea folk believe that your kin had something to do with their loss of magic—seagoing elves don't have any, to speak of—which naturally puts drow on their list of things to look out for. And that's what Xzorsh and Sittl do. They look out for the sea folk who live hereabouts."

"And for the *Elfmaid*, as well," put in Olvir, one of the crew. Until Fyodor's arrival, Olvir had been the ship's main storyteller. Though the man listened more than he talked these days—so eager was he to learn the new and wondrous tales that the young Rashemi offered—he was quick to jump in whenever an opening presented itself.

"Captain Hrolf is unnatural fond of elves, he is, seeing as how he had him an elf woman some years back. Well, about twenty years past, we come across a pair of Calishite vessels in the shallows, net spread between 'em. Seems they'd herded some young sea elves into the nets, planned to sell 'em down south as a curiosity. Hrolf now, he wasn't having any of this. A good fight, it was," Olvir noted dreamily. "Scuttled both the ships, we did, and fed the southern bastards to the shrimp."

"I was one of those young elves," Xzorsh said with quiet dignity. "I will ever remember this, as will my clan after me. The runes on the bottom of the *Elfmaid* identify her to the sea folk as Hrolf's vessel. We are pledged to protect him and all his crew."

The sea elf's eyes drifted to Liriel as he spoke, and his troubled expression said plainly that he was uncertain about the wisdom of including a drow in this pledge.

As well he should be, Liriel thought grimly. She would never forget the atrocities faerie elves had committed against her people, nor did she trust this particular male. For a long moment, the two elves regarded each other with wary curiosity.

"You could have killed me, but you did not," Xzorsh ventured at last. "You . . . you are not at all what I might have expected."

His words, and their puzzled tone, mirrored Liriel's thoughts exactly. The last things she would have expected from a faerie elf were mercy and honor. Yet Xzorsh spoke of a pledge as something so strong and immutable that his people would regard it with the pride a drow might give an inherited title. Liriel saw several possible explanations for this disparity: either the dark elves had misunderstood the nature of the faerie—or more to the point, had twisted the tales to their purpose—or this Xzorsh was naive beyond belief.

Either way, she did not know how to respond to Xzorsh's question. Liriel had no idea what stories the sea elf had heard about drow, but she was willing to wager that they hardly did justice to the evil and treachery that was her heritage. So Liriel merely shrugged and turned her gaze out to sea.

The sight before her stole her breath. Without a word she dove toward her pile of discarded clothes and weapons.

Hrolf had seen it, too. On the dark water, there were twin circles of reflected moonlight. The problem was, the sky held but one moon.

The captain roared orders to the crew as he lunged for the harpoon rack. He snatched up an enormous bolt of wood and metal and hauled it back for the throw. Before he could hurl the weapon, a long, silvery tentacle whipped forward and snatched it from his hand.

A spray of dark water exploded upward like a fountain as the creature burst from the waves. Its huge, bulbous head gleamed silver, and countless tentacles churned the water to keep it afloat. Two of the creature's arms spread wide and slapped against the starboard hull. There was a wet, sickening *slurp* as hundreds of suction cups found purchase.

"The eyes!" shouted Hrolf, pointing toward the bulbous orbs, each bigger than a man's head. "Shoot for the eyes!"

A storm of arrows rained toward the creature. Not fast enough. The enormous squid seemed to understand Hrolf's words, for as soon as he'd spoken, it sank below the waves to protect its vulnerable eyes. It did not loosen its hold on the ship, though, and the vessel rolled sharply to one side as the creature pulled it along. Liriel—along with most of the crew—was thrown to the deck.

She skidded along the wooden planks and slammed into the lower side of the ship with a force that sent sparkles of pain along her spine. The drow wriggled free of the tangle of sweat-scented limbs and frantically looked around for Fyodor.

He had somehow managed to keep his footing and was clinging to the mast lines with one hand. His naked black sword gleamed in his free hand, and his booted feet were planted wide on the sloped deck. Despite the danger, he appeared utterly calm. A faint smile curved the young warrior's lips, and he seemed to take on height and power before Liriel's eyes.

The battle fury was beginning.

Liriel let out a whoop of exhilaration. Fyodor's berserker rage was wondrous to behold, and she relished the prospect of seeing it unleashed upon a single, easily recognized enemy. He knew the crew now, and at any rate there was little danger that he could confuse a Ruathen fighter with a giant squid. She rolled onto her hands and knees and began the uphill climb to her friend's side.

Hrolf, meanwhile, was scrambling up the deck toward the port rail, shouting the names of several others to follow him. The men struggled upward, throwing their weight against the far side in an attempt to balance the faltering vessel. But the giant squid sank still lower, pulling the *Elfmaid* inexorably along. Frigid water sloshed over the starboard side.

A probing tentacle reached over the low rail and curled around one of the sailors. The squid lifted its thrashing victim high, then smashed downward into the crew. Again the tentacle arched up. This time the man hung limp in the squid's grasp. He made an effective bludgeon for all that, and with the second strike the screams of the injured mingled with the groaning protests of the battered ship.

As the squid raised the man for a third attack, Fyodor's sword traced a downward arc, cutting the lower end of the mast line free. Clinging to the line with one hand and suspended from the tilted mast, the young berserker swung out toward the water. He slashed at the flailing tentacle as he passed, severing it in a single blow. The captured sailor dropped heavily to the deck, still belted by a length of the writhing, silvery appendage.

The impromptu pendulum reached its outer limit, and Fyodor began to swing back toward the ship. To Liriel's astonishment, he let go of the rope well before he cleared the side of the deck. Holding his sword firmly in both hands, point downward, he fell directly toward the giant squid.

Fyodor landed on the creature's head, and the force of his fall drove his blade hilt-deep into the base of one of the tentacles gripping the *Elfmaid's* hull. The berserker began to wrench the blade back and forth, tearing an increasingly wide gash.

This attack seemed to confuse the squid. Other tentacles rose from the water, slapping out wildly in an attempt to dislodge the human. Fyodor continued to tear through the clinging tentacle, unmindful of the powerful blows that the squid occasionally managed to land.

As Liriel watched, with gleaming eyes and bated breath, she noticed that another warrior had entered the battle. Xzorsh had slipped back into the water and was sawing determinedly away at the second arm that clung to the ship. His efforts managed to distract the squid and, with a sound like that of a thousand boots pulling free of a muddy bog, the squid pulled the tentacle free of the hull. The squid then dipped the tentacle under the sea elf. With a quick, disdainful flick, it sent him hurtling out of the sea and up over the embattled ship.

Xzorsh hit the wooden deck with a painful thud. He rolled and somehow managed to find his feet. Pointing toward Fyodor, the elf called out a warning in a strange language of clicks and whistles.

Liriel did not have to understand the sea elf's words to perceive the coming danger. The tentacle Xzorsh had dislodged from the ship curled inward toward the squid's body, slowly and deliberately making a wide circle around the young berserker. The squid had changed tactics.

The tentacle closed in, wrapped itself tightly around the berserker's chest, and pinned his arms firmly to his side. With a quick, sharp motion—oddly like that of a warrior plucking an arrow

45

from his shoulder—the squid yanked Fyodor from his perch. This particular "arrow," however, was more persistent than most. Fyodor managed to keep his grip on the sword. As the creature pulled him beneath the waves, the berserker finally severed the tentacle that held the *Elfmaid* captive.

The ship righted itself abruptly, rocking wildly. Liriel clung to the rail of the ship and hauled herself to her feet. Her eyes fixed confidently upon the turbulent battle just beneath the waves. The water roiled and churned from the furious fight, and her keen eyes saw the spread of ichor in the moonlit sea. Steam rose from the icy water, a testament to the unnatural heat that suffused a berserker in full battle frenzy.

"You're calamari," she promised the injured squid, and her voice rang with wicked glee.

But Hrolf did not seem to share her confidence. The captain came to her side and placed a huge hand on her shoulder. "He's gone, lass," he said softly, "and I'm giving the order to flee."

"No," Liriel said calmly, not taking her gaze from the sea.

"There's naught that any of us can do for him. More good men will die unless we put some distance between the ship and that monster," Hrolf persisted.

"Give him time," the drow asserted. Despite her confident tone, Liriel began to feel the first raw edges of worry. Strength Fyodor certainly had, and courage and cunning. Time, however, was in dangerously short supply. Even a berserker needed air.

The sea calmed, suddenly and dramatically. "He is gone," Hrolf repeated, and nodded over Liriel's head to a grim-faced and watchful Ibn. The first mate took his place at the rudder and waved the men toward the oars.

At that moment the squid burst from the water, tossing its enormous head from side to side as if in mortal anguish. A small bulge rippled along the elastic carapace, working its way upward.

Xzorsh came to Liriel's side, his green eyes narrowed as he studied the creature. "The human is alive," the sea elf said with disbelief. "He is trying to cut his way through!"

"Fyodor is inside the creature, alive?" the drow said, hope and incredulity mixing in her voice.

"Squid are difficult to kill, even from the inside," Xzorsh explained grimly. "Had the human been swallowed by a vurgen, he could have cut his way out easily. Here, his only hope is to find the creature's eyes. We have nothing that can cut through that carapace."

Maybe *you* don't, Liriel thought. The drow scanned the deck, looking for the bag that held her throwing spiders. After several frantic moments, she spotted it tangled up in a length of rope. She quickly snatched up a handful of weapons: fist-sized metal spiders, their eight legs perfectly balanced, tipped in deadly spikes and fortified with the magic of the Underdark.

The drow hurled the spiders, one after another. The magic-enhanced weapons bit deep into the squid's carapace, forming a precise line and opening a wide crack. Before Liriel could stop him, Xzorsh picked up a harpoon and hurled it into the opening. The weapon sank deep into the wound, and the barbed point exploded from one of the creature's eyes. The squid finally went limp, and its tentacles rose to the surface like rays from a sun. The creature was dead, but so might Fyodor be as well.

Liriel whirled on the sea elf, speechless with rage.

"To show him the way out," Xzorsh explained.

Sure enough, a hand groped its way along the exposed shaft of the harpoon. In a moment, Fyodor's head burst from the ruined eye. He dashed the gore from his face and dragged in several long breaths. His foe was dead; the battle rage slipped away. For as long as a berserker rage lasted, he never felt pain, or cold, or exhaustion. Those things would come now.

With difficulty, the young warrior squeezed himself through the eye socket and began to swim with uncertain strokes for the ship. Xzorsh dove into the water to help, and a dozen hands reached out to help the day's hero aboard.

Fyodor slumped to the deck, pale as seafoam. His shirt had been ripped from shoulder to waist, and blood welled up from a dozen circular wounds. The sea elf began to tend the man, his movements so sure and deft that not even Liriel thought to interfere.

"Now there's a tale to tell your son's sons," Hrolf declared, shaking his head in disbelief. "It's lucky we are to have a berserker aboard!"

"It's *ill* fortune at work here!" the first mate said angrily. "Granted, the lad killed the creature. But by my reckoning, the squid never would have attacked if the female had not been aboard! And for that matter, what kind of man calls a black elf woman friend?"

It was a long speech for Ibn, and the sheer passion in his words brought sympathetic murmurs from the battered crew. Dark, furtive glares skittered toward the drow.

"What kind of man?" Hrolf repeated and then shrugged. "I also count the drow as a friend, and by *my* reckoning I captain this ship still. So speak your mind as you will, lad, but my orders stand."

There was nothing Ibn could say to that. He recognized his mistake at once. Every man aboard held the captain in high esteem, and most of them regarded the wounded berserker with something approaching reverence. They were willing enough to turn upon the drow, but not one among them could discredit what Fyodor had just done or would argue against the word or will of their captain. So the first mate contented himself with muttering, "Bad fortune!" as he stalked off in search of a dry pipe.

"Pay him no mind, lass," Hrolf advised Liriel. "Ibn is a good man, but slow to let go once he takes hold of something. He's not one for new ways, and yours are strange to us all." He cast a curious look at the young wizard. "During the battle you spoke a word—calamari—to the squid. What is that—a magic spell? A curse?"

"A meal," the drow returned slyly. Now that the danger had passed, her dark sense of mischief returned in full. She ripped the severed tentacle from the fallen sailor and strode across the deck to present it, still twitching, to Ibn.

"You wanted me to help with provisions? Fine. We will eat as drow do. Have this sliced, dipped in batter, and fried in rendered rothe fat. Calamari. It's quite good," she assured the mate, who was turning sickly green as he regarded the appendage.

"Ship's wizard," suggested a faint, strained voice.

The words came from Fyodor. He hauled himself up to a sitting position and cast a droll look at the first mate. "Consider her . . . ship's wizard," the Rashemi advised. He spoke with great effort, between ragged gasps for air, but his blue eyes sparkled with wry humor. "It's . . . safer that way."

The red-bearded man nodded, his distrust of magic momentarily thrust aside by the prospect of seeing that twitching tentacle on his plate. "Ship's wizard," Ibn agreed fervently.

Chapter 4

THE PIRATE'S LIFE

 he *Elfmaid* had been at sea for several days before the northernmost Moonshae Isles came into view. Fyodor was heartened by the sight of land and eager to explore. Yet the ship did not make port, but kept a careful distance from shore, cloaked into invisibility by the heavy spring mists.

"With winter's passing, the seas are opening, and the merchant ships will soon sail," Hrolf explained when Fyodor asked about the delay. The two men sat cross-legged on the deck of the forecastle, a torn net between them. Their fingers flew as they retied the knots with a rhythm of practiced ease. Barely missing a beat, Hrolf gave the young warrior a companionable swat on the back. "And after seeing you take on that squid, I'd say we'll pick off the merchants as easily as taking ripe currants off a bush!"

"I will not fight for you," Fyodor said quietly.

The captain paused, startled. "How's that, lad?"

"I fight only when I must, only to protect my land or my friends," the young warrior explained. "If the ship is attacked, I will stand with you. But I must warn you, if you attack another ship to rob it, I may well turn against you."

Hrolf's genial expression did not change, but his eyes turned hard. "A threat?"

"A warning," the Rashemi said calmly, but he cast a questioning glance at Liriel, who, lured by her friend's somber expression, had crept close to listen to the discussion. "Unlike my berserker brethren, I cannot always choose when the battle rage will occur. Did not Liriel tell you this?"

"That she didn't," Hrolf said ruefully as he eyed the wary drow. "Slipped your mind, lass?"

"You started the tavern brawl before I could get to that part of the story," Liriel said defensively. "I would have told you, otherwise. I'm fairly certain of that."

The captain sighed and tugged at his vast mustache. His good spirits returned suddenly, and he winked at the drow. "Don't look so downcast, my girl! Fighting's all good and well, but there're more ways than one to turn a profit!"

Later that day, the captain gathered together his crew to discuss the necessary changes to the usual lurk-and-attack strategy. The men agreed to Hrolf's plan readily enough, even though it involved Liriel and her dark elven magic. All of them had seen Fyodor fight; none wanted to face his black sword in battle. Moreover, they were accustomed to their captain's unorthodox methods, and they trusted him, if not Liriel.

It would not be the first time Hrolf achieved through bluffing what might otherwise have cost dearly in blood. In fact, the captain leaned heavily toward a benign form of piracy. If he could scare a ship into surrendering its cargo, so much the better. Hrolf loved a good fight, but he enjoyed fighting far better when the *Elfmaid* was well out of harm's way.

So the crew clustered around as Liriel explained the necessary spell. "It is a form of teleportation that will exchange one person for another. One of you will be sent aboard the ship to take our terms to the captain: half their cargo in payment for his man's return. Which of you is willing to go?"

"It's not just a question of who's willing, lass," Hrolf commented. "Think on this: what's to keep them from holding our man and going for an even trade or even refusing to trade at all? Don't get me wrong—your magic's a fine way to kidnap a man. It will put the other captain off guard, at least for a moment or two. But it's not enough."

"What, then?" Liriel demanded.

Hrolf smiled slyly. "The Ffolk of the Moonshaes are a hearty people, not easy to spook. Picture their captain finding himself face-to-face with a stranger who appeared all of a sudden on his ship. Who among us is most likely to strike head-numbing fear into the poor sod?"

All eyes turned to Liriel.

A slow, wicked smile spread across the drow's face, and she nodded her acceptance. Her eyes sparkled as she began to improvise the details of the plot. Soon the pirates were chuckling with delight. None argued or even frowned as she passed out their assignments with the absolute assurance of a battle chieftain.

Of all the men aboard, only two were not caught up in the

excitement: Ibn, who puffed stolidly away at his pipe, and Fyodor, who tried without success to hide his disappointment as he watched the shining, animated face of the plotting drow.

*　*　*　*　*

Liriel cast the spell at dusk. Although she was slowly becoming accustomed to the punishing glare of the sun and sea, twilight was a time of mystery, a time of natural magic that the drow recognized and intended to exploit. Sea and sky melded into one darkness, but the shadows resisted banishment. As they faded with the failing light, they seemed to leave an unseen presence behind. In the cusp between day and night, between shadow and dreams, anything seemed possible. This was important, for Liriel's spell depended upon her victims' capacity for awe as surely as it did her dark-elven wizardry. For such an enchantment, no time was more potent than twilight.

The Moonshae vessel was also ideally suited for Liriel's purposes. She realized this the moment the teleportation spell set her down upon its deck. She prowled silently about, her *piwafwi* cloaking her in invisibility as she studied the ship, observed the line of command. She even explored the cabins, the better to know her prey. One small chamber was littered with bits and pieces so odd they could only be spell components. Liriel quickly searched this cabin and, to her delight, found a small book filled with unfamiliar spells based upon sea magic. She pocketed the treasure and resumed her search.

The merchant ship was small but of a modern design, with a sturdy aft castle built as an original part of the ship rather than as a temporary, add-on platform. It had a sternpost rudder, steered with a tiller. The man at the tiller had to be told what to do, because he was under the after castle and couldn't see where the ship was headed. At the moment these orders came from the captain, who was perched in the crow's nest atop the ship's single mast. Ratlines—evenly spaced light ropes that formed ladders—ran up to the crow's nest from either side of the ship.

Silent and invisible, the drow scrambled up the lines and climbed into the crow's nest beside the captain. He was leaning over the edge, frowning as he listened to the agitated report of two of his men.

"What do you mean, Drustan is gone?" he called. "Gone where?"

"We have him," Liriel said, flipping open her sheltering *piwafwi*.

The captain straightened abruptly and whirled toward the sound of her voice. His face bleached in terror at the sight of a dark elf, close enough to touch.

"He is with my people," the drow continued and was rewarded by the look of horror that came into the captain's eyes. Clearly, he thought his man had somehow been whisked away to the fell, underground realm of the dark elves. All the better, Liriel thought smugly. She cocked an eyebrow. "We might be persuaded to return him."

The man tried to speak. No sound emerged. He licked his lips nervously and tried again. "What do you want?"

"Half your cargo," she stated. "Do not try to cheat us, for we will know. I am not alone," Liriel said, dropping her voice to a dramatic whisper. She pulled the folds of her cloak about her and blinked out of sight. The captain could not see her or the dagger she pressed against his throat, but the line of blood trickling down into the ruffles of his shirtfront was visible, and utterly convincing. Liriel saw in his eyes the terrified belief that his ship had been invaded by an unknown number of dark elves, a deadly and invisible force.

"We will do as you say," he said in a strangled tone, but there was a desperate cunning in his eyes that Liriel noted and mistrusted.

"It might save some unpleasantness if you know up front that your wizard is useless against us. No human spell can disperse our invisibility charms—magic slides off the drow like water from a seabird's feathers," she informed him coolly. "But any magical attack, however feeble, will be parried and answered. Believe me when I tell you that you do not wish to see drow magic tested in battle."

Liriel saw the light of last hope fade from the man's eyes and knew she had hit the target squarely. She gave him his instructions, making it clear that she would be at his side until all was done. If he gave the alarm, she promised, if he even hinted at the presence of the dark elves aboard ship, he would lose half his crew in addition to half his cargo . . . and perhaps his life as well.

The captain did as he was told, but the crew was slow to accept his claim that Drustan had somehow been magically spirited off the ship and that the cost of his freedom would be paid from their cargo. But they followed orders, lowering a large, flat-bottomed skiff and loading it with small oak casks.

"Make room for my people," Liriel hissed into the captain's ear. "Two will attend the skiff; the rest will stay to ensure there is no foolish attempt to cheat us of our toll. We will send your man back with the skiff, and then we will leave as we came."

While the captain bellowed down orders to rearrange the casks, Liriel, still invisible, floated silently down into the boat. As soon as the men were clear of the skiff, she cast a spell of levitation. The heavily laden craft broke free of the waves and rose slowly into the air. As the dumbfounded sailors watched, it glided silently off into the mist.

It was not an easy spell, but Liriel knew the value of an imposing exit. It would give credence to the captain's explanation, and the sense of wonder and fear that it inspired would occupy the humans' minds and keep at bay any thoughts they might otherwise have had about following the ghostly skiff.

When the boat touched down on the *Elfmaid*'s deck, Liriel slumped over one of the casks, drained by the powerful casting. The crew swarmed to meet her and to examine their haul. They were delighted to learn that the casks were filled with fine raspberry mead, a sweet and fiery honey wine scented with summer fruit.

"See our guest on his way, and then we'll tap a cask for the celebration. The rest we'll use for trade," Hrolf said with a wink.

The men set promptly to work, following the plan Liriel had laid out. The captured sailor had emerged from the teleportation spell into the darkness of the hold. Two Ruathen had awaited him there, armed with tiny darts from Liriel's crossbow. One quick jab had sent the sailor into a poison-induced slumber. He was still senseless when they brought him on deck and loaded him onto the skiff.

Liriel handed the precious spellbook into Fyodor's keeping and then joined the sleeping sailor in the skiff, for one step remained to complete the deception. It would not do to let the Ffolk know their ship had been held hostage by shadows, and that Ruathen pirates lay within easy pursuit. She watched as the *Elfmaid* rowed away, pulling farther back into the mist.

When the Ruathen ship was beyond sight, Liriel unstoppered a tiny vial that held an antidote to the drow sleeping potion. She poured a single drop into the sailor's slack mouth. He stirred, scratched, and then grumbled himself awake with a string of curses. His muttering ended in a strangled gulp when he saw a drow bending over him.

"Return to your ship," she commanded him and swept a hand in the direction of the merchant vessel. Instantly the faint, ghostly outline of the Moonshae vessel gleamed through the fog. Liriel had limned it with faerie fire to guide the sailor back and to further astound those who awaited him.

While the sailor gaped like a beached carp at his ship, Liriel cloaked herself with invisibility and slipped quietly into the sea. Her limbs felt heavy in the frigid water, and the heavy folds of her *piwafwi* dragged her down. Although she was a strong swimmer, it was a struggle for her to cover the short distance back to the pirate ship.

Several pairs of eager hands were outstretched to haul her aboard. Liriel barely registered the sailors' assistance, the feel of the deck beneath her feet, or the sight of it hurtling up to meet her.

Fyodor caught the drow as she fell and carried her down to Hrolf's cabin. He turned away while she listlessly stripped off her wet things, kept his eyes averted until the squeak of the cot's roping announced that she'd crawled under the covers.

"All went well," she told him in a drowsy voice, "but I have a feeling it'll be a while before that captain stops looking over his shoulder. He'll be seeing dark elves in every shadow for many days to come."

"You need rest," Fyodor said quietly. "I will leave you now."

There was something in his tone that cut through Liriel's haze of exhaustion. She hauled herself into a sitting position and studied her friend. As she'd suspected, he did not approve of this night's work. His eyes did not condemn her, but they held sadness, resignation. This stung the drow more than she liked to admit.

"I have tasted Moonshae mead before," Liriel said abruptly, "and I know its price." She leaned over the edge of the cot and fumbled through the discarded belongings on the floor until she found a small bag. She tossed it at Fyodor. It fell short of his reflexive grab and landed, with the unmistakable *chink* of many coins, at his feet.

"That is what the mead would have cost in the bazaars of Menzoberranzan. The captain will find an identical bag in his cabin. The ship's wizard has also been compensated. Trust me, you don't want to know the market cost of that spellbook," she grumbled. "The point being, none of those men suffered loss from this little game. In fact, they made an enormous profit, considering they were spared the cost and trouble of carting their wares into the Underdark!"

For a long moment, Fyodor stared at the unpredictable drow. "But why, little raven? Why go to such trouble if you intended only to buy the mead?"

Her smile was pure mischief, but he did not miss the flash of uncertainty in her amber eyes. "Do you think Hrolf and his boys would have been satisfied with a simple business transaction? They had their minds set on piracy! This way, Hrolf got to play out his bluff, the Moonshae merchants have their money, and everyone involved comes away with a good story to tell. No one is the worse for it."

Fyodor was floored by this revelation—for never had he seen anyone go through such lengths to hide an honorable intent—and he was deeply touched by Liriel's ill-concealed desire to please him. He closed the distance between them and took one of her hands in both his own. Her fingers were still icy cold; he began to chafe them gently as he considered his next words. There was much he wanted to say, but he was not sure any of it would make sense to the drow. Despite her convoluted mind and her delight in plots and intrigues, she had little understanding of the heart's complexities.

The silence between them was long. Liriel cocked her head and peered up at him in mock astonishment. "You are *thinking*," she accused him teasingly. " 'There are those who think, and those who dream,' " she said, quoting his own words back to him. "You're not changing sides, are you?"

His answering smile was rueful. "No. Just dreaming, as usual." He released her hand and turned to leave.

"Don't go yet." She sidled over to make room and patted the edge of the cot companionably.

Fyodor looked back over his shoulder. He let his eyes speak what was in his heart, but he kept a careful distance from her. "I am ever your friend," he said quietly. "But sometimes, little raven, you expect too much of a man."

Understanding flooded the drow's face, then consternation. Once, briefly, they had been lovers. The unexpected, unfamiliar intimacy of the encounter had torn Liriel from her emotional moorings, leaving her confused and shaken. Such things were dangerous— indeed, forbidden!—among the drow, and she'd readily accepted Fyodor's suggestion that they move beyond that interlude. The friendship between them was intense but difficult; they were still feeling their way through unfamiliar territory. Looking at her friend now, she realized that for him the matter was far from resolved. The thought both dismayed and intrigued her.

"Do you *want* to stay?" she asked bluntly.

Fyodor smiled gently into her stricken face. "Sleep well. I will see you next moonrise." And with that he left, closing the cabin door carefully behind him.

A storm of emotions buffeted the capricious drow: relief, frustration, and then a surge of purely feminine pique. She snatched a knife from under her mattress and hurled it at the door. It bit deep into the wood, quivering hard enough to give off an audible, twanging hum. The drow rolled over and buried her head beneath her pillow to muffle the mocking sound.

"He could at least have *said* yes!" she muttered.

* * * * *

At first light, the *Elfmaid* sailed into the Korinn Archipelago, a scattering of small islands north of the Moonshaes. There was an air of anticipation about the ship that Fyodor noted and mistrusted. Hrolf was especially jolly, full to overbrimming with boisterous humor and badly sung ballads.

The young Rashemi liked Hrolf, more with each day that passed, for the captain had an enormous capacity for enjoyment that was both disarming and contagious. Hrolf took whatever life offered—be it a sudden squall, a drinking horn full of mead, or a tale of adventure—with pleasure and gusto. Unfortunately, he also took more than was his by legal right. It was difficult for Fyodor to reconcile his growing affection for Hrolf with the man's fun-loving larceny, and he dreaded what might occur when they made land.

But the reception lavished upon the *Elfmaid*'s crew immediately put Fyodor's mind to rest. It was late afternoon when they made port on Tetris, a small island of rolling green hills and rocky, windswept coasts. The dockmaster greeted Hrolf by name and urged him to hurry along to the festival. As the crew made their way through the village—a cluster of stone-and-thatch huts that lined the river on its meandering way to the sea—many villagers called out cheery greetings. A small, well-rounded woman with glad gray eyes and cheeks like ripe apples ran to meet Hrolf, her skirts flying and her arms outstretched in welcome. The captain caught her up, spinning her around with ease and then enfolding her in a bear hug.

"His woman," explained Olvir, smiling indulgently as he nodded at the pair. He and Fyodor walked together, following the growing crowd that headed for the hills beyond the town. The two men had become good friends during the voyage, first trading tales of their homelands and then, slowly, confiding pieces of their own stories.

From his boyhood Olvir had longed to be a skald, but he could not reconcile himself with the lower status that his warrior culture assigned to their bards. So he went to sea, seeking a fortune to appease his ambitions while collecting the stories that fed his spirit.

"You come to this island often?" Fyodor asked.

"Five, six times a year. 'Tis almost a home port!"

"Still, that seems too seldom for a man and woman as fond as those two."

Olvir shrugged. "Moira will not leave the island, nor Hrolf the sea. They suit each other well; always are they glad to meet and content to part."

The sailor went on to other matters, describing the festival that would take place that evening. The Ffolk here followed ways long abandoned on most of the islands, ancient rites and festivals attuned to the turning of the seasons. Their druid, a doddering old gray-beard dressed in robes of an era long past, clung to the worship of ancient spirits of land and sea. Tonight the village would offer the yearly tribute to the river spirit and celebrate the coming of spring.

Fyodor stood with the villagers as the aged druid said his prayers and offered the yearly tribute into the waters: beautifully worked armbands, torques, and broaches of pure yellow gold. Fyodor was a little surprised to see that the pirates, too, stood by in reverent silence as the old man tossed a fortune in gold into the water.

Making the ritual more remarkable was the fact that Fyodor could perceive no magic about the place at all. Like many of his people, he had a touch of the Sight, and he was usually able to sense places of power. Here, he felt nothing. He resolved to ask Hrolf about this later.

With the setting of the sun, the ritual gave way to celebration. Hrolf and his men contributed several casks of their "stolen" mead. Bonfires dotted the hillsides, and around them the villagers and pirates danced to the music of reed flutes, drums, and small, plaintive pipes. Sooner than Fyodor expected, the frenzied, joyous pace of the festival gave way to pleasant languor. Some of the revelers crept away in pairs to seek the shadows beyond the flickering firelight. Those who remained danced and drank to exhaustion, then curled up near the fires and fell into contented slumber.

Taking advantage of the unexpected lull, Fyodor sought out Hrolf. The captain was seated in state upon a tree stump, his Moonshae wife on his lap and a large drinking horn in one hand. Hrolf roared out a greeting and pressed the horn upon the young man, insisting that he have his share. Fyodor drained the vessel—not a difficult task for one accustomed to the fiery *jhuild* of Rashemen— and then asked the captain about the day's ritual, explaining his perception that no magic lingered in the river.

The pirate shrugged. "Place spirits are not so common as they once were, that's true enough, but old ways die hard. And what's the harm of it? The river waters their fields, carries their boats to the sea, and gives them fish. That is worth more than gold to them!"

"Well said," Fyodor replied, pleasantly surprised by Hrolf's insightful and tolerant answer. Even so, he did not credit these words as being the whole truth, and he said so.

Hrolf responded only with a wink and a shrug. He refilled the drinking horn from the mead cask and handed it to the young warrior. "For a dreamer, lad, you worry too much! Find the bottom of this one and see if that doesn't steal your troubles!"

* * * * *

Liriel waited until well after midnight before leaving the ship. Although she agreed with Hrolf that the Ffolk might not take well to a drow's presence on their island, she could not resist the temptation to see this new land with her own eyes. Acting on impulse, she dressed as if she were participating in the promised festival, putting on a gown of black silk she had bought in Skullport and taming the wild waves of her hair into an elaborate arrangement of coils and ringlets. The Windwalker amulet she hid beneath the bodice of her gown, yielding the place of honor to a pendant Fyodor had given her: a smooth oval of glowing amber with a black spider in its heart. Thus garbed, she donned her *piwafwi* and crept, wrapped in invisibility, through the deserted village, making her way toward the dying bonfires on the hills beyond.

The drow had expected a festival; what she encountered more closely resembled a battlefield. Villagers and Ruathen alike were sprawled about like so many victims of a massacre, with one exception: the dead generally did not snore. The grating chorus resounding through the clearing bore vivid testimony to the evening's overindulgence. Hrolf, in particular, set the air vibrating with his raucous blasts as he lay asleep on his back, his boots propped up on one of several empty mead casks.

The drow's eyes narrowed as she studied the scene. She was frequently amazed at the odd weakness humans had for strong

58

drink. There was not a drow alive who couldn't drink three dwarves under the table, and even drow who overindulged could shake off the effects almost at will. Humans didn't have that type of fortitude, and it seemed to her that those humans least able to handle potent drink had the strongest taste for it. Still, she didn't see how so many humans could drink themselves into oblivion in such short order. Even Fyodor, who could swallow that wretched Rashemaar firewine without ill effect, had succumbed to the night's revelry. He lay in deep slumber. A half-full drinking horn had been thrust point-down into the soft ground beside him.

Liriel crouched at Fyodor's side and took up the drinking horn. She sniffed at the mead, caught the faint scent of the herbs that had been added to it. Since a knowledge of poisons was an important part of any dark elf's education, Liriel recognized the scent of a harmless—but potent—sleeping potion.

She was not at all surprised, therefore, when an owl-like hoot came from the "sleeping" Hrolf. At this signal the pirates scrambled to their feet like so many puppets pulled by a single string. The effect was both eerie and comic. Liriel could not help but think of zombies arising from a battlefield in response to a wizard's call.

The men stole down to the banks of a river. Wondering what Hrolf was up to now, Liriel crept along after the Ruathen. She watched, puzzled, as several of the younger men stripped to the skin and waded into the water. They dove repeatedly, coming up to toss small, shining items to their comrades on the banks. From their talk, Liriel pieced together the story of what had happened earlier that night and what was happening as she watched.

The sacrilege of this act of thievery troubled her, for no Underdark drow would dare to defile an offering to Lloth. From what she had learned since leaving Menzoberranzan, Liriel surmised that few deities were as vengeful as the Spider Queen. Still, it seemed a large risk to take for mere gold, and she decided to convince the pirates of their error.

Still invisible, Liriel walked among the men and watched as young Bjorn surfaced, a broad grin on his face. He waved a gold armband triumphantly overhead and then tossed it toward the shore. Liriel darted forward and caught the ornament, tucking it quickly beneath the folds of her *piwafwi*.

To the pirates, it appeared that the ornament had simply disappeared. They fell back from the invisible drow, bug-eyed with astonishment and fear.

"Captain, you said there was no river spirit!" a white-faced Olvir protested.

Bjorn was even more distressed. His thin hands fluttered like birds as he formed signs of warding, over and over. "May Tempus help us! We've angered their god!"

"We haven't thus far!" Hrolf returned, unperturbed. "Think, lads. We've been harvesting the gold every spring for ten years, regular as a crop of rye. No, any spirit that might've made this river a home is long gone!"

"What, then?" demanded Ibn.

The captain winked at his first mate, then held out one hand, palm up, as he faced the apparently empty air. "Hand it over, lass. You'll get your share later, same as us all."

Liriel smothered a grin. Hrolf's assurances to his men had put her mind at ease, and his quick-witted response to her prank pleased her. Still invisible, she tossed the bracelet to the captain. Its sudden reappearance dealt a second shock to the still-wary men. Then Bjorn figured out what was happening, and he began to chuckle. One by one, the Ruathen caught on. Not all of them, however, were amused by the joke.

"Damn female!" muttered Ibn as he turned back to the river. "Should ha' known it was her at the first sign of trouble."

* * * * *

By the time the sun rose, the gold had been safely stowed aboard ship and the pirates had resumed their places among the sleeping revelers. When finally the scene stirred to reluctant life, none of the Ffolk seemed to find anything amiss. The farewells between villagers and pirates were somewhat muted by the lingering effects of the mead, but Hrolf's crew took their leave in friendly fashion, amid promises to return soon.

The pirates' spirits returned in full once they were aboard the *Elf-maid*. Only Fyodor felt any ill effects from the mead, and although the young warrior was the target of much good-natured teasing, he felt too miserable to wonder why he was the only one so affected.

* * * * *

To Liriel's chagrin, the *Elfmaid* did not head directly for Ruathym. Hrolf set course for Neverwinter, a coastal city some three hundred miles to the north. The Ruathen wished to trade some of their stolen gold for Neverwinter crafts, but there was another, more practical reason for the diversion as well. Neverwinter was named for its unusually warm climate and a harbor that remained free of ice year round. This was in part due to the River, a current of warm water and air that swept eastward from Evermeet, over the island of Gundarlun, and narrowing until it touched Neverwinter's shores. So early in the spring, sailing the River was far safer than taking their chances against the ice floes that dotted the open sea. Hrolf planned to take to the River at Neverwinter, sail to Gundarlun to fish for spring herring, then travel due south to Ruathym. The expected profit was considerable, but this added time to the journey that Liriel had not considered. She had no idea how long the magic stored in the Windwalker might last, and she was anxious to reach Ruathym as soon as possible.

But the drow tried to make the best of the delay, using the time to study the book of sea magic and to add more spells to the Windwalker. Storytelling passed the time, too, and Liriel coaxed Hrolf and Olvir for information on their island home. As the days passed, she and Fyodor fell back into the comfortable routine of fellow travelers. Neither of them mentioned the moment that had passed between them in Hrolf's cabin, but Liriel thought of it often. She suspected that Fyodor did, as well.

At last the ship reached Neverwinter. The *Elfmaid* was received at the port by an armed guard. But after the dockmaster saw a sample of the pirates' golden treasure, she allowed the ship to dock—with the provision that Hrolf the Unruly remain under heavy guard on his own ship. It seemed that several taverns in Neverwinter had reason to remember the captain.

Liriel enjoyed exploring the city—walking at Fyodor's side, cloaked in invisibility. To her fell the task of browsing through shops displaying the water clocks and multicolored lamps for which Neverwinter's artisans were famed. Some of the stolen gold went to purchase a few of these treasures, which Hrolf would sell to wealthy Ruathen. It was a pleasant interlude, but the drow was not sorry when the *Elfmaid* put out to sea.

They sailed westward for two days before encountering another vessel in the warm waters of the River. Fyodor was on the forecastle taking a turn at watch when he saw it: a sturdy cog, leaning hard to the leeward, cutting through the water with almost reckless speed. He called an alert down to Hrolf, who was manning the rudder and regaling Liriel with stories of Ruathym.

"I know that ship," Hrolf commented, peering at it through an eyeglass. "She carries seal hunters. On their way back home, they are, and in a hurry."

His mustache lifted in a broad grin, and he winked at a pair of sailors lounging nearby. "Think of it, lads: a pallet of fine white fur. Now there's a gift to brighten your woman's eye and sweeten your welcome home!"

Liriel cast a quick glance toward Fyodor and shook her head. "Don't do it, Hrolf," she murmured. "You've seen him in battle only against a squid. I've seen him fight drow—and *win.*"

The captain scoffed. "What kind of fool do you take me for, lass? Think you that I'd risk turning a berserker's wrath upon my own ship?"

Hrolf pointed at the approaching cog. "I know her captain. Name of Farlow, used to be a sell-sword. A good man, if you like 'em quick to fight, and he knows us as pirates! All we need do is sail close enough to give Captain Farlow a good look at us and let him think what he will! And once they attack," Hrolf said slyly, "yon lad will stand with us, and at last we'll see him at play! It'll be an easy fight for the rest of us, by my reckoning!"

The captain's reasoning proved prophetic. No sooner had he finished speaking than the cog changed course. The heavy ship hurtled toward the Ruathen vessel at ramming speed, bowsprit leveled at them like the lance of a jousting knight.

"Take your positions, lads!" roared the captain with undisguised glee.

Such attacks were expected and anticipated, and every man leaped to the role that had been assigned him. Harreldson dropped the sail and joined several others at the oars. The ship was smaller and lighter than the attacking cog—a single collision could send the *Elfmaid* to the bottom of the sea. In such attacks, she was best served by her ability to change course quickly and by the fighting strength of her crew.

Fyodor snatched a large wooden shield from its hook on the forecastle. Five other men did the same, kneeling shoulder-to-shoulder to form a shield wall. Five more sailors, armed with arrows and longbows, dove for cover behind the wall. Liriel took her place at Fyodor's side, but her hands remained empty. If the need arose, she had more powerful weapons to hurl.

The cog closed in fast, and the seal hunters' first volley of arrows clattered against the wooden shields. Hrolf's men returned fire; then the *Elfmaid* turned hard astern and darted past the onrushing cog. Before the merchant ship could change course, Hrolf's rowers spun the ship in a circle and brought her alongside the cog. Two of the pirates twirled ropes that ended with heavy grappling hooks, then let fly. Both of the hooks found purchase on the larger vessel. A seal hunter leaned out to cut the lines; his body fell into the sea, bristling with Ruathen arrows.

Then came the grating shriek of wood against wood as the ships struck, then rebounded. The rowers set their oars and took up weapons just in time. Three of the hunters leaped over the narrow expanse of water that separated the two ships.

Hrolf barreled toward the invaders, roaring, his arms spread wide. He caught them before they could get their footing, and all four men plunged, with a mighty splash, over the side.

"Take the fight to them, lads!" The captain's voice came to them from the water below. "No need to be getting blood all over the *Elfmaid*'s clean deck!"

The pirates tossed boarding planks between the ships and began to swarm up the incline onto the cog. Weapons drawn, the more numerous hunters confidently awaited the pirates. Then, suddenly, the attackers' expressions of certainty melted into astonishment.

All of them had heard stories of Ruathym's berserkers, elite warriors who protected their homeland. Berserkers were never encountered at sea, much less aboard a pirate vessel. Yet the dark-haired warrior stalking toward them could be nothing less.

Fully seven feet tall, he brandished a black sword too large and heavy for most men to lift. There was an aura of magic about him, and his blue eyes burned with inner fire. Equally fearsome—and even more astonishing—was the drow female who followed the berserker like a small dark shadow. There was a long dagger in one slender hand, and a feral gleam in eyes as golden as those of a stalking wolf.

The seal hunters' hesitation lasted but a moment, for their black-bearded captain spurred them into battle with the point of his own sword.

The berserker went straight for Captain Farlow, backhanding two pirates out of the way with the flat of his blade as he strode up the boarding plank. He leaped onto the deck of the cog, swinging his black sword downward in a sweeping cut as he came.

Farlow snapped his sword up high to block the attack. His was a fine weapon—a hand-and-a-half sword of dwarf-forged steel, tested in two decades of mercenary fighting. The berserker's blade shattered it and sent deadly shards flying. Faster than Farlow would have believed possible, the berserker reversed the direction of his swing and batted a length of airborne steel toward one of the hunters. The shard flew end over end, like a thrown knife. It caught one of the hunters through the throat, nailing him to the wooden mast.

The captain glanced at the hilt in his hand and the jagged fragment of steel that was all that remained of his blade. He hoped it would be enough. Raising the ruined weapon high overhead, he flung himself at the deadly invader, putting his weight and his strength fully behind the blow.

Liriel saw the attack coming and shrieked a warning to Fyodor. Almost casually, the berserker reached up and caught the man's wrist, fully stopping his momentum. Then he twisted the captain's arm down and inward, and with one quick thrust he sheathed the ruined blade in the heart of its owner.

Surprisingly enough, the hunters did not abandon their fight with the death of their captain. They threw themselves at the pirates with astonishing ferocity. Liriel noted one in particular—a tall, red-haired man who fought with the zeal of a paladin as he faced off against Hrolf. The *Elfmaid*'s captain had managed to back the man onto the forecastle, but there both stood, neither taking nor giving ground, their swords ringing in a deadly dialogue.

The other hunters did not fare so well against the pirates and their berserker ally. In minutes, the cog's deck was slippery with blood, and few of the hunters had been spared Fyodor's black sword. Except for Hrolf's opponent, none remained standing.

Seeing that victory was theirs, Liriel let out a whoop and turned to Fyodor. One glance stole her triumph. Although only Ruathen sailors stood on the main deck, the killing frenzy had not yet left the young warrior.

"Throw down your weapons!" she shouted. "All of you!"

The berserker whirled toward the sound of her voice, his black sword cutting the air with an audible swish. Liriel had seen her friend in battle many times, but never had she faced him, or seen the fire and ice of his battle rage turned upon her. He towered over the tiny elf, for the magic of the berserker lent him an illusion of preternatural size and a strength to match. Liriel could see through the magic to his true form, but this was of little comfort. There was no recognition in Fyodor's eyes as he advanced on her.

Liriel dropped her bloody dagger and fell to her knees, holding her hands out wide, palms up in a gesture of surrender. From the corner of her eye, she saw that Hrolf and his chosen man still held their swords. They'd hesitated at Liriel's impassioned shout, but they eyed each other warily, neither willing to give up the advantage.

"If you value my life, Hrolf," she said quietly, "if either of you idiots value yours, drop your swords *now!*"

An instant's hesitation, then the clatter of falling steel shattered the tense silence. At last Fyodor's battle rage left him and, as the magic faded, he seemed to slip back into his own body. He stood there for a long moment, looking down with a puzzled expression into the drow's upturned face. Then the tip of his sword fell heavily to the deck. His eyes were haunted, his face ashen as he turned and walked away from the battle. Liriel understood and left him to his solitude.

The Ruathen sailors, however, swarmed gleefully over the captured cog. As Hrolf directed their efforts from the forecastle, they tossed bundles of raw skins onto their ship and carried aboard the stretching frames and barrels of lye needed to begin the process of tanning.

Bjorn struggled down the plank carrying a large oaken cask that proved too heavy for the slender lad. It slipped from his grasp and fell heavily to the *Elfmaid*'s deck. The lid cracked and gave way, and the contents spilled out. The boy stood there, gaping, his nearly beardless face pale.

"Captain, you'd better see this," he said at last.

Something in Bjorn's tone brought Hrolf at a run. The captain's ebullience disappeared as he gazed at the still, small figure on the deck: the body of an elf child, perfectly preserved by the pickling brine that puddled on the deck.

The macabre discovery brought the looting to an abrupt standstill. The pirates crowded around, not certain what to do. Their discomfort increased visibly when Hrolf tenderly gathered the dead child in his massive arms and wept, openly and without shame.

At length Hrolf laid the elfling gently aside and ordered his men to search the other barrels. His haggard face turned deadly as, one after another, the dead sea elves were laid out upon the deck.

"Call Xzorsh," he said grimly.

One of the men hurried below, returning promptly with a strange device that looked rather like a small hurdy-gurdy. Hrolf placed the thing in the water and turned the wooden crank. Instead

65

of music, the instrument gave off a series of clicks and whistles.

"A message to the sea elf," Bjorn whispered to Liriel. "Sounds travel faster and farther in the water than in air. There are creatures below who will hear and repeat the message until it reaches the sea ranger's ears. He will be here soon, and he will know what must be done."

When Hrolf rose to his feet, Ibn took the device from him and then nodded toward the cog. "What do we do with the ship and the men who yet live?"

"Scuttle it," Hrolf said tersely, "and leave the surviving scum to await Umberlee's judgment. But bind their wounds first, so the blood doesn't draw sharks or worse. The Lady of the Waves will do as she will, with no help from me!"

The captain's wrath sped the men about their work. They fell to, some loading the wounded hunters into a single small boat, others using battle-axes to hack gaping holes in the side of the cog. One of the survivors—the red-haired man who'd matched Hrolf blow for blow—tried to have words with the captain. Hrolf effectively silenced his protests; a single blow of his ham-sized fist dropped the fighter. The captain tossed the unconscious man into the little craft and gave the signal to set it adrift. In moments the mists closed around the condemned men, like a veil separating them from the mortal world.

Hrolf stood at the rail, looking out after the boat with grim satisfaction long after it had disappeared from view. Quietly, respectfully, the crew went about their duties. Few of them knew the full story of their captain's long-ago elven love, but there was not one among them who hadn't lost someone to the sea. There was not one among them who didn't send up a silent plea to Umberlee, asking the Lady of the Waves to take the wounded seal hunters to appease her wrath rather than someone else.

In these prayers, no one dared to name himself, or a friend or lover whom he wished to see spared. Those who lived with the sea were a superstitious lot, and they took their fate as it came. Yet not a man among them would deliberately place himself at the mercy of Umberlee, and not a man among them doubted what the seal hunters' fate would be at the hands of the sea goddess. And although they were Northmen, a people who as a rule held little love for elves, none of them believed that this fate was undeserved.

Chapter 5
THE AMULET

riel Baenre, the newly elevated ruler of Menzoberranzan's most powerful house, sat in state upon her black
throne. Faint purple light surrounded the young Matron
Mother, casting eerie shadows throughout the chamber
and forcing the eyes of the priestess seated before her into the light
spectrum. This Triel did by design, for light stole the nuances of heat
vision, masked the subtle play of emotion that dark elves were so
adept at reading. To the drow, absolute darkness revealed more than
it hid. Shadows were more useful for concealment.

It was important that Triel hide her distaste for her visitor, for
Shakti Hunzrin was a valuable tool, the first traitor-priestess in generations to successfully infiltrate the ranks of Vhaeraun's clergy. The
known followers of the drow god of thievery were few—in no small
part because suspected followers were summarily put to death—but
Triel believed that the so-called Masked God posed more of a threat
than Lloth's clergy liked to admit. As traitor-priestess, Shakti would
help ensure that this dangerous seed never bore fruit.

The Baenre matron was confident that Shakti's primary alle-
giance was to Lloth; indeed, Triel's powerful mind-reaving spells
revealed nothing more disturbing than fanatic zeal. Perhaps a bit
too much zeal, for unlike most priestesses Shakti held literal belief
in the Directives of Lloth. These so-called Directives—conquering
the Underdark and obliterating all elves from the Lands of Light—
were pleasant fantasies, useful for massaging the pride of the drow
masses and averting attention from other matters. Triel even
allowed that the Directives were worthwhile goals. Her attention,
however, was fully absorbed with more immediate concerns.

There had been recent challenges to her throne and whispers of
conspiracies to remove House Baenre from its long-held position.
Even the matriarchy, the system that had ruled for thousands of
years, was under attack. Indeed, all of Menzoberranzan teetered on
the brink of anarchy. Triel desperately needed something to offer

the struggling drow, something to rally them—something that, not incidentally, would help consolidate her own rank and position. The rogue magic wielded by her errant niece might well provide the key.

"What have you learned of Liriel's amulet?"

"There is good news," Shakti began. "The wizard Nisstyre is dead, and with him the plan to use the amulet for the furtherance of Vhaeraun's cause."

Triel nodded her approval. There were far too many rivals for this prize. "You have other contacts among Vhaeraun's ranks?"

"Many," Shakti lied smoothly, trusting in the mind shields that were among the most powerful of Vhaeraun's gifts to her.

"Then use them," the matron ordered. "Send them to the surface. Bring Liriel and the amulet back to the city."

"I have already sent my emissaries—no drow males this time, but creatures from another plane. *Not* the Abyss," Shakti said with easy confidence, "so you need not be concerned that other priestesses will know more of my plans than Lloth herself chooses to reveal."

Triel's countenance did not change, but Shakti saw the flicker in the matron's eyes as she registered the knowledge that a priestess of Vhaeraun had access to powers unfamiliar to most of Lloth's clergy. For the Hunzrin priestess it was a moment of pure gratification.

"Keep me informed," the Baenre matron said, her casual tone dismissing the subject as if Liriel and the mysterious amulet were of little consequence. "Now, on to other matters. You know Lloth has decreed that there are to be no wars between the houses. When the affairs of the city are back in order, this will change. It is possible that the fortunes of House Hunzrin will improve considerably."

Shakti carefully suppressed her glee. Triel's words appeared to hold out an offer of support from powerful House Baenre, but they might just as well be a test. Shakti knew that overambitious drow were often found dead in their own chambers.

"My mother, Matron Kintuere, will be pleased to hear that you are optimistic about Hunzrin's fortunes," Shakti replied carefully.

Triel dismissed this prevarication with a wave of one hand. "The alliance between Baenre and Hunzrin has been long and profitable; however, I have often found Kintuere difficult and tiresome." The matron paused, fixing a searching gaze upon the traitor-priestess. "Your older sister is dying. Soon you will be heir to House Hunzrin."

Shakti dipped her head in a bow of acknowledgment, but she kept her face—and her thoughts—carefully neutral.

After a moment, a rare smile crept through Triel's well-schooled facade. "Well done," she said wryly.

Perhaps Triel was complimenting her for an apparently successful coup, perhaps for passing some obscure test. Probably both, Shakti decided.

She took her leave of House Baenre soon after. The interview with Matron Triel had gone well, but Shakti did not feel at all complacent. The surface was a mere seven days' walk from Menzoberranzan, but to her it was an alien, unknowable world. Shakti had never ever set foot outside the city, much less the Underdark. She had no idea how difficult the task before her might be, or how long it might take.

When the magic of Liriel Baenre's amulet was hers to command, when she had washed her hands in her rival's blood—only then could she rid herself of the shackles of House Baenre and move on to the dual destinies that Lloth and Vhaeraun had laid upon her.

* * * * *

Xzorsh, the sea-elven ranger, was not surprised to receive Hrolf's summons. Before the final notes of the calling box had faded from the thin air, while the clicks and whistles still reverberated through the water, the ranger had the *Elfmaid* in his sights. He didn't have far to go; he'd been following the Ruathen vessel since its battle with the giant squid.

The sea elf was deeply troubled by the presence of a drow aboard ship, for he had pledged to aid all who sailed with Hrolf the Unruly. Xzorsh's sense of honor demanded that he mitigate the damage done by the pirates. So far, he had been able to do so without conflict, but the sea elf feared that he could not keep his pledge against the dark mischief a drow might work.

Yet Xzorsh was also intrigued by Hrolf's exotic passenger. Unlike most of his people, Xzorsh was fascinated by magic, and the drow female wielded it with skill and authority. The legends of the Sea People claimed that drow had stolen sea-elven magic; this only added to the ranger's curiosity. Above all, he wished to speak with the drow, to learn the truth of the dark elves. Perhaps even to barter with her for magical weapons. He certainly had the means—Xzorsh was skilled at scavenging sunken ships and lost cities for treasure, which he traded for forged weapons and other goods his sea-dwelling people needed. Xzorsh had long dreamed of possessing a bit of elven magic for himself.

But such personal goals would have to wait. Xzorsh had seen the approach of the cog and had witnessed at a distance the battle that followed. He did not interfere, for it was apparent from the outset that Hrolf and his men had matters well in hand. Nor did he rue the fate of the ship that drifted slowly toward the bottom of the sea. The merchant ship had attacked, unprovoked, for reasons that Xzorsh did not care to know. She had earned her fate.

As he neared the *Elfmaid*, Xzorsh saw, silhouetted against the sky, the dark ovoid bottom of a small ship. Survivors, he surmised, set adrift to await Umberlee's mercy. He did not disapprove. There were times when sea elves dealt with sailors in like fashion, for many seagoing humans posed a threat to all sea folk, and at times the elves were forced to strike back. Out of habit, though, Xzorsh came to the surface to check on Hrolf's recent handiwork.

Seven men were slumped in the small boat, all but one of them bearing wounds that had been tended and wrapped. The sea elf nodded, approving this evidence of fair play. Then his eyes settled on the red-haired man in their midst, and he recoiled in astonishment.

This man he knew. Caladorn, a Lord among the humans of Waterdeep, often held council with the mermen who tended the city's harbor. Xzorsh had frequent dealings with the merfolk and had seen the young human during one such meeting, albeit from a distance and through a filter of seawater. He had been impressed with Caladorn and considered him a man of honor. What could this man have done to provoke such a fate from the easygoing Hrolf?

Xzorsh swam cautiously closer. Sailors given to Umberlee were sometimes allowed to keep weapons so that they might not meet a fate other than that chosen by the Lady of the Waves. But these men were unarmed—further proof of some egregious offense.

"Lord Caladorn," Xzorsh called softly. The man jolted, then looked around for the speaker. His eyes widened as they settled on the sea elf, and Xzorsh gave the man time to absorb his presence. Few humans ever saw one of the Sea People, and those who were granted a sighting were usually overcome with wonder.

"I am Xzorsh. Like you, I am charged with the safety and well-being of my people," he said. "I would like to understand why you attacked the Ruathen vessel. Her captain is a friend of the sea folk and under my protection."

Caladorn nodded slowly as he took this in. The title of "elf-friend" was the highest honor that the People bestowed upon any human, given only to those who'd performed great service to the elves and who had a special love for and understanding of the fey race.

"That would explain why the Ruathen captain set us adrift," the man said thoughtfully. "Perhaps you can answer other questions."

Briefly Caladorn sketched the details of his grim discovery aboard the ghost ship, of Captain Farlow's hatred of the pirates and his inflammatory speech about supposed Ruathym atrocities against the sea elves. He described the battle, the incredible fury of the young berserker they'd faced, and Hrolf's grief at the discovery of the dead sea elves. "We had nothing to do with the death of these elves," Caladorn concluded earnestly, "yet the Ruathen captain gave us no opportunity to speak."

"Hrolf is impulsive," Xzorsh admitted, "and protective of the People."

"And now that you know our story, what will you do?"

The ranger pondered the matter. "My first duty is to the sea folk. I must learn who killed my people and why. When I can, I will send word to the merfolk of Waterdeep; perhaps they will see to your rescue."

"Then you also condemn us to death," Caladorn protested. The merfolk were capricious—they both knew that—and Waterdeep lay several days' travel to the southeast. "These men are wounded, some badly. We have no food and very little water. The merfolk—if they come at all—will be too late."

Xzorsh nodded his agreement of this assessment. "There is a group of small islands not too far from here. No humans make their home there, but you can survive there well enough until rescue comes."

The sea elf put both hands to his mouth and let out a high, piercing cry. There was a moment's silence, and then two gray fins cut through the water toward them. Caladorn instinctively reached for his empty scabbard.

"Not sharks," Xzorsh assured him. "These are dolphins—friends of the sea elves. They will pull you to safety faster than you could sail or row."

As Caladorn watched, intrigued, Xzorsh spoke with the creatures in a language of clicks and squeals. The sea elf took two ropes of braided reeds from his belt, tied one end of each to the boat and knotted the other into a loop. These he tossed to the dolphins. The creatures deftly caught the loops with their pointed snouts.

"I will travel with you throughout the night," the elf promised. He took a long knife from his belt and handed it to the human. "There are many dangers in these waters, some that I myself do not yet understand. You may have need of this."

Before Caladorn could speak, the ranger slapped the water sharply. It was a signal, apparently, for the dolphins set off toward the west, easily pulling the small craft.

When the first rays of the sun touched the surface of the water, Xzorsh turned back toward the pirate ship. There was no real urgency, now that he knew the nature of Hrolf's summons. Nor would the pirates be expecting him any sooner. He did not wish to explain why he'd been following the ship, or give words to his suspicions concerning the drow.

Never before had Xzorsh seen a drow take to the sea, and he doubted that this female had done so for a noble purpose. His people had suffered enough at the hands of the evil drow; Xzorsh was determined to do whatever he could to ensure that they would come to no further harm.

Even if the drow in question was under his pledge of protection.

Life's answers usually came easily to the young ranger, and the lines between what was good and what was evil usually ran straight and clear. But for once Xzorsh found himself wondering if things were truly as simple as he had always believed.

*   *   *   *   *

The morning hours passed slowly aboard the *Elfmaid*. There was little for the crew to do but await the arrival of the sea-elven ranger. The presence of the dead sea elves—even now that they were tucked discreetly in the hold—was a damper on the usually high spirits of the Ruathen sailors.

Fyodor did his best to distract them with tales of his homeland—of the place spirits that still lingered in springs and wells, of his adventures exploring the ruins of long-dead kingdoms buried in the thickly forested hills of Rashemen. The young storyteller did not understand why his tales of place spirits brought sly grins to the faces of the sailors, but on the whole the men seemed glad of the diversion he offered.

The first mate, however, concerned himself with practical matters. Ibn examined their haul, placing the valuable goods to one side and tossing the debris into the sea. He was about to send the broken lid of one cask spinning, but stopped suddenly and squinted at the markings on it. The mate pursed his lips, considered, and then examined the remaining barrels. He hurried over to Hrolf, who had spent the night at watch on the forecastle. The elven female was at his side, as she was too often for Ibn's taste, but the sailor had no time to indulge his prejudices.

"You must see this, Captain," Ibn said with uncharacteristic urgency and handed the lid to Hrolf. "That's the mark of Alesbane the cooper. The barrel is of Ruathym make. All the barrels holding sea elves had this mark."

Hrolf scowled and shrugged. "What of it?"

"Strange, it is," Ibn said. "What those seal hunters could want with Sea People is more than I know or care. I just hope no more pickled elves show up, and the blame for it put on Ruathym."

Liriel saw the point at once. Although she knew little of human politics, she could scent a plot in any form. "He's right, Hrolf. We should get those wounded men back and find out what they know."

The first mate did not look grateful for her support. His red brows met in a frown, and he leveled a glare at the drow. "You're to blame for this mess," he growled.

"What had I to do with it?" she said indignantly. "The sea elves were long dead before we found them."

"That's the way of ill luck. You never see it coming, but it finds you all the same!"

"Enough, lad," Hrolf said wearily. "Best that you find the men we set adrift and try to sort this thing through."

Liriel nodded. "I'm going below—the midday sun is still too bright for comfort—but call me when you find the seal hunters. I can get more information from them than they'd willingly give."

Ibn folded his arms and glared at her. "You won't torture a wounded man while I'm mate of this ship!"

"Spare me the sermon," she said dryly, "and do try to remember that magic gives options quite beyond those allowed by your crude imagination."

The drow swept past the mate, regal as a Matron. But she felt his baleful glare upon her as she made her way into the hold, and she wondered what he might do if he knew what she was about to attempt.

For Liriel had found unexpected inspiration in her own words. She *did* have the ability to extract information from the minds of the wounded seal hunters. Not from her wizardly magic, but with

73

clerical spells. Priestesses of Lloth could cast their sticky webs into the thoughts of another—even if that person had passed beyond the mortal realms. Why bother questioning the seal hunters, Liriel surmised, if she could speak directly to the spirits of the dead sea elves?

Of course, this was risky in the extreme. A powerful priestess could summon and command a spirit, but Liriel was a novice and had never tried the prayers and spells that would reach beyond death. She had no reason to believe Lloth would honor her request; indeed, her presumption might anger the Spider Queen. The spirits of sea elves would not be in the realms of Lloth, and Liriel doubted the drow goddess was on cordial terms with whatever elven deity sea elves worshiped.

After pondering the matter, Liriel decided that her best bet for success—not to mention survival—would not be to ask Lloth to summon the spirits, but rather to seek permission to enter the afterworld herself. It was a prospect that both chilled and fascinated the adventurous young drow.

Liriel crept into the corner of the hold where the dead elves lay, respectfully covered with a tarp. She knelt down and began to search the bodies, trying to find some clue that would tell her how they had been killed. There were no marks on any of them, beyond the slight wizening effect of the brine. Nothing to be gained there. At random, she chose one of the elves and held the cold hands between both her own. Since she had not known the sea folk in life, she needed contact with the body in order to track down the spirit.

The drow steeled her courage and began the intense concentration demanded of a clerical spell. She chanted softly, emptying her thoughts and pushing away the strands of magic that came so readily to her call. The magic she needed now was not the natural magic of the Weave, but the power of a goddess.

Suddenly Liriel was pulled from her body. There was a moment's bright, white pain, a quick wrenching as she was torn from the mortal world, and then . . .

Liriel had glimpsed the Abyss, had viewed all the lower planes through the scrying portals common among the priestesses of Lloth. The gray, mist-filled landscape before her was like nothing she had ever seen or, more precisely, like nothing she had ever *felt*. There was little to be *seen* here, yet all around her she felt the invisible passages that led to untold realms. The drow sent out her thoughts, seeking the sea elf's spirit.

There was a moment's touch. The exhilaration of success filled the drow's mind, and she urged her probing touch to go still farther. To her astonishment, there was nowhere to go.

Liriel's heightened senses perceived that something beyond the natural order had occurred. She encountered not the will of a god, but the art of a sorcerer. The spirit had indeed left the sea elf's body, but it was trapped somewhere on this plane. The drow deepened her concentration, narrowing her search to seek the spirit in the world she knew.

Suddenly Liriel stood at the gate of some terrible limbo. She felt the utter helplessness of the being she sought, felt the sudden surge of hope as the spirit felt her touch, felt the unseen eyes that pleaded with her for release. The drow's free-spirited heart recoiled from the terror she encountered, and instinctively she drew away.

I'll find you, Liriel promised silently as she eased back toward the mortal realm. I'll find a way to release you all.

"Damn female. Knew you was a part of this mess."

The voice, grim and triumphant, jolted Liriel from her trance. She spun to see Ibn watching her and only then realized she had spoken part of her promise aloud. So deep in meditation had she been that she hadn't heard the first mate's approach. He closed in now, his hand on the hilt of his knife.

Instinct took over. Liriel flung out a hand, fingers spread wide. Strands of magic flew from her fingertips, spun themselves into a giant web that spanned the hold. The blast of power caught Ibn, hurling him backward along with the magical trap. He hung there, bobbing slightly, stuck to the web like some enormous insect.

Liriel expected sullen wrath, or even a string of the colorful curses that were common aboard the ship. To her astonishment, Ibn looked pleased despite his ignominious situation.

"Attacked a ship's officer, you did. You're as good as dead," he promised her with dark satisfaction.

* * * * *

The memories of elves are long indeed, but to most of them the lost city of Ascarle had faded into the fabric of lore and legend. Many generations of elves had come and gone since the day Ascarle had disappeared—swept away by the rush of melting ice, then buried beneath the waves in the age when the great glaciers gave way to the northern seas. Few suspected that the glories of Ascarle continued, hidden deep beneath the waters off the northern coast of Trisk, a small island in the remote archipelago known as the Purple Rocks.

Few of those long-ago elves would recognize Ascarle now. Yes, most of the buildings remained intact—wondrous, gleaming structures magically grown from crystal and red coral. Even buried beneath the waves, the city looked as if it had been sculpted from fire and ice. Air still filled many of the buildings and the covered walkways that linked them. Treasures from ancient cultures furnished the luxurious rooms. Indeed, the only discordant notes in all of Ascarle came from its watery horizon and its current inhabitants.

Around the submerged city lived some of the most feared creatures in the sea. A hundred merrow—aquatic cousins of orcs—formed the core of Ascarle's standing army. The antechambers and tunnels that led into the crystal core were lairs to kapoacinth, marine gargoyles who lived for the enjoyment of causing pain. A band of evil nereids—beautiful, shapeshifting sirens dedicated to the destruction of seagoing males—flitted about the city, awaiting opportunities for mischief.

It was even whispered that a kraken made its lair in the submerged city. Of all the creatures of the sea, this gigantic and highly intelligent squid-creature was the most feared. In times past, entire cities, whole islands, had disappeared at the command of such beasts. Little was known about kraken, except that the creatures spent most of their lives in the unreachable depths of the sea, and that they at times amassed power that reached far beyond the waves. Even rumor of a kraken's presence was a formidable threat.

The apparent ruler of Ascarle, an illithid known as Vestress, certainly did nothing to discourage these rumors. A creature of immense magical power and shadowy background, Vestress claimed the title of Regent and ruled the undersea kingdom for the absent kraken. Or so she claimed, and so far none had dared to challenge her. For Vestress's reign was not limited to Ascarle. A far-flung network of spies and assassins known as the Kraken Society extended her power throughout the Northlands.

Vestress was an oddity among her kind. Illithids did not possess—or at least did not exhibit—gender, but this creature projected a mental "voice" that was decidedly feminine and a persona as regal as that of any queen. By human standards, illithids were hideous creatures that resembled some unholy pairing of squid and humanoid. Roughly man-shaped in form, the creatures had bald, high-domed heads, lavender hide, and white eyes devoid of expression. Four writhing tentacles formed the lower half of an illithid's face and concealed a sharp-fanged maw. Somehow, though, Vestress projected an elegance not in keeping with her ungainly form. Pale purple amethysts decked her three-fingered hands and studded the circlet of silver on her head. The full sleeves of her lavender silk robe whispered as she deftly moved the shuttle of her loom.

The Regent of Ascarle was currently at leisure. Weaving was her hobby and her passion, and she took to it whenever the demands of her position allowed. The illithid saw all of life as a tapestry, and she could spin nearly anything into thread: precious gems, stolen dreams. At the moment she sat before a tapestry that depicted a coastal town, peopled by former slaves that once had served her and maintained Ascarle's air-filled chambers. The weaving was her finest achievement, and Vestress gazed at it with satisfaction.

Then, to her astonishment, the sea-elven figures on the tapestry began to writhe as if in torment.

Vestress rose abruptly. This could not be. Not that she was adverse to tormenting the sea-elven spirits entrapped in the tapestry—far from it! What concerned her was that someone had attempted to contact the spirits of the dead elves. Someone powerful.

The illithid had expected that such an attempt would be made, but the seal hunters could not have reached Waterdeep so soon, and she knew that no clerics sailed aboard that vessel. Something had gone very wrong.

Vestress glided out of the weaving chamber and hastened to the room that housed her scrying crystals. With all the resources of the mysterious Kraken Society at her command, she would have an answer in minutes.

And before the day was out, the illithid's far-reaching tentacles would ensnare the priest or priestess who had dared to interfere with the Regent of Ascarle.

Chapter 6
STORM AT SEA

he Calling Conch, a dockside tavern in Luskan, served strong ale and hearty chowder at bargain prices. Tonight the patrons got even more for their coppers than they'd anticipated, and to a man they blessed Tempus for their good fortune. Rethnor, High Captain of Luskan, had been challenged to battle. The words had barely left the challenger's mouth before the Conch's patrons began busily clearing an impromptu arena, pushing chairs and tables against the walls. They ringed the room now, quaffing ale and placing bets as to how long Rethnor's opponent had yet to live.

The High Captain was an imposing bear of a man, with an uncommon breadth of shoulder and thickness of arm. A proud black beard cascaded down over his leather jerkin, and his thick brows slashed across his forehead in a single dark line. But it was his eyes, as blue and deep and icy as a winter sea, that proclaimed him a dangerous man.

At first Rethnor merely took the measure of his opponent. Their swords met in ringing blows as the Captain tested reach, strength, and resolve. The young man matched Rethnor's size and breadth, and he seemed well trained—no surprise in the warrior culture of Luskan—but he was still an unblooded youth with more enthusiasm than battle sense. Still, it promised to be an entertaining fight.

Rethnor lunged, his left-handed sword diving toward the heart of his young opponent. It was an obvious attack, and the fighter parried it easily with a flamboyant sweep that threw Rethnor's sword arm out wide. The High Captain expected this. Before the younger man could recover from the countermove, Rethnor stepped in close—so close the two men's beards were nearly touching, too close for either fighter to bring his sword into play. No problem for Rethnor—he had a dagger ready in his right hand.

With a deft flick, he severed the waist strap that held up the young man's leather thigh greave and then slashed down through the X-shaped side bindings that connected front greave to back. The protective garment flopped down over the fighter's boot, revealing an incongruously thin, bandy leg clad in leggings of faded red wool.

Mocking laughter and huzzahs filled the tavern, and the young fighter's face twisted with humiliation and rage. Rethnor danced back, savoring the moment and fully intending to play out the fight. This young cub had challenged him—*him*, Rethnor the High Captain, perhaps the finest swordsman in Luskan—and he intended to make the upstart pay for his insolence.

And so Rethnor was not at all pleased when the ring on his sword hand began to tingle with the familiar, silent summons. He needed to end the fight soon, so he might seek solitude before the large onyx stone revealed itself as the scrying crystal it was. Of course, he wore gloves to hide the device. Magic was not highly regarded by the Northmen, and it was imperative that Rethnor keep this secret from his fellow High Captains, but he could never know whether someone who secretly practiced the thrice-damned art of magic might be present during such a summons. If such a wretch detected an aura of magic around Rethnor, he or she would have a powerful weapon to use against him.

But of course the young fighter knew nothing of this, and he advanced on Rethnor with deadly purpose. "I'll have your guts to replace that garter," the swordsman promised grimly.

Rethnor's sigh of frustration hissed through gritted teeth. He parried the young man's furious overhead strike and countered with a feint. Quickly, skillfully, he worked the fighter's blade down low. Then once again he stepped in close, this time with his fist leading. A vicious uppercut to the jaw sent his challenger reeling back, both arms flung out wide. Before the younger fighter could regain his defensive stance, Rethnor dug his blade deep into an unprotected armpit. The youth dropped his sword and sank slowly to the floor, a look of surprise on his face.

It was a particularly brutal finale to the fight, but it suited Rethnor's mood. If he could not have the lengthy battle he desired, at least he could give this challenger a lingering death. The young man's lungs would slowly fill up with blood, and he would drown in his own stupidity.

The High Captain sheathed his wet sword and tossed a handful of silver onto the table to pay for his half-eaten meal. Then he strode into the night to see what information the Kraken Society considered so important that they would summon him, one of their most

79

powerful agents, at a time other than the specified safe hour.

Rethnor hurried to his house, impatiently waving away his wife's questions and the ministrations of his servants. He hastened to his private room and set flame to the wick of a whale-oil lamp. After bolting the door, he tugged off his gloves and regarded the scrying crystal on his ring. The glossy black color of the onyx had faded completely; in the small magic portal he saw the face of a beautiful, regal woman with impassive lavender eyes.

"Well?" he snapped, staring balefully at the tiny image. "Bad news or good, it had better be worth the interruption!"

You be the judge. The cool, feminine voice sounded only in his mind. No sound came from the ring; indeed, the woman's lips never moved. Rethnor often wondered why she bothered to show her face at all.

The seal hunters did not reach Waterdeep. The ship was intercepted by a Ruathen vessel. We believe it is bound for its home port.

Rethnor swore bitterly. He'd gone to a great deal of trouble and expense to set up this diversion: capturing the sea elves, delivering them alive to a secret drop on the distant archipelago known as the Purple Rocks, taking the bodies back to the coast in Ruathen barrels, putting them on a caravel set adrift in the known path of the Waterdhavian hunting vessel. It was but one of many acts Luskan had arranged and placed upon Ruathym's doorstep, just one step toward justifying Luskan's coming takeover of the island. But it was a particularly potent ruse, one that Rethnor knew would strike a responsive chord in the hearts of the Waterdhavian rulers. In fact, the idea had come from Waterdeep itself.

In recent months, reports of attacks on sea-elf communities had filtered ashore. Since it was well known that the Northmen of Luskan and Ruathym had no love for elves of any kind, the Lords of Waterdeep had made pointed inquiries. In truth, Luskan had had little to do with the sea elves' troubles; that did not stop Rethnor from exploiting them. If the elf-loving southern meddlers were determined to make this their affair, why not focus their indignation upon Ruathym? Yes, Rethnor concluded, this plan must be salvaged.

"What do you suggest?" he asked the tiny image.

Stop the ship, of course. We are told it left Neverwinter two days ago, sailing due west upon the River. Stop it, and do whatever you must to affix blame for the sea-elven troubles upon Ruathym.

Rethnor nodded. This would actually be easier than it sounded, for the channel of warm water known as the River was relatively narrow and the Ruathen ship had only two days' head start. The ships of Luskan were fleet; he could close the distance in mere days.

"I will handle it myself," he promised.

Take two ships, the voice suggested, *and as many fighters as they can carry. We have received word that there is a berserker warrior aboard the Ruathen vessel. He destroyed a giant squid, the emblem of the Kraken Society, and in so doing has earned our special enmity.*

The High Captain blinked, and for a moment his usually rock-steady confidence wavered. He had fought Ruathym's berserkers. They were trouble enough ashore; he did not relish the thought of fighting one in the close confines of a ship-to-ship battle. Still, berserkers were only mortal men, and they were even more eager than most Northmen warriors to take a seat in the mead halls of Tempus. He, Rethnor, would happily oblige this one.

"Three ships," he told the image with grim pleasure. "I sail at dawn with three warships."

* * * * *

For a long moment Liriel merely stared at the man trapped in her magical web, completed dumbfounded by Ibn's promise of death. She had acted only to defend herself—surely Hrolf would not turn against her for this! But Ibn seemed so certain, and he had sailed with the captain for years. And truly, what did she know about the strange ways of humans?

Liriel's drow instincts took over. Up came her hand crossbow, and a tiny dart flashed toward the first mate. The sleeping poison was potent; Ibn was asleep before he could finish the salty oath he'd begun to hurl at her.

The drow quickly dispelled the magic that had formed the giant spiderweb, and Ibn dropped heavily to the wooden floor of the hold. Liriel dug both hands into her hair and gripped her head as if doing so could contain her whirling thoughts. Granted, her impulsive action had bought her a little time. The potion would hold Ibn for several hours, but what could she possibly tell the others that would explain his enspelled slumber?

"Give him some mead," suggested a deep voice from the far end of the hold.

Liriel whirled at the unexpected sound. Her eyes narrowed as Fyodor rose from behind the remaining mead casks.

"What are you doing here?" she demanded angrily.

81

The Rashemi responded with a wry smile. "At the moment, little raven, I am trying to keep you alive. See the cask there with one side blackened a bit, as if it were placed too close to a fire? It holds some of the mead that put the villagers to sleep. Pour a bit of it down him, and a bit of it on him, and Hrolf will assume Ibn got into the stores and picked the wrong barrel."

The drow stared at him. A dozen questions clamored to be given voice; she picked the easiest. "You know about the mead? But how?"

"Remember, I was at your side during the trip to Neverwinter, paying the merchants for the goods you chose. The gold we used in payment was familiar—I saw some of the pieces when the druid threw them into the river." He shrugged. "Knowing Hrolf, I was able to find my way to the truth in time."

Liriel accepted both his plan and his explanation with a curt nod. She pried the lid off the half-empty cask and splashed some of the mead on the sleeping mate. "I can keep him asleep only until tomorrow morning," she grumbled. "Life would be so much easier if I could just kill him and have done with it!"

The drow looked up at Fyodor, and her eyes narrowed dangerously as she turned her thoughts to another matter. "You were spying on me."

"Not so," he protested. "I needed a place to rest, and the hold is quiet and dark. I . . . have not slept much of late."

She nodded, understanding. Since the Time of Troubles, when Fyodor's berserker magic had gone awry, he had often been tormented by dreams. When the battle frenzy faded, he seldom remembered the details of the battles he fought. But the faces of those who died by his sword came back to him by night. Liriel thought it extremely fortunate that drow, as a rule, did not dream at all. Most of the dark elves she knew would soon go mad if they were forced each night to face the consequences of their actions. But such thoughts were pushed aside as she focused on Fyodor. She'd hoped he'd overcome his remorse about turning on her during the last battle, but now she saw he had not. He was thinner, and there was a haggard look about him. Liriel suspected it was her face that had haunted his dreams of late.

A silence between them stretched until the tension became too great to bear. "You were chanting," Fyodor said softly, "but not words of magic. It seemed to me that you were praying. Is that true?"

Liriel nodded, surprised by the turn his thoughts had taken. "So?"

"You cast a spell through prayer; only a priest can do this." He paused, as if reluctant to continue. "I have seen you dance in the moonlight, touched by the shadow of Eilistraee. Tell me truly: have you become a priestess of the Dark Maiden?"

There was hope in his voice, but Liriel saw in his eyes that he did not believe this could be so. Eilistraee was the goddess of those drow who forsook the dark tunnels and evil ways, the goddess of dance and the hunt. The Dark Maiden encouraged her followers to create beauty, to aid travelers, to live in peace and joy beneath the sun and the moon. Fyodor knew that Liriel was a child of the Underdark.

Her fingers instinctively closed around the amulet of Lloth, as if to shield her friend from the Spider Queen and all that the goddess represented. "I was trained as a wizard from a young age," Liriel said steadily. "That is what I am. But before I left Menzoberranzan, I was sent to the clerical school. I was there but a short time, hardly enough to be accounted a priestess!"

"But your prayer was answered with magic," he persisted.

Liriel shrugged. "If a goddess is willing to grant me power, I'd be a fool not to take it!"

"But at what price?" Fyodor asked earnestly. "Liriel, I have heard many terrible stories of the drow and their goddess. You have given me to know that these stories are but a dim shadow of the life you knew. If this is so, what good can possibly come from such as Lloth?"

The drow thought carefully before speaking, for such questions were new to her and the answers were still forming in her mind.

"Do you remember what Qilué Veladorn asked me, when we asked her and the other drow of Eilistraee's temple to help us get the Windwalker back? She asked why I wanted to retain my drow powers—and what I intended to do with them. I am learning that there are many things that can be done. Stopping Nisstyre and his nest of Vhaeraun worshipers was one. Through the power of Lloth, I learned that the spirits of these elves did not move beyond the mortal realm. They were trapped through sorcery. If Lloth grants me the chance and the power to free these elves, I will take it!"

"But Lloth is evil, is that not so?"

"Of course," Liriel said without pause. "But Lloth is also powerful, and so my people worship her. I used to scorn the drow's constant scrambling for more and more power, like so many silly dragons collecting ever bigger heaps of gold. But I'm starting to see that power is also a tool," she concluded thoughtfully. "If I have it, and use it to worthwhile ends, does the source of it truly matter?"

Fyodor shook his head, not certain how to answer. He was deeply gratified to see how far Liriel had come; these were hardly the sentiments of the spoiled drow princess he had met in the tunnels of the Underdark. From the beginning he had sensed Liriel's potential, and through his Sight had caught fey glimpses of a destiny that might well rival the mightiest of Rashemen's Witches. He was proud of her growth, and he could not find words to refute her reasoning. But still he was uneasy.

"Come," he said at last. "Let us tell Hrolf that Ibn sleeps in the hold. That will buy a little time, but we must figure out what to do next."

Liriel smiled her thanks and slipped her arms around his waist. "Devious, you are!" she said teasingly. "Given time, you might make a creditable drow!"

He returned her friendly embrace and quickly disengaged himself. Not so much, this time, from the temptation her nearness presented, but because of the admiration in Liriel's voice. He was not proud of the deception he'd suggested, but to Liriel such acts were worthy of praise. She took great pride in her heritage and considered comparing him to a drow the highest possible compliment.

Fyodor's feelings of confusion deepened when he listened to Liriel explain the matter to Hrolf, for she spun out the web of deception with obvious relish. He could not help but wonder how far Liriel had truly traveled from the tunnels of the Underdark, and the ways of Lloth.

* * * * *

Xzorsh did not reach the *Elfmaid* until the following dawn, for he saw no need to hurry. Although he already knew the reason for his summons, the sea elf listened carefully to Hrolf's recitation of the facts. He briefly considered telling the pirate where the surviving seal hunters had taken refuge, but he knew there were no answers to be found there. The best Xzorsh could do for his slain kindred was to take them home to be buried with honor in the coral catacombs hidden deep in the sea. So he said nothing when Hrolf sent two men—his first mate, who was strangely groggy and the object of much teasing by his fellows, and the young warrior who'd killed the giant squid—out on a small boat to look for the adrift sailors. It was effort wasted, and it made Xzorsh's tasks as guardian more difficult, but the sea elf let it pass. He did not trust what Hrolf might do upon learning that Lord Caladorn and the others had escaped Umberlee's judgment.

Under Xzorsh's direction, the Ruathen sailors returned the slain elves to the sea. Far beneath the waves, sea folk from the nearest settlement awaited to take them to the distant city they had once called home. Sittl, Xzorsh's partner, had arranged all, and he awaited the ranger now in the depths. The other ranger would not come near the *Elfmaid*—his distrust of humans ran too deep.

At the moment, Xzorsh could hardly blame him. There was evil below the waves as well as in the world of humans, but the young sea ranger was deeply shaken by the brutal, senseless nature of these deaths. He was also troubled by the brief conversation he'd had with the drow. She had pulled him aside, told him of the strange fate that had befallen the spirits of the elves at the hands of some unknown sorcerer. Apparently she'd hoped he might be able to shed some light on the matter. But to Xzorsh such use of magic was horrifying and utterly beyond his understanding. He left the humans and their disturbing drow passenger as soon as possible to seek the familiar comfort of his friend's presence.

But Sittl's mood was even darker than his own. "I often think the world would be better if Umberlee took every human that so much as stuck a toe in the water," he said grimly in the clicks and whistles of the sea-elven dialect. "And I will never understand why you spend so much time and concern on that pirate!"

Xzorsh sent him a strange look. Sittl knew of his pledge. To sea elves, a pledge was an immutable bond! "Hrolf saved my life," he reminded his friend.

"So you have told me many times, but that was before we met. You were little more than a child then!" Sittl retorted. "The debt was paid in full long ago!"

"How can you say such a thing?" the ranger marveled, aghast that the practical, reliable Sittl could harbor such blasphemous ideas.

His partner turned aside. He did not answer for a long moment, but his mottled shoulders rose and fell in a deep sigh, sending an eloquent rift of bubbles floating upward. "One of the females was once my lover. The dead child was mine," he said flatly. "Forgive my harsh words against the human pirate; I am not myself."

Xzorsh reached over to clasp his friend's shoulder. "I'm sorry. If you had told me of your loss, I would have spared you this task."

The elf shook his head. "We have our duties," he said, and when he turned back to Xzorsh his face was composed. "What must we do now, to honor your pledge?"

"The others will see to the slain People. We two watch over Hrolf and his men. I need your help, for one of us must keep Hrolf's ship in sight, the other ensure that the two men who seek the seal hunters come to no harm. I cannot help but think," Xzorsh said slowly, "that the *Elfmaid* is in grave danger. There are forces at work that I do not yet understand."

"The drow?"

"Perhaps," the ranger said, and it was his turn to avert his eyes. This was as close to an untruth as ever he had told. Xzorsh did not trust the drow, but she knew magic and he did not. He would have to depend on her help to find and free the spirits of the slain sea elves. It was an impossible alliance and the most dangerous task he had ever considered.

Why then, Xzorsh wondered, did the very thought of it fill him with elation?

* * * * *

Three days passed, and neither the crew of the *Elfmaid* nor Ibn and Fyodor in their smaller boat caught sight of the adrift sailors. The two vessels tacked back and forth across the warm waters of the River, crossing paths repeatedly as they searched for the small boat. At last Ibn decided the effort was in vain.

"They're not on the River anymore, that's what," the first mate proclaimed. "Umberlee took 'em, and that's the end of it. We might as well get back to the ship."

Fyodor gave reluctant agreement. He hadn't particularly enjoyed the company of the taciturn sailor, but he hoped the time away from the ship had tempered Ibn's wrath against Liriel. The mate had not once brought up the matter. Fyodor took that as a good sign.

The two men rowed hard, and before long they had the *Elfmaid* in sight. Once on board, Ibn strode directly over to Hrolf.

"Call a Thing," he demanded, using the ancient word for a council of law. By Northman law any ship's officer had the right to request that such council be convened, but only to deal with matters of grave import.

Hrolf eyed the first mate warily. "What's this about, lad?"

"The female, that's what. She attacked me—a ship's officer—with her drow sorcery."

"You seem hale enough," the captain pointed out.

"Would you be happier if she'd left me dead?" Ibn retorted. "A hit or near miss, in the eyes of the law it's all the same, and well you know it!"

Perplexed by this development, the captain turned his gaze slowly over the men who had gathered to hear Ibn's words. Almost without exception, they nodded agreement to Ibn's assessment of the matter.

Hrolf sighed and turned to Fyodor. "You'd better bring her topside, lad. We've got to get to the root of this."

The young warrior nodded grimly and disappeared into the hold. He and Liriel returned to find the men seated in a tight semicircle on the deck.

"The Thing begins," Hrolf said, his face creased with regret. "You stand before the ship's council, Liriel Baenre, accused of attacking a ship's officer with sorcery. What do you say to this?"

The drow's chin lifted defiantly. "Whatever the man's position, has he the right to creep up on me, to threaten me with a knife? As you can see, Ibn is strong and well. I did nothing but stop his attack. If I'd attacked him, he'd be dead. If you doubt the truth of this, I'd be more than happy to demonstrate," she said, leveling a cold glare at her accuser. "And if using my so-called sorcery defies your laws, why did you not object when we came through the gates at Skullport?"

"Those are good points," Hrolf said hopefully.

Ibn folded his arms over his chest. "The charge stands," he growled. "She tossed me into a damned big spiderweb and shot me with one o' them accursed darts."

"But why didn't you come forward sooner, lad?"

"Yourself sent me off in that blasted little tub before my head cleared," Ibn retorted. "And don't think I'm happy about the rest of you lads thinking I got into the mead, or that I don't know good stuff from tainted. She musta splashed it on me!"

"Spiderwebs, darts smaller than your little finger, and a half swallow of *honey wine*—it's a wonder you survived all that," Liriel observed with acid sarcasm.

Some of the men chuckled, and Hrolf passed a hand over his bewhiskered mouth to cover a smile. But Ibn's face turned an angry red.

"I upheld your orders, Captain—I didn't lay hand on the wench. Not even when I found her casting magic in the hold, talking to them pickled elves like they was old cronies—holding hands with one of 'em! It was clear as sunrise that she knows more about all that than she's let on." The mate paused to let those words sink deep. "I been sailing with you a long time, Hrolf. I expect you to do right by me and by *them*."

Oh, well done, Liriel thought with grim admiration. She knew Hrolf well enough to realize that Ibn had touched several of the captain's sensitive spots.

A perplexed Hrolf chewed his mustache as he considered his dilemma. Most of the men had begun to accept Liriel's presence among them, and all of them seemed willing to grant her strange ways some leeway. But there were things that even he as captain could not ignore. If any other man had thrown weapons—of any sort—at the first mate, it would have been considered tantamount to mutiny. The standard punishment was a quick toss overboard. Granted, Ibn had pulled a knife on the lass, but it sounded as if he thought he had a good reason to do so.

"Three ships behind us, closing fast!" came the urgent voice of the man on watch.

The captain exploded to his feet, a look of intense relief on his face. "We're under attack, lads!" he roared out. "And Tempus be praised for it," he muttered into his beard.

* * * * *

Xzorsh and Sittl saw the approaching warships before the humans perceived their danger.

"Three to one. It does not look good for your human friend," Sittl observed.

The ranger shook his head. "Hrolf and his men fight well. They also have the magic of a drow and the might of a berserker on their side. I saw that human destroy a giant squid. All things considered, the odds are not so bad as they might seem."

Sittl considered this. "I think calling reinforcements would be a wise precaution. Since you will no doubt wish to stay in honor of your pledge, I will see to it." He smiled a little and placed a webbed hand on his friend's shoulder. "Promise me, though, that you will watch the battle from a safe distance."

Xzorsh nodded, grateful for the understanding and support. "But the sea elves are long gone. Whom will you summon?"

The other elf's smile broadened and turned wry. "You've been so concerned with the humans of late that you've forgotten there are as many peoples below the waves as above!"

The ranger acknowledged this gentle hit with a feigned wince. Sittl grinned, then turned to swim swiftly away to the west.

Left alone, Xzorsh turned his full attention upon the coming battle. As he watched the large warships close in, he wondered whether his assessment might have been overly optimistic, and he hoped Sittl's reinforcements would not be too long in coming.

* * * * *

Five days after his ships left the docks of Luskan, Rethnor spotted another vessel, far to the west and silhouetted against a twilight sky. The High Captain took up a spyglass and peered into it. He gave out a derisive sniff. For some reason the ship had dropped sail, and it had turned so that he looked straight at the ridiculous wooden figurehead—a garishly painted statue of a woman with elven ears and improbable curves.

"What in the Nine Hells is that? An elf ship?"

"Ruathen," one of his men put in, "That's the *Elfmaid*—I seen her before. Captain's one Hrolf the Unruly. He was run out of Luskan three years ago for tearing apart the Seven Sails Inn."

A slow smile crept over Rethnor's face. He'd found not only his quarry, but also a way to deepen the mist that concealed Luskan's plot against Ruathym. Waterdeep had forced Ruathym and Luskan to form the Captains' Alliance. Let the meddling southerners think their efforts had borne fruit and that the two groups of Northmen were working in harmony to tamp down the threat of piracy. He, Rethnor, would serve up Hrolf to both Waterdeep and Ruathym village, and in the process buy himself good faith with both cities. The elf-loving officials of Waterdeep would readily accept Hrolf in the role of villain. The man had a wild reputation—not to mention possession of those pickled sea elves. As for Ruathym—well, there had been many strange happenings on the island of late, and the beleaguered people might well grasp at any explanation presented them. According to Rethnor's sources on the island, Hrolf was considered to be something of a rogue.

The Captain sent orders to his two other warships to flank the Ruathen vessel, taking the central attack himself. "As soon as we come within range, fire the ballista over her deck. Take care not to sink the ship," Rethnor cautioned. "We need her whole, crew and cargo."

He raised the spyglass again and recoiled in astonishment at the sight before him. Standing on the deck of the ship, framed by a flying cloak that glittered darkly in the dying light, was a black elf. A female, at that. She was a tiny thing, all hair and eyes, with ears like a fox.

Rethnor swore under his breath. He'd amassed power and wealth through his ability to craft multilayered plots and through his ability to plan ahead for each possible move his opponents might make. Unlike most Northmen, he did not consider chess to be an effete pastime. But he played most of his games in the back rooms and the battlefields that led to power, with living beings as pawns and warriors. He knew all of his players and opponents well. He knew what to expect from the sailors and fighters of Ruathym and was even confident of his ability to overcome one of their berserker warriors. But despite the stories he had heard all his life—or perhaps because of them—he had no idea what to expect from a drow.

Chapter 7

DANCE OF THE *ELFMAID*

s Rethnor watched through the spyglass, the captain of the *Elfmaid*—a mountain of a man with pale braids and massive arms—hauled up a brightly colored square sail and sent men to the oars. The pirates were going to try to outrun them.

But the Luskan warships were built for speed. Two tall masts supported enormous sails that caught and held every breath of the wind, and the crews were chosen from the best the Northlands had to offer. Rethnor's lead ship, the *Cutlass*, plunged after the pirates, its bow leaping the waves like a dolphin at play, sending spray after spray of white foam flying.

As soon as Rethnor had the *Elfmaid* within range, he gave the order to fire. A ballista bolt—a giant, iron-tipped spear—traced an arc toward the pirate ship and tore downward through its gay sail. The bright cloth caught on the barbs of the ballista, rending from midsail to lower beam. The rip stole much of the wind from the sail, and the pirate ship slowed. Rethnor gave the signal, and two warships went wide to flank the Ruathen vessel. On three sides they closed in on the crippled ship.

But Hrolf the Unruly was not one to go down lightly. The pirate ship spun in a sharp turn—so sharp that Rethnor fully expected the ship to career. The Ruathen captain knew his *Elfmaid* well; the odd vessel righted and faced down her closest attacker, the ship approaching from Rethnor's left. The full strength of the wind caught what was left of the sail, and the oars bent under the force of the rowers' quick, desperate pull. The pirate ship lurched forward, so fast that the hull reared upward. Her sharpened bowsprit rammed broadside into the hull of the approaching warship. The lancelike beam bit deep into the wood of the Luskan ship.

The pirates immediately sent a storm of arrows toward the warship to hold back the Northmen fighters. Under the cover of Ruathen arrows, the black elf, nimble and surefooted as a squirrel on a

91

tree branch, ran up the tilted bowsprit and onto the warship's deck.

Northmen warriors charged to meet her with swords and battle-axes. The drow came steadily on. White fire spat from her hands and sent the warriors reeling back. She did not stop to press her magically gained advantage, but rose into the air.

As Rethnor gaped—he had no idea the damned fiends could fly—the drow floated to the very top of the masts. She pulled a long knife from her belt and cut the lines that held the sails aloft—first one sail, then the other, in less time than the telling would take. The massive sails plummeted down onto the fighters, burying them all beneath a blanket of heavy canvas.

Hrolf the Unruly was next to climb the bowsprit, and despite his massive size he was no less agile than the tiny drow. The captain leaped onto the deck and ran across the heaving, squirming canvas and toward the pair of masts. Meanwhile the pirates laid down boarding planks and swarmed up after him. They formed a ring around the outer edges of the canvas sail, stabbing down again and again into the trapped Northmen as they closed in toward the center. Here and there a dagger slashed up through the heavy canvas shroud, but the pirates easily cut down the sailors before they could emerge to stand and fight. It was not battle, it was butchery—and it was over in minutes.

Meanwhile the warship on the right flank closed in on the damaged warship, circling around to the west and pulling alongside the *Elfmaid*. Rethnor nodded his approval. His ship was approaching from the east. The Ruathen vessel would be trapped, pinned to one warship and tightly flanked by two more.

The *Cutlass* came in fast, swinging around at the last moment so that her port side struck the trapped pirate ship with a solid thud.

"We got 'em now!" crowed the boatswain.

Rethnor responded with a grim smile. He was no less confident of the eventual outcome, but he'd fought Ruathen before, and he wouldn't consider them dead until their own funeral services were over and done with.

At a roar from their captain, most of the pirates hurried back aboard their ship. Hrolf the Unruly remained were he was, boots planted wide on the bloody canvas as he braced himself for the second impact as the western ship closed in, battle-ready warriors clustered at the rail. From his perch aboard the higher warship, Hrolf looked down at his *Elfmaid*, and at the three ships that surrounded her like the spine and covers of a book. But his gaze did not falter, and his massive chest was flung out as if to receive the expected blows.

Odd, thought Rethnor. Northmen sailors usually preferred to die on their own ships.

As the High Captain watched, the dark elf floated down to the deck and then scampered over to the *Elfmaid*'s bowsprit. She straddled it, holding on with both hands and bracing her feet against the hull of the impaled warship, as if she intended to push the pirate ship free. To Rethnor's astonishment, she did precisely that.

The drow threw back her head and sent a single high, keening note soaring toward the darkening sky, an eerie sound that sent a prickle of dread running down Rethnor's neck. Immediately there was a flash of light and sound, like lightning and thunder enmeshed in one combined burst of power. A spray of multicolored sparks bounced off the broken hull of the warship, and the *Elfmaid* shot backward. With a mighty splash, her up-tilted bow dropped back down to the water.

While the Northmen fighters gaped at this marvel, Hrolf the Unruly cut through the boom lines on the foremost mast. The pirates who'd remained aboard the warship with him rushed to his side. Muscles knotted and straining, they gave the heavy beam a mighty heave. The boom swung out, sweeping over the bow and continuing around toward the westernmost warship. So close was the ship that the tip of the swinging boom reached over the rail and into the fighters gathered there. Several of the men were swept off the deck and into the sea. As if that weren't bad enough, the boom continued its path—tracing a wide arc back toward ship's rear mast. Like a giant quarterstaff, the second mast parried the blow, but the crash of impact sent a shudder through the damaged warship. A grinding creak rent the air; then, slowly, the rear mast leaned and toppled into the sea like a felled tree. All that remained was a few jagged splinters and a tangle of lines.

Rethnor turned to his second, the warrior who served as battle chief. "Do not board the pirate ship. Bring the battle to us," he ordered.

The Northman responded with a curt nod, clearly understanding the High Captain's reasoning. On familiar footing, the Northmen fighters had better chance of success, for who could know what deadly magical traps that damnable drow wizard might have waiting for them on the *Elfmaid?*

A dozen or more men took up grappling hooks and sent them

twirling toward the retreating pirate ship. Line after line fell into the sea, but finally one, then two more hooks caught hold on the low rail. The Northmen attached the lines to winches and drew the ship in as they would a hooked fish. Archers kept the pirates pinned down behind their shield wall so they could not cut the lines.

The capture of the *Elfmaid* brought roars of anger and protest from her captain. Still aboard the damaged warship, Hrolf yelled out colorful challenges to his enemies' manhood and ancestry, brandished his mighty broadsword, and demanded battle.

"Oblige him," Rethnor commanded the steersman, and the *Cutlass* once again closed in on the damaged ship. The pirate captain needed no invitation to board; when the warship came within reach he vaulted over the watery divide and hurled himself, sword first, at the nearest fighters. His men swarmed in behind him, all of them as eager for battle as their captain.

Rethnor stayed on the forecastle, watching the fight and biding his time. He wanted the Ruathen fighters on this ship. *All* of the fighters. Yet some men remained on the pirate vessel, standing ready to defend her against attack.

The High Captain turned to his ombudsman and gave an order to be relayed to the other warship. The man picked up semaphores and waved the signal. In response, the Luskan fighters on the far ship sent volley after volley of arrows raining down on the pirates. The choice was clear: the Ruathen defenders could stay where they were and die, or take the fight to the ship that was reeling them in. When the *Elfmaid* was close enough to her captor, the pirates leaped onto the warship and flung themselves into battle.

All of the Ruathen were doughty fighters, but Rethnor saw no sign of the expected berserker. With mixed disappointment and relief, he picked his first victim: a dark-haired youth who stood out among the fairer Ruathen. An easy kill—the lad could hardly lift the black sword he held.

Rethnor stalked in, intending to gut the young fighter before he could parry the first blow. The Captain hauled back his blade in preparation for a backhanded slash.

But he did not swing, for astonishment knotted his arm muscles in place. Suddenly his sword was no longer aimed at the young man's torso; it was more on a level with his opponent's thigh.

Rethnor looked up. The young fighter appeared to be at least seven feet tall, with shoulders as wide as the too-large sword he now held with frightening ease.

"Berserker," breathed Rethnor. His moment of fear passed, and the anticipation of battle swept through him like a fever. He raised his sword to his forehead in a gesture of challenge.

In a movement almost too fast for the eye to register, the black sword mirrored his salute. Then it cut downward with an audible swish. Rethnor blocked, ignored the surge of bone-numbing pain that leaped up his arm and into his shoulder from the force of the impact. He spun, gripping his sword with both hands and lifting it high overhead to parry the next slashing blow. The swords met with a shriek of metal. Rethnor continued the turn, coming around to face the berserker and using all his strength and weight to press the black sword down toward the deck. He lifted a heavy-booted foot above the joined blades and kicked out.

The Northman's foot connected hard—a gutter fighter's move that should have doubled his opponent over in deeply masculine agony. The berserker did not so much as blink. His black sword whistled up, throwing Rethnor's sword arm out and wide. Faster than the High Captain would have believed possible, the berserker changed direction to slash straight down.

So fast did the blade descend that Rethnor heard the clatter of his falling sword before he realized what had happened. Pain as pure and bright as molten steel exploded in his mind and his arm. He looked in horror at the dripping stump at the end of his sword arm. With one stroke the berserker had cut through gauntlet, bracer, flesh, and bone. Rethnor's severed hand lay on the deck in a spreading pool of blood.

Several of Rethnor's men ran to their captain's aid, and the berserker turned to answer the new threat. Dimly Rethnor was aware of the skinny young pirate who scuttled in to claim the grim trophy, only to hurl it into the sea. He felt a belated surge of loss as his hand splashed into the waves; then he turned and stumbled toward the hold of the ship.

There, in the galley, was a circular stone firepit. A large kettle was wedged into the pit, embers from the evening meal still bright beneath it. With a kick, Rethnor sent the kettle flying. His remaining hand shook as he pulled a broad dagger from his belt and thrust it into the hot coals.

The High Captain waited until the metal glowed red; then he set his jaw against the pain to come. He fully intended to live, but to do so he had to stop the flow of blood. He took up the dagger and pressed the hot metal against his bleeding stump. A brutal hiss and the stench of seared meat filled the room.

Rethnor fought back the waves of agony and nausea and struggled to remain conscious. Again he heated the dagger and cauterized the wound, and then once again. Finally he slumped to the floor to await the battle's end. He knew that, for him, the fight was over, but there was no thought of defeat in his mind.

His war chief was a capable commander. One ship had sustained serious damage, but nearly two-thirds of his fighting force still stood. The pirates were outnumbered nearly seven to one. Not even a berserker or a drow could even those odds.

Then he heard the whine of some unknown missile, the shattering explosion as it hit some target to the west. Even down in the hold the crackle of fire and the smell of burning wood and flesh came to Rethnor. Only two ships left, he noted dimly as the room began to spin out of control. Still, the odds favored Luskan, and he was confident.

* * * * *

Liriel prowled about the warship, wrapped in her *piwafwi* and invisible in the surging waves of battle. Again and again her dagger slipped between some Northman's ribs, or slashed a hamstring. Perhaps it was not the most noble of battle techniques, but Liriel was pragmatic. As the drow saying went, "The unseen knife cuts the deepest."

Trusting Fyodor's battle rage to keep him safe, she sought out Hrolf and silently decimated the circle of fighters around him. An expression of almost comic outrage suffused the pirate's face when he saw his opponents had inexplicably fallen. He spun on his heel and went roaring off in search of new playmates. Liriel stepped over the body of the man she'd just slain, intending to follow Hrolf—for where the captain went, so did most of the action.

A strong hand seized a handful of the drow's cloak and hair, then yanked her sharply backward. She stumbled, tripping over the fallen man behind her.

The agile drow recovered quickly. Catching herself before she could fall, she dropped to the deck and threw herself into a side roll. The move wrenched her *piwafwi* from the hand of her attacker, but it also threw the cloak open and dispelled the invisibility charm. Liriel came up into a crouch, a knife in each hand, ready to throw into the eyes of whatever canny Northman had perceived and attacked her.

To her astonishment, Ibn stood over her, a grim smile on his red-bearded face and Fyodor's distinctive driftwood cudgel in his hand.

The drow's first thought was that Fyodor had fallen in battle, despite the power and prowess granted by his battle frenzy. It did not surprise her that Ibn would bring her the news—of all Hrolf's men, only he would find pleasure in delivering such a blow.

Fear tightened, like bands of mithril, around her chest and throat. She rose to her feet, her face a dark and regal mask, her eyes steadily fixed upon the mate's gloating face.

Before the stunned and grieving drow could guess his intent, Ibn hauled back the cudgel and swung it fiercely toward her. The rock-hard driftwood club caught Liriel in the middle with a strength that folded her over and forced the air from her lungs. She collapsed to the deck, completely unable to draw breath.

Ibn snatched up a net and tossed it over her; then he stooped down and plucked her off the deck. Holding her easily in his arms, the sailor covered the distance to the rail in two steps. Without hesitation, he threw the bound and helpless elf into the sea.

* * * * *

"It is fire, and it is ice."

Once, not so long ago, Fyodor had used those words to try to tell Liriel what the berserker rage was like. Never had the words rung so true as at this moment.

The battle fury burned fierce in Fyodor's blood, and his sword seared its way, like a black flame, through the throng of fighters. Just as powerful, and every bit as deadly, was the ice. The magic that sped Fyodor's sword arm also seemed to freeze time itself, slowing the movements of all those around him to a sluggish crawl, giving him time to think and react. The frenzy enhanced some of his senses and benumbed others. Although his body bore the mark of many wounds, he felt no pain. Nor did he tire. Each swing of the heavy sword came as easily as the last.

Yet the ice was a prison, as well, a fastness to rival any dungeon stronghold. Fyodor could not help but fight; he had to fight until no more stood against him. He could do nothing *but* fight. And so he had to watch, helpless in the grip of his own killing fury, while the treacherous first mate threw Liriel to her death.

Elaine Cunningham

His worst fear—that Liriel would someday find her way into his nightmares—had come true. The berserker curse kept him from going to his friend's aid. Perhaps her blood was not on his sword, but it was on his hands. In the small part of his mind that was still his own, Fyodor knew a loss deeper than any he'd ever felt or feared. Some instinct of self-preservation reminded him that he would remember none of this at battle's end. This was no consolation to the young man, for the dead returned to haunt him whenever he grew too weary to keep himself awake. He would relive the horror and helplessness of Liriel's death, again and again, for as long as he lived and as often he slept.

A roar of rage and grief tore from Fyodor's throat. He whirled, slashing out viciously as he spun. The blow severed the head of a Northman warrior and sent it flying. Fyodor lunged after it and caught one of the red-blond braids in his free hand. He began to whirl the gruesome trophy overhead like a macabre bolo, then let fly at one of the dead man's horror-struck comrades. The missile flew straight and true. Bone connected with bone, and the man went down in a splash of gore, his own skull shattered by that of his friend.

An enormous, axe-wielding Northman waded toward Fyodor over the thick carpet of the slain. The fighter called out to Tempus as he came, and to the warriors who had gone before him, exhorting them to prepare him a welcome in the mead halls of their god. The warrior clearly knew he would die, and he came on determined to go out in glory and honor. Shrieking a final battle cry to Tempus, the axeman lashed out with religious fervor.

Fyodor stepped forward to accept the wicked bite of the steel. The axe never came close. Almost against his will, the berserker pivoted sharply away as the blade descended. He continued his spin, whirling in a complete circle and swinging his sword at waist level as he went. The black blade cut through the Northman's protective leather jerkin and chain mail, sliced deep into his body. Instantly dead, the man slumped forward, the heavy weight of his body pinning the sword firmly between two bones of his spine.

The berserker tugged, but even his magically enhanced strength could not dislodge the weapon. Another Northman, seeing that the dangerous fighter was momentarily vulnerable, came at a run.

Fyodor kicked out hard, catching the dead warrior under the chin and sending the lolling head snapping back. There was a sharp

98

crack as the spine fully gave way; then the two halves of the dead warrior slid apart, freeing Fyodor's sword and spilling blood and entrails onto the deck. Fyodor calmly sidestepped as the attacking Northman charged into the horrible mess. The man slipped, arms windmilling, his momentum taking him on a slide toward the side of the ship. Fyodor sped his progress with a slap from the flat of his sword. The man hit the rail hard, and his booted feet flew up as he toppled headfirst into the sea.

The berserker swept a glance over the wild, surging melee. Over a hundred Northmen still stood, against less than a score of Ruathen. But Fyodor would fight until he'd killed them all, or until he himself was slain.

The young warrior no longer cared which came first.

* * * * *

Fearful and impatient, Xzorsh watched the battle raging overhead and waited for Sittl to arrive with reinforcements. The Ruathen pirates seemed to be doing well. At least, none of the bodies that sank past the sea elf wore familiar faces.

Then, suddenly, someone he *did* know plunged into the sea. The drow, tangled in netting, dropped near the startled sea elf. Her strange golden eyes settled on him for a moment; then she reflexively drew in seawater in a deep gulping breath. The amber orbs rolled up, and her thrashing limbs went still.

Xzorsh snatched up a handful of net and swam frantically for the surface, dragging the drow with him. He shook the water from his eyes and, taking stock of the battle, saw that the deserted *Elfmaid* was the safest place to revive the drow. He swam around to the far side of the pirate ship to avoid detection, then nimbly climbed up, dragging the unconscious female after him. Not wasting any time removing the netting, he placed both hands on her rib cage and began the rhythmic pumping that would empty her lungs of water.

Tense moments passed before his ministrations took effect. The drow coughed, sputtered, and then gave up the water she had inhaled. She recovered faster that Xzorsh expected. Seizing his hands, she pulled herself up into a sitting position.

"The net," she gasped in a raw-edged voice, struggling to tear it away, her eyes as frantic as those of a trapped animal.

Xzorsh reached for his knife, then realized that its place was empty—he had given it to Lord Caladorn. Seeing this, the drow told him there was a knife in her boot and wiggled the one foot that was not entangled in webbing. Xzorsh found the knife and went to work. It was the finest blade he'd ever held, and it cut through the ropes with astonishing ease. In moments the drow was free. She hauled herself to her feet and staggered over to the rail.

The warship that she had attacked with a massive fireball had drifted away from the battle. Flames leaped toward the darkening sky and licked at the sea as the ship burned down to the waterline. Two of the attacking vessels remained, and the battle was being waged exclusively on one ship. The other warship—the one that had lost a mast—managed to press in close. A line of Northmen stood at the rail, holding long spears and pikes and harrying the pirates whenever they came within reach, herding them back toward the midst of the battle.

And the battle itself was not going well. Fyodor raged like a whirlwind across the deck of the warship, and wherever he went Northmen fell before his blade. But his shirt hung in tatters around him, and his hair and clothes were dark with blood. Liriel suspected that much of it was his own. Even a berserker had limits, and when Fyodor fell, so would the Ruathen who were protected by his fury.

Xzorsh came to her side and handed her the knife. "Never have I seen so sharp a blade," he said tentatively. "Perhaps this is a foolish question, but do you have anything that can cut through the hull of a ship?"

Liriel spun to face him, her golden eyes distant as her thoughts raced over the possibilities. Suddenly she smiled and tore a bag from her belt. She shook out the contents; a dozen or so crab-shaped metal objects clattered to the deck. Xzorsh recognized them as the things she'd hurled at the giant squid. They had cut through the tough carapace of the creature, but the sea elf did not see how they would help him now. They would not fly through water as readily as they spun through the air.

Closing her eyes, the drow held her hands over the strange metal crabs and began to chant. They began to glow, taking on the red color of a winter sunset. At length the drow stooped and gathered them up.

"These are throwing spiders," she explained quickly. "I've changed the enchantment slightly. Put them on the hull of the ship—or anything else, for that matter—and they'll dig their way through. I want them back," she cautioned the sea elf as she handed them over.

Xzorsh nodded and pointed to some of the pike-wielding Northmen. "When their ship is at the bottom of the sea, I will retrieve your weapons and return them to you."

Liriel gave him a fierce grin and a companionable swat on the shoulder—a gesture she'd no doubt learned from Hrolf. "Send them to Umberlee," she said with dark glee.

The sea ranger nodded and dove into the water, hugging the bag of precious magical weapons close to his heart.

Left alone on the *Elfmaid,* Liriel paced the deck as she contemplated her next move. Invisible or seen, she could fight well with a sword but not well enough to turn the tide of battle. Her strongest weapon, her magic, was the best option. But she could not hurl fireballs without hitting some of Hrolf's men.

Liriel's fingers closed around the Windwalker, and she frantically reviewed the arsenal of spells she had stored in the amulet. None of them, in and of themselves, seemed equal to the task. She needed . . . She did not know what she needed.

Suddenly her eyes focused on a familiar object. Inspiration sparked, then caught flame. She let out a single whoop of excitement and then got down to the serious business of spellcasting. A spell similar to the one she'd used on the throwing spiders—one that would animate an object and subject it to her will—was stored in the Windwalker. She had never tested it, but there was no time for such precautions now.

Liriel raced over to the figurehead and placed one hand on the ten-foot statue. With her free hand, she clasped the Windwalker and began to chant.

Stored magic poured through her body and into the carved image of the elven maid. The garish paint under Liriel's hand took on more realistic hues; then the lifelike colors spread out in all directions until the entire statue took on a semblance of life.

A shudder rippled through the giant elven female, and the figurehead stirred. Wood cracked like thunder as the elf maid tore herself away from the ship that bore her name. At Liriel's bidding, the wooden warrior strode toward the rail and dove into the sea.

Massive wooden hands broke the surface with a force like that of a breaching whale. The elf maid gripped the rail of the warship and hauled herself aboard, setting the ship rocking crazily. Northmen and pirates alike lost their footing and tumbled to the deck. The fighters quickly scrambled to their feet, but the sight of the approaching statue sent them reeling back. For a moment the din of battle gave way to stunned and profound silence, broken only by the heavy tread of the elf maid's wooden slippers upon the deck.

The animated figurehead advanced steadily, weaponless but without fear. She plucked up a Northman fighter and hurled him into the sea, then backhanded another and sent him flying into the ready sword of a waiting pirate. On and on she went, a fearful killing apparition.

Hrolf was the first to recover from the shock. A grin of sheer, boyish delight split his face, like that of a child whose favorite toy had been brought inexplicably to life. He called out a fond greeting to the thing and bade her tend the troublesome axemen massed on the port side. The elf maid turned at once to do his bidding.

Liriel noted this with a surge of relief, and she gladly relinquished her creation to Hrolf's command. The powerful magic she had cast, the terrifying plunge into the sea, had drained her strength. She felt the pull of exhaustion and slid slowly to the deck, giving herself at last to sweet, deep darkness.

Chapter 8

SEA FOLK

he sky was still dark when High Captain Rethnor emerged from his pain-racked slumber. His cabin boy darted forward with a flask of water and held it while the captain took a few tentative sips. As soon as he could summon breath and voice, Rethnor immediately demanded that the war chieftain be brought to him. He was not at all happy to learn the man was dead. Rethnor asked for the first mate, then the boatswain, and received the same answer.

"Well, damn and blast it, bring me the highest-ranking man still standing!" he roared. The cabin boy scurried off at once to do his bidding.

To Rethnor's extreme dismay, the highest rank belonged to that of the ship's physician—not a normal fixture aboard Northmen ships but one that, given their mission, Rethnor had considered a wise precaution. It seemed his instincts had been sound, for the physician had obviously found work to occupy himself. The healer was spattered with blood, and he looked unspeakably weary, much older than his fifty-odd winters. And the tale he told was grim indeed.

Two of the mighty warships had been lost, one to fire, the other inexplicably scuttled. All of the warriors—all!—had been slain or badly wounded. Only a few of the crew, barely enough to sail the ship, had escaped the *Elfmaid*'s wrath.

The pirates had proven to be fearsome and inventive fighters. Their captain's blade alone had claimed at least a score of the Northmen. But it was the berserker, and then the magically animated figurehead, that had utterly decimated the Luskan fighters.

Rethnor listened with growing horror as the story of the battle unfolded. When at last the telling was done, he absently allowed the physician to check his wounded arm and to change the dressing. His thoughts raced as he considered all he had heard.

The unthinkable had happened. A single Ruathen ship had over-

103

come his trio of warships and was even now bound for her island home with this news. The Luskan snips had covered their name-plates and had flown plain sails and no port flags, but it was possible that someone among the pirates might have recognized the man who'd led the attack. Rethnor was not unknown among the Ruathen. As High Captain, he had attended many meetings of the Captains' Alliance and had often sat across the table from the island's battle chieftains, the so-called First Axes of Ruathym.

Rethnor determined that come what may, word of this attack could not reach Ruathym. Granted, the island's people were unlikely to unravel the tangled plot he'd woven to enmesh them, but Rethnor was not willing to give them a chance.

"Who steers the ship?" he demanded. "Where are we bound?"

"One of the sailors—I know not his name. Rest easy; we sail for Luskan," the physician replied in a soothing voice.

Rethnor threw aside the coverlet and rose to his feet. He thrust aside the protesting healer and made his way up to the starlit deck and confronted the astonished tillerman.

"Turn her about," he ordered in a voice that forbade argument. "Set a direct course for Trisk."

The sailor blinked but promptly relayed the order to the scant remaining crew. None of the men openly questioned Rethnor—to do so at the best of times would have meant their deaths—but to a man they wondered whether the sword that had severed the High Captain's hand had also stolen his wits.

Trisk was one of two large islands in the distant cluster known as the Purple Rocks. The islands lay west of Gundarlun, and past the warm waters of the River. Ice floes were still a hazard at this time of year, but even more fearsome were the strange and deadly sea crea-tures who were said to lair near the islands.

These stories were told only on solid land, preferably far from the sight of the sea and in the warm security of a crowded and firelit tavern. The tillerman did not want to remember those stories now. He was a Northman, and he did not fear to die. He just wished he could be certain there was a path between the mead halls of Tem-pus and the bellies of the sea creatures that surely awaited them.

* * * * *

Liriel slept through that night and well into the next day. She awoke with a start, surprised to see sunlight pouring in through the portal and Hrolf keeping vigil beside her cot. He grinned broadly when he saw her eyes upon him.

"It's glad I am to see you awake, lass! Lie still, now," he admonished her as she struggled to sit up.

"The lad is well enough, but sleeping," Hrolf continued, guessing what her first question might be. "He took a few cuts, none of them past stitching, but tired himself out something fearful. I've lived on Ruathym all my days and seen berserkers in frenzy many a time, but never anything to equal that!" he said with awe.

"It gets worse each time," Liriel managed to say.

Hrolf nodded, his jovial face suddenly very somber. "He doesn't have many more like that in him, does he?"

The drow shook her head. Her eyes drifted shut, but not before the pirate noted the uncharacteristic despair in their amber depths.

"What do you plan to do about it, lass?" Hrolf asked softly. "I figured some time back that you're looking to Ruathym for answers. Might be that I can help you find them."

"It's a very long story," Liriel muttered.

Hrolf folded his arms and leaned back against the wall. "You got until moonrise to tell it," he said calmly. "The lads bade me keep you here till then. They're working on a surprise for you."

"Carrying out the verdict from the Thing?" Liriel inquired with a touch of bitterness.

The captain grinned. "You might say that. But it's naught to fret about, trust me on that. Now, let's hear your tale."

Trust was not something that came easily to the drow, but Liriel found comfort in Hrolf's bluff assurances. Indeed, she had not realized until this moment how fully she'd come to trust the pirate. Without hesitation she told him the story of the Windwalker. Stolen from one of Rashemen's Witches, the amulet was an artifact from some ancient time, its magic little understood even by the powerful Witches who had worn it over the years. She told of the series of events that had introduced her to rune lore, the ancient magic shared by ancestors of Ruathym and Rashemen, and the story of how she'd come to possess the amulet. Finally, she told him of the quest that drew both her and Fyodor to Ruathym. The Windwalker was crafted for two things: to store "place magic" for a time, and to carve a newly learned and unique rune upon the ancient and sacred oak that stood on Ruathym. Liriel's innate drow powers and ready spells attested to the Windwalker's potency. She hoped that the journey to Ruathym—the lessons she learned, the trials she endured—

would form the needed rune in her mind and heart that would grant her permanent possession of her dark-elven magic, and Fyodor control over his berserker strength.

"I've heard tell of ancient rune quests," Hrolf observed when at last she paused for breath. "Let's say the shaping of the rune does come to you. Do you know how the casting of it should be done?"

Liriel shook her head. "I know a lot about wizardly magic, but this is completely different."

"Might be that I can help you there," he said thoughtfully. "You're right in saying that much about rune lore has been forgotten, but bits and pieces of the old ways can still be found if you know where to look. Some in my family still pass down the old tales." He paused and gave Liriel a grin and a wink. "You might ha' noticed I don't go about things the way most people seem to think I ought. That current runs deep in my family. I got a cousin, a good friend since we was boys, calls himself a shaman. Him and me will have a sit-down and talk it out, see what can be done for you and the lad."

The drow nodded her thanks, but the despair did not fade from her eyes. "If we make it to Ruathym in time," she said softly.

Hrolf considered this. "You know," he said, "I've been thinking about the plan to stop by Gundarlun. Herring fishing is nasty work. I'd just as soon do without it this spring. We've provisions enough to take us to Ruathym, and our trade goods won't spoil before the next trip. So how about we sail straight for home?"

Liriel's startled gaze flew to the pirate's face. "You would do that for us?"

"That and more, and don't you be looking so surprised about it!" The pirate reached out and gently cupped her chin in his massive paw. "You're a right smart lass, but you've yet to learn a thing or two. You and the lad have stood by me, and the *Elfmaid*, time and again. Don't you be thinking I'll soon forget it."

Hrolf gave her cheek a gentle pat and then sat back. "If you're feeling up to visitors, there's someone powerful eager to talk to you."

Liriel lifted an inquisitive brow.

"Xzorsh," the pirate responded, grinning broadly. "The elf's been swimming alongside since sunrise. Got something for you, he says, and won't give it into any hand but yours. I'm thinking that he's a bit taken with you, lass."

Liriel responded with a derisive sniff.

"Well, why not? He's a likely-looking lad," Hrolf teased, "and you with a fondness for swimming!"

"If I thought I could hold my breath long enough to make it worth my while, I might be tempted," Liriel responded wryly. "But I might as well see what he wants."

Still grinning, the captain left the cabin and clopped up the ladder to the deck. A few moments later, Xzorsh came quietly to the door, a familiar bag in his webbed hands.

"Your magic crabs," he said, placing the still-wet bag on the floor. "They are all there."

The sea elf looked as if he wished to say more, so Liriel waved him into the room's only chair. There were things that she, too, wished to discuss.

"Was it hard to find the throwing spiders? The magic crabs," she amended, remembering the name Xzorsh had given them.

"Not too hard. I often search lost ships for items of worth," the elf said eagerly. "I am considered skilled at such tasks and often find things useful for trade." He reached for his belt and unclasped a bracelet attached there—a heavy gold band of ancient design set with large oval sapphires. He offered the bauble to Liriel. "Would you take this in exchange for the knife you lent me? And would you name a price for one of the magic crabs? Or other weapons of magic, if you have them to spare?"

Liriel waved away the gaudy bauble. "Take the knife, and welcome," she said absently. "I've a dozen like it. As for the magic crabs, it so happens that I do have a price in mind."

"Before I was tossed overboard," she began, "I saw enough of the battle to recognize which man led the attack. A big man, dark-bearded, left-handed. My friend Fyodor fought him and cut off his sword hand. It went into the sea. Find the severed hand and bring it to me."

A look of horror crossed the sea elf's face. "What could you want with such a thing?"

"Can you get it or not?" Liriel asked impatiently. She had her reasons, but she certainly didn't intend to speak of them. By Lloth's eighth leg, *thinking* about them was bad enough!

During her short career in Arach-Tinilith, Liriel had learned that Lloth's priestesses possessed spells to rival those of the most powerful necromancers. Even if the dark-bearded man still lived, his *hand* was certainly dead, and there might be answers she could get from it, powers that she could wield over him. The needed spell was powerful, and as usual the risks were correspondingly great.

Elaine Cunningham

Liriel was not certain she could control such a spell even if Lloth chose to grant it.

"It is *possible* that I could find it," Xzorsh admitted. "But the sea is full of creatures, and most likely a severed limb has been . . ."

"Eaten," the drow finished curtly. "Well, do your best. I'll make it worth your time. In fact, why don't you take a couple of the magic crabs with you now as advance payment? The rest we'll negotiate upon your return."

Hearing the dismissal in her words, the sea elf claimed his treasure and rose to leave. He paused at the door. "The lost spirits of my people. How can I help you find them and set them free?"

"Get the damned hand," Liriel repeated emphatically. When the male did not look convinced, she added, "Doesn't it seem strange to you that three ships and nearly two hundred fighters came after a small fish like the *Elfmaid?* They wanted something from us, and they knew enough about us to bring a large fighting force. I don't think they were after Hrolf's cache of Neverwinter clocks."

Xzorsh stared at her. "The attack was prompted by the slain sea folk?"

"It's possible. Once we find out who those men were and what they're up to, we have a chance of finding out what happened to your people. For that," she concluded testily, "I need that hand."

The sea elf nodded as he absorbed this. "Forgive me, but I do not understand why you trouble yourself with the problems of sea folk."

The drow shrugged, not having any reason to give that she herself understood. When she offered no explanation, Xzorsh suggested one.

"I have heard many grim tales about the dark elves. You are not at all what I expected of a drow. It seems to me that I have been taught in error."

A vivid image flashed into Liriel's mind—the inevitable result that would occur if this noble-minded but utterly naive sea elf ever encountered one of her dark kindred. In a heartbeat, she snatched a handful of throwing knives from under her mattress and hurled them in rapid-fire succession at the too-trusting elf. The blades bit deeply into the wooden door, tracing a dangerously close outline around the startled Xzorsh.

"You are too slow to think and too quick to trust," she snarled at him. "Now get out, and return only when you can bring me what I want!"

The ranger ducked out of the room and disappeared. With a sigh, Liriel fell back onto her pillow. It was a necessary thing, but she had not enjoyed doing it.

* * * * *

As he swam back toward the site of the recent battle, Xzorsh could not rid his mind of the drow's words. There was much truth in them, he admitted. He was ever one to see things as all good or all evil, qualities that he considered as distinct and separate as sea and sky. The drow had fought for Hrolf and fought well, and she had shown concern over the fate of the slain sea folk. This had banished Xzorsh's doubts and established her in his mind as a friend to be trusted. She was right in saying that he thought too little and trusted too much.

On the other hand, if Liriel truly was what she wanted him to believe of her, why had she bothered to point any of this out to him?

Such thoughts continued to trouble Xzorsh throughout the day and well into the next night. Then he came upon the charred ruins of the ship that Liriel's magic had set aflame, and the remains of the vessel that he himself had scuttled, and he had no more time to devote to such musings.

The task the drow had given him was difficult. Many were the bodies trapped among the wreckage, and sifting through them for a single, severed hand was grim and dangerous work. Xzorsh had no way of knowing what other scavengers might have been drawn to the wreckage, or what creatures might even now be watching him.

So he went about his work quickly, ignoring the treasure in weapons and jewelry and concentrating on the macabre prize that the drow had commissioned. To his astonishment, he found what he sought. Entangled in a web of torn lines was a large, severed left hand. Dark hairs covered the back of it, and two fine rings decked the fingers. Xzorsh pocketed these rings—he could use them for trade—and placed the hand in a small bag.

Although intent on his discovery, Xzorsh quickly sensed the dark figures that emerged stealthily from the wreckage. There were four of them: hideous, man-shaped creatures with thick scale-covered hide and webbed hands and feet. They were merrow— aquatic cousins of ogres, but faster and more fierce than their land-dwelling kin. These four were an elite force; all had small ivory horns protruding from their foreheads, the mark of the most

109

powerful males. Keen black tusks curved up from their underslung jaws, and they were armed not only with their black talons—the traditional weapon of the merrow—but also with human-made spears and even the silvery trident of a triton.

Xzorsh reached over his shoulder for the short spear strapped to his back and awaited the attack. As he expected, all four came at him in a swimming charge, their weapons leveled at him.

The sea elf waited for the last possible moment. Then he twisted, agile as an eel, in a downward circle that took him below the reach of the weapons. As he went, he thrust out with his spear. He felt the impact, then the sudden softness as the point plunged through the merrow's scaly armor to the flesh below.

The three surviving creatures dropped their weapons and closed in, taloned hands reaching down for him and jaws flung open wide in preparation for rending bites. Xzorsh snatched at the trident as it floated down past him and braced the long handle against his hip. The lead merrow backpaddled fast to keep from impaling itself on the weapon. This was the opportunity Xzorsh wanted; he leaped upward, thrusting out high and hard.

The trident's middle prong sank deep into the merrow's unprotected throat and up into its head. Xzorsh pushed until the prong met the back of the creature's skull; then he whipped his feet forward and planted them against the dying merrow's chest. He shoved with all his strength, pulling the trident free and sending himself hurtling back through the water, beyond reach of the grasping hands and snapping jaws.

Xzorsh whipped the trident around to face the two remaining sea ogres. The creatures were more cautious now; circling their prey like humanoid sharks, they waited for an opening.

The sea elf thought frantically. He had seldom encountered merrow—most of the creatures lived in fresh water, and the few that had adapted to the sea usually laired in caves and shallow waters. Stupid creatures who lived only to kill and to eat, merrow sometimes fell in with more powerful beings who offered opportunities for murder and plunder beyond the ogres' limited imagination, or payment in glittering trinkets. Xzorsh had no idea who commanded these merrow, but one of them carried the weapon of a triton—a creature from the elemental plane of water. The implications of this were utterly beyond the sea elf's ken, and suddenly he wished the drow were with him. If anyone he knew could make sense of the twisted alliance this suggested, it would be she.

110

A quick, searing pain slashed across the sea elf's shoulders. Xzorsh arched backward, teeth gritted against the sudden agony. One of the merrow had managed to get within talon's reach. The sea elf whirled and stabbed out with the trident, but his attacker had already retreated beyond range. Xzorsh's fighter's instinct kicked in, and he looked back over his shoulder to find himself nearly face-to-fang with the second merrow. The elf pushed back hard with the butt of the trident and caught the merrow in the gut. The silver handle thudded against the creature's scaled abdomen, pushing the merrow away and buying Xzorsh a moment's time.

The sea elf reached for one of the drow's magic crabs and tore it free from the braided reed that secured it to his belt. He darted under the merrow's grasping hands, twisting around to swim up behind it. With a quick one-two move, he placed the crab-shaped object between the merrow's shoulder blades with one hand, and with the other hand punched down hard. The barbed legs sank deep into scales and flesh, then began to move as the enchanted weapon dug its way through.

The merrow spun to face the sea elf, its hideous face contorted with astonishment. Its fanged mouth opened again and again in grating, bubbling screams as the magic crab tore through its chest. The crab burst free in a spray of blood, a still-beating heart clinging to one of the barbed legs. When it met no further resistance, the weapon became inanimate metal once again.

Xzorsh snatched up the fearsome thing, brandishing it in the face of the last merrow. The creature halted its attack, regarding the unexpectedly resourceful sea elf cautiously. Then it turned and fled.

The ranger watched the merrow go, relishing thoughts of the report that the creature would give to its unknown commander. Let them know, Xzorsh exulted silently, that magic has come once again into the hands of the sea folk!

* * * * *

Patience was not among Liriel's strengths, and she had a good deal to say about Hrolf's insistence that she stay abed until moonrise. The captain merely laughed at her diatribes, promising her that the price of waiting would be paid in full.

At last the twilight colors beyond the cabin's portal gave way to darkness. Liriel leaped from her cot and quickly dressed and armed herself. Although Hrolf clearly thought the surprise would be a good thing, Liriel could not forget that not all the pirates had intentions that mirrored those of their captain.

Fyodor was waiting for her at the top of the ladder. He met her with a smile, but his eyes were deeply shadowed. She gave him a quick, cautious hug—for he moved stiffly and was bandaged in a dozen places—and an inquisitive look.

"It is nothing," he said softly. "A dream."

"Something about Ibn tossing me overboard in a tuna net?" she whispered back. She'd wondered if anyone had seen the attack, but Hrolf had said nothing to her of Ibn's treachery, and the first mate stood at the rudder, his red-bearded face as inscrutable as usual.

Fyodor recoiled. "It is true, then. I promise you, little raven, the traitor will not live out the day!" he said with grim earnest.

The drow smiled and claimed her friend's arm. "Oh, yes he will, and many days to follow! There's an old drow saying, 'Revenge is a dish best served cold.' That usually means revenge is more fun if you take the time to cool down, to plan and savor the act, but it works in other ways, too. Let Ibn wonder and worry. That will serve him better than hot steel and a quick death. And he is needed until the *Elfmaid* makes port; for all his faults, he's a capable sailor," the pragmatic drow added. "In the meanwhile his failed attack will keep him in line—although it might be wise to let him know that you are aware of what he did, so he doesn't think his secret will die with me. Now, let's see Hrolf's surprise!"

Fyodor looked doubtful, but he held his opinions to himself and led her through the broadly grinning pirates, up to the prow of the ship. Bjorn stood there, clearly embarrassed to be the focus of all eyes. His face gleamed red beneath the yellow tufts of his virgin beard, and behind him loomed his latest—and largest—work of art.

The elf-maid figurehead, inanimate once again and back in her proper place, had been repainted to resemble a drow with golden eyes. The flowing wooden locks were now white, and the still-wet paint of the face a glossy black. Some attempt had even been made to whittle the figurehead's lavish curves down to something more closely approximating Liriel's lithe form.

An unfamiliar emotion tightened the drow's throat as she gazed up at her own likeness.

Hrolf came to drape a massive arm around her shoulder. "Looks good on the old girl, doesn't it?" he said happily. "And by Tempus, won't the new elf maid spook damn near anyone we happen to meet! Umberlee take me if I shouldn't ha' thought of this years ago!"

Chapter 9
STRANGE ALLIANCES

he *Cutlass* sped toward the Purple Rocks, its skeleton crew spurred to exhaustion and beyond by their grim-faced captain. Rethnor was determined to reach Trisk in record time, for there was much at stake. He had lost not only his sword hand, but also his magical onyx ring—his only means of receiving messages from the western command center of the Kraken Society.

The captain could send missives—the magic pendant that he wore hidden under his tunic would relay his words to the western outpost—but this was not enough to meet his needs. He sailed to Trisk, not only to replace the scrying device, but also to enlist the help of Kraken agents who lived on the remote island.

Or, more to the point, *around* the island.

Rumors were plentiful among the people of the Kraken—this was to be expected in an organization that dealt in information brokering. Many of these were whispered tales of the strange magics and deadly beasts that haunted the western outpost. Even allowing for poetic license and the usual tavern boasting, there was no denying the dangerous nature of the waters around the Purple Rocks. Rethnor believed many of the rumored sea creatures were real and that some of them answered to the bidding of the Kraken Society. And more importantly, he had come to suspect that small and modest Trisk was in reality the primary base for the entire network of spies and assassins.

Rethnor intended to demand an audience with the leader of the society, and he did not think he would be refused. No matter how powerful the dark network of the Kraken might be, the base itself could not survive without trade. And Luskan was the island's strongest trade partner. In Rethnor's estimation, he had more than enough leverage to warrant all the demands he intended to make.

The captain pulled his magic pendant from its hiding place and began to dictate his orders into the shining disk, sending messages across the sea to the Purple Rocks and to hidden outposts on the mainland. For the first time he understood why the unknown, unnamed woman with the lavender eyes appeared to him in his scrying crystal. Without such reassurance, it was hard for him to accept that the magical messages truly reached their destinations.

As he looked out over the icy sea, the Northman—despite his inbred distaste for things magical—found himself wishing he had some knowledge of the art so that he could sense the far-reaching ripples that carried his commands to distant shores. Power he had, wealth in abundance, great strength and remarkable fighting prowess. But it occurred to him that these things provided little protection against the might of magic. The thought was new to Rethnor, and deeply disturbing. For some reason it chilled him, and he felt as if he'd heard the call of an unseen raven—the harbinger of a warrior's death.

The High Captain shook off his dark thoughts and fixed his eyes firmly on the western horizon. No doubt there was magic at work around the Purple Rocks, but there was power to be had, too. If he had to face the one to gain the other, he would take his chances as they came.

*　*　*　*　*

The town of Yartar was an important crossroads of the Northlands, located as it was on the River Dessarin and the trade road between Triboar and Silverymoon. Many important goods came through this town, not the least of them information.

Baron Khaufros, Lord of Yartar, was an ambitious man. He had inherited his wealth and title, but he'd earned his position as ruler of Yartar by his ability to build alliances of trade and politics. He was a steadfast member of the Lords' Alliance, that group of cities that tied their interests closely to those of Waterdeep. Khaufros was also a member of the Kraken Society, and the hidden chambers and tunnels under his mansions were frequent haunts of those spies and assassins who did the society's dark work.

At the moment, the baron was alone, engrossed with the pile of messages on his desk. Late spring brought a thawing of the Dessarin and a flow of messages from many towns—and many sources.

Khaufros absently tossed back the contents of his goblet and read the missive from his unknown Luskar contact once again. The plot against Ruathym was proceeding nicely, but for reasons unspecified it was decreed that the blame for many of the island's troubles was to be affixed upon a certain rogue sea captain of Ruathym. Khaufros was to do whatever he could to augment and support the new "facts" that spoke against this man. The Kraken leader from Luskan was also calling in all markers, demanding that the Ruathen ship be stopped by any means possible before it reached its home port, for the accusations could not be as easily made if the man lived to refute them.

"My lord baron."

Khaufros instinctively crushed the damning message in his hand and looked to the door of his study. The entrance was flanked by two suits of Cormyrian plate armor, priceless things forged of mithril and tested in battle against the Tuigan horde. Standing between them, utterly dwarfed by their martial glory, stood his elderly and impeccable steward, Cladence.

"The diplomatic courier from Waterdeep is here, m'lord, awaiting your pleasure."

The baron smiled and leaned back in his chair, the needed plan already forming in his mind. "Show him in, Cladence, and send my scribe in with him. Shut the door after them—we may be in conference for some time."

The messenger was a young man of common stock, too ignorant of court ways to change his travel-stained gear before seeking audience. Since this was the last mistake the lad was likely to make, Khaufros was inclined to let it pass. The baron accepted the letter from Waterdeep, broke the seal, and quickly scanned the contents. Routine information, for the most part, some of which he had already heard in greater detail from his Kraken Society contacts.

Khaufros looked up, his eyes focusing on a point somewhat behind the waiting courier. "Semmonemily, if you will, please," he said politely.

There was a metallic creak of plate against plate, and one of the empty armor suits stirred to life and began to advance on the messenger. The young man turned toward the sound just as a spiked metal gauntlet lashed out. His head snapped sharply to one side, and bits of broken teeth clattered to the floor like so many bright pebbles. Before the messenger could cry out, the empty metal hand struck again, and then again. Calmly, efficiently, the armor suit went about its grim task.

The baron and his scribe looked on with impassive eyes, for

115

they were too accustomed to such events to feel much of a response. Once they'd watched such executions with horrified fascination and just a touch of perverse pleasure. Now it was mere routine. Nor did either man blink when the armor suit blurred and melted, reforming itself into the mirror likeness of the dead messenger. This, too, was a commonplace event.

Semmonemily was a doppelganger, a shapeshifting being able to adopt any form it chose. By taking the place of the slain courier, the doppelganger could return to Waterdeep with altered missives.

The creature was one of the baron's most valued allies. The other was the wizened scribe seated at the writing table, bottles of various-hued inks before him and quill poised. This scribe was also a shapeshifter of sorts, for he could perfectly duplicate the writing of any man alive. As Khaufros spoke, the scribe bent over his parchment, transmuting the original messages into unimpeachable copies, subtly changed to reflect the baron's will.

Information was power; that was the basic tenet of the Kraken Society. But those who wished to know true power understood that it was not enough to gather information—one had to control it. And, upon occasion, create it.

★　★　★　★　★

Shakti Hunzrin was becoming accustomed to annoying disruptions. Since the day she had entered Triel's service as traitor-priestess, she had been expected to attend the Baenre matron's every whim. But this night's summons was by far the most abrupt and the most unusual.

The Black Death of Narbondel, the dark hour of midnight and the time when Menzoberranzan's magical timepiece was enchanted anew, had come and passed. Shakti had been comfortably asleep in her bedchamber, her door guarded by vigilant golems she'd enspelled to ensure that her dreamless slumber would end with the coming of the new day. Such precautions were not unusual among future matrons who had no wish to mysteriously die in their sleep.

But this night the stone guardians did not attend their given task. Shakti awoke with a start, literally shaken from slumber by one of her own golems. Its stone fingers closed around her upper arms; its impassive stone eyes returned her startled gaze.

Then she was hauled out of bed and thrust toward a glowing door that had appeared in the center of the bedchamber. Before she

116

could so much as curse the offending golem, the thing gave her a shove that sent her reeling through the luminous gate.

Shakti landed on her rump, her night robe hiked up around her plump thighs and her hair flying in wild disarray around her furious face. By the Mask of Vhaeraun, she vowed grimly, Triel would pay for this indignity!

"Welcome, priestess," said a cold and unexpectedly masculine voice.

The Hunzrin priestess froze. She knew that voice, as did all of Menzoberranzan. Those who cared to listen heard it every day, when the archmage celebrated the darkest hour by casting a spell of renewal upon Narbondel. But what, she wondered with extreme foreboding, did Gromph Baenre want with her? And by all that was dark and holy, how many Baenres would she be forced to endure?

"I am delighted to entertain one of my daughter Liriel's former classmates. Please, take a seat," Gromph continued, his manner an ironic parody of the gracious host. "I'm sure you can find one that is more to your liking than that carpet."

Shakti scrambled up and smoothed her robe decently back into place. Mustering all the dignity she could, she seated herself across from the archmage's polished table. Never had she been so close to the dreaded Gromph Baenre, and only with great effort did she refrain from staring. He was an exceptionally handsome male, young and vital in appearance despite his reputed seven centuries of ill-spent life. His eyes were of the same rare amber hue as his daughter's, but Shakti had never seen that expression of icy calculation in Liriel's golden eyes.

The wizard reached for a bellpull on the wall. "Will you have wine? Or tea?"

"Nothing, thank you," Shakti returned flatly. His polite manner was a subtle but obvious form of mockery, and the proud priestess bitterly resented any male—however powerful—taking his amusement at her expense. "I would not presume to take so much of your time."

"Ah." Gromph laced his fingers and placed them on the table before him. "You fit my sister's description well; she says that you are ever one to attend to the business at hand. Matron Triel is seldom wrong, of course, and I readily admit you have worked wonders in matters of agriculture. Your contribution to the restoration of the farms and rothe herds has not gone unnoticed. But I must draw your attention to another matter, one that remains unresolved."

The archmage held out his hands to her, palms up. Although they had been empty a moment before, cradled between them was a tiny bowl of dark red crystal. It grew rapidly until it was identical in every respect to the scrying bowl given to Shakti by the drow god Vhaeraun. The priestess stared, too stunned to hide her astonishment.

"You are acquainted with my daughter," Gromph continued in his cool, measured tones. "Yet I doubt you understand the half of Liriel's value. She is a wizard of no little ability. Did you know I arranged and supervised her training myself? And do you think I would go to such trouble for no purpose?"

Shakti could do no more than shake her head, but Gromph seemed to consider the answer sufficient.

"I am sure that you, of all people, can understand the importance of one who has a foot firmly in two camps. Of course I knew that Liriel would someday attend Arach-Tinilith, would be trained as priestess to Lloth. But I had her first, and the earliest marks on the mind cut the deepest! Liriel was created to be one of my strongest supporters—a Baenre priestess who is first and foremost a wizard. Despite the recent unpleasantness with the amulet, she still could be useful to me," Gromph concluded, "and I want her back."

The archmage leaned forward, his amber eyes intent upon Shakti's face. "It has come to my attention that you have sought assistance from beings from the elemental plane of water. If, as you suspect, Liriel has taken to traveling the waterways of the surface, this was not an unwise choice. Yet I understand that your threats and blandishments met with rebuff, is that not so?"

Shakti managed to mutter something in the affirmative.

"Not surprising. As a priestess of Lloth, you are accustomed to the creatures of the Abyss—entities of pure evil. The creature you have summoned is more complex; thus your methods must be more subtle."

Shakti's mind reeled as she tried to take in the implications of Gromph Baenre's words. How could he know so much? And more importantly, what did he plan to do with this knowledge?

The archmage plucked a bit of parchment from the empty air. "In the interim since your foray into the plane of water, I have gone to no little trouble to learn about the creature you summoned. On this parchment is written her true name. Use it only as a last resort, for there are easier ways to command the loyalty of this being. She calls herself Iskor, and she deals in information. She is messenger for a god worshiped on the elemental plane and, apparently, by many creatures of the sea. As you surmised, Iskor is not content with her role and wishes to amass power of her own. Thus she also carries information to creatures that make their homes in the surface waters. Promise to be her eyes and ears into the Underdark, and demand that in return for your aid she will seek out Liriel."

"You want the amulet," Shakti stated, more to buy time to gather her thoughts than for any true purpose.

This seemed to amuse Gromph. "Of course. Who would not? But I also want *Liriel*. See that she is returned alive."

The archmage rose to his feet. "That will be all. You should have all the information you need. If you require more, I will know. Kindly do not approach me directly. That might be . . . inconvenient."

Shakti could well imagine why. She would never accuse the archmage of Menzoberranzan of consorting with Vhaeraun, but what other explanation could there be? Where else could Gromph have acquired that scrying bowl? Or have learned so much about her plans? Or have gotten past the god-given wards on her chamber? Yes, she had a very good idea why Gromph Baenre had no wish to be seen in the presence of his sister's traitor-priestess.

But no matter what powers he might command, what information he possessed, Gromph needed someone like Shakti. The archmage was tied to Menzoberranzan by the task of enchanting Narbondel—an honor that was also a chain with links forged anew with the coming of each midnight hour.

The young priestess found no pleasure in this realization, for it was well known that no one who had dealings with Gromph ever did better than break even. For that matter, few survived. There was nothing to be gained by this enforced alliance, and much at risk.

Shakti had little choice but to agree to the archmage's demands. But if some means of escape presented itself, she vowed to take it.

* * * * *

Iskor, the water wraith, slipped into the door that led from her home on the elemental plane of water to the hidden city of Ascarle. The passage was brief but exhilarating—like swimming through a cloud of merrily roiling bubbles. On the other side she emerged from a pond filled with brightly colored fish, exploding upward into the dry and brittle air with the exuberance of a playful sea lion.

Iskor liked this new world and her role in it. She even liked the

119

illithid that watched her with expressionless white eyes. Evil and ambitious Vestress was a marvelous creature, even if she *was* an air-breather.

The water wraith assumed corporeal form little by little as she emerged from the water. Her face and body took the form of a sylph—a beautiful water nymph—but with skin and hair as transparent as finest glass. Iskor would have been invisible, but for the tiny, effervescent bubbles that whirled through her. She looked like a fountain contained within some exquisite sculpture.

Iskor smiled at the illithid and came forward to grasp both of the creature's purple hands in her glassy fingers. "Oh, Vestress, you will be so pleased at my news!"

The illithid disentangled herself as inconspicuously as possible. *By all means, continue. Good news has been scarce enough of late.*

"I recently met a most unusual traveler to my home plane," the water wraith continued with girlish enthusiasm. "A drow! A priestess who makes the Underdark her home! At first she was rather tiresome—all threats and demands—but now she offers information on her dark realm in exchange for services that only creatures of the sea can provide. Would she not make a wonderful addition to the Kraken Society?"

Indeed, Vestress was more than a little intrigued by the prospect of adding a drow to her band of informants. The illithid herself had left the Underdark many, many years ago, under circumstances that did not permit her to maintain ties with her homeland. It would certainly be very useful to have such an informant. But Vestress did not like to offer Iskor too much encouragement, lest the annoyingly bubbly creature spin off into new heights of euphoria.

And what might these services be? the illithid inquired, her mental voice projecting extreme disinterest.

"The priestess seeks the return of a drow female who escaped the Underdark. She was last seen in a city known as Skullport. Do you know it?"

Well.

"Splendid! The runaway is a drow wizard by the name of Liriel Baenre. She is young and easily marked by her golden eyes. It is believed that she took to the sea—where bound, no one knows. Upon this drow's return to the Underdark, my new contact—Shakti—will pledge herself to the Kraken Society. I took the liberty of telling her about the society and offering her this honor," Iskor concluded, beaming.

You may tell your contact we will see to Liriel Baenre, Vestress agreed, steeling herself for Iskor's response. The water wraith, predictably enough, gave out shrieks of glee and spun in a giddy little dance.

In all, this struck Vestress as a promise easily kept, for the illithid had already received Rethnor's report and she knew that a female drow sailed aboard the Ruathen ship that was inexplicably causing so much trouble. Vestress intended to send forces to intercept the pirate ship and capture the drow; as it happened, she had need of the services of a drow wizard.

The only part of the bargain Vestress disliked was that she must return the wizard to the Underdark. But, no matter. Iskor's new acquaintance sounded promising: devious, innovative. It might be amusing, mused the illithid, to bring this Shakti to Ascarle, as well. Surely one of them—wizard or priestess—could rid Vestress of her little problem on Ruathym. If there was an existing conflict between the two elven females, so much the better. In the illithid's opinion, there was nothing like a deadly competition to sharpen wits and skills.

And so Vestress waited calmly until the water wraith's glee wound down, and then she laid out to Iskor the terms meant to entice an Underdark drow to travel to the realm of the Kraken.

* * * * *

Xzorsh pursued the *Elfmaid* with all possible haste, for he was eager to rid himself of the grisly trophy in his bag. He was also concerned by the sudden appearance of the merrow, for he suspected those four might be part of a larger band. He had his duty to Hrolf, but he also wished to return to the ranger outpost to see what had become of Sittl. The promised reinforcements had not arrived, and Xzorsh feared for this friend's safety.

It was night when the sea elf found the ship. The drow girl stood alone at the rail, gazing out over the water as if deep in thought. But Xzorsh did not doubt that she was watching for him, or that she knew he was near—drow eyes were reputed to be even sharper than those of the sea folk. She gave no indication that she saw him, but she stretched languidly and dropped her cloak to the deck, then spun away and began to dance in the moonlight. Never had Xzorsh seen anything so entrancing as the drow's graceful, lyric move-

121

ments, and he gazed at her with wonderment. Many moments passed before he realized that he was not the only one so affected: the eyes of every sailor still on duty were fixed upon the elf. Suddenly it occurred to him that Liriel's dance had taken her—and the attention of the crew—to the far side of the ship. Xzorsh understood that she wished to keep their meeting a secret.

As stealthily as possible, he crept aboard ship and eagerly donned the glittering cloak she had left there for him. He knew it was a cloak of invisibility, but this knowledge did not fully prepare him for the experience of wearing it. It was odd, unnerving, to look down at his feet and see nothing but the small, wet prints he left on the deck. Wonderingly, Xzorsh held his webbed hand at eye level and spread the fingers wide. Nothing. He grinned, glad the drow could not see his antics.

Liriel concluded her dance with a whirling leap, falling to her knees with her head flung back and her hands outstretched toward the moon. She held the position for a moment as her long white hair swirled around her like a storm-tossed cloud. Then, with an abrupt change of mood, the drow stood and nonchalantly smoothed her wild locks back into place as she bade a good-night to the open-mouthed young sailor who stood watch. Xzorsh, still grinning with delight, followed the drow down into the hold and into Hrolf's cabin. She shut and bolted the door, then turned to him and held out a hand for her *piwafwi*.

"All this time you could see me?" he asked with a touch of embarrassment.

Liriel lifted one snowy brow. "You're standing in a puddle," she pointed out.

"Oh." Both relieved and chagrinned, the sea elf shrugged off the borrowed cloak, then handed over the bag.

He knelt near the cot and watched, fascinated, as the drow went to work. She spread a small mat on the cot and sprinkled it with some dried, spicy-smelling herbs. On this she dumped the contents of the bag. After sharply bidding Xzorsh to keep his distance and hold his tongue, she closed her eyes and began a soft and rhythmic chanting. Her dark form swayed. One of her hands clasped the engraved black jewel that she wore as a pendant, the other entwined fingers with the severed hand in a grotesque parody of a lovers' handclasp.

Then, to his astonishment, Xzorsh *felt* the magic in the room—a strange, cold tingling that made the thin air almost as alive and expressive as water. He felt it flow toward the drow, and he watched with shining eyes as she continued her chant and bent the eldritch current to her will. Then abruptly she fell silent, and the magic was gone. Xzorsh felt an odd sense of loss.

"Tell me," he entreated. He was immensely impressed by the female's ability to channel such a force and eager to learn what information it might have yielded.

Liriel turned her eyes toward him, but Xzorsh doubted that she saw him. Her gaze was troubled, distant.

"Nothing," she murmured.

Xzorsh studied her, puzzled by the strange effect the casting of the spell had on her. "Nothing at all?"

She blinked several times, and at last her eyes focused on him. "The man still lives. Where he is, or what he intends, I do not know. But I got the feeling that he is not yet finished with me, that he and his want something from me. As does Lloth," she added in a distracted whisper.

It was in Xzorsh's mind to ask her about this Lloth, but at that moment a hideous face appeared in the cabin's portal and sent all other thoughts into instant banishment.

"Merrow!" he said as he leaped to his feet. When Liriel shot him a puzzled look, he repeated urgently, "Merrow. Ogres of the sea."

"Damn!" spat the drow. She reached under her mattress and pulled out a long, keen knife, one even finer than the one Xzorsh had coveted. "Seems like a good time to break this in," she said with a touch of grim humor as she pressed it into his hands.

And then she was gone, sprinting through the hold and up the ladder to the deck, shouting an alarm as she went. In the cramped quarters beyond her cabin, pirates spilled out of their hammocks and seized weapons.

"What are we fighting, lass?" Hrolf asked happily, tucking his shirt into his breeches and falling into step with the drow as she hurried toward the rack of harpoons.

"Sea ogres."

Hrolf stopped in midstride. "*Merrow?* What in the Nine Hells are they doing in these waters?"

Before Liriel could answer, six pairs of enormous webbed and scaly hands slapped onto the ship's rail. Six merrow leaped onto the deck, quick and nimble as giant frogs.

"Mother Lloth," Liriel breathed as she looked up at the hideous faces. The merrow were as large as their land cousins—all were

123

well over nine feet tall—and they moved with a speed and agility that no ogre could match.

The largest of them, a male with two ivory horns protruding like hideous thumbs from its forehead, took a step forward. "Where be the dead elveses?" it demanded in a low-pitched gurgle. "Want them, we do!"

Xzorsh, his hand resting easily on the hilt of his new knife, went forward to face the merrow chieftain. Though he was but half the creature's size, his eyes offered a challenge that the sea ogre did not disdain. "The People are no longer on this ship," he said firmly. "They have been returned to the sea. You are relieved of the task of taking them to your master, whoever he might be."

The merrow chief actually looked pleased by this news. It turned and grunted something to the others.

Liriel listened carefully—ogre slaves were common in Menzo-berranzan, and she knew enough of their dialect to make out a few words of the merrow's guttural speech. Her eyes widened in shock as she divined this one's intentions. She barely had time to whip the harpoon up in a defensive position before all six merrow darted toward her.

The chieftain lunged at Liriel, massive arms spread wide. Her ready harpoon clunked into its scaly abdomen, but skidded across the tough hide without penetration. Fortunately for Liriel, the harpoon was longer than the creature's reach, and it kept those lethal black talons from closing on her. Even so, the speed and force of the attack sent the tiny drow reeling back. The butt of her weapon hit the mast hard, and the onrushing merrow supplied the force needed to push the barbed weapon through its scaly hide.

Liriel let go of the harpoon and rolled aside as the impaled mer-row came crashing to the deck. But five of the merrow remained, and all were as fast as the drow. A large, webbed hand slapped down and seized her ankle. She was dragged facedown across the deck and then swept up, kicking and cursing, into a merrow's arms. The creature easily slung the thrashing elf over its shoulder. It dropped into a half-crouch, then sprang up over the rail and into the sea.

They plunged deep into the icy water. Above her Liriel heard two more splashes, and then no more. The pirates were no doubt dealing with the merrow remaining on board. This gave her a cer-tain amount of grim satisfaction, but did nothing to improve her situ-ation. Not that she faulted the humans—the attack had taken no more than a few seconds. The sea ogres were incredibly fast fighters. They were even faster in water. Hrolf's men tossed out nets in a desperate attempt to ensnare and retrieve the merrow and their captive, but the merrow were beyond reach almost as soon as they hit the water.

Suddenly her captor thrust her away. Liriel wriggled beyond its reach and swam frantically toward the surface, her lungs burning for air.

But the sea ogres were not through with her. Two of the creatures flanked her and seized her wrists. They pulled her taut between them so she could not reach any of her weapons or even get in a decent kick. The third merrow produced a small silver ring and jammed it onto the middle finger of her hand. Then, grinning horribly, it punched her in the stomach.

The drow doubled over, expelling the last of her precious air with an audible *oof!* and a rush of bubbles. Water flowed into her lungs to fill the void. To her astonishment, she found that she could breathe it!

So *this* was how the merrow intended to kidnap her, she realized. From some unknown and powerful source, they had acquired a ring of water-breathing. She had heard of such trinkets. The trio encircled her, indicated with grunts and gestures that she was to accompany them.

Now that the immediate threat of death was past, Liriel's mind began to race over possible ways to escape. She would have to outthink them; she could not overcome three creatures of such size and power in battle.

Then, suddenly, something exploded, with a cracking of ribs and a spray of blood, from her captor's chest. Liriel recognized one of her own throwing spiders. She seized the weapon—ignoring the clinging bits of flesh and sinew—and whirled upon the nearest sea ogre.

But the creature was fast and in its native element; the drow's movements were slowed by the unfamiliar heaviness of the water. The merrow seized Liriel's wrist. The drow slapped downward with her hand, but the spider did no more than touch the ogre's scaly forearm.

Then Xzorsh swam into view, his spear held ready. With a quick thrust, he struck the spider and drove its barbed legs deep. The enchantment triggered, and the spider began to burrow its way through the sea ogre's flesh.

Immediately the merrow let out a gurgling yelp and dropped its hold on Liriel. Bracing its wounded arm against its hip, the ogre seized the spider's metal body and frantically tried to pull it free. If the merrow had had the time and wit to consider the matter, it might have realized the folly of this strategy. Whereas the spider might have eaten through the arm and been content, it now continued on its path and dug its way deep into the creature's groin.

It was odd, Liriel thought as the merrow's howls echoed through the water, that she'd always thought of the sea as a silent place.

She left the merrow to its fate and swam toward the two fighters that grappled in unequal combat. Pulling her short sword, she prepared to even the score against the sole surviving merrow. To her way of thinking, two elves just about made up one of the sea ogres.

But Xzorsh seemed to have the battle well in hand. His new knife flashed and wove in a compelling—if entirely unfamiliar—pattern as he nimbly dodged the merrow's lunging bites and the swiping blows of its taloned hands.

As Liriel watched, she began to make sense of the battle. The sea elf shadowed many of the larger creature's movements, using the currents and eddies caused by the merrow's attacks to speed his own knife. It was a complicated and multilayered school of swordplay, one the drow had not even considered. Of course, there was little call for underwater combat in Menzoberranzan. Yet Xzorsh, in his native setting, was fully the match of any drow fighter Liriel had seen at play.

At last the elaborate dance of feint and double-feint came to a close. Xzorsh buried his knife to the hilt in the base of the merrow's skull. Bloody bubbles gushed from the creature's mouth, and the massive arms floated limply out to its sides. The sea elf braced both feet against the dead merrow's back and pulled his knife free.

Liriel retrieved the now-dormant throwing spider and swam to the sea elf's side. "Your magic crab," she told him, smiling delightedly at the sound of her voice bubbling through the water. By way of explanation, she held up her hand, wiggling the fingers to show off her new ring.

Xzorsh might not know much of magic, but he realized the power of the ring. For a moment the elves merely faced each other, smiling as they shared the exhilaration of a battle won. Then the ranger tied the precious magic spider to his belt and held out a hand to Liriel.

"Come. The others will be worried about you," he said.

126

Without hesitation she took his hand—or, more accurately, his wrist, for the ranger's webbed fingers forbade a traditional hand-clasp. As they swam together toward the starlight, Liriel marveled at the strange turns her journey had taken. Not long ago, she had looked to the tunnels beyond Menzoberranzan for adventure. How narrow that ambition seemed now that she could see the wonders of the night sky, walk upon the surface lands, and swim the sea as effortlessly as a fish! Strange, too, were the friends she had picked up along the way. She'd never given much thought to faerie elves, beyond the realization that if she ever met one she'd probably have to kill it. The possibility that she might actually consider befriending such a being had never entered her imagination. Nor did she ever imagine that she would have a friend such as Fyodor—a human, and a male at that—or that the ebullient Hrolf would come to regard her with the sort of fatherly pride and affection she had always sought, tentatively and with utter futility, from her drow sire. How odd it all was, Liriel mused.

Stranger still was the rune that was beginning to take shape in the drow's mind, little by little with each day that passed. Every tiny line and curve was clear to her, although the whole was far from complete. The shaping of it was not of her making. In fact, Liriel felt a bit like a spellbook, receiving the ink from the pen of some cosmic scribe. Nothing in her wizardly training had prepared her for this or for the feeling that this magic was not so much a force to be exploited, but an outcome woven from the threads of her life. It was all foreign to the drow, and she did not understand the half of it. But exciting, it was! she concluded happily.

A contented sigh escaped her, sending a ripple of bubbles racing toward the starlit sky.

Chapter 10
THE PURPLE ROCKS

he illithid's purple hands gripped the arms of her throne as she sent a brief burst of mental power toward the merrow warrior—just a puff, just enough to send the sea ogre reeling back a step. Merrow were proud creatures, and this one had not wanted to admit that its band had met failure. Foolish creature, to think it could hide anything from the Regent of Ascarle!

Then came a second puff of energy, and a third. Bit by tantalizing bit, the illithid forced the merrow back toward the large oval pool at the rear of her audience chamber. The merrow knew full well the fate that awaited it there; its horror only made the exercise more delightful.

Vestress prodded the merrow until it was a but few feet from the edge of the pool, and she froze it there. Its mind—such as it was—she did not touch. Another game awaited, and for that the merrow would need possession of its limited wits.

The illithid sent a silent summons into the deep water. After a few minutes the surface of the pool rippled, and a pair of long, thin tentacles snaked out onto the tiled floor. Like thin arms they flexed, heaving and straining in an effort to drag the rest of the creature out of the water. Another pair of tentacles emerged to join in the struggle, and finally an enormous, bulbous head protruded. A large tail, fluked like that of a whale, flailed and slapped at the water as the creature humped and wriggled and dragged its way out onto the marble tiles.

The aboleth—for such it was—turned its three slitlike eyes upon the immobilized merrow. These eyes were stacked one above the other, and they glowed with a strange purple light that intensified as the creature began to cast a charm. The sea ogre's face went vacant at once as it fell under the spell, but several moments passed before it took the first jerky step toward the fishlike creature. Sometimes it took a good while for the aboleth's innate magic to wrest its prey from the grasp of the illithid.

This was a game Vestress and the aboleth played often. It amused them both and gave them what they most coveted. The illithid watched as one of the aboleth's tentacles curled back and snapped, whiplike, toward the merrow. The sea ogre jolted as the incredibly potent venom coursed through its body and shuddered convulsively as the poison took effect—rapidly transforming the merrow's thick and scaly hide into a slimy, transparent membrane. The creature's innards were clearly visible, but just for a moment. Bone softened, and the merrow's form began to sag like a melted candle.

Still under the aboleth's spell, the sea ogre oozed its way over to the edge of the pool and splashed into the water. The aboleth dragged itself back to the water to feed. For all its fearsome appearance, the aboleth did not have any teeth, and its mouth was hidden on its underbelly. It could consume only victims that had been reduced to the consistency of mucus, and it could not eat except in the water.

Vestress sat calmly while her playmate sucked the merrow dry. The wait was usually well rewarded. The aboleth might be ungainly, but it was one of the most potent sources of information in all of Vestress's vast network. An aboleth acquired all the knowledge possessed by any creature it ate. No aboleth willingly gave up these secrets, but Vestress was exceptionally skilled—even for an illithid—at pulling information from an unwilling mind. The aboleth enjoyed the challenge of going mind-to-mind with the powerful illithid, and occasionally it agreed to hunt and consume some intelligent seagoing creature that might yield up—posthumously—information of special interest to Vestress. In all, it was an arrangement that suited them both.

Again the aboleth dragged itself out of the pool, moving more slowly now that it had gorged itself on a nine-foot ogre. It locked stares with the illithid, and the battle for mental supremacy began.

Vestress reached out with her psionic powers, touching the impressive shields that guarded the sea creature's mental treasure trove. She pressed, nudged, battered at the wall—all to no avail.

At last the illithid turned away, admitting defeat. Sometimes she won, sometimes not. It was no coincidence, however, that she usually lost when the prize was a creature such as this merrow—and *after* she had extracted from its mind any information of value.

The aboleth did not seem to care about such distinctions. The victorious fish-thing slithered back into the water, leaving a trail of gray slime on the marble tile, and then disappeared into the depths beyond the pool. Oddly enough, it was this disgusting substance that had prompted Vestress to summon the aboleth in the first place. Although the slime smelled disgustingly like rancid lard, it was useful in making potions of water-breathing, and Vestress had it collected after each of the aboleth's visits.

Vestress sent a mental summons into the antechamber for her newest slave. The slave was human, a strong, pale-haired female who'd fought entertainingly against the illithid's mental control. No matter—the female had succumbed as did all. Now docile and efficient, the woman knelt on the tile and began to scrape up the grayish slime. When the marble floor was spotless and shining, the well-trained slave took the bottled slime and headed off for Vestress's alchemy chamber, where it would be transformed into a potion of water-breathing.

The illithid was in particular need of such a potion. Her last one had been used to create a ring of water-breathing, a valuable item lost to the drow whom the slain merrow and his band had failed to kidnap. This drow—indeed, the entire crew of the Ruathen ship—had surprised Vestress more than once. That situation, however, was about to change.

The Regent glided toward the pool that led to Iskor's watery realm. She would summon the water wraith and persuade her to bring the drow Shakti to Ascarle at once. What better, more entertaining way to learn more about her new drow foe—and her new drow ally—than to pit them against each other?

*　*　*　*　*

The *Cutlass* made port on Trisk, the main island in the Purple Rocks archipelago, in record time. With the assistance of an efficient dockmaster, Rethnor sent a messenger to the palace requesting an immediate audience with King Selger, the nominal ruler of Trisk. As he suspected, the monarch sent a coach at once to bring the High Captain of Luskan in state.

This was Rethnor's first visit to the island, and as the royal coach crested the rocky hillsides of the coast and rolled through the green valley beyond, all that he saw confirmed his suspicions about the island's place in the Kraken Society. The people of Trisk were cheerful and industrious. Never had Rethnor encountered so pristine a harbor, or farms and homesteads so well tended. At first glance, the island appeared to be a place of remarkable contentment—a paradise.

But Rethnor had not achieved his position by accepting first appearances. He noticed the strain behind the smiles, the frantic striving at excellence, the watchfulness on every face. And he noticed that the emblem of the Kraken Society—a many-tentacled purple squid—was worn in some form by every person he set eyes upon. Rethnor did not think that these simple, isolated folk had become Kraken agents through personal ambition, or even by choice.

So much the better.

He found King Selger to be much as he'd expected—delighted with the impromptu visit, eager to please, clearly aware of the importance of maintaining Luskan's goodwill. Rethnor intended to see how far the king would go to keep it.

The High Captain waved away repeated and lavish offers of food, mead, and various entertainments. "My time is short. I need to meet with the head of the Kraken Society," he said bluntly.

Stunned silence met his words, then carefully worded disclaimers. Rethnor would have none of it. He badgered, ordered, threatened—and finally King Selger yielded.

"We will do what we can to aid you," the king said cautiously, "but upon your own head be the consequences."

"I accept them," Rethnor said, and then added dryly, "Perhaps it will set your mind at ease to know that these consequences, whatever they may be, will not affect the island's trade status with Luskan."

The king's face turned deep red at these words—even a puppet monarch had his pride, Rethnor noted—but he did not try to deny their truth. His only caveat was that Rethnor must wait for low tide. Nothing the captain could do or say would make Selger budge on that point.

And so shortly before the following dawn, a servant summoned Rethnor and showed him to the royal stables. The two men selected their mounts from among the stout, shaggy ponies indigenous to the island, and then rode off in silence. Rethnor tried to extract information from the servant, but the man did not speak the Common trade language and Rethnor knew only a few words of the obscure dialect spoken on Trisk. The High Captain suspected the servant had been chosen specifically for his lack of linguistic skills. Although King Selger had little choice but to cooperate with this powerful ally, he apparently intended to do all he could to protect the secrets entrusted to him.

The two men rode in silence to the island's northern coast. It was a dismal, deserted place, a long stretch of rock-strewn sand that was eerily devoid of life. No seabirds wheeled and quarreled overhead, no crabs scuttled along the still-damp sand. Rethnor's lone escort took him to a rocky ledge that dropped off suddenly and dramatically into the sea. He pointed out the caves that were revealed only when the tides were at their lowest ebb.

As soon as Rethnor swung down from his mount, the servant seized the pony's reins. Wheeling his own mount about, he bolted back toward the safety of the town.

Rethnor briefly considered throwing a knife into the coward's back, but the man was out of range too quickly. With a curse and a shrug, the Luskar let the matter pass. He took a pine-pitch torch from his pack and lit it; then he dropped into the water.

Even at low tide, the sea was waist-deep at the cave's entrance. Holding the torch high, Rethnor slogged onward into the darkness. The cave was larger than he had anticipated, and the vast blackness seemed to swallow the flickering light. Just as the Captain began to wonder whether the king had sent him on a fool's errand, the chamber narrowed, and the light of his torch reflected off the walls of a wondrously carved stone passage.

Thick pillars lined the walkway, and curving buttresses met overhead in graceful arcs. All surfaces were carved with intricate designs, detailed scenes, and the curving script of some long-forgotten language. The artistry was breathtaking, and Rethnor could not help but calculate the market price of some of the artifacts he passed as he waded through the silent halls. Just the gargoyles alone would bring a fortune to rival that of the most corrupt Waterdhavian noble.

Rethnor raised his torch for a better look. Marvelously detailed and endlessly varied, the gargoyles perched atop the pillars like silent sentinels watching over the passage. Looming over him was a particularly fearsome statue—a goblinlike creature with an owl's beak and feet, and wings like a cross between those of a bat and a manta ray. As the torch's flickering light touched the gargoyle, the stone statue stirred to life. The massive wings snapped out into a tight arch, and the creature leaped from its post. Down it glided toward the stunned man, the talons on its enormous feet flexed and eager.

Too late Rethnor realized his error. These were not statues, but living creatures—kapoacinth, a marine variation on the pure evil that was a gargoyle. As the creature bore down on him, Rethnor flailed at it with his torch. But what weapon was fire to a creature of stone?

As the kapoacinth swooped in, Rethnor understood what a hare must feel just before the strike of a hawk. Giant stone claws closed on the Northman's shoulders, biting through the protective layers of fur overcoat and leather armor. Rethnor gritted his teeth against the pain as the creature dragged him from the water. His torch flew from his hand and died with a feeble hiss.

The gargoyle flapped heavily into the air with its prey and then glided down the passage. After a time the man's eyes adjusted to the darkness. He noted that the passage was one of many, each with side tunnels branching off haphazardly on either side. The kapoacinth took many turns, following a convoluted path that Rethnor could not hope to remember. Then, to the High Captain's greater horror, the creature changed path once again and dove straight for the water. The man filled his lungs with air just as the icy impact struck him.

After the cold, Rethnor's first sensation was that of incredible speed. The water rushed past him with a force that threatened to tear him from his captor's claws. Then, suddenly, the motion stopped. Cautiously Rethnor opened his eyes. They had emerged from the tunnel into a large, deep basin. In the dark water ahead Rethnor could make out the shapes of what appeared to be the ruins of a city wall. Once again the kapoacinth dove like a stooping hawk. The creature glided through the remains of a massive portcullis, then swiftly made its way through an enormous labyrinth of ancient stone.

In moments the inner city lay before them—not ruins, but a marvel crafted from crystal and coral, beautiful beyond telling. Like a diamond with a heart of flame, the city lent an eldritch glow to the surrounding water.

The kapoacinth swooped down to a marble walkway that ended in a gleaming arch. Its talons opened, and Rethnor dropped heavily onto the path. With a sharp slap of its barbed tail, the creature sped him through the magic doorway. Rethnor stumbled through the portal and emerged in an air-filled room. The entire underwater journey had taken little more than a minute or two, but the shock of it had quickened his heart and emptied his lungs. Another moment more would have been too much for him. Yet even as he dragged in much-needed air, he placed his one remaining hand on his sword hilt and surveyed the room for potential danger.

Rethnor found himself in a place of surpassing beauty, an antechamber that would have graced any palace in twenty realms. The crystal walls whorled upward in intricate patterns to the peaked ceiling, giving the impression that the room was contained within an enormous gem. Exquisite marble of pink, green, and white was inlaid in exquisite designs on the floor and walls, and rare statues graced the alcoves. Most fair of all was the servant who came to greet Rethnor, a woman of the North, dressed in silken robes that matched the pale gold of her hair. In a strangely toneless voice she bade him follow, her movements wooden as she led the way through ever more wondrous rooms.

Unaccustomed to such splendor, the High Captain was keenly aware of his sodden clothing and bedraggled appearance. He had little thought to spare for such petty emotions, for nothing in this unnatural place felt right, and his warriors instincts screamed out a warning. As the beautiful slave led him down a long passage toward the audience chamber, he strove to still his mind and prepare his wits for the encounter to come.

But nothing could have prepared Rethnor for what awaited. The vast room was dominated by a marble dais and a crystal throne the color of pale amethysts. Seated upon this was a regal—if hideous—creature. A silver diadem rested on its high-domed lavender head, and the four tentacles that made up the lower half of its face writhed in sinuous, graceful patterns.

Well met, Rethnor, intoned a familiar, feminine voice in his mind.

The High Captain gaped at the strange creature, unable to hide his distaste. *This* was the regal woman who had guided so many of his recent plans? Was it possible that this malformed beast was the famed head of the Kraken Society?

We thought you might be more comfortable conversing with a form similar to your own, the illithid explained. *In answer to your rather tactless, if unspoken, question, I rule this place as Regent. Do not underestimate my power, or that of those I serve.*

Rethnor's left arm jerked up to one side, without his will and of its own accord, revealing the stump where his sword hand had once been.

We see you have been careless with the scrying ring we gave you, the illithid continued. *It is well we had the foresight to provide you*

*with a second device. But let us speak on matters of import. You have
come to seek assistance. We are ready to provide it.*

A silent summons from the illithid brought two more, even
stranger creatures into the room. A glasslike nymph glided toward
the throne, and at her side stalked a female drow.

Rethnor had no opinions on nymphs, but he held a Northman's
dislike of elves, drow or otherwise. They were scrawny, wispy, ugly
things, to his mind more like shadows than real creatures in the way
they flitted about, utterly despicable for their effete dependence
upon magic. But this female was more substantial than any elf he'd
ever laid eyes on, with a tread you could hear and a solid form that
approached human proportions. She was plump and curvy enough
to draw the eye of any hearty male, but there was not a bit of softness about her. The drow's eyes were red, as hard and cold as
rubies, and bright with feral intelligence. On the dark canvas of her
face was painted barely controlled fury. Despite his innate prejudices, Rethnor was intrigued.

*We will provision your ship and provide you with fresh sailors and
fighters from among the people of Trisk, so that you might continue
your pursuit of the Ruathen ship. These two will go to help ensure your
success.*

"What need have I of two females?" Rethnor demanded,
appalled by the very idea of setting sail with these creatures aboard.

*Iskor, the water wraith, can speak with the creatures of the sea and
locate the ship you seek in moments. She can also summon powerful
beings from her native plane. Perhaps such can succeed where you, to
date, have not. Shakti, the drow, has yet to prove her worth, but you
will take her all the same.*

Rethnor glowered at the elf. His fierce glare had turned aside
powerful warriors, cooled the battle ardor of hardened Northmen.
But the drow's strange red gaze did not falter; indeed, she seemed
to grow only more angry as she regarded the man.

"This insult is past bearing," she spat, speaking in harsh, badly
accented Common. As she spoke, she fingered the silver cuff that
clung to one pointed ear—no doubt some magical device that translated her speech, Rethnor surmised.

"I sought partnership with a water wraith, offering value for
value, and how am I repaid?" the drow continued bitterly. "Taken to
this . . . faerie city and apprenticed to a human? A male!"

*Do you not wish to capture your runaway drow? She is on the ship
this man seeks. You need him, and he you. I strongly suggest you find a*

way to work together, the illithid commanded.

The Northman and the drow locked stares, taking furious measure of each other. Rethnor was the first to speak. "When we find the ship, the berserker warrior is mine to slay. Keep your foul magic away from him," he ordered.

"What is a human fighter to me? But touch the yellow-eyed bitch, and you die!" snarled Shakti in return.

Well, well, observed the illithid's mental voice, showing the first note of humor Rethnor had ever perceived in it. *It would seem that you two have found common ground already.*

* * * * *

The *Elfmaid* kept a steady course upon the warm waters of the River, rounding the island of Gundarlun without incident and then turning southward toward Ruathym. Despite the loss of the large profit the herring would have brought them, the crew seemed cheerful and eager for the return home.

All but young Bjorn, who usually spent the long days at his carving or painting. Unusually restless, he paced the deck for hours at a time, looking toward the sky as if there were words written there that only he could read.

At twilight of the third day, Hrolf could bear no more of this. "Out with it, lad! If there's a storm coming, say so and be done with it!"

The young sailor looked troubled. "Not a storm," he said hesitantly. "But something. I know not what." He shrugged, sheepish as a child pressed to confess the details of an unremembered nightmare.

The answer was soon to come. Liriel saw it first, for the range of her elven vision was longer than even that of the farsighted sailors. A dark wall of water raced toward them from the northwest, gaining height and power as it came.

The pirates watched its approach stoically, knowing their seamanship to be no match for the killing wave. Liriel was not so accepting of her fate. She seized the Windwalker and began to chant, calling upon the strongest defensive sea-magic spells she had studied and stored in the amulet. A bubble of energy, glowing faintly with the faerie fire of drow magic, encircled the ship like a giant dome.

"To retain air around the ship, and keep us from being swept under," Liriel explained tersely. "It gives us a chance, no more."

Hrolf wrapped an arm around her tense shoulder and gave her a quick, grateful squeeze. "That's more than we had a moment earlier. Grab ahold, lads, and prepare to get bounced around some!" he roared.

As the echoes of his voice reverberated through the magical bubble, the captain dropped facedown to the deck and took hold of a secured rope line. Elsewhere, the other sailors followed his example, bracing themselves as best they could for the coming onslaught.

The wave swept under the *Elfmaid* and lifted her up with breath-stealing speed. To the astonishment of all, the ship did not plunge back down into the sea; the massive wave continued to hold them aloft.

Then the wave shifted and began to take on humanoid form. Eyes the size of war shields gazed down at the stunned crew, and enormous watery hands cradled the ship—which was still encased in its glowing orb—as easily as a child might hold an oversized plaything. With an odd, undulating movement, the creature began to move toward the northeast, its arms and body lengthening and shortening as it went, like the ebb and flow of the tide.

"What in the Nine bloody Hells *is* that thing?" Hrolf demanded. His usually ebullient voice was reduced to a harsh whisper.

"An elemental," Liriel returned. She had seen stone elementals and knew the incredible strength of such creatures. She even had the magic to conjure and command such a being. But it had never occurred to her that such could be called from the other elements, and she was astonished by the sheer size and power of this one. The elemental's fluid shape was hard to measure, but she guessed it stood at least twenty feet above the waves, with arms at least twice that long.

The ship settled down into a gentle swaying motion, and one by one the sailors left their secure holds and came to cluster around their captain. Their expressions were fearful, but confident.

"How d'we fight this one, Captain?" Olvir asked for them all. Despite the tremor in his voice, the seagoing skald asked the question with the tone of one who fully expected an answer. Their captain had led them through many unorthodox adventures and provided Olvir with tales enough to while away the nights of the longest winter.

But this time the light of battle did not come to Hrolf's eyes. The captain felt an unaccustomed lack of optimism. The *Elfmaid* had lost five good men to the fighting so far on this trip, bringing their number down to under twenty. There were enough remaining to man the ship—barely—but not enough to take into battle against such a foe. Indeed, Hrolf had no idea how a force of *any* size could trim the sails of this watery monster. But he stifled his own fear and faced the men with a confidence he did not feel.

"No fighting just yet," he said firmly, casting a stern glance in Fyodor's direction. "We're not exactly under attack, to my way of thinking. Seems as if this thing wants to take us for a ride. We wait it out, weather this delay same as any other storm. Go about your business best you can, but keep your weapons sharp and ready. Once this wet bastard puts us down," he promised with a touch of his customary battle glee, "it had best be ready to block, duck, or bleed!"

The men responded with a halfhearted cheer. Hrolf sent them off to do little-needed tasks. When all were occupied, he pulled Liriel aside. "Can you do aught to stop this thing, lass?"

The drow shook her head, thinking of the unlearned spells in her pilfered book of sea magic. "Not yet. I'll check my spellbooks for ideas, though."

Hrolf cast a glance at the sky. His weathered brow creased as he made some calculations. "Looks as if you'll have time to ponder over it. Unless I miss my guess, from the direction we're headed I'd have to say this thing plans to take us to the Purple Rocks."

"What are they?"

The captain met her curious gaze without a trace of his usual humor. "A place best avoided," he said grimly as he placed one hand on her shoulder. "Go look through them magic books, my girl. But read fast, or Umberlee will have us all."

Chapter 11
ESCAPE

o you know anything about this?" demanded Khelben "Blackstaff" Arunsun, archmage of Waterdeep, as he thrust a sheet of parchment into his nephew's hands.

The young man scanned the elegant, slanted script that could only have come from the quill of Baron Khaufros, one of Waterdeep's staunchest northern allies. "I don't believe it," he said flatly.

"Oh? And what basis have you for doubt?"

"I have met the drow in question, and my instincts where women are concerned are impeccable," the younger man declared comfortably, laying down the parchment so that he might attend to a blond lock that had strayed onto his forehead. His fastidious preening only deepened the archmage's scowl.

"She caused a bit of trouble down in Skullport," Khelben reminded him.

"My point precisely. According to the Dark Sister, this lovely young drow played a pivotal part in the raid that took out a nest of Vhaeraun worshipers and freed a shipload of children destined for slavery. Oh, I've been following her progress," he said in response to the archmage's incredulous gaze, and his voice lost every hint of its lazy drawl. "Did you think I would send a strange drow to the Promenade Temple and not follow through to ensure that my original judgment was sound?"

Khelben ceded this point with a nod, but the worry lines creasing his forehead did not disappear. "I do not doubt that you did your job, Danilo. But did you know that this drow also singlehandedly rescued a criminal from Skullport's dungeon, then booked passage upon this man's pirate ship and used some sort of powerful gate spell to remove it from the underground port?"

"No," the youth admitted and grimaced. "I stopped gathering information after the battle, assuming that the lovely lady had achieved happily-ever-after, as the bards are wont to say."

Khelben lifted one eyebrow at Danilo's reference to bards, but for once the archmage refrained from giving his opinion on the matter of bardic reliability. "It is the drow's magical escape from Skullport that concerns me and gives credence to the baron's report. Anyone who commands power enough to bypass Halaster's gates is a potential danger."

The young man nodded somberly as he picked up the parchment. Once again he read the reports of increased drow activity in the area of the River Dessarin. There had been sightings of a raiding party traveling the Dessarin, and the bodies of several drow males had been discovered in the hills east of the river. Several different bands of human adventurers were apparently squabbling over bragging rights for this victory. The small town of Trollbridge had claimed an attack by a drow female who wielded powerful magic and who had apparently enspelled a young swordsman to do her bidding.

Danilo did not doubt that the pair described were the same he had met less than a month before. By all accounts, the pretty little drow had been busy. But he could not credit to her the atrocities that Baron Khaufros reported or accept the baron's suggestion that the dark sorceress would take over the wills of whatever men she happened to meet. But he *did* understand Khelben's concern about the girl's magical ability. A powerful wizard, drow or otherwise, was always a wild card, and the game currently playing out in the northern seas was complicated enough.

"She should be watched," Danilo admitted.

"She should be stopped," the archmage retorted and then paused. "There is something else you should know. We have received word from the harbor merfolk that a Waterdhavian hunting vessel known as the *Cutter* was scuttled by pirates. There were no survivors; all of the men aboard were put to the sword. The captain of the attacking ship was Hrolf the Unruly, the man your drow rescued from Skullport's dungeons."

The young man's face went very still. "Wasn't Caladorn aboard that ship?"

"I'm afraid so," Khelben said somberly. "Since the young fool has his mind set on adventuring at sea, the Lords of Waterdeep sent him north to gather information. For some time now, we have been receiving reports of attacks upon sea-elven communities and increased raiding activity by factions within the Northmen. Shortly before his ship was lost, Caladorn managed to relay by magical means that he'd found something of importance and was returning with it to the city. I find it uncomfortably coincidental that a Ruathen pirate ship, by all appearances dominated by a dark-elven wizard, would stop him from doing so, and by such brutal means. In light of all we know—and all that we have yet to learn—we cannot allow this particular dark elf free run of the Northlands."

Danilo took a long, steadying breath as he absorbed this news. Caladorn Cassalanter was a member of his own set and a close friend of Danilo's oldest brother. The young nobleman struggled not to give Caladorn's loss undue weight in his consideration of this matter, for he had learned painful lessons about the grim consequences of taking quick vengeance. Even with all emotion aside, however, Danilo found it hard to discount the dire predictions coming from Yartar.

The domain of Baron Khaufros was on the Dessarin River, and much information flowed to his small town from the wild interior of the Northlands. The baron's keen eye and nearly infallible grasp of local politics and events had repeatedly averted disaster. Just a few seasons past, Khaufros had investigated scattered sightings of orc tribes on the move, plotted their paths, and predicted that they would convene in a single, remote valley. This advance warning had enabled the Lords' Alliance to stop the orcs before they could form a rampaging horde.

Perhaps this lovely drow wizard was another potential threat, one that could cause untold damage if she were allowed to run unchecked. The lore books were fat with tales of powerful, ambitious wizards and the devastation they left behind. Every young mage knew the risks, and the temptations, that lay along the path he or she had chosen. Danilo had ample reason to know the dark face of power, for in his own past were dire secrets known only to him and to the stern man who awaited his response. These secrets lay heavy between them as they contemplated the damage that another powerful young wizard might do, and considered what should be done to prevent this eventuality.

Danilo blessed the fact that he himself did not have to make such decisions. He was young—barely into his twenties—and completely absorbed with his magical training and his fledgling efforts on behalf of the Harpers. Hiding behind the persona of an idle nobleman, a fop, and a flirt, he was becoming expert at gathering information. It was enough. He wanted—he would accept—no more power and responsibility than this.

"What will you do?" he ventured, when at last Khelben's watchful silence became too much to bear.

The archmage turned away, his face inscrutable. "It is already done. The pirate ship was recently spotted rounding the northern coast of Gundarlun—they cannot be far from the island and are no doubt following the River due south toward Ruathym. We have contacted a Waterdhavian ship wintering on Gundarlun, one specially equipped for dealing with piracy. Grandassian is the ship's wizard. You know his skills; I daresay he is at least the equal of this drow."

"He will kill her?" Danilo demanded, aghast.

"He will bring her back to Waterdeep, so that we might ascertain her abilities and know her purpose."

Danilo shook his head as he remembered that chance meeting and envisioned the dark elf's golden eyes. The wild spirit behind those eyes had convinced him that the drow at the masquerade was no Waterdhavian noblewoman in a magic-enhanced costume, but the genuine article. A hawk would sooner present its wings to be clipped, a panther walk willingly into a cage, than this untamed girl would submit to defeat and capture.

"He will kill her," Danilo repeated softly, and he wondered at the surge of loss that followed in the wake of this realization. For the first time in his young life, he wished his instincts concerning women were not quite so infallible.

* * * * *

Throughout the day the water elemental carried the *Elfmaid* toward the northeast, bent low with its enormous burden yet showing no sign of slowing or tiring. The pirates made an effort to go about their usual business, but there was, in truth, little for them to do. At length they fell to drinking and the telling of grim tales.

For once Fyodor took no part in the storytelling. The old legends of Rashemen, however, were very much on his mind. He took a solitary post on the forecastle, gazing at the horizon with sightless eyes as he sought inspiration in his country's rich treasury of lore. Fyodor had learned that no matter what puzzle life offered him, he could usually find an answer in the remembered deeds of ancient gods and heroes.

Alone in Hrolf's cabin, Liriel frantically studied her book of sea magic for the means to overcome a water elemental. There were no spells listed that could accomplish this feat. Nor could she send it back to its home plane—apparently the preferred method of dealing with such creatures—for few drow studied the elemental planes, and water was hardly their favored element. Liriel knew little of the sea, and less about the plane of water and its creatures. The drow resolved to redress this lack, if and when she reached Ruathym. At the moment, though, she was severely taxed by the double effort of maintaining the bubble shield that enclosed the ship and devising a way to escape from the elemental.

The day was nearly spent when Fyodor's shout roused her from her reverie. Liriel heard his distinctive bass voice calling out something about an approaching ship. Armed with her newly learned spells and those stored in her Windwalker amulet, the drow hurried to the deck to investigate this new development.

There were actually two ships—a large two-masted caravel sailing from the west and a tiny dot on the northern horizon that was still well beyond the reach of any eyes but hers.

"The ship is fully armed!" Fyodor exclaimed, pointing to the arsenal of catapults and ballistae on the decks of the approaching caravel. "Perhaps they can help us escape from this creature."

Ibn glowered at the young warrior. "Help, from a Waterdhavian ship? It's well that you can *fight,* boy, since you haven't the good sense the gods gave a clam. That's plain enough by the company you keep," he concluded, casting a significant glance toward Liriel.

The drow ignored the sailor's insults in favor of more important matters. Her eyes narrowed as she gazed at the approaching ship. There was an aura of magic about it. Strong magic.

Since leaving her home city, Liriel had noticed that her eyes were becoming more and more attuned to the nuances of power. Menzoberranzan was permeated with magic. She could no more see magic there than she could employ her heat vision when the midday sun turned sea and sky to pale blue fire. Magic was hardly unknown on the surface world, but it was comparatively rare, and Liriel was finding that she could sense its occurrence and gauge its power. So she did not doubt the instinct that warned her of a mighty spellcaster aboard the approaching vessel. Since it stood to reason that a ship's wizard would know more of sea magic than a drow, Liriel planned to take full advantage of the unknown wizard's skill. But first, she had to wrest the *Elfmaid* from the elemental's watery grasp.

The drow faced the creature and began to chant the words to a part-water spell, her body swaying as she drew power from the weave of magic and reshaped it into an invisible sword. She flung one arm up high, instinctively falling into a battle stance as she lashed out with her eldritch weapon.

But Liriel was near exhaustion, and sea magic was new to her. Her usually lethal aim failed her; the spell, which should have parted the elemental neatly in two, merely lopped off an arm.

Water gushed, like a mighty waterfall, from the wound. The *Elfmaid*, still in its protective bubble, was swept away on the flow. Sailors tumbled to the deck and rolled toward the bow of the ship. Fyodor, high atop the forecastle, was thrown from his perch and into the air. He hit the bubble of force and slid down its curved surface toward the water. At once he saw his danger: if he fell into the water he would slip down to the lowest part of the magical globe and be crushed between the ship and the bottom of the bubble. His flailing hands found a hold—the wooden bodice of the figurehead's low-cut gown. Fyodor hauled himself onto the perch offered by the elf maid's ample bosom. Holding fast to the statue's pointed ears, he hung on for dear life as the ship plummeted into the sea.

A solid wall of seawater splashed over the domed shield as the ship dropped under the surface of the water. But Liriel's spell held; the air-filled bubble bobbed to the surface, the *Elfmaid* rocking wildly within its protective shield.

Now that the ship was free, the exhausted drow dropped the magical defense. Too soon—a vast wave of water flowed upward and re-formed into the elemental. Ignoring the approaching caravel, the elemental once again closed on the *Elfmaid*. But the creature had only one arm; it apparently was unable to tap the inexhaustible supply of seawater to regenerate its form. Liriel took note of this, then dove deep into the concentration needed for her next casting.

Her intended spell was a summoning, very like the dark-elven magic that raised an army of spiders from the creatures that lurked in every cranny of the Underdark.

The result was immediate and spectacular. Every sea creature within attacking range came to her call, forming the strangest army the drow had ever seen. A pod of gray whales began to nudge and prod at the elemental with their enormous, barnacle-encrusted heads. The elemental batted at them with its one remaining arm, but the whales persisted, pushing the creature inexorably northward and away from the Ruathen ship.

The efforts of the smaller creatures were also taking effect. They swam up into the water that comprised the elemental's bor-

144

rowed body, turning the sea-colored creature dark with their shadowy forms. Hundreds of small fish busily schooled, swimming in fast, tight circles as if they were in some enormous fishbowl. The dizzying current seemed to confuse the elemental, and it swayed drunkenly as it flowed toward the north.

Other, more deadly creatures joined in the attack. Long-snouted barracudas darted about inside the creature, snapping and tearing as they sought the essence of the creature contained within the seawater. One of them managed to rip through the elemental's watery hide and was shot, with a sudden gush of fluid, from the creature's body. With the force of a ballista bolt, the fish slammed into the side of the *Elfmaid*. Its body splattered, leaving a dark streak behind as the remains of this strange warrior slid slowly into the sea.

The elemental's watery form flowed in to close the wound, but the creature had lost a bit of stature with the attack. It seemed weaker, too, and it no longer fought the determined whales that nosed it steadily away from the Ruathen ship.

By now Fyodor had climbed down from his perch, and he came to Liriel's side. The drow was swaying, drained by the powerful magic she'd cast, and he slipped a steadying arm about her waist. "You cannot fight it alone," he told her quietly.

"It becomes smaller with each attack," the stubborn elf responded, pulling away from her friend's embrace.

"Just so." Fyodor fixed a determined gaze upon her. "In my land, there are tales of an ancient sword whose strike could freeze the blood and flesh of an enemy. Put such an enchantment upon my sword, and I will carve frozen pieces from the creature for as long as I am able."

Liriel stared at the young man, understanding what he intended to do. He did not expect victory over the elemental, but he was fully prepared to die in battle against it if that would cut the creature down to manageable size. It was not the first time Fyodor had taken on suicidal odds to spare her, and Liriel had yet to understand how this could be so. Self-preservation was the first law of the drow. A mixture of awe and confusion sparked the girl's ready temper.

"Your confidence in my ability is touching," she snapped, thinking of the years of crafting, the incredibly powerful spell-binding, that went into making a weapon such as the one in Fyodor's tale. "But you have no idea what you're asking! Before we try conjuring magic swords, let's give the fish a chance. Oh, look—there's a good one!"

Elaine Cunningham

A large black creature that looked strangely like an Underdark bat spiraled upward through the elemental's liquid body and into the head. The long tail whipped about, thrashing and probing. The elemental reeled, its one hand clutching at its temples as if it were in agony.

"Manta ray," Hrolf told her, a grin of dark satisfaction on his bearded face. "Got a poisonous sting to its tail with enough power to sink a small whale. Now *that'll* slow the critter down, and give him something to regret come morning!"

The Waterdhavian ship, meanwhile, had changed course to close in on the wounded elemental. A catapult lever sprang forward, sending a grapeshot load hurtling toward the creature—crystalline particles of some sort that caught the last rays of sunlight like so many glittering gems.

"Uh-oh," Liriel murmured. Without bothering to ask for details, the pirates dropped to the deck and flung their arms over their heads.

The whine and thud of the catapult's machinery caught the attention of the tormented elemental, and it spun just in time to face the incoming spray of crystals. Instinctively, the elemental threw up its one arm to ward off the attack, and it began to sink into the protective waves.

Not soon enough. A geyser of steam billowed into the darkening sky, filling the air with a tremendous hiss and the overwhelming stench of cooked fish. The Waterdhavian ship changed course immediately to veer away from the deadly cloud, but the faint cries coming from it indicated that some of the sailors had been scalded. The pirates leaped to their feet, cheering and shouting at this double victory.

Nevertheless . . .

"They will pursue," Ibn pointed out, his tone grim.

Hrolf shot a significant look at Liriel. "Not if they think there's nothing left of us to chase."

The drow considered this, her fingers closing around the Windwalker as she reviewed the spells contained in the amulet.

"Enough!" Fyodor demanded, his voice tinged with anger. "Look at her. She is barely able to stand. How much magic do you think one person can channel and live?"

"She's stronger than you think, lad," the captain said stoutly, wrapping a fatherly arm around the girl's shoulders and giving her a squeeze.

146

The young warrior stood his ground. He had seen the Witches of Rashemen pour forth their magic in battle, draining their power and essence until there was nothing left of them but piles of drifting dust and empty black robes.

"It is better that we take on the ship in battle," Fyodor insisted.

Liriel sniffed. "You don't want to face off against the wizard who melted that elemental, trust me on that. And it's not *one* ship, but two." She pointed to the northeast; the distant vessel was now close enough for human eyes to discern.

Hrolf snatched up an eyeglass and trained it on the approaching ship. "Damn and blast it, it's one of them warships we fought before!"

"And the elemental was taking us to them," the drow added. "Believe me when I say that anyone who can summon elementals is bad news. Hrolf and Ibn are right. Whoever those people are, they will pursue us until we are dead—or they think we are. You," Liriel demanded, whirling to point at one of the sailors, "bring me a sea chart with our current location marked on it. Harreldson, take the rudder and set course for Ruathym. The rest of you, to oars! Put some distance between us and that caravel!"

The men scurried to do her bidding. Even Fyodor took a place at the oars, for he knew that no argument would sway the stubborn drow once her mind was set upon a given course of action. The row of oars dipped and pulled, and the nimble *Elfmaid* leaped toward the south. Tracing a stately arc, the caravel changed course to pursue.

Liriel stood alone on the main deck, her eyes closed and her hands curved before her as if she were holding an invisible globe. Slowly, as if in graceful dance, her hand turned palms-out and her arms stretched high, then went out wide. A sheet of darkness, a vast impenetrable curtain of black, fell between the *Elfmaid* and her attacker.

"It worked," Liriel muttered with relief. She had never tried to reshape the drow globe of darkness into another form, and until this moment she had no idea whether or not it could be done. Taking no time to exult, she turned to the next part of the spell. The sailor she'd sent for the chart hovered nearby, his eyes round with wonder as he stared at the summoned darkness. Liriel snapped her fingers impatiently, and he darted forward with the chart.

"We're here," she mused, touching one black fingertip to the point on the map that the sailor had marked and sliding it down as far as she dared. "What are we likely to bump into here? Rocks?

Shoals? Anything?"

"Nothing but open sea," the sailor said, and his face blanched as he understood the drow's intent.

"I'm not real happy about it myself," she grumbled, for the gate spell required for such an escape would have challenged her even if she'd approached it fresh and rested. Still, there was something to be said for the power of desperation. And by the time the *Elfmaid* was ready to take the dimensional plunge, their situation would be desperate indeed.

The fingers of the drow's right hand curved around the Windwalker, and she flung her left hand toward the black curtain. Magic fire spat from her fingers, forming a fireball that tore through the darkness and beyond. There was a moment's silence, a thud of impact, then shouts from the other ship and the faint crackle-and-hiss of a fire quickly extinguished.

Again Liriel attacked, and this time came the unmistakable *pop* of a fireball glancing off a magical shield. Good, she thought grimly. The enemy ship's wizard was every bit as powerful as she'd suspected. She was almost certain what his next move would be, and she readied herself in preparation.

Summoning every fireball in her arsenal, Liriel braced her feet wide and set off the first small missile, much as a drow armsmaster might send out a scouting party of kobolds to test the enemy's range and resolve. She heard the magic fire strike the unseen shield, and she began to count rapidly. An answering flash exploded from the darkness—her own weapon, rebounded back. The fireball, diminishing in size and power as it came, fell short of the *Elfmaid* and disappeared, with a weak fizzle, into the water.

A smile of triumph flashed across the drow's weary face. She now knew precisely how long she had between attack and escape. Again she stretched out her hand, and again magic fire erupted from her fingers. A barrage of fireballs spewed forth, so many that the sky was brightened as if by festival fireworks, so quickly that it appeared as if a single line of multicolored lightning flashed from her outstretched hand.

With the last of her fireball spells gone, Liriel swayed and then dropped to the deck like an arrow-shot raven. But she struggled to her knees, both hands clasping the Windwalker and her face set in determination. Quickly she called forth the gate that would take the pirate ship several miles to the south and to safety.

Nothing.

A scream of pure, primal rage tore from the drow's throat. Never had magic refused to obey her call! Anger lent her a moment's strength; she snatched up her obsidian pendant and raised it high even as her scream ended in a shriek of prayer— a brief and fervent oath in the ancient Drow tongue, a final, desperate plea to Lloth.

Utterly spent, Liriel fell silent and watched with dull eyes as her own weapons rebounded toward the pirate ship in a colorful storm, whistling as they burst through the curtain of blackness and hurtled downward like falling stars. The illusion she had hoped to create— the destruction of the *Elfmaid*, her death, and those of her friends— would soon be all too real.

And then the lights and the sound were gone.

The *Elfmaid* was surrounded by swirling gray mists, by heavy air as dank and foul as that of a despoiled crypt. Although she'd been temporarily blinded by the fireballs, Liriel had her other senses in full measure, and she caught the familiar scent of giant fungi and a whiff of sulfur and brimstone. Faintly, as if from some unfathomable distance, came the echoes of roars too terrible to have come from mortal throats and of shrieks that spoke of torment and despair. Liriel's eldritch senses were fully aware, too, and she sensed the palpable cloud of terror and gloom that pressed heavily upon all those unfortunate enough to enter these realms. She also sensed the core of dark fire that was the heart of this fell domain, felt the frigid obsidian hand that reached out to touch her and to claim the offered prize.

Lloth had answered her prayer.

Relief mingled with horror in the young drow's heart. She and her friends would escape their deaths, but oh, the price! In that desperate moment, Liriel had pledged herself as priestess to Lloth, and she had been accepted.

A mere novice in Menzoberranzan, Liriel had not been required to make such a pledge, but considering the many challenges she faced, it was a step she logically should have taken long before this. Not a problem, the drow told herself, and nothing outside the realm of her experience and expectations. She had merely agreed to become a conduit for the Spider Queen's power, as had her fore-mothers for centuries untold, and vowed to work for the glory of Lloth. Power was power—she would accept what she was given and make the best use of it that she could. And yet, as the oppressive gloom of the Abyss crept into her soul, Liriel wondered for the first time what the price of this power might be.

And then the mist parted to reveal a sparkling night sky and a calm, black-satin sea. Liriel turned her eyes upon the humans. To a man, they were frozen in place and looked as if they'd been chilled to near-death by the touch of a vengeful wight. She fervently hoped they did not realize where they had been.

Finally Olvir managed a weak grin. "And I thought the last magical trip was bad! Don't get me wrong—I'm glad to have come out of that with my hide in one piece—but give me a choice, and I'll take a stormy sea anytime."

"Aye!" Hrolf agreed, his voice less hearty than usual. "Don't exactly know why, but Umberlee take me if I don't feel like I just slept with a lichwoman!"

The analogy was apt, and it sent visible shudders running through the men of the *Elfmaid*. But the matter was over, and the sailors shook off the eerie lethargy and went about their tasks with a gusto that spoke loudly of their pleasure to be back upon the open sea.

But Fyodor was more perceptive of magical matters than the Northmen. He came to Liriel's side and knelt beside her on the deck. "Where *were* we?" he asked in a low voice. "Never have I felt such power in a place . . . or such sorrow."

The weary drow tried to answer him and found she could not. Liriel was drained, empty, numb—and utterly defenseless against the despair that was the Abyss and the churning chaos that marked the touch of Lloth. She had never expected to feel so horrified by something that should have been a matter of course—indeed, the greatest honor a drow could know. Her dark-elven assumptions were profoundly shaken, her drow magic temporarily exhausted, her natural resilience stretched to the breaking point. It was all too much. An unfamiliar moisture gathered in the corner of her eyes and spilled over onto her cheeks. For the first time in her life, Liriel wept.

For a moment Fyodor merely stared at her, utterly dumbfounded. Then he swept the drow into his arms and carried her down into the privacy of the hold. She buried her face against his chest, clinging to her friend as if borrowing his strength until the silent tears had run their course. By the time Fyodor reached her cabin, Liriel was asleep in his arms, her thin body still shaking from the convulsive sobs.

Fyodor stayed with her a long time, for her fingers gripped his hand as if it were a lifeline. In truth, he would have stayed regardless. During their travels he had frequently watched over her so, for Fyodor was often unable or unwilling to sleep. In slumber Liriel looked tiny, fragile—utterly unlike the fierce, powerful being who channeled such fearsome magic. At such moments she was his alone. He needed that feeling tonight, and he clung to her hand as fervently as she clasped his.

Yet try as he might, Fyodor could not conjure the wistful deception. Liriel knew things, experienced things, that were far from his understanding. She was as much a mystery to him, and as far beyond his reach, as the mighty Witches who commanded his land. He sensed that something of great and dire import had happened this night, something that took the girl still further from him. The pain this brought him was as nothing, however, compared to his concern for her.

The fey gifts that were the inheritance of the Rashemi had granted Fyodor a bit of the Sight, and the things he had glimpsed in that dreadful place had chilled him to the soul. He could not help but wonder what the more magically sensitive drow had felt and seen. As he watched over Liriel's sea-deep slumber, he thanked the ancient gods that drow did not dream.

* * * * *

Rethnor lowered his eyeglass, and a smile of grim satisfaction crossed his black-bearded face as he savored the scene of destruction he had just witnessed. The strange curtain of darkness was gone, and the troublesome *Elfmaid* was no more. Perhaps Rethnor had not bested the young berserker himself, but the man was dead for all that. In his mind, all was well enough.

"Turn her about," he ordered the helmsman who stood at the wheel of the *Cutlass.* "We return to Trisk at once."

But Shakti whirled on him, her scarlet eyes blazing. "We were to capture the ship! What of the prisoners? Yours, mine?"

"There *is* no more ship, and anyone we might have captured is now food for the sea creatures. I am satisfied with the conclusion. If your prize has been destroyed, what is that to me?" he taunted.

To Rethnor's surprise, the elf woman laughed in his face. She snatched the eyeglass from his hand and smacked him in the chest with it.

"Fool!" she spat out, punctuating the remark with another sharp blow. "Look again. There is nothing but a cloud of steam, caused when rebounded fireballs struck the water. If the ship had exploded, there would be more heat lingering in the air, and burning wreckage and blood to warm the waters. Fool!" she repeated scathingly as she hauled back the eyeglass for another attack.

The captain reflexively seized her wrist, and he stared at her in disbelief. "You can see *heat?*"

"You cannot?" she retorted and pulled free of him with an expression that suggested his very touch was distasteful.

Rethnor was not accustomed to such insolence from a mere female, and his black brows pulled down into a stern **V** of disapproval. "Mind your tongue, woman."

The drow glowered at him. "Your eyes are worse than I had suspected, if you mistake me for a woman! I am Shakti, matron heiress to House Hunzrin. You should know the name of the person who brings your death, and I swear by the Mask of Vhaeraun that I will kill you if you presume to lay hands—*hand*," she sneered pointedly, "upon me, ever again."

He shrugged off this warning. "You are certain the ship has escaped? But how is this possible?"

"The drow I seek is a wizard. She is . . . powerful," Shakti admitted from between gritted teeth, and then she struck the ship's rail with her balled fists and let out a string of what Rethnor took to be drow curses.

"The wench is not out of reach, not even on Ruathym," the captain said, surprised to find himself giving assurance to the angry elf. "You will have your prisoner yet."

The drow stopped in midtirade and eyed him warily, as if weighing his words on some scale of her own. He returned her stare, letting her measure him as she would.

"I had never given thought to how persons might be shaped by the world around them," she mused. "The underground home of the drow is complex, riddled with layers and full of unexpected twists and turns. And you—you are as cold and as deep as this sea, are you not?" she said with obvious approval.

"But little good will that do me!" she mused, her mood turning dark once again. The drow snatched Rethnor's left sleeve, and before he could guess her intent, she lifted the maimed limb mockingly high, as if raising an imaginary sword in a gesture of challenge.

"You wish to kill the man who took your hand," she scoffed, "yet you have not bothered to have it replaced! Only a fool would go into battle without his sword hand!"

152

Again Rethnor stared at the drow, this time with a stirring of fascinated interest. "Replaced?"

"Or improved, if you prefer," Shakti said smugly. "In my homeland, our priestesses could regenerate a limb to its original state, only younger and stronger. Or our artisans could build you a new one—or several, each to suit a different purpose—of steel and mithril that is nonetheless as supple as flesh. Of course, if we *were* in my homeland, you would by now be either dead or enslaved."

The captain ignored this taunt. "Could you do this?"

"Not here," she admitted. "The needed tools and magic remain in the Underdark. But I *could* replace your hand with that of another human."

"No man would consent to such a thing!"

"I never imagined that one might," Shakti said dryly, not understanding the captain's horrified reaction. "But there are human slaves in Ascarle, are there not? And I assume a slave's consent would hardly be needed. When we return, choose one that pleases you, and I will see to the rest."

Rethnor fell silent as he pondered the drow's macabre suggestion, and he wondered what kind of being could speak of such things so casually. He had heard there were spells like this—usually wielded by necromancers, those wizards who dealt in death. He'd even heard rumors of a hideous slave trade in which healthy men were captured and sold for such purposes, their bodies auctioned off piece by piece as if they were mere swine to be divided into hams and chops and bacon. This notion went against all Rethnor's Northman sensibilities, for how could a man unwhole hope to enter the halls of a warrior god? And the very thought of integrating the flesh of another man with his own utterly appalled him.

And yet . . .

"The hand," he began tentatively. "How much skill will it hold? Will I be able to wield a sword again? Not just lift it and flail about, but will I be a master?" he demanded, his voice gaining passion as he spoke.

The drow eyed him with a dour expression. "It depends. How skilled were you before?"

"Very. The best."

"Good," she said flatly. "You would be amazed at how many restored fools ask if they'll be able to play the harp now and, when advised they can, admit they were unable to before. Even among the drow, there are those who cannot open their lips but a bad jest emerges. Bah!"

"I do not care much for jests of any sort," Rethnor said by way of reassurance. "But puzzles intrigue me, and so I cannot help but wonder why you would offer to do this for me."

Shakti smiled in grim approval, shielding her eyes against the starlight with one hand and turning her gaze far out over the dark waters. "You doubt my motives. That is good."

He waited, but the drow did not add to this. "You consider it wise to go into battle with only strong allies," he guessed.

Her eyes darted, like two mocking red flames, to his face. "If you like. That explanation will do as well as any."

Although Rethnor was not accustomed to verbal fencing, he was a skilled swordsman, and he knew a parry in any form. A familiar exhilaration came over him as he met the challenge in the elf woman's crimson eyes. He had not had a good battle for many days, and he hungered for the thrust and retreat, the bold attack and the clever treachery that made for a truly good match. Here, in a guise stranger than any he had ever imagined possible, was a foe truly worthy of battle.

And perhaps, he thought as he considered the ample curves beneath the elf woman's somber dark robes, this one was worthy of conquest, as well.

"How do you propose to capture the wizard?" Shakti demanded, shattering his pleasantly salacious musings and returning him to the task at hand.

"She will no doubt head for Ruathym. I have spies on and around the island." He hesitated, not sure how much he should reveal. Enough, he decided, to gain this one's confidence. There was a new hand to be gained and perhaps a bit more.

"There is a portal between Ascarle and Ruathym," he said. "Recently discovered, it is an ancient magical path, probably conjured by the elves who once lived in both lands. Messengers use the portal to carry orders. When your enemy reaches the island, we will know of it."

Shakti stared at him as she absorbed this. "Why doesn't the illithid use this portal to launch an attack?"

"You have much to learn of the Kraken Society," he told her. "Information is the weapon it provides, not warriors. Vestress asserts that it is better for all if Ruathym appears to collapse largely under the weight of its own lawlessness."

The drow sneered. "And you believe that? There is one reason alone why the illithid does not use the portal for conquest: *she cannot.*"

Rethnor did not dispute her words, for he himself had occasionally wondered why his Kraken contact—whom until recently he had visualized as the woman in his lost scrying ring—had insisted that the portal could be used only by her fey messengers.

"What type of beings carry your orders?" the drow demanded, her words echoing his unspoken thoughts.

"Nereids. They are vain and malicious creatures from another world—"

"The elemental plane of water," she interrupted. "Yes, I know all about those. But what about mortal beings? Humans, elves? The illithid's sea ogre troops? Can *they* pass through?"

Rethnor considered this. "I do not know."

Shakti gave a derisive sniff. "Perhaps we should find out." She jolted suddenly as if a new and illuminating thought had struck her.

"Liriel has proven herself skilled at managing portals," she mused. "If she can move an entire ship, surely she could find a way to pass through the gate that leads from Ruathym to Ascarle."

"Ah," Rethnor said, smiling a little as he nodded his approval. "You plan to lure this drow through the portal to Ascarle."

"Try not to be any more of an idiot than you must," Shakti advised him coldly. "Of course I would not risk such a prize in an untried portal! But think on this: by now the illithid knows Liriel Baenre as well as I myself do! Vestress has asked me many questions about the rogue wizard and has no doubt taken any information from my mind that I did not speak aloud. I now understand the illithid's interest. Mark me, Vestress needs the yellow-eyed bitch as much as I do!"

"To help her open the portal," Rethnor reasoned.

"It is the only possible explanation," Shakti agreed in a glum tone. The illithid had brought Shakti here, ostensibly to learn about recent events in the Underdark. Shakti, in return for this information, had been given surface contacts to the vast trade and intrigue network of the Kraken Society. It had seemed a worthwhile exchange for both. But as she reviewed her conversations with the illithid, Shakti realized Vestress had shown an inordinate amount of interest in Liriel and her adventures. Whatever worth Shakti had to the illithid was temporarily overshadowed by the promise of Liriel's wizardly skill. This deeply angered Shakti. Despite her newfound power and confidence, she found that her resentment of the Baenre princess was as keen as ever.

The drow seethed with deep frustration as she measured the delay Liriel's escape would bring. Shakti wished to return to Menzo-berranzan as soon as possible. She could not do so, however, on her own power. The water wraith had brought her to the elemental plane of water, and from there to the undersea city. Shakti had expected a brief meeting with the head of the Kraken Society, not an extended stay. The demanding Baenres—Matron Triel and that wretched Gromph—might accept a brief absence while Shakti met with surface conspirators, but this delay was becoming untenable. The longer Shakti stayed away from Menzoberranzan, the more important it became that she return with a captive Liriel in tow. She could not wait for Rethnor's spies to find the wizard. It was time for her ally from the elemental plane to make good on their deal.

"Where is Iskor?" she demanded.

"The water wraith? She disappeared when the water elemental was destroyed, and I say good riddance to them both," Rethnor responded.

A wise move on Iskor's part, Shakti thought grimly. The priest-ess was losing patience with the flighty creature and had started contemplating ways by which she might shatter the water nymph's glassy form. But those pleasant thoughts aside, Shakti needed to find Liriel, and soon, or her own welcome in Menzoberranzan would be less than cordial.

Neither Matron Triel nor Gromph were known for patience.

Chapter 12
RUATHYM

iriel knew she would never forget her first glimpse of Ruathym. They reached the island at twilight, and the setting sun framed the land with a spectacular display of brilliant clouds and gilded sea. But the image that would ever cling to Liriel's memory was not that of the island's rugged coast and fingerlike coves, or the picturesque villages and rounded green hills beyond, or even the deeply forested mountains that cast long purple shadows in the dying light. It was the look on Fyodor's face: joy mingled with poignant longing.

"One would almost think you were returning home," she commented.

Fyodor nodded, not taking his rapt eyes from the hills. "It is very like. If indeed my ancestors came from this place, I think I know how they must have felt when first they saw Rashemen."

His dream of homecoming was contagious, and for a moment Liriel missed the familiar tunnels and caverns of the Underdark. A stab of pain—and jealousy—pierced her. In all likelihood, she would never again see her ancestral home, and it troubled her that Fyodor was so clearly eager to return to his. Not that she begrudged him his homeland. She simply realized, suddenly and forcefully, that their shared journey was all she had. Now Ruathym was within their sights. After they reached their long-sought goals, what then?

This thought had never occurred to the drow before. She was not much given to introspection, and she found it deeply troubling. Since the day she had been thrust from Menzoberranzan, Liriel had thrown herself into the perilous journey, following a rune quest meant to culminate with the permanent possession of her drow powers and Fyodor's ability to once again control his berserker might.

But indeed—what then?

Liriel had little time to ponder this troubling thought, for the *Elfmaid* swept toward the island with breathtaking speed. It was a dangerous passage. Large, barren rocks thrust upward from the sea, much like the stalagmites of her homeland, forming a lethal maze that only the best—and best informed—sailors might navigate. And the harbor beyond lacked conventional docks; a rounded cove with a sweep of pebble-strewn beach served as the only landing. Shallow-keeled boats, both large and small, had been drawn up onto the beach, and a few massive piles had been driven into the sea floor to provide mooring for deeper ships. To one of these Hrolf headed, flying toward land with an abandon that had the fearless drow staring with astonishment.

Then the square sail dropped, and the oars fell deep into the water. The *Elfmaid* slowed abruptly, and Hrolf and his men leaped the rail and dropped into the chest-high water of the cove. Ibn stayed to secure the ship to its mooring; the others waded for shore with joyous haste.

Their approach brought a glad rush from the village beyond. Children, some of them already nightshirted for bed, evaded their mothers' grasping hands and splashed into the water to throw themselves into the arms of returning fathers or brothers. The Ruathen women, for the most part, were more decorous, awaiting their menfolk at water's edge with calm faces and shining eyes.

As agreed, Liriel and Fyodor hung back until Hrolf had a chance to explain their presence. The drow could hear the captain's bluff, hearty voice raised in a storytelling cadence, but his words were muffled by the crowd who gathered around him to listen. There was no mistaking their response, however; an angry murmur began, like the rumbling hint of a summer storm, and soon erupted into a loud and bitter argument.

Liriel waited and listened, her face stoic. Fyodor's concern, however, was written clearly in his troubled blue eyes.

"Olvir has told me much about the village," he said. "Hrolf is much loved, but he is considered odd by his people. Sometimes they listen to his schemes, sometimes not. There is no telling how they will receive us."

"Regardless, we have come too far to fail now," Liriel said coldly. "We have come to this island, and the people can like it or not."

Fyodor's worried expression deepened, and he took the drow by the shoulders and turned her to face him. "Little raven, do you trust me?" he said urgently.

Liriel scowled. This was unlike Fyodor. The young Rashemi seemed to sense that proclamations of this sort were beyond her dark-elven sensibilities, and he usually respected her emotional boundaries.

"What's your point?" she demanded.

He responded by sweeping a hand toward the wildly beautiful island, the snug wooden cottages, the grim-faced folk dressed in simple, brightly colored clothes.

"These people are my far kin. From all I have heard, their ways are very like those of my ancestors. You must believe me when I tell you to tread carefully."

Liriel eyed him coldly. She might not like his words, but she had to admit there was wisdom in them. No stranger to Menzoberranzan could hope to understand its intricate layers of protocol and intrigue; this place no doubt had its own peculiar customs. She accepted Fyodor's advice with a brusque shrug.

"What do I do?"

"Do not use magic unless you have no other choice," he cautioned her. "I am sure Hrolf has told them you are a wizard, and many will be watching you. Do not give them any more reason to fear you than they already have. Try to remember that everything about you is strange and frightening to these people—your magic, your elven features, the reputation of your people, the silence of your step, the sound of music and wind in your voice. For a time, it is best that you speak but little. Listen and watch. Allow me to speak when it is time to tell them of our quest."

"*Tell them?* This is wise?"

Fyodor nodded somberly. "It is best to speak plainly. Warrior folk prefer words that are simple and direct. Nor should we try to hide our purpose; they would not take kindly to dishonesty. Also, Olvir has given me to know that they are likely to welcome a Rashemi warrior on *dajemma*," he said, naming the coming-of-age journey taken by all young men of his homeland. "Like my people, the Ruathen enjoy hearing of far places, and a wandering warrior is expected to carry tales of valor."

"But you said you weren't sure how they would receive us. What you really meant was not *us*, but *me*," Liriel observed.

The young warrior shrugged. "It is much the same. We travel *dajemma* together; I will not go where you cannot. Hrolf will surely make this known to them."

Liriel absorbed this in silence. She had indeed come to trust Fyodor, but she had never imagined she might have to depend so completely upon him or any other person. The proud drow was accustomed to controlling her life, making her own way. She accepted that Fyodor's grasp of the situation was probably accurate, but it grated on her nonetheless.

"There is one more thing," Fyodor said hesitantly. "Olvir tells me that the womenfolk of Ruathym tend to hearth and family, leaving most other matters to the men."

The drow sniffed. "So they are fools. What of it?"

"You will need to show proper respect." When Liriel continued to regard him blankly, Fyodor elaborated. "You have told me the womenfolk rule in your land. In Ruathym, the tables are turned, and you might expect the same sort of treatment a drow male might receive in your homeland."

"Nine Hells!" the drow muttered, clearly appalled by this revelation. She turned a defiant glare upon her friend. "I will limit the magic and listen more than I speak, but I'll be damned as a yochlol if I'll bed any bearded human he-rothe that beckons for me!"

Fyodor blinked and fell back a step as he absorbed this new fact about drow culture. "Perhaps I was hasty in comparing the lot of dark-elven males and Ruathen women," he said with a bit of wry humor. "Believe me when I say you need not fear anything of the sort."

"Because . . ." Liriel prompted, hearing the rising tone in Fyodor's voice.

Again the young man hesitated. "Since you and I travel together, they will assume you are my woman. Trust me, it is better than the only other assumption they would make about a lone female aboard a pirate ship. There is more," he said, raising a hand to cut off Liriel's ready tirade.

"In this land, warriors hold the highest rank. The people will consider a Rashemi berserker worthy of honor. Although they might not understand my choice of companion, if they accept your presence it will be in respect of what they consider to be my property."

For the first time since he'd met her, Liriel was completely and utterly dumbfounded. Fyodor quickly turned his gaze toward the shore so she could not see the laughter in his eyes. Her befuddlement was comic, in a dark sort of way, but it was also precisely the response he'd hoped to elicit. The shock dulled some of the light in the drow's wild golden eyes and silenced her caustic tongue. For the moment, at least, Liriel more closely approximated the stoic calm expected of the women of the Northlands.

"We may go ashore," he said, pointing to a broadly smiling, gesticulating Hrolf.

"Kill me now," Liriel muttered darkly as she climbed the rail and jumped into the sea. Sloshing ashore, a "respectful" pace behind her friend, she railed silently and bitterly over this new twist in their journey. Taking a secondary role was annoying enough; more disturbing still was the suspicion that this, too, was somehow part of the rune she must form.

These matters filled Liriel's thoughts so completely that she found she had little difficulty keeping silence that evening—not that any words she might have wished to speak would have been heard in the noise of the celebration.

It seemed the entire village of Ruathym—the island's largest town—turned out to welcome home the travelers. In the center of the village, surrounded by neat wooden homes and workshops, was a cleared area large enough for all the people to gather. Here, Hrolf told her, the Thing—their court of law—was held, as well as many of their celebrations. Tonight the clearing was bright with bonfires, and the scent of stewed meat and roasted fish filled the air. Raucous laughter competed with loudly told tales as the villagers jostled and thronged about, drinking horns or wooden mugs in hand.

Never had Liriel felt more at odds than in this strange company, and she was grateful for the steady presence of both Hrolf and Fyodor. Among her people she was considered stately—she surpassed the five-foot mark by nearly three inches—but the islanders loomed over her. Almost without exception they were tall and fair, with sky-colored eyes that regarded her with a mixture of hostility and curiosity. Even the women who, unlike drow females, were usually smaller than the males of their race, stood closer to six feet than five. These women might have made fearsome warriors, yet they carried few weapons, and they garbed themselves without any concession to combat practicalities. Long, straight tunics of brightly colored and much-embroidered cloth covered their gowns—and hampered their movements. All of the women wore soft fabric boots, crudely fashioned jewelry, and demure expressions. Liriel was not pleased when one of them, a young female with braids of palest yellow gold, approached her. What had *she* to say to one of these pallid, insipid wenches?

To Liriel's relief, the fair-haired islander did not address her, but merely fixed a wide-eyed stare upon her that the drow found insulting in its directness.

"Dagmar!" roared Hrolf happily, scooping the girl up into a brief, ebullient embrace. Keeping an arm around her waist, he turned a beaming smile to the watchful drow and her companion and quickly made the introductions. "This winsome lass is kin to me," he explained, "the daughter of my cousin, Ulf the shaman, and herself soon to be the prettiest bride on the island!"

"Not so, Uncle," the girl said in a low voice.

Thunderclouds began to gather on Hrolf's brow. "Don't you be telling me Thorfinn has taken back his pledge! He took Ygraine's death hard, I'll grant him that, but so did we all. You're Ygraine's sister, and heir to the prophecy! Thorfinn's troth and rank are yours by right. By Tempus," he swore, pounding a fist into his open palm with a resounding smack, "I'll trounce that young scoundrel within an inch of his worthless life!"

"Thorfinn is dead," Dagmar said bluntly. Her face was pale but controlled, her blue eyes steady as she regarded the angry Northman. "He was killed as he slept. No one knows who did it, or why."

Remorse flooded the pirate's face. "Ah, lass, I'm sorry. I hadn't heard."

"There is no reason you should have. We celebrate the *Elfmaid*'s return. The time to speak of the dead will come later," she said softly.

Something in her tone brought new concern to Hrolf's eyes. "You speak as if Thorfinn's death was but one of many. There has been battle?"

"Would that there *had* been battle!" the girl said bitterly. "The warriors of Ruathen should die with honor against a worthy foe, not as pawns of the gods!"

"Tell me," Hrolf insisted gently.

Dagmar took a long, steadying breath. "There have been accidents, strange happenings. Men have drowned—fisherfolk who could swim before ever they took a step: Grimhild, Brand, Drott, Fafnir. Some of our mightiest hunters have been found torn to ribbons by the claws of unknown beasts; our finest trackers go missing. Fishing boats return to shore as driftwood. Children at play simply disappear."

"Strange indeed," he muttered, appalled by these revelations.

"There is more. Ancient spirits have returned to the wells and springs; fearful creatures haunt the ruins. Only the most daring youths and maids dare go near the old sites now. There are dark forces at work," Dagmar concluded somberly, turning her eyes to the drow and her companion. Then, unexpectedly, her grim face broke into a smile. "It is good that you have come, Fyodor of Rashemen. Dark times make for great deeds, and we of Ruathym gladly welcome such a warrior to our midst. Be at home for as long as you choose to tarry."

Her words had the ring of ritual; formal, too, was the demure kiss she bestowed on Fyodor's cheek. The young warrior accepted her tribute with a nod, and returned her clear, candid gaze—so like his own—as he placed one hand on the hilt of his dark sword.

"I am pledged to protect my homeland. Your troubles are now mine; for as long as I walk this land, Ruathym will be as home to me," he promised.

"Is it just my imagination, or have we fallen into a large vat of honey?" Liriel inquired icily. "For cloying sweetness, this moment lacks only tremulous viols and a shower of flower petals!"

Dagmar stared at the drow with amazement, much as a child might regard some curious, mythical beast who had inexplicably broken into song. "The *dock-alfar* talks!" she blurted out with artless delight.

"Aye, that she does," Hrolf said with a chuckle. "And I've a fair idea what she might say next! Come along, lass," he said, wrapping an arm around the astounded drow and steering her firmly away from incipient mayhem.

Dagmar watched them go, her blue eyes frank and curious. "I never thought to see a *dock-alfar*—a dark elf—on this island. Indeed, I had thought them to be only legends. How strange she is, and how very small! Yet she speaks the Common tongue nearly as well as a real person. She is your thrall?"

"No," Fyodor said, a wry smile lifting his lips at the very idea. "Liriel is slave to no one. She is as free as a wild mountain cat and not nearly so tame!"

"Your concubine then," the young woman concluded in a matter-of-fact tone. "Well, that is the way of men. But a warrior must also have sons. Have you a proper wife in Rashemen?"

Fyodor merely shook his head, for he was speechless in the face of the Ruathen girl's blunt inquisition. And yet, he realized suddenly, Dagmar was not so very different from the maids of Rashemen. He'd merely become accustomed to the contradictions and complexities of his drow companion. Dagmar's direct manner was as bracingly familiar as a drink from a cold mountain stream.

"No wife. Well, perhaps you will take a woman of the north back to Rashemen," Dagmar continued, smiling artlessly. "And if not, at least you will enjoy your stay while it lasts! There are many youths and maidens in the village, and much merriment and adventure even in these troubled days. Some of us," she added, dropping her voice to a whisper, "leave for Inthar with tomorrow's dawn, to seek answers to the trouble that besets the island. Will you come? Bring the *dock-alfar*, if you like—I will see that none of the others object."

The Rashemi considered the invitation. The ruined keep known as Inthar had featured largely in Olvir's shipboard stories. An ancient stronghold shrouded with magic and mystery, it might well be the place for him and Liriel to begin their quest. Fyodor accepted the invitation. Before he could ask Dagmar for more detail about the expedition, the call of hunting horns cut through the din of the crowds.

Instantly the villagers stopped their merriment and made their way in silence to the central bonfire. They ringed the leaping fire and sat cross-legged on the ground in a well-ordered circle. The groupings were apparently based upon clans, for Dagmar led him over to the place where Hrolf and another man enough like him to be his twin sat with an assortment of fair-haired women and children. Beside Hrolf sat Liriel, her face as composed as that of an obsidian statue, but her eyes burning with a heat rivaling that of the central fire. The drow, Fyodor noted with a touch of foreboding, was not enjoying her first night on Ruathym.

In truth, Fyodor's observation was only partially correct. Ruathym and its customs were utterly foreign to Liriel, but that very strangeness whetted her curiosity. At the moment, she was focused entirely upon the scene unfolding in the middle of the clearing.

Before the bonfire stood the largest warrior Liriel had ever seen. The drow shaded her sensitive eyes with one hand as she studied the man. Nearly seven feet tall he was, in late midlife but still in prime strength. His lined face and knotted muscles reminded Liriel of a weathered oak. His fair hair had faded to gray, but his eyes were bright and blue and proud. Liriel was accustomed to the smooth perfection of drow beauty, but she sensed the history in that face—challenges met, battles won, character tested and tried until it was as strong and steady as the oak he resembled. Liriel knew instinctively that this man was an important leader among his people, even before he lifted his voice to speak.

"I am Aumark Lithyl, First Axe of all Ruathym. Let any who would challenge step forward."

The words seemed to be a formality, for none of the younger warriors so much as blinked. In Menzoberranzan, status-conscious soldiers would have cheerfully slain their brothers and climbed over the still-warm bodies for such an opportunity. Liriel studied Aumark Lithyl as he spoke, trying to understand what there was about the man that could inspire such unnatural loyalty.

But the leader spoke only a few words before yielding the floor to the village skald, a white-haired gnome of a man who declaimed songs about Ruathen heroes of recent and ancient times. The scald, in turn, called upon Hrolf to share news of the wider world.

To Liriel's way of thinking, Hrolf was fully the equal of any storyteller she knew. Even though she had lived through the events he described, she listened, entranced, as the captain told the story of the *Elfmaid*'s trip—the battles they had seen, their unusual escapes, the treasures they brought to the island through trade and thievery. There was a glow of pride about the captain as he described Liriel's contributions to the adventure, and although the drow noted that the villagers shifted uneasily as Hrolf described her feats of magic, the looks they cast over her changed from grim curiosity to wondering awe. It was, in her opinion, a vast improvement.

When at last Hrolf paused for breath, he called upon Fyodor. The young warrior rose, completely at ease before the large crowd as he began to speak of his own quest. He spoke of Rashemen, of the Time of Troubles when long-dead heroes and ancient gods walked the lands—a terrible time when magic went awry and the people were tormented by horrendous nightmares. Then came the Tuigan invasion and the devastation of his land. He told of his own part in the war, his growing acclaim in battle, and the ever-increasing strength of his battle frenzies. Candidly, he described the need to control his berserker rages and his hope that the Windwalker amulet, and the drow spellcaster who carried it, might restore him to himself, and to his homeland.

This, also, seemed to raise Liriel in the estimation of the Ruathen, for many nodded with pride and approval as Fyodor spoke of the drow's efforts to learn their ancient lore, and of the rune quest that had led them both to this place.

The fire had burned down to glowing embers by the time Fyodor's tale came to a close. At a signal from Aumark, the people slipped quietly away from the gathering to their own cottages, many of them carrying sleeping children. Hrolf's cousin, whose stern expression seemed out of place on a face so like that of the jovial captain, rose and stalked from the clearing without so much as a word to the pirate. Dagmar expressed a wish to linger, but her father spoke a few sharp words in a language Liriel could not understand. The Ruathen girl's jaw set with displeasure, but she nonetheless rose and obediently followed her sire, leaving Hrolf alone with Liriel and Fyodor. For the first time since setting foot on Ruathym, the drow had a chance to speak her mind.

"Well, what's to come of all this?" she demanded.

Hrolf grimaced and shrugged. "You're here, lass, and so far no one's taken it upon themselves to run you back into the sea. That's more progress than you'll know! And the lad's words helped. But my kinsman Ulf—good-looking lad, but stubborn as a snail—didn't take to the idea of teaching rune magic to an elf woman."

This news was not unexpected, but it was nonetheless disheartening. Liriel's shoulders slumped, and she hissed a drow curse from between clenched teeth.

"Now, don't you be fretting," Hrolf admonished her. "Ulf will come around! He's a good lad and not one to be following the thinking of other men. Give him time to make up his mind about you."

"And until then?" she inquired bitterly.

"Let me see," the captain mused, stroking his beard in a parody of thoughtfulness. "You must've gone clean through those books of yours during the trip. Might it be that you're wanting more?" he asked slyly.

The drow's eyes lit up, and Hrolf grinned. "Then tomorrow I'll take you to the Green Room. We've a fine library, filled with books and scrolls from all over. Don't rightly know what's in it, myself, but you're welcome to root around."

"I had not heard Ruathym to be a place for scholars," Fyodor observed.

The pirate shrugged. "Didn't set out to be that, but you never know what treasures you might find when boarding a ship or raiding a keep. To most folk here, the Green Room is just another kind of treasure heap. Valuable as gems those books might be, but they're of no practical use to us simple sailors and fisherfolk."

"Can you wait until later in the day to explore this treasure?" Fyodor asked the drow. "We have been asked to go with some young folk to Inthar come morning. I think we should go."

"Bad business, that," Hrolf cautioned. "Best to keep away from those ruins."

"Are my ears failing me, or did an old woman's words come from the lips of Hrolf the Unruly?" inquired a new and jovial voice behind them.

The three friends turned to face the newcomer. The man approaching them had thick braids of pale ash brown, and a bluff and cheerful face marked by keen gray eyes and a well-tended short beard. He was taller than Fyodor by a handspan and had the same stocky, thick-muscled frame. He was dressed in leathers and armed as if for battle. A broadsword was strapped to his back, and a well-loaded weapons belt encircled his waist and crossed in an **X** over his massive chest. A one-handed battle-axe hung on one hip, and a large iron hammer—tipped with a broad, flat disk of mithril on one side and a wicked, spiked claw on the other—bounced on the opposite side.

"Wedigar!" roared Hrolf in welcome, extending both hands to clasp the man's wrist in a warrior's greeting. "It's glad I am to see you again, lad. What brings you to the village?"

The man's bearded face turned sober. "You know that Thorfinn was killed," he began.

"Aye, Dagmar told me. A great loss."

"More loss than you know," Wedigar said grimly. "He was to have been First Axe of Holgerstead after me."

Hrolf's brows rose. "Is that so? I knew Thorfinn as a fine fighter, but I hadn't heard he'd joined the ranks of the *hamfariggen*—the shapestrong," he translated for the benefit of Liriel and Fyodor. "Holgerstead is a village to the north. Our berserkers live and train there. The mightiest among them can take on the form of beasts during a battle rage. A sight to behold, that is, though not so common now as in olden times."

"Thorfinn was the last, after me," Wedigar agreed somberly. "There are no more *hamfariggen* upon Ruathym, and therefore no one to lead when I have gone to the halls of Tempus. The old women who read omens believe the shaman's daughter is, of all our women, most likely to bear shapestrong sons. Since Thorfinn is dead, I came to the village to court his pledged bride."

"You don't sound very happy about it," Liriel observed with more pleasure than the situation truly demanded.

"I have a wife," the man said shortly. "She has borne me only daughters, but I am content. There can be no peace with two women in one house."

"Precious little of that with just one woman," Hrolf agreed with a grin.

"What of you, Fyodor of Rashemen?" inquired Wedigar, clearly eager to change the subject. "Are your people also *hamfariggen?*"

"No, and may the ancient gods be praised," Fyodor said with such fervor in his voice and horror on his face that Wedigar fell back a step and regarded the young man with puzzlement.

Afraid he had insulted the ruler of Holgerstead, Fyodor hastened to explain. "You have heard me say that the rituals of Rashemen no longer control my battle frenzy. I would not like to think I could become a beast against my will, like some wolf-bitten man at the coming of the full moon!"

Wedigar considered this. "Since the shapeshifting gift is not of Ruathym, it has no part of the magic that rages within you. But it might be that you could learn *our* rituals. You would then have a berserker power you *could* control."

"A good idea," Liriel agreed promptly, but Fyodor looked unconvinced.

"Think on it, and we will speak of these things again another time. But come, lad. Let's test your strength and skill," Wedigar invited with a good-natured smile as he drew his sword.

The Rashemi shook his head. "I dare not fight you," he said bluntly. "Even a friendly contest might bring the rage upon me."

"Hammers, then," the First Axe suggested, tucking his sword away and unhooking the hammer from his belt. "We throw for distance."

Since he had no excuse for this, Fyodor agreed. Wedigar handed him the weapon, and the young Rashemi hefted it experimentally. It was heavy, but much lighter than the hammers he himself had wielded at the forge. He tossed it high into the air and watched as it spun, considering its speed and balance. Although Liriel and Hrolf instinctively ducked out of the way of the falling weapon, Fyodor stood his ground and easily caught the polished handle.

Wedigar lifted a brow. "You have done this before."

"Seven years at the forge," the Rashemi agreed. "I was apprenticed to a swordsmith as soon as I could stoke a fire and hold tongs. Never have I used a hammer in battle, but we often threw for sport when the day's tasks were done."

Fyodor hauled back the weapon for the throw. Sighting down a tree at the edge of the clearing, he heaved for all he was worth. The hammer spun toward it, end over end. The clawed tip bit deep into the wood.

The First Axe nodded, visibly impressed. "You must come to Holgerstead. It is your place," he said simply.

"I would like to see more of Ruathym," Fyodor agreed. "Tomorrow we go to Inthar, and I wish to see more of the surrounding hills and forests—perhaps to hunt. I have been too long away from the land," he said wistfully. "But in a few days, I will come."

"I will tell your warrior brothers to expect you," Wedigar said heartily, clapping him on the back. "But the moon rises high, and we must sleep. The unmarried men of the village sleep in the Trelleborg—the barracks. Let us go there now; there is a place for visiting warriors, as well."

Fyodor cast a quick glance toward Liriel, but Hrolf was already ahead of him.

"Don't you be worried about the lass, now," he said, dropping an arm around the drow's shoulders. "In this land, unmarried women stay in their father's houses. I've got me some warehouses at the edge of the village and a snug cottage of my own with an extra room that should suit my girl here. Never had me a daughter before, but I'm thinking I'll get the knack of it soon enough."

"She couldn't want better care," Fyodor said, deeply touched by the sincere warmth in Hrolf's words.

"Oh, don't mind me—just go ahead and make all the arrangements!" Liriel snapped. The drow shrugged off Hrolf's embrace and spun away to stalk into the night. After several paces she stopped, turned, and glared at the pirate captain. "Well, are you coming or not?"

Her two friends exchanged knowing glances and furtive grins. "There's one important thing to keep in mind when dealing with elven females," Hrolf confided to Fyodor in a droll whisper. "They're just like women, only more so!"

* * * * *

The rising sun was still clinging to the distant edge of the sea when Liriel and Fyodor caught their first glimpse of Inthar. It was a vast and sprawling keep, ancient beyond reckoning. An enormous curtain wall of thick stone surrounded the site, its many gaps testifying to the ravages of time and battle. Inside this first perimeter was a maze of walls and buildings, most of which had been reduced to tall, tumbled piles of rocks. Above it all soared a single round tower, as remote and forbidding as the widow at a warrior's funeral. The explorers—Fyodor, Liriel, and three young Ruathen—stood for a long moment in somber contemplation of the grim site.

"That is the best way to enter." Ivar, a young man with a bowl-shaped mop of yellow hair, pointed to a gap in the curtain wall. "The area has been explored and secured."

"Secured from what?" Liriel asked warily. An aura of magic, as visible to her senses as the thick morning mist, clung to the ruins. It was best that she knew now what sort of magic-wielding creatures they might face, so she could prepare the needed spells.

"From time to time wild beasts lair in the ruins," Dagmar responded in a voice one might use to soothe a frightened child. The young woman drew a small bone knife from her sash and handed it to the drow. "You will not need to use this, but carrying it might make you feel better."

Liriel stared at the feeble weapon and then up at the woman. To all appearances, Dagmar was serious. The drow's eyes narrowed.

Sensing the coming storm, Fyodor hurriedly took the knife from Dagmar's outstretched hand and tucked it into Liriel's boot. "You may find a use for it," he murmured, then immediately regretted his choice of words. The drow's grim smile suggested that she had one already in mind.

Then a low, quavering moan started somewhere in the depths of the maze of stone, rising slowly into a thin wail. The sound was faint and distant, but it carried an eldritch chill that sent tremors through every member of the exploring party.

"A spirit," Ivar said, his voice pale with dread. "There are many in these ruins."

"Not just any spirit," Liriel corrected him. "That's the cry of a banshee—the evil remnant of an elven female. I wonder what causes it to linger here."

Fyodor caught the musing tone of her voice and remembered her pledge to find and release the trapped spirits of the sea elves. Although he appreciated her devotion to her promise, he did not see how there could be a connection between the two matters. "Was this place once an elven stronghold?" he asked.

The fifth member of their party—Brynwolf, a young warrior with reddish-brown braids and beard—let out a scornful laugh. "I doubt that even Inthar is that old! There are no elves on this island, nor have there been since the days of the Rus," he boasted.

"All the same, the elders have said we are not to go into Inthar when the groaning spirit cries," Dagmar said in a disappointed tone. "Sigurd and Kara ignored the warnings."

Liriel had no need to ask about the fate of these explorers; the grim expressions on the faces of the three youths—and her own knowledge of banshees—told her what had happened. Without magic to shield them, the humans had no doubt been slain by the banshee's keen. Liriel mused that it was well for her companions that dawn had broken; the banshee's wail was chilling at any time, but it could only release its deadly keen at night. Even so, the touch of the creature, the mere sight of it, could be dangerous.

But a priestess of Lloth—even a reluctant one—had no need to fear the undead. Liriel had proved that in the dungeons under Skull-port. She tugged her obsidian pendant from its hiding place beneath her tunic, and she prepared herself to face once again the power and confusion that was her dark goddess.

"I'm going in," she informed Fyodor.

The young man nodded as if he had been expecting this. He turned to his new friends. "We will meet you back in the village."

The three Ruathen argued and threatened, but they soon realized that neither Fyodor nor his strange little companion could be dissuaded. With many a backward glance, they strode away and disappeared into the forest, reluctantly leaving the Rashemi and the drow to their fate.

"The keep?" Fyodor asked when at last they were alone.

Liriel nodded. Banshees were known to hoard treasure, and the keep was the most likely stronghold. Holding firmly to her holy symbol, the drow slipped into the stone maze and made her way toward the tower. Fyodor followed closely, alert for any beasts that might be crouching amid the stones and shadows.

They got to the foot of the tower without incident. A single arched portal, empty where the wooden door had long ago rotted away, led into the keep. Beyond, all was darkness. Liriel conjured a globe of faerie fire and followed the bobbing ball of light into the dank interior.

Inside the keep was a courtyard, hints of its former splendor remaining in the carved marble of the walls and floor. Liriel noted the indentations where gems had been pried from the stone and the distinctive elvish design of the low wall that surrounded a mineral spring bubbling up in the center of the yard. But there were no signs of treasure or of the spirit.

The drow wandered over to the spring and sat down on the crumbling marble. A sensation of cold assaulted her at once, though the bubbling spring sent wisps of mineral-scented steam into the stagnant air. With intense foreboding, Liriel looked deep into the water. Gazing back at her with malevolent red eyes was the face of an elven hag. Wizened skin stretched tight over angular bones, and strands of sparse hair writhed, like a tangle of serpents, in the churning water. Clawlike hands extended up, reaching with deadly purpose toward Liriel.

The drow leaped to her feet, her pendant in her hand, as the banshee burst from the water and flew into the air.

"Magic you have, and magic I crave—but the living may not pass," the spirit hissed, swirling around the stunned pair like a wild-cat circling its prey.

As the drow brandished her holy symbol, the banshee responded with mocking, hate-filled laughter. Liriel frantically mouthed the words of a clerical spell, one that would drain power from an undead creature. But the banshee's wild mirth only increased, and at last Liriel understood what she faced.

This spirit had once been drow.

While it was possible for an elf of any of the surface races to turn to evil and become a banshee, dark elves excelled at evil, strove for it—*bred* for it! A drow banshee was among the most feared of all undead. A high priestess might have had the power to turn such a creature; Liriel did not. And the only thing that might kill a banshee—an enchantment that could dispel evil—was beyond her as well. That spell was not taught in Menzoberranzan. Considering the nature of Lloth's clergy, such magic could be suicidal.

Liriel turned to Fyodor. "Run," she said succinctly.

He did not debate the matter. The friends fled from the tower as the banshee's laughter rose into short, wailing bursts, a mocking sound that pursued them as they ran wildly along the edge of the sea cliffs. They did not slow their pace until the tower of Inthar was long out of sight and the banshee's voice was no more than a lingering chill in their souls.

The Rashemi was the first to stop. He leaned over, hands on his knees as he drew in long, ragged breaths. "Better a hundred armed men than such a creature," he gasped out.

Liriel nodded absently, her eyes turned out to sea and her thoughts still puzzling over the strange encounter. Banshee lairs invariably housed whatever the elf had valued in life. What magic was the banshee guarding, and why had it insisted that the *living* might not pass? There was a mystery here that both disturbed and intrigued the inquisitive drow.

Suddenly some movement on the rock-strewn beach below

caught the distracted drow's eye. Two figures walked along the shore—obviously lovers, judging by their entwined hands and the solicitous way the large, fair-haired man bent over the much smaller woman. Liriel peered more closely at the female who, despite her yellow hair and pale skin, did not have the look of a Northwoman. She was too small, too slim, and far too impractical, clad as she was in a clinging gown of cloth-of-gold, a fabric more appropriate to a royal wedding than a seaside tryst. The wind blew cold off the sea, yet the woman wore no cloak—only a fringed shawl of white silk knotted about her shoulders. The two faced the sea, and since they were too far distant for even Liriel's elven eyes to discern their identity she did not bother pointing them out to Fyodor. Nor did she truly wish for him to contemplate such contented lovers.

"Let's take the forest path," she said abruptly and spun away from the cliff's edge.

They had walked in silence for nearly an hour when, without warning, Fyodor stopped and drew his sword. Liriel instinctively followed suit, pulling her dagger and falling into battle stance at his back.

"What is it?" she demanded, her voice just above a whisper.

"The forest," he replied in kind. "It has gone silent."

The drow strained her ears. Sure enough, the strange sounds of the forest creatures—the chirp of insects, the cry of birds, the scolding voices of the little furry things that Fyodor called squirrels—had disappeared. The only sound was the wind in the restive leaves.

Then, suddenly, a rush of wind and wings spun down toward them. Instinctively Liriel dropped and rolled. Fast though the drow was, her attacker was faster still. A scorching pain slashed her shoulders, followed by a sharp, wrenching stab as a lock of her hair was torn from her scalp. Liriel ignored both and rolled into a crouch. Her eyes widened at the sight before her.

Fyodor had his sword out before him, holding it in two hands as he faced off against a man-sized hawk. The enormous bird and the warrior moved in a slow, eerie dance, circling together as each sought an opening. A white, wavy strand of Liriel's hair was tangled in one of the hawk's daggerlike talons, and its bright, silver-hued eyes regarded its opponent with feral intelligence. When Fyodor shot a quick, concerned glance toward his drow companion, the hawk seized the moment and darted in, beak diving for the human's heart.

Liriel sucked in a startled gasp; there was no time for her to deflect the attack. And no need—even without the battle rage,

Fyodor was a capable fighter. Up came the black sword, blocking the strike and slapping the curved beak sharply to one side. For just a moment, the hawk's neck was exposed. But without the berserker frenzy to speed his movements, Fyodor could not move the heavy sword fast enough to take advantage of the opening.

The giant hawk fell back a few hopping steps, spreading its wings wide in preparation for the next attack.

Liriel snatched a bolo from her belt, whirled briefly, and let fly. The weapon spun and wrapped itself around an enormous leg. The whirling weights struck with a satisfying *crack*, and the hawk staggered to a stop. For a moment the drow dared to hope the leg bone had broken, but the giant raptor recovered its balance and came on again, this time advancing on Liriel with an odd, hopping gait.

The drow snatched up a handful of throwing knives and squared off against the thing. She'd once seen a normal hawk drop to the ground, seize and carry off a rabbit nearly as large as itself. She did not doubt that this gigantic raptor had similar intentions, and her throbbing shoulders suggested she was its intended prey.

Her arm pumped as she tossed four knives at the attacking hawk. All the weapons flew straight and true, sinking to the hilts in the bird's dappled breast feathers. But the depth of muscle beneath kept the blades from touching a vital spot. The hawk merely shrieked again and darted in, listing to one side a bit but still moving faster than Liriel would have dreamed possible. The smell of carrion assaulted her as the hawk's open beak closed in.

The drow threw herself into a backward roll, came up on her feet, and dove to one side. Meanwhile, Fyodor advanced, battering at the creature with his cudgel. This bought Liriel a moment's time. Shielding her eyes with one hand, she summoned a fireball and hurled it at the still-advancing hawk.

The missile exploded with a burst of light and a wild spray of feathers. Fyodor reeled back, blinded by the sudden brightness and gagging from the horrid stench of singed hawk.

A shrill cry ripped through the forest, a chilling sound that for sheer power competed with the fireball's blast and the banshee's rage. Enormous wings buffeted the air as the wounded hawk rose into the sky, trailing wisps of foul smoke as it flew unsteadily westward into the deep shadows cast by Ruathym's mountains.

Liriel rose to her feet, weaving drunkenly as she regarded her friend. He was unhurt, but the exploding fireball had showered him with soot; his face was nearly as black as her own, and singed feathers clung to his hair and shirt. He coughed, spat out a pinfeather, and then spoke.

"In my land we have many odd sayings, and as you know, I use them all too often. But mark me, one of these I will never again speak lightly, now that I know the full truth of it!"

The drow frowned, puzzled by the odd track her friend's thoughts had taken. " 'There are those who think, and those who dream'?" she guessed, although she saw no connection between Fyodor's favorite adage and the current situation.

"Not so," he said with a droll smile. " 'Close' only counts in horseshoe games and fireball spells."

Chapter 13
SHAPESHIFTERS

t Liriel's insistence, Fyodor left the village that afternoon with a group of hunters. She could sense his eagerness to explore the forests and hills, and she had no desire to keep him at her side to fuss over her small injuries. Hrolf did more than enough of that. The captain clucked and scolded like a whole barnyard full of broody hens as he pillaged his warehouse for salve and bandages.

After ordering Liriel to take a seat on a large barrel of ale, the captain rummaged among his store for a keg of his special herbal brew. It seemed that the same stuff he'd used to drug the Moonshae mead was also deemed good for cleaning wounds and deadening pain—not to mention waterproofing the underside of ships—and he kept it in quantity. After carefully cutting away the drow's torn leather jerkin, Hrolf poured some of the stuff onto a cloth and began to dab at the shallow gashes that scored both her shoulders.

Liriel sat through these ministrations with uncharacteristic patience. In truth, she rather enjoyed the unfamiliar and undemanding affection her "adopted father" had lavished upon her since the day they'd first met. But the treasures of the Green Room beckoned her, and Liriel soon found herself glumly wishing she'd sent the oversolicitous pirate off with Fyodor.

"Still haven't got shed of the female, I see," observed a dour voice from the warehouse doorway.

Hrolf glanced up at his red-bearded first mate. "Ibn! Haven't seen you since we made port, lad. Had trouble sleeping, have you, and come to help yourself to a bit more of the mead?"

The man snorted at the teasing reference to his enforced shipboard nap, and he cast an angry look at the drow. "Bad business," he muttered as he took his pipe from his sash. "Thought we had our share of ill fortune aboard the *Elfmaid*. Seems like trouble followed us ashore."

"Don't be lighting that thing in here," Hrolf cautioned him, pointedly ignoring the mate's insinuations. "There's enough of that newfangled smoke powder stored hereabouts to drop all of Ruathym into the sea!"

As Ibn tucked away his pipe and flint, he cast a measuring gaze around the warehouse. The building was stuffed with crates and kegs piled haphazardly together in no discernible order. "Good thing you know what all you got in here, Captain. No one else does, that's certain."

"Is that why you've come, lad?" Hrolf asked mildly. "To insult my girl and tell me how to run my affairs?"

"To warn you," Ibn returned, returning the pirate's cold gaze without flinching. "I was out with the fishing boats early this morning. Thought I saw a sea elf."

"Xzorsh?" the captain asked, surprised by this news.

"Might'a been. They all look much the same to me. The morning's catch was none too good. Some of the nets were cut. There's mischief in the waters hereabouts, make no mistake."

"What're you saying, lad?" Hrolf demanded.

"Might be I wasn't the only one to see the elf. If people start thinking your friend's behind some of the recent troubles, might be they'll come looking to you for answers." The mate paused, and once again he turned a pointed gaze upon the drow. "Might be, Captain, that you should start thinking about what those answers could be."

"Might be, lad," Hrolf returned in a grim imitation of the first mate, "that you should haul your sorry ass out of my warehouse before I kick it up between your shoulders."

Ibn shrugged. "We been sailing together a long time, Captain. Thought I owed you the warning—do with it what you want." With those words, he spun on his heel and stalked out of the warehouse.

"That one's no friend of yours, lass," Hrolf cautioned Liriel. "I've always liked Ibn—as much as he'll let me, at any rate—but he does take on some strange moods from time to time. Mark me: he bears some watching."

This warning rang through Liriel's mind as she made her way to the long wooden building that housed Ruathym's stolen literary treasures. She hadn't spared a thought to Ibn since making land the day before, and that realization troubled her. No drow survived long by ignoring an enemy. And the sheer number and variety of these, she mused darkly, was making it difficult for her to keep up!

By the time the late afternoon sun cast long shadows over the village, Liriel had a somewhat better idea of what she faced. She'd searched the Green Room for every scrap of information she could find about the elemental plane of water. Since one of her unknown enemies had the ability to summon a water elemental, it made sense to learn what she could of such powers. The more the drow read, the more impressed she became with her shadowy foe and the forces he or she might command. One passage in particular seized her attention, fascinating in its implications—and its possibilities.

"*Nereids,*" she read aloud. "Shapeshifting beings from the elemental plane of water, they live to trick and drown unwary sailors. Often taking the form of beautiful women, they cast a charm over men and lure them to their doom. A nereid carries a soul-shawl that contains its essence. If this shawl is taken, the creature is enslaved by the possessor. A wizard can coerce an enslaved nereid to do his bidding, even force it to act as a guide to the elemental plane of water."

"Legend," observed a terse, deep voice. "A skald's tale and nothing more."

Liriel lifted her eyes from the book to regard the village shaman. She was impressed. Ulf was a large man, but she hadn't heard him enter the room.

"More than legend," she said bluntly. "I think I might have seen one myself, just this morning, walking along the shore with some man. At the time I thought something about the female was wrong, but I did not know until this minute the truth of it."

Ulf looked skeptical. "If this is so, what became of the man? The tales say nereids charm men to drown them, but no one has turned up missing this day."

The drow shrugged, admitting the point but not willing to abandon her theory just yet. She twisted the silver ring that her sea-ogre abductors had placed on her hand. If the unexplained drownings were indeed due to sea sirens, it might be a good idea to give Fyodor her ring of water-breathing. Men, it seemed, were far more susceptible to the charms of such a creature than were females. Naturally.

"Why have you come here?" the shaman demanded with typical Northman candor. "What do you hope to find on Ruathym?"

"All that Hrolf and Fyodor have said of me is true," Liriel said. "I came on a rune quest, and when the rune is complete, I will use the Windwalker's magic to carve it onto Yggsdrasil's Child."

Ulf scoffed. "Do you know the rituals of casting? Can you so much as find the sacred tree?"

"Show me."

"I will not teach you," the shaman stated bluntly. "It cannot be done. No frail elf has the strength or the will needed to shape a rune."

Liriel bristled. "You speak without knowledge. Name a challenge. If I fail—and I will not—*then* you may claim to know the measure of my strength!"

A spark of interest kindled in the shaman's cold blue eyes. "You are willing; that much can be said for you. But no, I will not name a test. If your rune quest is a true one, your needed trials will come to you as they must."

"And when I succeed, you will teach me?" Liriel demanded.

"You have not yet succeeded," Ulf said coolly, "and I have little faith you will. There is always a price to be paid for a new rune, a price far higher than most are willing to pay."

Before the drow could respond, the wooden door of the library was flung open and a yellow-haired youth ran into the room. Liriel recognized Ivar, one of the young men who had accompanied her and Fyodor to Inthar. His tunic was stained with blood, and his eyes were wild in his beardless face.

"You must come!" Ivar said urgently, tugging at the shaman's sleeve. "The hunters! Some are dead, and Aumark Lithyl—"

"The First Axe was slain? How?" demanded Ulf.

"No, he yet lives, but needs tending. A wild boar came upon us near the ravine. Aumark was gored, and badly."

The shaman's face turned grim, and he swiftly followed the lad, the curious drow close on his heels. A crowd had gathered around the door of a round wooden hut, but parted at once to allow the shaman through. Liriel hesitated, then pushed her way in behind him. She reasoned the shaman had more important matters on his mind than shooing her away, and she took a place against the rounded wall where she might observe.

The wounded chieftain lay in a rapidly spreading circle of blood. There was a deep gash in his side where the boar's tusks had slashed him. Ulf chanted as he bandaged the wound with soft cloths and smeared a paste of herbs on the surrounding skin. He threw yet more herbs onto the fire; at once the room was filled with fragrant smoke. Liriel noticed with interest that there was a subtle magic in the herbs, the scented steam, and the words of the chant. But Aumark's wound was deep, and the magic of the Northlands would not staunch the flow of blood in time. Already the thick dressing had turned crimson.

The drow came to crouch beside the laboring shaman. "Let me," she commanded. Ulf tensed, then yielded with a terse nod.

Liriel tore aside the dressing and placed one slim black hand over the gaping wound, the other on her amulet of Lloth. She closed her eyes, envisioning the fey darkness of her ancestral home—the stronghold of the Spider Queen—and then brought to mind the words of the clerical spell. And as she did, she frantically searched her imagination for something to offer the dark goddess in exchange for the gift of healing she was about to request. Lloth, the chaotic deity of the evil drow, would have no interest in a human warrior unless she, Liriel, could give one.

"Conflict is coming to this land," Liriel murmured, praying aloud in the drow tongue. "I sense this, though I do not yet know the names of all those who will fight. Heal this battle chieftain, and I will stand with him in battle and fight as a priestess of Lloth. The drow pursued a surface war and lost. But let *this* war be fought in your name and *won,* that those who live under the sun's light may know at last the true power of Lloth!"

The amulet in her hand tingled with fey power, and Liriel knew she had piqued the interest of the proud and capricious goddess. Quickly she chanted the words to the clerical prayer, steeling herself as dark magic coursed through her and into the still, pale form of the Ruathen chieftain. There was a searing hiss, and she felt the torn flesh beneath her hand knit together. Aumark's body contorted briefly from the brutal healing, and then lay still.

Drained and dizzy, Liriel opened her eyes and slowly tapered off the stream of healing power. She noticed with relief that the chieftain's breathing was deeper now, and the ruddy color was beginning to return to his weathered face.

"For what you have done, all of Ruathym is grateful," the shaman said slowly. "I say truly that never have I seen such powerful healing magic. But still, I will not teach you."

For a moment the drow merely stared at the man, utterly baffled by his stubborn refusal. Then with a quick, angry movement she rocked back onto her feet, rose, and stalked out of the hut. The villagers, some of whom had witnessed her feat of healing magic, fell back in awe as she passed.

Fyodor was also there, waiting for her. Belatedly the drow remembered that he, too, had been on the deadly hunt, and she tugged the silver ring from her hand. Taking one of his hands in hers, she slipped the ring onto his smallest finger. "Do not take this off," she admonished him in a low voice. "Your life may well depend upon wearing it."

He responded with a wry smile. "It seems that you, too, have been busy. Come, little raven—we must talk."

The two friends left the village and made their way westward along the shore, wrapped in their cloaks against the chill of the coming night. Fyodor was clearly troubled, but he did not speak until the sunset colors had faded nearly to silver. Then, abruptly, he asked the drow if she had told anyone of that morning's attack.

Liriel blinked. "Just Hrolf. If he has spoken of it to another, I know not. Why?"

"The boar that gored Aumark," Fyodor began. "It might have been a natural beast, but I doubt this. I have hunted wild boar in Rashemen. Always they are dangerous, but this one was canny beyond belief. I would swear that it lay in wait for us, as if it knew the path the hunters would take. And I *saw* something," he added, giving the word the emphasis that indicated he spoke of the fey Sight of his Rashemi heritage. "There was something familiar about the boar. It was—it was as if the beast cast a shadow other than its own, one whose shape I could not quite make out. I felt much the same thing when we faced the hawk."

"So?"

"*Hamfariggen*," he said grimly. "I fear the hawk and the boar were two forms taken by the same man."

"Wedigar," Liriel breathed, nodding as she added this piece to the puzzle taking shape in her mind. "Yes, that would explain many things! The attacks on the hunters, even the missing children."

"But why?" Fyodor demanded. "Why would such a man attack his own?"

The drow cast a sidelong glance at the young berserker. He was not going to like what he was about to hear. "Like you, he does not choose," she said bluntly, and then she told him what she'd learned about the nereid, and her suspicion that such a creature might have cast a charm over the Ruathen shapeshifter.

Fyodor stared at her, appalled by the possibilities. "You are certain?"

"No," Liriel admitted, leveling a challenging gaze up at her friend. "But I think I know of a way we could find out."

* * * * *

Elaine Cunningham

Moonlight touched the sea with silver fingers and cast a pale, luminous glow over the rock-strewn shore. It was the sort of night that Sune, goddess of love, might have fashioned especially with trysts in mind, yet Fyodor wandered silent and alone at the water's edge.

Then a faint song, like that of someone singing softly for her own pleasure, came to him on the wind. The young Rashemi paused to listen, entranced by the artless beauty of the song. Quietly he made his way around a tall pile of dark rocks, rounding a point that curved in to form a small cove.

The singer stood on a large rock at the very edge of the sea, looking out over the water and singing softly in a language Fyodor did not recognize. She was a young woman, fair-haired like a North-woman but more delicate—nearly as slim and small as an elf. Very beautiful she was, with pale skin that glowed like pearl in the moonlight and soft ripples of gold hair flowing free over her shoulders. She started like a fawn when she caught sight of Fyodor and lost her footing on the wet rocks.

Fyodor instinctively darted forward to catch her as she tumbled from her perch. For a moment, the golden singer filled his arms, and the dull ache the warrior always carried with him was forgotten. She drew away—too soon!—her hands nervously smoothing the white shawl knotted about her waist.

"Do not fear me, lady," he said softly. "Your song drew me, but I have no wish to harm you or even to disturb your solitude. If you wish, I will leave you."

A slow smile came to her face. "You are kind," she said in a shy, sweet voice. "In truth, I would welcome your company—indeed, would you be willing to see me safely home? I was lost in the song and did not realize until just now how dark the night has become."

The last words were spoken with an odd mixture of apprehension and innocent flirtation. Fyodor took the hand she offered him, steadying her as they made their way along the shore. The girl began to sing again as they walked, silvery music that melded with the moonlit waves until sea and sound were as one. Fyodor did not know exactly when it was that they stopped walking, or when the girl came again into his arms. His mind registered the soft caress of the waves lapping against them both and the sweet, salty taste of her lips on his. Or was it the sea? He did not know or care.

A shrill, anguished scream split the air and shattered Fyodor's dreamlike haze. Cold assaulted him like a blow, and he saw with astonishment that he stood knee-deep in the icy waves. Not far away was Liriel, a grimly triumphant smile on her dark face and a white silk shawl fluttering like a victory banner in her hands. The golden singer knelt in the water before the drow, her hands outstretched beseechingly as she wept and pleaded for the return of her shawl.

Slowly the details of their plan returned to his benumbed mind, and Fyodor realized with intense chagrin how completely he had succumbed to the nereid's charm. Had he truly been alone, the siren would have tried to drown him as she had no doubt slain the missing fisherfolk. Yet so beautiful was the nereid, so utterly human her appearance and so heartbreaking her distress, that Fyodor had a difficult time remembering she was a thing of evil. Liriel, however, had no such problem.

"Be still!" she hissed, brandishing the shawl in the weeping nereid's face. "By this token, you are *mine*. Accept your servitude and remain in the sea—silent and unseen—until I have need of you."

The nereid covered her face with her hands, wailing pitifully as she sank below the water, disappearing as she went.

Fyodor turned incredulous eyes upon the drow. "You will keep her enslaved?"

"Of course," Liriel said casually. "You never know when a nereid might come in handy. Nice job, by the way, bringing her out into the water toward me. I wasn't sure you would realize that I followed you in the water so as not to leave footprints in the sand."

He *hadn't* realized that, but he wisely decided to let the matter stand. Despite the success of their plan, he could not help but be dismayed, not only by the ease with which Liriel consigned the nereid to servitude, but also by her willingness to use the nereid's services despite its evil nature.

"Come," he said shortly. "We must speak to Wedigar at once."

*   *   *   *   *

They found the First Axe of Holgerstead asleep in the room he and Fyodor shared in the Trelleborg barracks. Wedigar came awake quickly, with a warrior's trained alertness. His eyes narrowed in puzzlement when they settled on the Rashemi's somber face and on the dark-elven female at his side.

"What is this, lad? It is unseemly to bring a woman into the Trelleborg!" he admonished Fyodor.

183

"Women are not the issue here. More exotic females seem to be the order of the day," Liriel observed coldly as she pulled the shawl from her bag. "This belonged to your girlfriend. Look familiar to you?"

The warrior stared blankly at the length of fringed white silk, then up at Fyodor. "What is this about?" he demanded.

"Do you remember nothing about a golden-haired girl? Liriel thought she saw you walking with one along the shore," he urged.

"The shaman's daughter? What of it? You know I came to the village to court her."

"Not Dagmar, but a magical creature," Fyodor corrected him, "one who can charm a man so completely that he would gladly kill himself and, perhaps, others as well.

Wedigar's eyes narrowed dangerously, but he kept his control. "Explain yourself," he said evenly.

"This morning, shortly after dawn, we returned from Inthar along the shore cliff. Liriel saw a man and a maid walking along the water's edge. Not long after, we were attacked by a giant hawk, nearly the size of a man. It was not a natural hawk," Fyodor said softly, "but a creature such as the ones you spoke of when you told me what form a *hamfariggen* fighter might take."

"You are a stranger to this land," the First Axe of Holgerstead said in a stiff voice, "and because you do not realize the insult in your words, I will not call challenge upon you."

Liriel let out a soft, exasperated hiss. "Fine. Don't. But you will explain *this*." Before either man could react, she lunged at the warrior and seized the neck of his nightshirt with both hands. With a quick, sharp movement she tore the garment open to the waist.

Across the warrior's chest, in a neat straight line, were four small, shallow puncture wounds. Below them was a large circle where the dark hair had been singed away and the skin raised in a large, red blister.

"Explain those," the drow suggested coldly.

For a moment Wedigar sat in silence. "I cannot," he admitted.

"Then permit me," Liriel said. "I threw four knives at the hawk who attacked us, as well as a small fireball. Lucky for the bird, its chest muscles were too deep for the blades to do much damage, and the feathers protected it from most of the effects of the fireball. Your wounds are smaller than I'd expected, but then the target has shrunk considerably. No offense intended," she added with a glance at his heavily muscled torso. "I also threw a bolo at the thing's leg, and Fyodor hit it repeatedly on the back and right side with his cudgel. There should be some fairly impressive bruises in those locations."

"There are," Wedigar muttered.

Liriel cast a disbelieving look at her friend. "You weren't exaggerating when you said these people are no good at lying," she said dryly. "This one won't even make an attempt!"

"I speak the truth," the warrior told her bitterly, "at least, what little of it I can remember! Yesterday morning I did go to the shore intending to meet the shaman's daughter when she came ashore after the morning's fishing. You know she labors with the fisherfolk. But I did not see the boats return. I believed only that I misunderstood what cove I should seek and thought no more of it. The morning passed quickly. Now that I think of it, a bit too quickly."

"You didn't notice the pain? The wounds?" she persisted.

"I did," he said tersely. "Of them I could remember nothing."

"What about this afternoon? Where were you during the hunt?"

"I remained in the Trelleborg most of the afternoon. I can neither walk nor hold a sword without pain. How could I hunt?"

Fyodor cast a puzzled look at Liriel. "Then he could not have taken the form of the boar that attacked Aumark!"

"There is a way," Wedigar admitted. "Those who are strong in the shapeshifting rage can sometimes take a *hamfarir* flight. The body stays behind; the spirit goes forth in animal shape. It is possible I did what you believe, for in spirit form my injuries would not deter me from doing this, though my body would bear any wound that might be given the spirit-animal. Tell me," he demanded abruptly, "did someone manage to wound the boar? A spear wound in the hindquarters?"

Fyodor nodded, and the warrior's shoulders sagged in despair. "I had feared this might be so. But how was this done, and why can I remember nothing?"

"I can help you remember," Liriel said confidently. "The truth of your actions is hidden in your mind, which, by the power of my goddess, I can read."

Without waiting for Wedigar's consent, the drow retreated into herself and silently spoke the words of the clerical spell. The result was sudden and dramatic. Usually the spell yielded a peek into another mind—an image, an impression, perhaps a few words. This time the wall built by the nereid's charm tumbled down, and Liriel knew the whole truth of the warrior's part in the troubles that beset the land he helped to rule and defend.

And so, apparently, did he.

Wedigar groaned and buried his face in his hands as the horrors he had committed came back to him in a single, vivid rush. He sat in tortured silence for many long moments, but when at last he lifted his eyes, they were set with determination.

"I will call a Thing," he said firmly. "I will own up to what I have done and accept the ruling of the people I have betrayed."

An exasperated Liriel cast her eyes skyward and then turned to Fyodor. "You talk to him."

"I understand your decision," the Rashemi began. "Your sense of honor demands that you face your actions and accept punishment. Yet your duty to your homeland demands otherwise. Strange things have happened to us and to the people of Ruathym—more than can be explained by the curse the nereid placed upon you. No, there is more at work here, and we must know what. If there is a single dark purpose behind all these things, would it not be wise to bide your time in silence until the answer is found?"

"You ask me to put the lives of my people at risk!" Wedigar protested. "I would rather die in battle than let this foe continue his work!"

"But how will you fight? Who is the foe?"

The First Axe shrugged helplessly, utterly at a loss for an answer. Fyodor put a hand on the man's shoulder. "What is needed now is patience and skill at intrigue—both of which are foreign to the Northman warrior. But the drow are bred and trained for just such things. Bide your time in silence and let us seek answers. It might be this work has been laid upon us as part of the rune quest that brought us here," he added suddenly, and for some reason he was certain the words were truth.

Liriel nodded agreement, her eyes deeply reflective as she added this new insight to the growing pattern.

Wedigar threw up his hands. "I will do as you say," he muttered, "but I like it not."

Fyodor could not help but agree, for he could not rid himself of the lingering cloud of despair that Liriel's clerical spell had left behind. He had seen Liriel in prayer before, and her link with the dark goddess of the drow troubled him deeply. This time the thread of power had been much stronger. As she'd cast the spell that allowed her to peer into the shapeshifting warrior's mind, Fyodor had been assaulted by a sense of seething chaos and overwhelming evil. The moment passed quickly, as did all glimpses given him by his limited Sight, but he knew he would remember it always. He knew Liriel's strength of spirit and her uncanny resilience, but he did not see how she could remain untainted by such evil.

Wedigar's unwitting deeds in animal form had been many and terrible. Fyodor's own transformations into a berserker whirlwind would probably bring about his death. But even these things paled before the Rashemi's dawning fear that Liriel, in her quest for power, might undergo another, even more deadly type of shapeshifting.

Chapter 14
CALL OF THE DEEP

scarle was a city of rare beauty and ancient wonders. Shakti, however, was not impressed. When not in conference with the illithid regent, the drow priestess spent many hours pacing about the marvelous marble corridors, seeking places that were not too scorchingly bright for her drow eyes to endure, seething with impatience as she waited for the tangled plans of the others to sort themselves out, and pondering ways to best turn them to her personal advantage. On her own, Shakti was a canny manager, but she had no notion of how to mesh her goals with those of her new allies.

At the moment, Shakti was taking a meal in the company of the illithid's other "guest." The priestess cast an angry glare at the man who was seated at the far end of the long table, calmly eating some sort of overcooked seafood by the light of a single candle. She noted, with a touch of pride, that his new hand was functioning nicely. That had been a pleasant interlude—selecting the slave who'd serve as a donor, inflicting the painful rituals, indebting the arrogant human to her in ways he could not begin to understand. Still, that pleasure did little to dispel the worry and boredom that had become Shakti's lot.

"How long must I wait for my prisoner?" she snarled at Rethnor. "What purpose this delay?"

The black-bearded human regarded her somberly for a long moment; then he pushed back from the table. "Come," he said and strode from the dining hall.

Shakti hissed a curse, then rose to follow. The man led her through a labyrinth of corridors to the most peculiar room the drow had yet seen. Her first impression was annoyance. She was assaulted by faint green light too bright for comfort and too thick with energy to be anything but magical. The air was humid, and heavy with the scent of salt and of growing things. This piqued Shakti's interest. Agriculture was, after all, her original passion and area of expertise.

The drow edged into the strange room. It was a vast chamber whose walls and high-arched ceiling were made of thick, translucent crystal. The entire room was filled with rows of long, narrow vats. Curious, Shakti stepped closer and peered into the nearest container. It was full of salt-scented water, in which was growing a curious type of weed.

Rethnor reached in and plucked off a bit of the plant, a tightly whorled frond at the end of a long stem. "This is a kelpie," he informed her. "A rare form of seaweed. They are grown here, and sprouts such as this one are sent to Ruathym, where they are placed into the waters surrounding the island."

"What is that to me?" demanded the drow.

The Northman beckoned to a nearby slave, a fair-haired man nearly his own height and girth, and ordered him to approach the large vat at the far end of the room. The slave's eyes widened in terror, but he did not disobey.

"Watch carefully," Rethnor advised the drow. "You should find this most entertaining."

As the curious priestess looked on, lank strands of weed rose, of their own accord, from the vat, writhing sinuously in the humid air. They quickly took the form of a green-clad woman. It was not an impressive illusion—the innate magical immunity of the drow allowed Shakti to see through it at once—but the slave's face took on a look of rapt obsession as he contemplated the creature before him, as if the rather pathetic imitation were the true embodiment of his deepest, unspoken longings.

"A charm spell," Shakti muttered, watching as the kelpie woman beckoned the slave into her embrace. He went to her eagerly, and they tumbled together into the vat of water. There was no struggle, no sign of life but for a rift of bubbles that ended soon enough. The surface went still and remained so. The man had drowned—quickly, quietly, blissfully content with his fate.

"Kelpies," Rethnor repeated. "They have lured many Ruathen warriors and sailors to their deaths. This is but one of the strategies used against our foe. In due time, they will weaken, and we will attack."

"Very impressive," she sneered. "You have demonstrated that human males are fools, but this I knew already. I want the Baenre princess, now!"

As do I, said a calm and feminine voice, speaking directly into the drow's mind. Both Shakti and Rethnor turned as the illithid glided toward them, her lavender robes trailing behind her in a silken whisper.

The conquest of Ruathym is important. We are agreed on that, Vestress continued. *The Kraken Society would benefit from a western outpost, and we also wish to reward Rethnor's efforts. Luskan is an important trade partner, and you have proven yourself a valuable agent. But mark me, Lord High Captain: we grow impatient with your tactics. The pirate ship escaped you. You should pray that her captain did not recognize you or your ship, and that he is not even now spreading word of Luskan's perfidy among his people. The task of conquest will be more difficult if the islanders are forewarned. Do not delay much longer; else you lose all we have worked to accomplish.*

The man scowled. "Then why do you not attack at once?" he demanded. "I have seen your forces—a hundred sea ogres, twice as many human and elven slaves, gargoyles, strange water creatures from other worlds. Send them through your portal, if you can, and let them lay waste the island this very day!"

Do not presume to instruct me, Vestress advised him, her mental voice icy. *Bring me the drow wizard soon, or see the valuable resources of Ascarle and the Kraken Society slip forever beyond your grasping hands!*

With royal hauteur, the illithid swept from the chamber. As Shakti watched her go, her dark fingers clutched the pendant hanging over her heart, a small disk of obsidian, engraved with the shape of a half-mask.

"It is as I thought," she said in a deeply troubled voice. "The illithid needs Liriel Baenre's wizardly spells to open that portal. And she will have them, caring not whether Liriel is alive or dead at the time."

Rethnor's lips tightened in a small, hard smile. "I have often thought the only good wizard is a dead one, but I fail to see how this one's death will aid Vestress."

The drow turned a somber crimson glare upon him. "The illithid can read your mind; through the power of my god, I can read *hers.* Vestress will have Liriel, whether you manage to deliver her up or not. There are more ways than one for her to gain knowledge of the magic the wizard wields. And if Liriel dies, I lose my prey."

"What is that to me?" Rethnor replied mockingly, turning Shakti's recent words back against her.

The drow's eyes narrowed.

A tingling shock of pain exploded in Rethnor's new hand, sending the five fingers jerking out straight. He watched, horrified, as the fingers curved and reached for the handle of a knife tucked into his weapon belt. Without his will, *against* his will, the treacherous hand began to lift the knife toward his own throat. Rethnor strained the muscles of his left arm, seized the advancing wrist with his own strong right hand and tried to force it away—all to no avail. The hand that had become as much a part of him as his implacable ambition had utterly betrayed him. He felt the cold, sharp sting of the knife against his throat, felt the warm welling of blood as the blade slid gently across his skin.

"I will not lose my prey," Shakti said softly, emphatically, her eyes glowing with malevolent satisfaction. "Do whatever you must, but bring Liriel to me alive!"

With that, the drow priestess spun and stalked out of the kelpie nursery.

The knife clattered to the floor as Rethnor's arm fell to his side. He flexed his fingers, bent his arm and bunched the formidable muscles, and was relieved to find that all were once again at his command.

For now.

*　*　*　*　*

Xzorsh was in a quandary. The young sea ranger had received disturbing reports through the Relay—the complex chain of information that intelligent sea creatures passed along great distances with astonishing speed. Hrolf's ship had been attacked off the coast of Gundarlun by yet another creature of the elemental plane of water. The sea ranger had seen many things in his years of patrolling the waters, but the strange happenings of recent days lay far beyond his ken.

Even more astounding was the news that the beleaguered ship had simply disappeared. Xzorsh suspected the drow girl's magic was behind this, and he was eager to know the truth of the matter. His curiosity, however, was but one of his motivations. He had his pledge to Hrolf to consider.

And therein lay the dilemma. Xzorsh had not seen Sittl since the day the *Elfmaid* had been attacked by three warships, and then later by the band of merrow. The reinforcements Sittl had promised to send had not appeared. Nor had any of Xzorsh's inquiries yielded information on Sittl's whereabouts. Not even the Relay had news of the missing sea elf. Xzorsh was worried about his partner, fearing mightily that the other ranger might have fallen foul of the sea ogres. With two friends in trouble, which was Xzorsh to seek out?

After much deliberation, the ranger set out for the west, heading for the remote cluster of islets where he had delivered the surviving seal hunters. Beneath these islands, in vast water-filled caverns, was hidden a sea-elven city. The coral catacombs in which they entombed their dead were in the open seas nearby. Xzorsh hoped Sittl might have made his way there, perhaps to mourn his slain lover and child. The ranger believed he might find his friend there. Not coincidentally, the islands also lay along the shortest route to Ruathym.

With all possible speed, Xzorsh set out for the nearest island in the tiny archipelago. Here, in a rock formation hidden in a sheltered cove, he and Sittl often left messages for each other that were too sensitive to trust to the open Relay. There was nothing, and he cast his eyes toward the sky in a gesture of frustration that he'd learned from his human charges. To his astonishment, a familiar ovoid shape floated overhead: the skiff that had brought the marooned Waterdhavians to the island!

The sea elf swam for the light and waded quickly ashore. Not far from the water's edge, three men were huddled around a small fire. One of them, a tall man whose haggard, sunburned face was nearly the same shade of weathered reddish-brown as his hair, rose when the ranger approached and faced him down.

"Lord Caladorn," Xzorsh murmured. "I had no idea you and your men would still be here!"

"Only three of us remain," the young lord said coldly. "The others have died waiting for the merfolk of Waterdeep harbor to inform the city of our survival. Or did you even so much as try to send word?"

Xzorsh nodded, but his worry increased fourfold. Sittl was supposed to have handled this matter. "My deepest regrets, Lord Caladorn, but you must believe me when I tell you that the Sea People did not forget you! Something has gone very wrong; I fear for the safety of my messenger. But I myself will find a ship to return you to the mainland," he promised. "Ruathym is the nearest land. I should be able to reach the island in a few days. Sooner, with the help of sea creatures who are even faster than I."

The man's ravaged, accusing visage softened. "I thank you for this, but I know of the Northmen's hatred of elves. Even for the chance to see Waterdeep again, I would not have you put yourself at risk."

"Do not fear for me; there is no need," Xzorsh said simply.

"Are you so certain of this? The barrels holding your slain kindred were of Ruathen make."

"That may be so, but none of it was Captain Hrolf's doing. Yet I thank you for your warnings." The sea elf paused, and a smile lit his thin, intense face. "You are much akin, you and Hrolf. Both of you possess a degree of honor that—forgive me—is rare among humankind. You may trust in him, and in me."

Caladorn was silent for a moment; then he extended his hand to Xzorsh as to a comrade. "Then we will await your return."

The sea elf nodded acceptance of the man's trust, but waved aside the offered handclasp. "I cannot," he said with a wistful smile, holding up his own hand and spreading the fingers wide so Caladorn could see the webbing between. Then he turned and dove once again beneath the waves.

As he swam rapidly toward the west, Xzorsh found himself contemplating his hands, wondering if his webbed fingers could learn to shape magic. What was it, he mused, that kept the sea folk from learning this art? All his life, he had been fascinated with magic and felt for it the same deep affinity, albeit unfulfilled, that a land-dwelling elf had for starlight. And he could *feel* the magic, like an eldritch current in the usually thin and lifeless air, when the drow wizard had summoned it. Perhaps this meant he had some small aptitude. Perhaps Liriel would agree to teach him.

A rueful smile came quickly in the wake of this thought. Try as he might, Xzorsh could not imagine the fiery drow in the role of tutor. But he did not abandon such thoughts altogether, for they sweetened his dreams and sped his way toward Ruathym.

*   *   *   *   *

The kelpie stretched, watching idly as her graceful fronds undulated in the still, cold waters. A passing fish nipped at one of the green limbs, tearing off a chunk of bloodless, leafy flesh. The kelpie grimaced but did not, in truth, feel pain. She was well accustomed to grazing sea creatures. If anything, the hungry fish served to remind her that it had been far too long since she herself had fed.

The kelpie swirled in the water, tearing up the shallow roots she put down from time to time, and began to drift in closer to the shore. Somewhere, out beyond the waves, was some hapless male as ravenous as she. She'd possessed two such men herself, and she had dim memories of the eager meals her parent kelpie had consumed. All those victims, she remembered, had had eyes that were bright with a strange hunger. The kelpie didn't quite understand this, for they never attempted to feed upon her.

A stirring of the currents drew the kelpie's attention from the shoreline ahead. To her surprise and delight, a male swam toward her. And she had not yet attempted to charm him!

Long, supple fronds reached out to enfold him; the male batted them away. When she persisted, he drew a knife and began to hack away at her. Puzzled, the kelpie cast her charm. The male's flailing arm slowed, and the knife slipped from his webbed fingers. His eyes widened as he looked upon her, then darkened with desire. She wondered, briefly, how he perceived her: as a woman, or a green horse, or perhaps a hippocampus—a sea mount that appeared to be a cross between a giant seahorse and a dolphin. But as he gazed at the illusion-enhanced kelpie, he spoke an unfamiliar word in a harsh, sibilant tongue, a name that suggested his heart's desire was something other than the usual choices. No matter. The kelpie smiled and waited expectantly for her latest conquest to drown.

He did not oblige her.

This confused the kelpie, and she released the strangely resilient creature. But the charmed male seized one of her longest fronds, entwined himself with it, fought passionately her every attempt to dislodge him.

The kelpie considered this odd turn of events for several long moments, and decided it might not be such a bad thing. The male would protect her from hungry fish, perhaps even hunt for her. Surely there was other, similar prey in these waters. Let him find her another like himself, that she might eat.

* * * * *

Dawn had not yet silvered the water when the fisherfolk dragged their boats into the sea. It was early for such labor, but the waters around Ruathym, usually so benevolent, had become as miserly as a dwarven moneylender. Feeding the village was growing ever more difficult, and the Ruathen in their little boats ventured farther out than usual into the icy waters in hope of finding food.

The fisherfolk of two boats stretched a large, weighted net between them, rowing gently as they trolled the deeper waters in hope of ensnaring more than the few spiny and inedible fish that all too often comprised the day's catch.

Suddenly the net swept back and taut; something large had found its way into the trap. But the fisherfolk's smiles of elation quickly disappeared. The net did not move. Whatever they had caught was beyond struggling.

"Not again," whispered young Erig as he regarded the silent net with horror. His partner for the morning, the shaman's pale-haired daughter, nodded grim agreement. They both had seen other large and lifeless catches hauled ashore. Each death had weighed heavily upon Dagmar, she who had lost her twin-born sister in a summer squall. Yet she fell to work at once, dragging up fistfuls of the heavy net. Shamed by the girl's stoic fortitude, Erig joined in the effort.

The two boats drifted closer together as the rising burden drew them in. The circle of the fisherfolk tightened, and soon they could make out the two still forms entangled in a mass of seaweed. Fearfully, Erig reached out and began to strip away the fronds that obscured the identity of the drowned men.

A hand shot out of the seaweed and seized the young man's wrist. Erig let out a startled yelp and fell back. It was as if a corpse had suddenly leaped from its bier, with one terrifying addition: the figure that tore free of the seaweed was a sea elf with long plaited hair, a face twisted with rage, and a long keen knife in his webbed hand.

So unexpected was the attack, and so strange the attacker, that for a moment even the warrior-bred Ruathen were frozen with shock. Dagmar, however, had the presence of mind to use the oar in her hands. She swung hard, and as the elf leaped into the boat she met his rib cage with a sharp crack. The blow halted the momentum of the attack. Erig seized the moment and punched out, landing a blow that sent the slightly built elf reeling back. Once again he struck, and at last the elf dropped senseless into the sea.

The second elven figure entangled in the seaweed seemed more interested in freeing himself from the green mass than attacking, but the Ruathen were in no mood for making fine distinctions. Dagmar lifted the oar high and smashed down, again and again. The elf—a male with short hair as green as the kelp—ceased his struggles and fell limp.

For a long moment the fisherfolk merely stood and stared at the

195

strange beings in their nets. Finally Valeron, the oldest among them, leveled an accusing finger at the unconscious sea elves.

"There's the answer for the poor fishing and torn nets, or may Umberlee take me! Mayhap these sahuagin-spawned fish-elves know something about the drownings, too."

"Take them to land. Make them tell us what they know." This opinion was voiced from one of the other boats that had drawn near to observe the spectacle.

The taboo against sea elves was strong, and Dagmar tried to convince the others this course was not wise. But the voice of a woman was soon lost among the males' clamor for justice—and vengeance. The elves were dragged aboard, and all thoughts of fishing abandoned as the folk turned back to Ruathym with their catch.

*   *   *   *   *

"Xzorsh, my friend, can you ever forgive me for what I have done?"

The ranger shifted painfully; he was bruised and battered from the pounding he'd taken at the Northwoman's hands, and the wound from Sittl's knife made his shoulders burn and throb—but he managed a wan smile.

"It was not your fault," he said, and not for the first time. "You were under the charm of a kelpie—of course you would fight to protect the creature. What I do not understand is why you ventured so far west in the first place, and why you did not leave word for me!"

His partner grimaced. "After I left you to tend your pledge to the human pirate, I was waylaid by a band of merrow. They brought me here; I do not know why. I managed to escape while they quarreled among themselves. When this happened, I cannot tell you, for I do not know how long I was under the kelpie's spell. Nor do I know what other things I might have done," he added in a voice tight with foreboding.

Xzorsh patted his shoulder. "I remember my first view of the kelpie lair. There were no other victims entwined among the creature's fronds, so you may rest easy."

"Rest easy? Not until we find a way to free ourselves from this place," Sittl said, casting a fearful look at the stout wooden walls of their prison.

The ranger sighed. He spread his fingers and regarded his hands. They had been out of water for little more than an hour, and already the delicate webbing was dry and fragile. His lungs burned from the effort of breathing the thin, dry air. It was an effort he could not long continue; in his dizzied and weakened state, he fancied he could actually see his life-force drain away, like an ebbing tide slipping away from the shore.

A sudden, cold splash struck him, dragging him back to full awareness. Xzorsh shook the water from his eyes and gazed with amazement up at Liriel. The drow girl stood over him, an empty bucket in her hands and an impish grin on her dark face.

"Thought you might be getting homesick," she said lightly.

"How are you here?" Xzorsh demanded. "I did not see you come in."

"No one did," the drow returned. "And I don't think they'd be pleased if they knew about it. You two are neck-deep in trouble."

"Where is Hrolf? Surely he can tell them we mean no harm!"

Liriel's face turned grave. "I don't know. No one has seen him all day. He has been known to go off alone now and again, but he couldn't have picked a worse time! A few of the *Elfmaid*'s crew are willing to speak for you, but their words are not heard over the blathering of that wretched Ibn!"

"Hrolf's first mate does not have much love for elves," Xzorsh admitted.

"Do tell," Liriel agreed with a touch of sarcasm. She had ample proof of that from her personal experience with the man, and she felt an unexpected twinge of kinship with the captive and misunderstood sea elves.

Even so, she herself was not entirely certain the Ruathen's accusations were unfounded. She had come to think of Xzorsh as an ally, perhaps even a friend. Yet she had been raised to distrust all the fair races of elves, and her drow indoctrination had left its mark.

"Why did you come to the island?" she asked bluntly.

"I heard the *Elfmaid* had disappeared. You know I am pledged to protect Hrolf and his crew. I wished to know he was safe. I also wished to learn how such a thing was done."

Liriel tipped her head to one side as she considered the sea elf. To all appearances, he was sincere. Yet there was something in his eyes—a touch of hunger, a hint of some personal agenda—that set off alarms in her dark-elven mind.

Her fingers crept up to her clerical symbol, and she silently cast the spell that would enable her to know whether his motives were more closely allied with aid or evil. Looking into Xzorsh was an odd experience—like being drawn deep into the heart of a flawless gem. The facets were there to add interest, but the color and substance within was consistent with the surface beauty. Like Fyodor, this male was what he appeared to be.

The drow turned to Xzorsh's friend, whose dull eyes regarded her with a mixture of fear and contempt. The last time she'd seen this elf he'd hurled a spear at her; his disposition did not seem to have improved in the interim. But as she cast the spell of knowledge a second time, she expected a brief swim in his suspicious but otherwise nobleminded depths. To her surprise, the results of the spell were anything but positive.

A hideous image popped into her mind: a fish-man creature with green-scaled skin, black fins, and enormous round eyes bright with malevolence. A nimbus of vicious, sadistic energy crackled around the creature—the aura of pure evil.

"Sittl, no!"

Xzorsh's despairing cry tore Liriel free from the disturbing spell. She blinked, focusing in on the sea elf's sullen but otherwise handsome face. A moment passed before she realized that his eyes were dry and fixed, his breathing a barely perceptible gasp.

"He is dying," the ranger said, and his green eyes pleaded with the drow. As Liriel met his gaze, she suddenly realized that Xzorsh was looking none too well, either.

The drow snatched up the empty bucket and chanted the words to a simple spell. She upended it over Xzorsh's head, sending a fall of life-giving water cascading over both the males. After a few moments of this, the unconscious elf began to stir.

"Put the bucket down," Xzorsh said urgently. Liriel did so, and to her astonishment the ranger plunged his partner's head into the water. She quickly saw the reason for this: the sea elves apparently could breathe air only for short periods of time. She watched, fascinated, as water poured from the gills on the elf's neck with each breath of the water. Several moments passed before the submerged elf had revived enough to sit up.

"We must get him back to the sea at once," the ranger said.

Liriel hissed with exasperation. "There's a line somewhere between nobility and foolishness, but I've yet to find it! No offense, but you're looking lower than whale droppings." When Xzorsh regarded her blankly, she pointed to the still-full bucket. "Breathe some of that, while I think of a way to get you out of here."

While Xzorsh at last tended his own needs, the drow quickly

debated what she should do. The hideous image she'd seen troubled her, but there was no time to speak of it now. She doubted the sea elves would survive much longer, and she certainly didn't relish the idea of explaining to Hrolf that she'd let his friend wither up and die.

"Can you breathe ale?" she asked abruptly.

Xzorsh and Sittl responded as one; they jumped, as startled as boys caught at some little prank. They exchanged a sidelong glance and a sheepish grin.

"I see you've tried it," the drow said dryly, then explained to them what she had in mind. Xzorsh grinned, utterly delighted with the plan, but his friend refused to have anything more to do with drow sorcery.

"Have it your way," Liriel said with a shrug. But she pulled a small object from her bag—a dried starfish she'd found on the shore, apparently stranded when the tides went out—and tossed it into the recalcitrant sea elf's lap. She raised one white brow in an eloquent arch.

"I will do as you say," Sittl agreed grudgingly.

The drow nodded and fell into the concentration needed for the casting of a powerful spell. She had learned much from her stolen book of sea magic—and from the scrolls and spellbooks in the Green Room—and she'd made a point of studying water elementals. She planned to summon two such creatures. Unfortunately, the sea elves' wooden prison was on the innermost edge of the village, too far away from either the sea or the cold freshwater spring that served as village well. Water was needed to form the elementals' bodies, yet apart from Liriel's enspelled bucket, there was little water to be had in the immediate vicinity. Ale, however, was available in quantity. Hrolf's warehouses stood next to the prison.

The sound of splintering wood announced that Liriel's summons had been answered. She winced as one expensive cask after another shattered to provide the fluid needed for the elemental to take corporeal shape. Still, she knew instinctively that Hrolf would shrug off the loss.

"Remember what to do," Liriel admonished the elves; then she drew her *piwafwi* close around her and blinked out of sight. She slipped out the door—she had left it slightly ajar after picking the lock—to see what her magic had wrought.

Her eyes widened with delight at the sight of the two amber-colored creatures undulating toward the prison. The elementals were not large—no more than seven or eight feet in height—but they were perfect for the task ahead.

Liriel closed the door behind her and stood off to the side.

The drow watched as the elementals smashed down the prison door and sloshed inside. She sent out a command to the summoned creatures, holding firm against their indignant response. After a brief struggle, the elementals yielded to the power of her magic and burst out of the prison into the street. Encased within the amber form of each was a sea elf, sharing the liquid body with the essence of the elemental creature.

The elementals did not seem happy about this new partnership, and they set a determined pace toward the shore. Many of the Ruathen took up weapons against the strange invaders. But the elementals barely seemed to notice the blows, so intent were they on their journey. When it was clear the creatures did not intend to attack—indeed, had no interest in doing battle at all—the villagers ceased their defensive efforts and merely watched. Some fell in behind, and an ever-growing crowd followed the liquid creatures toward the sea. Liriel slipped behind a thick-trunked walnut tree and dispelled her invisibility charm, then openly joined the bemused throng that followed in the elementals' wake. It seemed wise to her to do so; otherwise, her absence might be noticed and her involvement in the matter suspected.

After a while, the rolling gait of the elementals began to falter. The creatures' paths started to weave, and they looked for all the world like ships tacking back and forth to catch a particularly capricious breeze. None too soon, the elementals stumbled into the surf and fell gratefully into the sea, like a pair of drunken sailors falling facedown into their beds.

Liriel lifted a hand to her face to hide her smirk. She understood now why the sea elves had reacted as they had to the suggestion of breathing ale.

Fyodor came to her side. He wrapped an arm around her waist and leaned in close. "Well done, little raven!" he whispered in her ear. "The sea folk will wake up with a headache the size of the northern sea. But thanks to you, at least they will awaken!"

* * * * *

Nor was Fyodor the only one to come to this conclusion. Smoke burst from Ibn's pipe in angry little puffs as the sailor observed the strange escape.

He'd long suspected that the drow female was in thick with the sea elves; this proved it. Hrolf, the damned fool, was too besotted with the long-eared wench to see it, and the villagers were too awed by her healing magic to listen to words spoken against her. And he, Ibn, was hardly in a position to press the matter. The elf woman had made sure of that, keeping secret his attack against her.

Ibn spun on his heel and made his way to Hrolf's cottage. Once before he had taken matters into his own hands. The attempt had failed. He would try again, and again, until at last the elf woman lay dead. He could not do otherwise, for there was far too much at risk.

Chapter 15

THE RAVEN'S CALL

 yodor left for Holgerstead later that day. Wedigar had sufficiently recovered from the injuries he'd incurred while in animal form to feel ready to travel, but he was hesitant to do so alone. Fyodor and Liriel tried to convince him he was free from the nereid's charm, but Wedigar was haunted by the things he had done while under the evil creature's seductive power. He would not risk the possibility that he might again turn upon his own people, and he exacted a pledge from Fyodor to watch over him and stop him should he prove a danger. The young Rashemi could not deny him this, for he himself had lived with such fears for many months.

With both Hrolf and Fyodor gone, Liriel felt alone and exceedingly restless. She buried herself in the Green Room's treasures, learning all she could of Ruathen lore and history, but the knowledge of rune magic that she needed remained just beyond her grasp.

Unlike the magic she knew, runes could not be learned through reading and study. *Life* was the necessary conduit for such knowledge. Some simpler runes could be taught and had been passed on from master to seeker from time beyond memory. A few were gifts from the gods, but the most personal were shaped through the questing journey.

This Liriel knew, and her frustration increased as she read. Her journey, to all appearances, had come to an end. What, then, was she to do now?

And there was also the matter of the hideous creature she had glimpsed behind the face of Xzorsh's sea-elf friend, and the chilling evil that surrounded him. Liriel could not rid herself of the feeling that she ought to warn the sea ranger. It would not be an easy task, for it was plain that Xzorsh was fond of his companion, and she doubted he would hear words spoken against him. And what proof did she have, except for the Lloth-given vision?

With a heavy sigh, the drow opened a lore book and began once

202

again to study the turbulent history of the Northlands. But the saga of slain heroes, endless warfare, and titanic sea battles could not hold her attention. At last she thrust the book aside and hurried from the Green Room to the cove where the *Elfmaid* was moored.

Liriel quietly slipped aboard and searched the hold for the device that Hrolf had used to summon the sea-elf ranger. She dropped back into the water on the seaward side of the ship and turned the crank on the small box. A series of clicks and squeaks ensued, and the drow leaned back against the *Elfmaid*'s hull to wait. Liriel suspected Xzorsh had not gone far, but even so the wait was painful, and for the first time she regretted her decision to lend her ring of water-breathing to Fyodor. If she'd had it, she might have gone out in search of Xzorsh.

Perhaps an hour passed before she saw the dark shape moving swiftly toward her. Liriel took a deep breath and plunged beneath the water, swimming out to meet the summoned ranger.

The first blast of power took her unaware. Like an iron fist, it thrust into her mind and gripped her will, dragging her closer. But Liriel had in full measure the dark-elven ability to shake off magical attacks. She thrust aside the mental intrusion and pulled her dagger. Just in time—the creature who'd attacked her rounded a stand of waving seaweed and came into full view.

The creature was fishlike, with an enormous, bulbous head and three vertically stacked eyes. Faint purple light shone from these eyes and cast an eerie nimbus in the water. Slender tentacles rippled behind like locks of hair as the creature's sharklike tail propelled it forward with terrifying speed.

Liriel drew in a startled gasp of seawater. An aboleth! Such creatures inhabited the hidden waters of the Underdark, but she had not thought to encounter one here. She spun and with frantic haste swam for the surface, speeding her way with her innate powers of levitation.

The drow shot from the water, coughing and sputtering. Seizing the rail of the ship, she hurtled over and dove for the deck. She rolled several times, as fast as she could, putting as much distance between herself and the lethal beast as possible.

A long, thin tentacle snapped into the air with a whip-like crack. Seawater flew in a sharp spray, mingled with dark droplets of venom. Liriel shielded her face with her arms and prayed that none of the drops would find her. When no stinging pain came, she dared to look up.

Two tentacles gripped the rail. With a mighty tug, the aboleth heaved itself upward. The ship rocked wildly, and Liriel began to slide toward the rail. She grabbed a knife from her sleeve, thrust it deep into the crack between two boards, and hung on for her life.

A silent shriek tore into her mind, a mental blast that spoke of rage and pain and frustration. The aboleth's massive body splashed fully back into the water, but the clinging tentacles remained where they were, twitching uncontrollably.

Liriel leaped to her feet and ran over to the rail. Two of her throwing spiders clung to the severed tentacles, their killing magic spent. The water below churned wildly, thick with swirling ichor and the flashing of silver weapons. Then Xzorsh came into view, his green head breaching the surface along with the heaving, struggling aboleth. The ranger straddled the creature, the knife in his webbed hands flashing as he stabbed down repeatedly.

Nor was his the only weapon brought to bear against the aboleth. The drow's keen eyes made out the forms of several other fighters—man-shaped, but with silver-green skin and legs that ended in fins rather than feet. Each of these warrior wielded a three-pronged silver pitchfork, and they wheeled and darted like eels as they attacked the enormous monster.

Liriel whirled and ran back to the weapons rack. She seized a harpoon and leaped into the neck-deep water. The fighters—all but Xzorsh—scattered at once. The drow lunged at the aboleth's eyes, putting her full weight behind the blow. The weapon sank deep into the middle orb, and the creature's struggles finally ceased. With a grimace of disgust, Xzorsh slid away from the dead monster.

"Who were those people?" Liriel demanded, shielding her eyes with one hand as she gazed out into the water, hoping for another glimpse of the strange warriors.

"They are tritons," the ranger replied in a troubled voice. "Of them little is known. They do the sea elves no harm, and sometimes they come to the aid of goodly folk. And just as often, not. My people believe they come from the plane of water, and that their purposes originate there. I suspect their interest is not in you, so much as in the elemental creatures arrayed against you."

The drow nodded thoughtfully as she took this in. In her opinion, the ranger's fears were well-founded. Elemental creatures of any sort were rare; she had encountered far too many for mere coincidence. Most had fought against her and her friends; these tritons had come to her aid. Liriel knew with the assurance of one born and bred to Menzoberranzan-style intrigue that she was caught up in something bigger than she could yet comprehend.

"Tell me all you know," she demanded.

Xzorsh told her of the merrow who had wielded the weapon of a triton. The tritons were skilled and fierce warriors, unlikely to be overcome unless the merrow had attacked in large numbers under a commander with more intelligence and battle knowledge than sea ogres usually possessed. He told her Sittl had been abducted by a band of merrow and brought to the shores of Ruathym.

The drow nodded thoughtfully, thinking of the nereids that haunted the waters near Inthar and the elemental that had kidnapped the Ruathen ship. For some reason, Ruathym seemed to be the focus of extraplanar creatures. But who commanded them, and to what purpose?

"A wizard could have summoned that water elemental," Liriel mused, "but no wizard commanded that nereid. The creature still possessed its soul-shawl. There are creatures of the Underdark about, too. A banshee—the spirit of a really nasty drow female—has taken up residence in a well, though how in the Nine Hells it got there without anyone noticing is beyond me. Banshees generally tear up the countryside for a while before finding a lair and settling down. And an aboleth, of all things! What in the name of Lloth's twisted legs are we dealing with?"

The ranger shrugged helplessly. "Strange happenings have been occurring below the waves, as well. A message Sittl sent to the mermen of Waterdeep harbor was altered before it reached its destination. Seldom is the Relay tainted so! Innocent men's lives were lost as a result. And I must see Hrolf, else three more will soon die. Where is he? Wasn't it he who summoned me?"

"No, that was me. Hrolf's still off fishing in the mountains, or so his kinsman believes." Liriel took a deep breath and plunged in. "I needed to warn you about Sittl. With my magic, I can glimpse into a person's mind, determine his motives. I did that just before I set the two of you free. You passed, more or less; he didn't." Quickly she described the creature she had seen and the sense of evil that surrounded it.

Xzorsh listened in tight-lipped silence. "I have heard of this drow goddess of yours. You will forgive me if I don't trust the visions she sends."

The drow had no argument to counter this. "But what was that creature? And how do you explain what I saw?"

Elaine Cunningham

"I cannot," he said shortly. "Nor do I wish to discuss this further. Sittl and I have been friends and partners for years. He has given me no reason to distrust him, and I will hear nothing more said against him." He paused and eyed Liriel with sudden curiosity. "You said I passed your test, *more or less*. What evil thing did you see in me?"

"No vision of strange creatures, if that's what you mean. But it seemed to me you wanted something more from the situation than you were admitting," she said with uncharacteristic candor.

The sea ranger's eyes lit up. "That is so! All my life I have wished to learn more of magic, and I dared to hope you might teach me. I have heard magic is expensive to learn and to cast, but I can pay. Perhaps these might be a start?" So saying, he took two large rings from his bag and dropped them into the drow's hand.

Liriel glanced at the jewelry, then did an astonished double take. One of the rings, a thick band of gold set with a large flat-cut onyx, exuded an aura of powerful magic. The other was a signet ring of silver, with a raised symbol that was reminiscent of the house insignia worn by most of Menzoberranzan's nobility. Something about the ring was familiar, and she studied the design: a stylized, simple picture of five ships with single, triangular sails. She knew that design; she had just seen it reproduced in the lore book that spoke of the Northmen's ceaseless warfare. It was the official seal of the High Captains who ruled Luskan, a port city north of Waterdeep and the blood-rival of Ruathym. This was important information. She only hoped it had not come too late.

She raised blazing eyes to the sea-elf's face. "Where did you get these?"

"From the severed hand you asked me to retrieve," he responded, puzzled by her vehement reaction.

"And you didn't see fit to mention them?"

"You asked only for the hand. I did not think gold and gems would serve your purpose, else I would have given them to you," Xzorsh said.

Liriel threw up her hands in exasperation. Yet she had no time to vent her ire, for it was possible she held in her hands the clue to Ruathym's troubles. Luskan was a rich and powerful port—perhaps powerful enough to command the forces that were arrayed against the island. The problem would be to convince anyone that this might be so.

"I've got to get back," she said abruptly.

The elf caught her arm when she turned. "Three men are stranded on a small island not too far away—some of the seal hunters Hrolf set adrift. I promised them I would send a boat for them."

Liriel sniffed and pulled free. "And who will ask for this boat—you or I? You just broke out of their prison, remember? They think you and your friend conjured the magic that ruined a good door and a whole lot of ale, and they're not too happy about any of it. Show up in Ruathym, and one of those axe-happy villagers will chop you into fish bait before you can say two words. Me they avoid, or treat like an unweaned child. They might have listened to Fyodor, but he's away." But even as she spoke, her gaze skimmed the pebble-strewn shore. "Can you sail one of those small boats?" she asked, pointing.

When he nodded, the drow immediately began wading toward the shore. She made her way to a trim little craft and held both hands out, palms down. Xzorsh saw her lips move, and then the boat rose into the air—just a bit—and floated silently off the beach and out over the water. The boat settled down beside him, so gently that it barely made a ripple. From the shore, Liriel cast a look over each shoulder and then indicated with emphatic gestures that he should leave at once.

Xzorsh hesitated for only a moment. Theft was not part of his creed, yet he saw no other way to rescue the men than to borrow this boat for a time. As he raised the sail, he vowed he would see the boat returned to its owner as soon as possible. He pulled taut the lines and set the little boat on an eastward course.

It occurred to him, some time later, that Liriel had not answered his request for teaching. The sea-elf's shoulders rose and fell in a deep sigh. At least she had not said no. For now, at least, he still had his dreams.

* * * * *

As Liriel hurried back to the village, she debated who best to approach with her information. The men of the *Elfmaid* might support her; after all, they had been attacked by three warships led by a High Captain of Luskan. Yet she doubted anyone had recognized the man, or they surely would have spoken of it. Hrolf would certainly listen to her and, with the help of the ring she held in her hands, he could almost certainly convince the other villagers. But Hrolf was not here.

Who, then? Ibn was entirely out of the question. The scheming first mate would probably try to turn her efforts against her. Bjorn? Of all the men aboard, the young artist had been most accepting of her—even admiring, in a shy sort of way. Yet he was a mere lad, and a rather frail and scrawny one at that. Liriel had noticed that in Ruathym only warriors were truly taken seriously. Finally she settled on Olvir, the would-be skald. The storytelling sailor was the most likely member of Hrolf's crew to possess knowledge of other lands and the leaders who ruled them. Olvir had a fondness for tales and would listen to her and perhaps help, for Fyodor's sake if for no other reason. It had not escaped Liriel's attention that the two men had become friends during the long voyage.

The drow repeated her request for directions a dozen times before she found someone who would tell her where Olvir's cottage lay. Some of the villagers snubbed her outright, others were too awed by the very sight of the drow to pay heed to her words, and still others showed keen suspicion about her purpose in seeking out the man. Liriel had no doubt Olvir would be amply forewarned of her coming.

Indeed, the seagoing skald met her outside the cottage, while his wife and children looked on curiously from behind the half-shuttered windows. He listened politely enough, but he merely shook his head when she asked him to accompany her to speak with the First Axe.

"This is one keg you don't want to tap," he said bluntly. "Ruathym and Luskan have a treaty—the Captains' Alliance, some call it. The last war with Luskan near to grounded us, so many ships were lost, and we're in no shape to take on another battle. Aumark Lithyl is a warrior, but he knows this to be true."

"He may have no choice but to fight," Liriel pointed out.

"So you say. But even if this ring is what you believe it to be, did you see it on the hand of the warship's commander? *When* the hand was attached? Well then, seems like all you got is a sea-elf's word. That won't hold much water around these parts—less now than usual, what with all the good ale those pointy-eared, magic-casting bastards poured into the sea!"

Nor would they listen to a dark-elven female. Olvir was kind enough not to speak the words aloud, but Liriel heard them nonetheless.

Frustrated beyond words, she made her way back to the Green Room to search for more pieces to the puzzle. Perhaps if she could present a more detailed and reasoned whole, the stubborn males who ruled this place would give her a hearing.

One very important part of the puzzle was the myriad of strange creatures she had encountered. Liriel brought to mind the image of the hideous fish-man, and she set to work finding all the information she could about such creatures. Even if Sittl was all Xzorsh thought him to be, the long-haired sea elf was in this to the tips of his green ears. Someone considered him important enough to have him abducted and brought to the shores of Ruathym. If, indeed, he'd been "abducted" at all.

It didn't take Liriel long to find a familiar-sounding description, for creatures known as sahuagin were apparently frequent scourges of the northern waters. She wondered why Xzorsh had not mentioned this. He must have recognized the creature she was describing. Puzzled, she continued to read, burning candle after candle. The night was nearing the dark hour of Narbondel—midnight, the humans called it—before she thought she understood what prompted the stiff, angry expression on the sea ranger's face when she'd spoken of the creature she'd glimpsed beneath his friend's handsome facade.

Some sages believed the evil sahuagin frequently gave birth to mutated young, babies that resembled sea elves in all things but a rapacious nature. It was supposed that most of these children were slain at birth. Liriel nodded as she read this; the drow killed all babies born with the slightest defect, and they would certainly destroy any child who was identical in form to a racial enemy. But some of these mutated sea children were spared, raised as sahuagin but with the knowledge that they would in time live among the sea elves. As spies and assassins, these sahuagin, known as "malenti," could do untold damage to the sea-elven enemy.

Liriel could well imagine why Xzorsh had rejected her suggestion so vehemently. Sahuagin and sea elves were mortal enemies. How could he believe this of his friend and partner? The resemblance between malenti and sea elves also suggested a shared ancestry, and Liriel was not a bit surprised to read that many sea elves denied the very possibility that malenti existed. Drow would slay anyone who so much as suggested the dark elves might bear an ancient kinship to kua-toa, the fish-men creatures of the Underdark. Liriel suspected that surface- and sea-dwelling elves were not without similar pride.

Yet she could not reject the idea that Sittl might be such a creature.

209

She had to know if this was possible, and the best way to do so would be to see a sahuagin with her own eyes, to see if the resemblance ran true to the Lloth-granted vision.

As was usually the case with Liriel, action followed quickly upon decision. The young wizard hurried back to Hrolf's cottage. She cast a longing glance at her bed. Since leaving the ship she had been able to follow no set pattern of waking and sleeping hours, and the rumpled covers looked wonderfully inviting.

No time, she decided as she took from her pack a copy of the spellbook her father had given her. Any spell in that book could take most of the night to learn and cast.

Liriel paged to a particularly difficult spell—the one that had first introduced her to the priestesses of Eilistraee. The first time she had ventured to the surface, the wizard who served as her tutor had insisted that she seek out a company of dark elves. The spell had been attuned to search for such beings and to carry her to an open place a safe distance away. It was an unusual spell, every bit as difficult as she remembered. This time she did not have the assistance of her powerful drow mentor. It was nearly dawn when Liriel at last was ready to try.

The drow began to chant softly, swaying as she did, her hands weaving in a seemingly random, seeking pattern. She felt a sudden chill, the sharp tang of a cold northern wind, and knew the casting had worked. Exactly where the spell had taken her, she could not know.

All around her was the sound of the sea. She opened her eyes and scanned the shore. Here it was rocky and wild, with no natural harbor. Above her was a sharp cliff; beyond that wisps of smoke drifted lazily into the sky. Liriel wrapped herself in her *piwafwi* and floated up to the top of the bluff so that she might investigate the settlement beyond.

A glance told her she was still somewhere in Ruathym. The cluster of cottages were built of wood and decorated with intricate, interlocking arches and high-peaked roofs, a style identical to the buildings of a Ruathym village.

In the village, all seemed well. The cottages were silent; hounds slept undisturbed in the courtyards. Yet Liriel trusted in the spell that had brought her to this place, and she swept a seeking gaze over the village and the shore beyond.

Her keen eyes caught the shimmering ripple as something broke the surface of the sea. A hideous, fishlike head with huge round eyes and ears like small black fins emerged from the water. With quick, furtive movements the creature pulled itself out onto the rocks and scanned the bluff above. Roughly man-shaped, it was covered with dark green scales. Fanged jaws, like those of the deadly *pyrimo* fish found in Underdark waters, opened and closed as the creatures spoke sounds Liriel could not hear. It was a signal, apparently, for at least a score of other creatures crept from the waves and began to scale the cliff that separated the sea from the village.

"Sahuagin," Liriel whispered excitedly. There could be no doubt. These were the creatures described in the lore books, identical to the thing she had seen when she'd looked into Sittl. The long-haired sea ranger was almost certainly a malenti—a mutated sahuagin passing as a sea elf—and Xzorsh's life might well depend on her ability to convince him of this.

The drow's first impulse was to reverse the spell that had brought her here so she might warn the sea ranger at once. But as she watched the creatures scale the cliff, her resolution wavered. One of them, smaller and slower than the others, failed to find a secure hold for its webbed foot. It slid painfully down the rocky incline, and the claws on its feet grazed one of its elders as it went. The larger sahuagin lunged like a striking snake, jaws snapping viciously at the offending creature and sinking deep into the soft tissue beneath its rib cage. After tearing off a large chunk of flesh, the big sahuagin calmly chewed and swallowed. Its now-dead comrade continued the slide, falling unnoticed to the rocks below.

Liriel swallowed hard. She had little love for the patronizing, stubborn humans of Ruathym, but neither did she like the idea of abandoning them to the murderous sahuagin. Yet she could not warn the villagers; they would likely fear her as much as they did the fish-men. No, she'd have to handle this one on her own.

The drow reviewed what she had learned of the creatures. They hated light—they were as pained by it as any Underdark drow—and they feared spellcasters. That would do for a start.

Liriel readied the spells she needed and waited until all the creatures had scaled the bluff. In precise and orderly formation, they crept past the invisible drow toward the sleeping village, their bulbous black eyes bright with fierce anticipation.

At Liriel's command, a curtain of yellow faerie fire blazed up along the edge of the bluff, cutting the sahuagin off from the sea and casting their long, hideous shadows into the village beyond. Instantly the sahuagin stopped their advance, casting frantically about for some means of escape. But there was none. The sudden bright light roused some of the villagers, and cries of alarm began to spread. In moments the warrior-bred Ruathen poured from their cottages, fully armed and ready to do battle.

One of the sahuagin, the large and casual cannibal, whistled out some sort of command. The others fell into a wedge-shaped formation, their weapons—a motley and no doubt stolen collection of spears, tridents, and hauberks—snapped up before them. Liriel noted that the big sahuagin took up a position at the very rear, and that the creatures got progressively smaller as they neared the forward point. This did not surprise her—drow did not expend their leaders in battle, either. The sahuagin were apparently ranked according to size and strength, with those of lesser rank taking the greatest risks.

Liriel once again called upon drow magic and limned the sahuagin chieftain with faerie fire, so that it blazed like a green torch. The creature clacked and whistled frantically as it pawed at itself with its clawed hands, as if trying to extinguish the flames. The others, momentarily deprived of command, faltered, and the strict formation fell apart. But then the Ruathen were upon them, and the sahuagin knew what to do. They fell into battle with vicious delight, attacking the humans with their slashing talons, rending jaws, and stolen weapons.

The drow tossed back her cloak and advanced on the leader. She dropped the faerie fire that surrounded the large sahuagin and pulled her long dagger in preparation for its attack. But the creature merely stared at her, its fishlike eyes intelligent beyond her expectations, and filled with rapt awe. To Liriel's astonishment and chagrin, the sahuagin fell to its knees and briefly touched its scaly head to the ground in an unmistakable gesture of adulation.

Liriel did not even want to think about the implications of this. She kicked out hard, catching the sahuagin under its scant chin and sending it sprawling backward. Instinctively the creature drew a knife and parried her first lunge. Leaping nimbly to its feet, the sahuagin faced her down and presented its long knife in a weird parody of a drow challenge. Liriel responded with a feint and a quick, slashing cut. The sahuagin blocked, blocked again, then riposted. Its movements were fast, fluid, and oddly elven. As the battle progressed, Liriel was hard pressed to hold it back, though she was by far the better trained. The unlikely opponents stood toe to toe, exchanging swift and ringing blows. Liriel was relieved that this one, unlike its brethren, did not employ the sahuagin's darting, deadly bite in battle. She was fully occupied by its swordcraft!

At long last she slipped past the creature's guard and sank her dagger deep into its gut. She gave the weapon a vicious twist and wrenched it out, then thrust in again. The dying sahuagin's knife dropped from its nerveless claws, and the creature once again fell to its knees, its eyes bright with adoration and fixed upon Liriel's dark, elven face. The drow delivered a backhanded slash to the creature's throat, ending its misery and quenching the incomprehensible, fervid light in its black eyes.

The strange encounter left Liriel feeling shaken and somehow tainted. She shook off the lingering, queasy dread and whirled to address the nearest opponent.

A large sahuagin had managed to toss a weighted net over a red-clad warrior and was poking at the trapped man with a long spear. None of the thrusts hit a vital point; the fish-man was toying with its prey with obvious and sadistic glee.

Without thought, Liriel conjured a small fireball and hauled it back for the throw. Startled by the sudden burst of light, the sahuagin spun to face her. Its viciously grinning jaws fell slack with astonishment as it faced the magic-wielding drow, and terror froze the creature in place. Pitiless, the young wizard hurled her weapon with deadly accuracy. The fireball flew unerringly into the creature's enormous mouth. The explosion sent a spray of gore and ichor flying, and the headless sahuagin dropped heavily to the ground.

Liriel stepped over the body and crouched beside the wounded man. Her dagger flashed as she quickly cut him free from the entangling net. Although he bled from a dozen shallow wounds, it was apparent that he could yet fight. The drow pressed one of her own knives into his hands. Hauling him to his feet, she gave him a firm shove in the direction of the nearest sahuagin. The man tossed a quick, grateful nod toward the drow and then flung himself into battle, roaring an oath to Tempus as he went.

A brief, faint smile curved Liriel's lips. The Ruathen were warriors to the core, ready to respect and accept another warrior who had proven worthy—perhaps even one as strange as she. The thought brought her a moment's warmth, and then it fled as the crush and turmoil of battle closed in about her.

The drow fought alongside the Northmen, using all the battle skills at her command. Her bolos spun around the legs of the fishmen and sent them sprawling; her throwing knives buried themselves in the eyes and throats of the sahuagin; her dagger dripped with greenish ichor. When at last the invaders lay dead, the eyes of all the Northmen settled upon their strange ally.

"You are *dock-alfar*, yet also a rune-caster," one of them ventured in an awed tone. "It has been long years since such a rune-casting warrior led this village in battle, but in ages past it was ever so. Most of the people of Ruathym do not much care for magic, but here we remember the ancient ways and honor them. How are you called?"

For some reason Fyodor's special name for her danced ready on her tongue. "Raven," she said simply.

This brought approving nods from the warriors. Liriel remembered the tales Fyodor and Olvir told, ancient stories that claimed ravens visited the battlefields to guide the spirits of the slain into the afterlife. Yes, it was a good name for a drow among Northmen.

She let the men lead her into the village, which, it seemed, was only a few hours' walk north of the village of Ruathym. They promised to show her the way back after the songs were sung to honor the slain. And so she sat in a place of honor beside the village chieftain—the man she'd saved from the sahuagin's net—listening as the village skald spun out the lineage and deeds of the men who had fallen during the sahuagin attack, and watching as sparks from the funeral pyre leaped high into the clear blue sky.

It was a strange ceremony, yet the drow found it oddly moving. In Menzoberranzan, the dead were usually interred in small, airtight stone crypts dug into the solid rock that lay north of the city cavern. This was a matter of practicality, not respect. The bodies were simply stored there until a need arose for battle fodder or slave labor, at which point a wizard would be called upon to animate the corpses. Only priestesses of Lloth were cremated. Here on Ruathym, this honor was apparently extended to all, even the lowliest thrall.

The day was nearly spent before Liriel saw the high-pitched roofs of Ruathym village. As she walked, one of the skald's songs echoed in her memory—a newly composed ballad that honored the little warrior known as the Raven.

For the first time, the adrift and restless drow felt a tendril of herself reach out and take root in this strange land. And one more curving line was added to the rune that was slowly taking shape in her mind.

214

Chapter 16
THE CAPTAIN'S CONSPIRACY

he Regent of Ascarle bent low over the scrying crystal attuned to her aboleth ally, staring into the smooth surface long after the vision had faded away—along with the creature's life-force. The illithid was not pleased by the loss of the aboleth, or by the fish-thing's failure to kill and consume the drow wizard. Vestress wanted the powers wielded by Liriel Baenre, and learning of them secondhand from the aboleth had seemed a reasonable approach to take.

The illithid had witnessed Liriel's escape from the aboleth's charm spell, and she was intrigued that a single drow could command so much strength of mind and magic. She was not in error in suspecting that this drow, with her wizardly spells and her Underdark magic, might yet provide the answer to a vexing problem.

For all her power, despite the myriad secret tentacles that probed into the affairs of much of the Northlands, Vestress had lost her ties to her own ancient heritage. She was a rogue illithid, cast off from the city where she'd been spawned, denied the community of collective minds that sustained her kindred. The self-proclaimed Regent of Ascarle was desperate to establish contact with others of her kind. She had tried, many times before. Some of her efforts had failed entirely; most succeeded at least in expanding the reach and the power of the Kraken Society. But as the illithid's power grew, so also did her frustration and her obsessive desire to overcome anything that stood against her. One failure that weighed heavily upon Vestress was that which had been exiled to Ruathym.

Many years ago, Vestress had wrested the city of Ascarle from other hands. Fell creatures and evil spirits had haunted the near-ruins buried in the watery depths north of the Purple Rocks. Most fearsome was the banshee who watched over the sunken treasure. The creature had been a wizard, a member of a drow army that had marched against the elven city in centuries beyond memory, only to be destroyed in turn when the rush of melting glaciers swept Ascarle away. The drow wizard had remained beyond death, transformed into a banshee, protecting the lost magical treasures of the city from any who might try to claim them. Vestress had overcome the banshee in a titanic magical battle and banished the undead drow to some unknown place. Thus had things remained for many years.

Then came Iskor, the water wraith, and the influx of extraplanar creatures such as nereids to add to the strength of Ascarle. Vestress was pleased—more so when these creatures inadvertently discovered a watery portal between the subterranean city and the distant island of Ruathym.

Midpoint between the Purple Rocks and the Moonshaes, due west from Waterdeep and lying on the warm river of water that ran eastward through the sea from the elves' island stronghold of Evermeet, Ruathym would be an important strategic addition to her empire. Vestress determined to add the island to the lands held in the grip of the Kraken Society. But when she tried to send her armies, she came up against an ancient and implacable enemy: the banshee, which had taken up residence in the watery portal.

Mindless in its purpose after the passage of centuries, the undead creature refused to let any living creature through the portal and spent its remaining power keeping the magic gateway closed. Not one to be outdone, Vestress quickly changed tactics, employing her powerful and ambitious Luskan agent to aid in the fall of Ruathym. Only recently had Vestress discovered that the elemental creatures, such as Iskor and the nereids, were beyond the banshee's magic, and the illithid had added the efforts of these extraplanar allies to the coming conquest, sending them to the island to quietly decimate Ruathym's fighting forces. But these intrusions had made the elven spirit restive. Vestress, too, was growing restless, and the illithid was eager to see the illusive banshee overcome once and for all. And when the banshee was gone from Ruathym and the portal open, all the armies of Ascarle would pour through. Ruathym would be hers to rule.

The Regent of Ascarle turned abruptly and glided from the scrying chamber that linked her to every corner of her hidden empire. At this moment, the frustrated illithid felt need of her loom. The intricate patterns of her tapestries, the interaction of warp and weft, was something she could control utterly.

But the weaving room was not unoccupied. Shakti stood in the chamber, studying the nearly finished tapestry stretched out on the loom. The priestess looked up as Vestress approached.

"An interesting scene," the drow said, pointing to the picture of sea elves staked out on the dry ground, writhing in torment in the harsh light of the sun. "It seems to me, though, that the human over in this corner was not in the picture yesterday. He looks very like one of the slaves."

From time to time, I must eat, the illithid said calmly.

A weird light flashed in the drow's eyes. "Then it is as I thought! You have found a way to capture the spirits of these . . . creatures upon your tapestry!" The drow reached into the coils of her hair and took from it a stiletto, four inches long but slender as a needle. This she poised over one of the tormented sea elves. "May I?"

The illithid nodded permission, and Shakti plunged the weapon into the weave of the tapestry. The impaled sea elf writhed and twisted, his mouth open in a silent shriek.

"Fascinating," murmured the drow as she took a few more experimental stabs. "Such a thing would command a fabulous price in Menzoberranzan!"

Once Ruathym is under the rule of Luskan and your wizard captured, perhaps I shall make you a present of it.

Shakti tucked away the stiletto with obvious regret and turned a measuring gaze upon the illithid. "As to that, I know your true intentions, even if that fool Rethnor does not," the drow stated calmly. "You will allow Luskan to conquer Ruathym, but not rule it."

We are pleased with your acumen, the illithid agreed, honestly enough. *It is true that we are using Luskan. It would not do at all for news to get out that the island of Ruathym had been overrun by some mysterious force, and for enterprising adventurers to trace the invasion back to Ascarle. No, let the blame rest entirely upon the humans. We will not risk revealing the location of this city.*

"What part in this have you assigned to me?" demanded the priestess. "Do not try to deny it—you would not keep me here, else."

Vestress considered the drow for a long moment before responding. *We wished to observe and measure your abilities. When the conquest of Ruathym is completed, we will bid Iskor to return you to Menzoberranzan so that the Kraken Society might have a competent pair of eyes in the Underdark. Your service will be rewarded through information. The vast network of spies, thieves, and assassins that make up the Kraken Society will be at your disposal.*

"This you have said before. But what of the other portion of our bargain? What of Liriel Baenre? Does she yet live, or have you managed to kill her?"

My, my, mused the illithid, *perhaps you have abilities we have not yet considered. But rest easy—the wizard lives.*

"Bring her to me alive, and I will see that you get from her what you need. If she proves too strong of mind and will to yield to your mental magic, I will bring to bear upon her the power of Vhaeraun, the drow god of thievery, to snatch the needed knowledge from her. And in return, you will show me how *this* is done," Shakti demanded, one finger thumping a sea-elf child imprisoned on the tapestry.

Vestress inclined her purple head in a nod of agreement, then sent out a silent mental summons that brought a pair of merrow slaves scurrying to the chamber. She sent the sea ogres to fetch refreshment—raw fish and spiced green wine for the drow, a cringing sea-elven slave for herself. Upon reflection, Vestress decided this might be a pleasant way to spend the afternoon: dining on an elven brain, tormenting the spirits of the sea elves entrapped on the tapestry, and conspiring with this deliciously evil drow. This interview had already yielded one delightful idea. Despite her assurances to Shakti, Vestress had never faltered in her decision to slay the drow wizard, but it occurred to the illithid that she might add Liriel Baenre's spirit to those captured on the tapestry. As a captive lich, the drow wizard's magic would be there for the taking. And when she had no further need of Liriel and her magic, Vestress might well give the finished weaving to Shakti. The drow priestess would no doubt consider this to be base treachery, but certainly she was accustomed to such treatment.

Until such a time, they might as well enjoy each other's company. Even a Regent was entitled to moments of leisure.

*   *   *   *   *

Rethnor, meanwhile, was busy with his own preparations. He had left the undersea stronghold and was now a guest in King Selger's palace. From there he dispatched messages to Luskan ships patrolling the northern seas, gathering the forces needed to mount a surprise attack against Ruathym.

The time was near for conquest. One thing yet remained—the decimation of the Ruathen berserkers. Once the mighty warriors of Holgerstead were out of the way, the rest of the island would fall easily enough. Rethnor, despite his passion for battle, had no desire to face a tribe of berserkers defending their homeland. Let them fall to one of their own—let their deaths be dealt by a treacherous and familiar hand. And if the dark-haired youth who'd taken Rethnor's hand died along with the rest of them, so much the better.

* * * * *

Exhausted by her sleepless days, the rigors of battle, and the long walk back to Ruathym village, Liriel made her way to Hrolf's cottage and stumbled straight for her bed. She stripped down to her tunic and took hold of the rumpled covers. Her fingers touched something small, furry—and familiar. Instinctively she jerked her hand back, then snatched up her dagger and used the tip of the weapon to throw back the blankets.

Hidden beneath the layers was a small black spider, of a sort Liriel knew quite well. The tiny red hourglass on its back marked it as a widow, a spider whose poisonous bite could kill a large man. The Underdark variety was much bigger and more canny; this one looked confused and rather forlorn.

"You poor little thing," Liriel murmured. This spider was no real danger to her—dark elves had an affinity for arachnids and a natural immunity to many spider poisons. But whoever had put the spider in her bed could not have known this.

Absently the drow began to stroke the widow's black-and-red back with the tip of one finger, much as a Ruathen child might caress a hound puppy. The spider seemed strangely listless, so Liriel gently picked up the fragile creature and slipped from the cottage. First she would take it into the forest, so it could spin its traps and feed. Then, she would seek out the one who wanted her dead and repay him in kind.

The drow searched her room for nearly an hour before her efforts yielded two clues: a stray flake of ash on the floorboards and a single thread of wiry, flame-colored hair, nearly hidden in the bright weave of the blankets. As she suspected, her attacker was Hrolf's red-bearded, pipe-smoking first mate.

The drow sank down on the edge of her bed and considered her options. She could accuse Ibn outright, but who would listen? She could attack him, but this would hardly endear her to the villagers and would certainly destroy her chances of winning over the stubborn shaman. Yet she could not let the attack go unacknowledged. She had to put Ibn on notice, let him know she was aware and alert.

Liriel closed her eyes and began to softly chant the words to a clerical prayer. It was a simple spell, a boon that Lloth granted even to drow outside her clergy. In response to her summons, hundreds

219

of arachnids would creep out of the woodpiles and crevices to converge on the hut were Ibn lay sleeping. They would not form an attacking swarm—she would not endanger the delicate and sacred creatures so—but they would spin throughout the night and drape the sailor's bedchamber in layers of gossamer webs.

When the spell was cast, Liriel crawled into her bed and dropped almost immediately into exhausted slumber. Her final thought—an image of Ibn coming awake in a tangle of spider silk and frantically batting his way through—curved her lips in a smile that lingered long after she had fallen into a dreamless sleep.

* * * * *

Liriel came awake the next morning before dawn, sitting bolt upright in bed and gripped by the terrifying conviction that something was very wrong.

Then she heard it—the traditional chanting song that sped the spirit of the slain to the afterlife that awaited. Entwined with the unfamiliar words that spoke of the man's lineage was a name she knew, a name written deeply upon her heart.

The drow threw aside her covers and raced from the hut, not bothering to dress or arm herself. Clad only in her tunic, she frantically followed the mournful cadences of the song to the village center, where a solemn group gathered around a large, pale form. Liriel registered the familiar, deep timbre of the shaman's chanting voice—so like that of his dead kinsman—and the group of fisherfolk still clad in the rough boots and aprons they donned each morning before plying their trade. Among them stood Dagmar, grim-faced and pale as death. Some of the women wept silently; Hrolf's young kinswoman looked as if she had no tears left to shed.

A wail of pure anguish cut through the somber chant of the shaman. Dimly, as if through a mist, the realization came to Liriel that the voice was her own.

Without thought, without will, she found herself kneeling at Hrolf's side. She smoothed his wet, disheveled braids, picked up one cold, massive hand and cradled it against her cheek. She began to keen softly, a high and haunting chant she had heard in the tunnels near Skullport, when the faithful followers of Eilistraee—the Dark Maiden, the drow goddess of song and the hunt—mourned the comrades who had fallen in battle.

Ulf's song faltered and then fell silent, for the shaman recog-

220

nized a loss deeper than his own. He watched as the *dock-alfar* chanted, rocking mindlessly in time to her eerie song. Her grief was all the more terrible for being tearless, and her strange golden eyes seemed to burn against the darkness of her skin. Next to the stoic calm of the Northmen, the dignified tears of their womenfolk, the elf's wild mourning was almost frightening in its intensity. Yet it was clearly genuine, and Ulf stood by in respectful silence, even in gratitude, that Hrolf had been so beloved.

The shaman was grateful, too, for the belated insight the little drow gave him into his lost kinsman. He and Hrolf were sons of twin-born brothers, and they had grown up together. No brother could have been more dear to him, yet never had Ulf understood his kinsman, especially Hrolf's youthful—and nearly disastrous—passion for an elven woman. Ulf had been aghast when Hrolf took in this black elf maid as a daughter. Suddenly he could see why. They were strangely akin, the pirate captain and the little drow wizard—both wild and untamed, approaching all of life with a natural exuberance the Northmen usually knew only in battle. Even in her mourning, the elf was utterly unfettered by convention, as Hrolf had been his whole life long. It was a farewell the pirate would have appreciated.

After several moments the shaman waved the fisherfolk away, then came to place a hand on the grieving drow's shoulder. "I have lost a friend and kinsman," he said softly, "but it seems to me that you have lost a father. This land is no longer foreign to you; forever will a piece of your heart remain in Ruathym."

The drow nodded; instinctively she knew this to be true. She had fought to protect the Ruathen village from the sahuagin attack, but Hrolf's death had bound her to the island as nothing else might have done. Only once before had Liriel known such an overwhelming sense of desolation and loss. She had been little more than a babe when Gromph Baenre, her drow sire, had ordered that her mother be slain so he might take sole control of his talented daughter.

"No rune comes easily, even to a god," Ulf said somberly as if he followed the pathways her thoughts had taken. "The cost is always high, and it will no doubt be higher still before you are finished. Do you still wish to learn?"

Liriel lifted blazing eyes to the shaman's face. "You can ask this of me?" she demanded. "Hrolf is dead. I will have the knowledge to learn why—and the power to avenge him!—whether you teach me or not."

This answer seemed to please the grim shaman. "Then we will begin."

221

Chapter 17
YGGSDRASIL'S CHILD

he funeral for Hrolf was to take place that very day. Most of the villagers took part in the preparations, for there was much to be done. The *Elfmaid* had to be cleaned and provisioned, her planks and timbers doused with whale oil; songs needed to be written to commemorate the man and his deeds; driftwood gathered for an enormous bonfire; food and drink readied for the feast—a lavish and lengthy affair meant to remind those left behind of the reward awaiting them in the mead halls of Tempus.

By Ruathen custom, a captain's first mate was to oversee the preparations, but Ibn was nowhere to be found. So Liriel took over the details. The villagers followed her directions without question or complaint, not seeming to care they were being led in this matter by a female, and an elven one at that. She fell into the role of leadership instinctively, for she'd had ample practice at planning and organizing large and elaborate events. It was odd, she thought more than once throughout that long and hectic day, that the skills she used to honor Hrolf had been honed in the decadent festhalls and mansions of Menzoberranzan.

The colors of sunset spilled into the sea by the time all the village gathered by the cove to see the pirate captain on his last voyage. As Ulf and Olvir took turns chanting the songs of farewell, Liriel looked on, as coldly composed as the *Elfmaid*'s wooden figurehead. When the ceremony finally came to an end, the drow gave the signal to set sail.

Hrolf's crew somberly went about the task of setting the rudder and raising the sail—not the usual gaily colored square, but an enormous banner of triumphant blue, upon which young Bjorn had painted the holy symbol of Tempus.

The chill breezes that announced the coming night caught the sail. It fluttered, then snapped taut, and the ship glided slowly out to sea. When it had reached the far outer edges of her range, Liriel dipped an arrow into the many-colored flames of the driftwood bon-fire and fitted it to a longbow. She sent the flaming missile arching high into the sky. It plummeted down like a falling star and disap-peared behind the *Elfmaid*'s low wooden rail. There was a moment's silence; then the oil-soaked ship blazed like a torch.

The Ruathen watched in somber, approving silence as the sparks from Hrolf's funeral pyre leaped up to meet the setting sun. This was an ancient ceremony, seldom done in these times, but all those present sensed its rightness. Everyone there knew of the pirate's great love for his *Elfmaid*; no one could imagine another captain walking her decks. And those who watched took strength from the rituals. In every detail, they had honored the ancient cus-toms of the Northmen. The ceremony brought to mind the glorious times of ages past and ignited the flame of pride in the hearts of the battered islanders. Whatever they had endured of late, they were descendants of a proud and strong people, and they would prevail.

In uncanny echo of these thoughts, the wooden figurehead on the prow of Hrolf's ship suddenly stirred to life amid the flames. The enor-mous elven maiden raised high her blazing sword. Before the wonder-ing eyes of the villagers, the figure's appearance shifted: no longer a ten-foot drow, but a broad-shouldered Northman with pale braids and an enormous mustache, and blue eyes ablaze with a wild passion for life. For a moment, Hrolf the Unruly lived again for them all. A proud smile crossed the figure's wooden face, and his chin lifted to a tri-umphant angle as the ship sank at last into the waves.

Every eye turned in awe to the little drow in their midst, mar-veling less at the magical feat than at the fact that a stranger—an elf—could understand so completely their warrior sensibilities. Although none had given words to the thought, all felt there was something vaguely shameful about death by drowning. In giving Hrolf a warrior's funeral, the black elf maid had reminded all pre-sent of the man's love of battle and his fighting prowess and, in doing so, had restored to him his honor.

Ulf walked over to the silent drow and placed a hand on her shoulder. "Come," he said softly. "We will join the others at the feast-ing later. Before night falls, we must take your belongings to my house."

Liriel eyed the shaman suspiciously. "Whatever for?"

"You should not be alone at such a time."

"Nonsense. I've been living alone for nearly half my life!"

"It is the custom of this land, about which you already know

223

much. The apprentice stays in the house of his or her master. We begin your training tonight."

The drow started to protest. She was exhausted and heartsick, in no frame of mind for the study of rune magic. And yet, this was why she had come to Ruathym. Her need, and Fyodor's, had not diminished, nor would the time allotted them expand to allow for personal sorrows. So she responded with a curt nod and followed the shaman to Hrolf's cottage.

Much later that night, when the feasting was over and the sated villagers had gone to their beds, the shaman and his student made their way into the forest. They walked without speaking, climbing a large hill that was crowned with a flat, grassy bluff. Overhead the moon was a mere sliver of silver light, and the celestial shards that followed it through the sky shone like glittering tears.

"There is unseen power in the land and in the sea," Ulf began. "He who would be a shaman must learn to feel this power before he can learn to gather it and shape it into a rune. In this place the magic is strong. See what you can do to find it."

With those words, he turned and began to stride from the clearing.

"That's *it?*" demanded Liriel, incredulous. "This is the teaching you promised me?"

The shaman turned to glare at her. "Find the power. Even the great ones—even the gods—are not given runes lightly. How can you hope to learn the casting of runes if you cannot learn to attune yourself to the source of their power?"

Since Liriel could not refute this reasoning, she spun away and stalked into the center of the clearing. She closed her eyes and began to breathe deeply, clearing her mind and readying herself as she did before the casting of any powerful spell. As a wizard, she had learned to use chants and gestures and spell components to shape magic to her will; now she attuned her thoughts to the Weave itself—the intricate and invisible web of magic that encircled all of life.

Elves do not use *the Weave; we are a* part *of the Weave.*

Where this thought came from, Liriel could not say, but she acknowledged it as truth. There was power she could claim as her own, power that was *her*. She envisioned the fabric of magic, like so many intricately woven silver threads, and searched for her place within it all. After a time, her seeking thoughts found this place, and she engraved the memory of it on her mind.

Not stopping to ponder this new and marvelous insight, the

drow persisted in her silent quest. She sought the magic that belonged to this place alone. The vision, when it came to her, was not one of invisible threads, but of a fabric even more delicate and magical. Moonbeams traced a silvery path from the skies to this clearing, forming a powerful connection between land and sky. Liriel thought of Qilué and the other priestesses of Eilistraee who worshiped the Dark Maiden in song, in dance, and in the hunt. Moonlight was a holy thing to them, a symbol and a source of their goddess's magic. They would feel the power of this place and know the magic it held.

Instinctively, Liriel began to dance—slowly at first, her body swaying and her arms reaching up toward the silvery path. Then she circled the clearing, her feet moving in an intricate pattern she had not realized she knew. It had been too long since Liriel had danced, and her deep and innate love of it swept her deeper into the gathering ecstasy of the dance. She whirled and dipped and leaped, finding the pattern and moving with it.

Caught up in the magic and movement, the drow did not know time. For her, there was only the dance. Only when the moon had disappeared behind the distant mountains did she stop, her heart beating wildly and her tunic clinging to her glistening body.

A faint sound came to her from the forest nearby, and the drow whirled, dagger in hand. Ulf emerged from the leafy hiding place, his bearded face suffused with awe. He walked up to the drow, ignoring the blade in her hand, and gingerly reached out to touch one of her damp curls.

Liriel's gaze followed the movement of his hand, and her eyes widened. Her hair, which had always been whiter than fine parchment, shone with faint, silvery light. Beyond doubt, it was a sign of Eilistraee's favor.

Joy flooded the drow's heart. The pervasive, smothering sense of evil that had gripped her since the day Lloth had claimed her as priestess parted like mist before the sun. Then, just as quickly, the darkness snapped shut around her, oppressive, yes, but heavy with the promise of power. The shining light disappeared from Liriel's hair as abruptly as if someone had blown the flame from a candle. Lloth had reclaimed her own.

"Never have I seen such a thing," marveled Ulf. "I would not have thought it possible, but it may be that you are ready to face Yggsdrasil's Child now—tonight! I will show you the way."

"No need," the drow responded evenly. Although the gift of

Elaine Cunningham

Eilistraee had been snatched from her, she now understood that all places and persons had a magic of their own, and she remembered the shining path that led to the sacred oak. And so she turned and pushed her way into the forest, the incredulous shaman following in her wake.

Liriel made her way unerringly through the thick woods, following the lines of power that led to the sacred tree. Finally she stopped before an enormous oak. It was ancient, far older than even the long-lived drow could hope to become, yet there was nothing about its thick truck and fresh spring leaves that set it apart from other, equally large trees that they had passed by.

"This is it," she said positively.

"But there are no runes carved upon it," Ulf pointed out.

In response the drow closed her eyes and extended both hands before her. She wasn't certain her wizardly spells could reveal magic of this nature; the shaman's sharp intake of breath spoke of her success.

Liriel gazed upon the tree. Carved on the massive trunk were dozens of complex markings—runes, each one completely unique. She ran her finger over one of them and felt the ancient indentation. The marks were carved into the physical tree, but the magic of Yggsdrasil's Child shielded them from casual gaze.

"You have done well," Ulf commended her. "There are five ritual questions that must be spoken before you begin. First: What is Yggsdrasil's Child?"

"It is a symbol," Liriel responded, quoting from the books of lore she had studied. "The Tree of Yggsdrasil holds all of life; entire worlds are like fruit in her branches."

"Why have you come?"

"To carve on the sacred tree a rune of power," the drow said, picturing in her mind the elaborate pattern that had been taking shape for many days.

"How was this rune formed?

"From life comes magic; from life, therefore, must a rune be formed. I went on a long journey, to see and to learn and to let life shape the rune."

"With what will you carve the rune onto the sacred tree?"

Liriel took the Windwalker amulet from her neck and grasped the hilt of the tiny dagger. She twisted it, and it came free of the sheath to reveal not a dagger, but a tiny chisel. "I will carve the rune with this artifact from a time long past, enchanted by rune-casters

226

and blessed by the ancient gods."

"And how will you do the casting?"

This final, elusive answer was not something she had learned from book or scroll; it had come to her this very night in the moonlit clearing. "By the power of the land upon which Yggsdrasil's Child grows, and the strength of the oak, and the magic I call my own," Liriel answered.

The shaman nodded. "You may begin."

Liriel turned to the ancient tree, ran her fingers over the weathered trunk as if seeking a spot that was hers alone. When it felt right, she raised the chisel and closed her eyes, bringing to mind her rune and letting it fill her thoughts.

Long moments passed, but still she did not move. The pattern was not yet complete—the rune had not fully taken shape. Dismayed and puzzled, Liriel stood unmoving, searching her thoughts for what might yet be missing.

Fyodor.

The answer hit her like a blow, but she knew it at once to be true. She could not do this without Fyodor, for he was an integral part of the rune she must cast.

Liriel opened her eyes and released a long, tremulous breath. This was almost too much for her to absorb. The young wizard had always thought of herself as the keeper of both quests—hers and Fyodor's. She had come to accept him as a partner and a friend, but for the first time she began to realize their destinies were entwined in ways she could not yet begin to understand.

Without a word, the drow turned and walked away from the sacred oak.

Ulf did not question her; indeed, he seemed to understand the matter better than she. "When you are ready, you will try again," he said calmly. "But next time, you will not have need of me."

Chapter 18
HOLGERSTEAD

iriel awoke at sunrise after a scant hour or so of slumber, startled from sleep by the clamor coming from somewhere below her. A moment passed before the usually alert drow remembered where she was, and why. Grumbling, she tossed aside the blanket and crawled out of the cot she'd been given in the loft of Ulf's cottage. Quickly she dressed and climbed down the ladder that led into the large central chamber that served as kitchen, meeting area, and sleeping quarters for Ulf's family.

The room bustled with activity. Ulf's wife, Sanja, a thick-bodied Northwoman whose usual expression suggested she'd recently drunk large quantities of sour milk, looked positively pleasant as she went about her work. She was dressed as if for a festive occasion; her braided hair was wrapped around her head with ribbons and fixed in place with pins of yellow gold, and she wore a bright red shift over a blouse of much-embroidered linen. The woman busily packed pots and clothing and household linens into an enormous chest, all the while happily scolding the thralls who attended the packing and the usual household chores. Dagmar moved to do Sanja's bidding also, but Liriel noticed that the girl was pale and tight-lipped as she went about her work.

"What's going on?" the drow inquired as she helped herself from a bowl of wild berries.

"My daughter travels to Holgerstead today," Ulf replied. "She will enter the household of Wedigar, the First Axe of that village. When the moon is full, they will be wed. It is a great honor to this household," he said, casting a stern glance toward the girl.

Liriel did not need to ask Dagmar's opinion of the honor being dealt her. It astounded the drow that no one seemed concerned by the young woman's obvious distress. Liriel was not certain whether she should feel sorry for the girl—who was clearly being sent away and married off against her will—or whether she should try to slap some sense into the spineless wench.

There was little time for either. Liriel abandoned her meal to watch as two burly thralls lugged the chest out and hoisted it up onto a flatbed wagon, to which were hitched two pairs of oxen. Several barrels and crates had already been loaded and strapped securely into place.

Sanja crossed her arms over her bosom and surveyed the heavily laden cart with a critical eye. "Well, Dagmar, all that's lacking are the traditional barrels of oil and meal. Those you can fetch from Hrolf's warehouse before we leave. Not even a First Axe could quarrel with my daughter's bride price," she said with deep satisfaction.

Liriel's eyes widened with astonishment and rage. A female was expected to bring a *dowry?* In her land, not even the lowly males were subjected to such indignity. Drow males were chosen as mates for whatever merits the females happened to see in them. They were discarded just as easily, true, but at least their families didn't sell them to whatever priestess put in the highest bid!

Before Liriel could speak her mind, Sanja stripped off several of the golden bands encircling her plump arms and gave them to her daughter, along with a spate of motherly admonitions about a wife's duties. The speech was blunt and detailed enough to startle even the fun-loving drow. Dagmar made her escape as soon as she decently could, her face corpse-white except for the livid stains of embarrassment that slashed across her cheeks.

"I'll go with you to Hrolf's warehouse," Liriel said abruptly.

The young Northwoman only nodded, clearly eager to be away. She took up the lead rope and began to guide the oxen down the road that led toward the warehouses. Liriel fell into step, and they walked in silence past the small buildings that housed the ducks and rabbits that supplied the family's table.

Dagmar paused near the edge of the yard and cast a long look over the kitchen garden. Tending this, Liriel had learned, was one of Dagmar's responsibilities. Between gardening and fishing, the girl was as much a servant as any of the slave-born thralls who served the household. And this was the life of the only daughter of an important and relatively wealthy man! The drow couldn't help but wonder what type of servitude awaited Dagmar in another woman's household.

Two large wooden boxes stood just off the path, full of sand and salty water. Liriel caught sight of a burrowing clam—it seemed that many of the villagers kept a supply of shellfish and edible seaweed handy. She absently plucked a bit of kelp—a tightly whorled bud of some sort—from the water and began to nibble it as she searched her mind for anything that might ease Dagmar's situation. A look at the girl's stricken face, however, banished all thoughts of diplomacy.

"You don't have to do this," Liriel said bluntly. "Fight your way out of it, if you have to. I'll stand with you. I won't see another female served so badly!"

But the young Northwoman shook her head. "I must go," she said in a distracted voice as she flipped a pale yellow braid over her shoulder. "The First Axe needs a *hamfariggen* heir who can lead the berserkers in battle. It is my duty to provide one.

"You heard Hrolf speak of Ygraine," Dagmar continued softly. "She was my twin-born sister, lost last spring in a sudden squall. The night we two were born, the old women who read the oracles said Ygraine would bring the shape-strong magic back to Ruathym and help restore the ancient glories we have all but lost. And what other path to glory is given a woman of the North, but through the man she weds and the sons she bears him? Ygraine's betrothed was the last young *hamfariggen* warrior on the island. He is dead. The only shape-strong man on Ruathym is Wedigar, and he must have sons. Ygraine would have gone to him willingly. This destiny now falls to me; can I do less than she?"

Liriel threw up her hands in disgust. If Dagmar was going to take that attitude, there was no helping her!

"But there is something you can do for me," the girl murmured. "I wish to go to Holgerstead quietly, and alone. Leave me now and wait for a time before returning to my father's house, so they do not know I have left. Else, they will travel with me and hand me with great ceremony into Wedigar's unwilling hands. That, I think, I could not bear."

The request seemed reasonable enough, so the drow nodded and slipped off into the nearby forest. After an hour or so passed, she'd wander back to the cottage with news of Dagmar's escape.

A grin of wicked anticipation spread across Liriel's face as she pictured Sanja's astonishment and ire. The stolid Northwoman could throw an impressive tantrum. Liriel had observed a most entertaining example of Sanja's talents earlier, when she and Ulf had crept into the cottage in the waning hours of night. Granted, the woman's rage was not as colorful and violent as those favored by drow priestesses, for the dark elves could punctuate their shrieking diatribes with the lashes of a snake-headed whip and bursts of magical fury. But the Northwoman did what she could with the resources she had—Liriel had to grant her that!

It was something to look forward to, anyway, in a day that had unquestionably gotten off to a bad start.

* * * * *

Rethnor was still abed in his room in Vestress's palace when the door to his room exploded inward. The portal shattered into a storm of sparkling crystal that showered his bed and clattered to the marble floor. One jagged shard pierced the arm he instinctively flung up to shield his face.

The High Captain swore as he tore out the splinter and cast it aside. He leaped to his feet and lunged for the sword that he kept always ready beside his bed. Bringing it up in guard position, he faced down the intruder.

Shakti stood in the ruined doorway, clutching a smoking pitchfork in her hands as if it were a spear. Her dark face was livid as she advanced on the captain.

"Three days you have been in the Night Above," she shrieked, "and what have you accomplished? You have returned to Ascarle without Liriel Baenre. Show me how you will bring me my prey, or die now by my hands!"

In response, the captain lunged forward, blade leading. He stabbed between the pitchfork's tines and then spun his body sharply to one side. The speed and strength of his attack tore the weapon from the drow's grip. It fell to the floor with a sharp clatter.

"Die by your hands?" he taunted her.

"Or yours, if you prefer," the drow hissed from between clenched teeth. She thrust both hands out, thumbs entwined, and then slapped her palms sharply together.

A familiar tingle started in Rethnor's new hand and sent a shiver of dread into his very soul. Once again the treacherous limb abandoned him to the power of the dark elf's foul magic. He watched in helpless rage as his sword hand lifted his blade and placed the edge against his throat.

"How will you deliver Liriel Baenre?" demanded Shakti as she stalked in closer. "Tell me all you have done, and plan to do, or die now!"

Rethnor did not doubt the drow's sincerity of purpose, and he spoke with all candor. "I have contacted my spy on the island and know at last the drow wizard's weakness. She has a human lover—

the very warrior who took my hand," he admitted grudgingly. "By all reports, the elf woman is very loyal to her friends. If this man is captured, she will certainly come after him."

The priestess looked doubtful. "She is drow. Why would she care for the welfare of a human male?"

"You have a better suggestion?" Rethnor asked this with less sarcasm that he might have employed—it seemed a prudent choice, considering the sword at his throat.

"Kill him," Shakti advised coldly. "If he is an interesting lover, the loss will anger her, and she will seek vengeance."

Rethnor considered. This reasoning struck him as sound, given his own rather casual attitude toward his bedmates, and his experience with this particular dark elf.

"It will be as you say," the captain promised. "The time for the invasion nears, and tonight the berserkers of Holgerstead will die. All of them," he added with grim satisfaction.

"Really? By whose hand?"

The Northman glanced down at the sword at his throat, and his lips tightened in a small, hard smile. "By the hand of treachery," he said softly. "I have learned how effective that can be."

A strange light entered the drow's crimson eyes. "Effective, but too efficient for my liking," she stated with dark glee, and she reached for something tucked into her belt, something that looked like the handle of a whip.

As she pulled it free, several thick ropes emerged from among the folds of her skirts. They rose up, swaying sinuously, and regarded Rethnor with pitiless, reptilian eyes. To his horror, the High Captain realized that the whip was made up of living snakes. Five of them—all with eager, open jaws and fangs dripping with venom.

Shakti drew back her arm and then lashed forward. The snake heads dove in, and their fangs sank deep into the High Captain's flesh. Jolts of icy, numbing pain shocked through him, and he dropped to the floor, nerveless and limp.

Again the priestess flung back her arm, ripping the snakes' fangs from him. She stood poised for an agonizingly long moment as Rethnor steeled himself for the second strike.

"That will do for now," the drow said with obvious reluctance. "But remember the price of failure and do not risk awakening my anger!"

Shakti tucked away the whip; the snakes immediately snuggled back into their hiding places. She retrieved her pitchfork and stalked from the room. The man regarded the shattered door, his deep puncture wounds and torn flesh, and he marveled that the drow did not consider these to be acts of rage. He wondered with deep foreboding what might occur if she should ever become truly angered.

A thought flashed in Rethnor's pain-numbed mind, one too full of possibilities to ignore. The thrice-bedamned priestess had turned his own body against him. But perhaps there was some treachery he could yet deal her. Shakti wanted the drow wizard. Very well, he would deliver her to Shakti, but in such a rage as might well level all of Ascarle.

A proverb from, of all places, Waterdeep, came unbidden to his mind: "The gods look with pity upon two sorts of people, those who don't get what they want, and those who do."

* * * * *

Sanja's reaction to her daughter's defection was all Liriel could have wished. After a time, however, the woman's ranting ceased to be entertaining and became merely tiresome.

Apparently Ulf shared Liriel's opinion, for he curtly told his apprentice it was past time for them to resume her studies. The drow nodded and followed the grim-faced shaman out toward the forest. Once they'd left the boundaries of the village behind, however, Ulf sent a brief, conspiratorial grin in her direction. Liriel smothered a smile—it seemed the shaman was not so unlike his rowdy kinsman, after all.

But the shaman quickly sobered and got down to business, long before Liriel could sort though the mixed feelings of warmth and pain that remembrances of Hrolf brought her. "Tell me of the magic you have stored in the Windwalker," he demanded.

Liriel explained what she could of the Underdark's strange radiations, comparing it to the place magic the shaman knew and understood. "This magic fades in the light of the sun, but once my rune is cast, the magic will be mine as long as I live and no matter where I go," she concluded.

Ulf considered this. "But why is this so important? You wield other magic: that of spells, and of runes, and even, I think, that given by the gods. When you danced in the moonlight, you found the magic of the place and something else besides. Upon whom did you call? Selûné?"

"I don't know of any goddess by that name," Liriel said

233

uncomfortably, unnerved by the questions about her theology. She did not like discussing Lloth with people outside her race, and she was not sure how the jealous Spider Queen would respond to any mention of Eilistraee. "As to dark-elven magic, it is what makes me what I am. Would you willingly abandon the power that comes from your homeland, to live as a spellcasting wizard in some southern city?"

The shaman nodded to concede the drow's point, then looked at her keenly. "Northmen are not religious people, at least not by the standards of the mainlanders. We call upon some of the gods—Tempus before battle, Umberlee during a storm, and Auril when the cold weather proves a threat—but you won't find us bowing the knee and moaning out prayers. Our dealings with the gods are more honest. We name a bargain. If the god doesn't hold up his end of the deal, we call it off and go our own way."

"But the gods demand worship!" Liriel protested.

Ulf shrugged. "If a man dealt falsely with you, would you continue to do business with him? Why should we hold mortals to higher standards than gods?"

The drow considered these words of blasphemy. Strangely enough, they made a certain amount of sense. It was true that the Spider Queen demanded high payment for any of her favors. She herself had successfully bargained with Lloth, when in exchange for the *Elfmaid*'s escape, she had pledged herself as priestess.

Liriel knew a shining moment of hope—and heresy—as she wondered whether it might be possible for her to be free of this pledge.

But no. The Spider Queen had fulfilled her part of the bargain. Liriel recalled that terrifying moment when the drow goddess had snatched the ship from certain death—and carried it into the Abyss. The *Elfmaid* returned to the mortal world before any but Liriel could know where they had been, but Liriel would never forget the horror and the despair of that place, and the dark seductive power in the evil that ruled it.

"Now rune magic, that's another thing entirely," Ulf continued, breaking into Liriel's troubled thoughts. "Don't try to make a bargain with Yggsdrasil's Child."

"Why not?" the ever-curious girl wanted to know.

"Why bother? What could you possibly promise that would matter to an oak tree?"

The drow stared at the shaman for a long moment before she perceived the glint of laughter in his eyes. "You might *look* like Hrolf," she groused, "but living with Sanja has thoroughly warped

234

your sense of humor!"

"I will not try to deny that," Ulf agreed as he turned to leave. He paused and placed a hand on the girl's shoulder when she moved to follow him. "Stay here for a time. Might be that the answers you need will come to you while you dance. Not that Northmen hold with such, but I've heard tell elves do some of their best thinking that way."

Liriel nodded absently. There was some truth in his words, and she had seen—and experienced—the healing and power and joy that the followers of Eilistraee found in their moonlit dances. But what she needed now was not the power of a drow goddess, but something even more dangerous and frightening.

She needed the love of a human man.

* * * * *

Fyodor's days in Holgerstead passed swiftly, for he'd found much to occupy himself. He spent many hours working alongside the village swordsmiths, sharpening the edges of blades and axes. Despite his youth, he had known bitter warfare for more than five years, and he could scent a coming conflict as surely as young Bjorn could sniff out a storm. To his mind, the strange events of recent weeks could only be a prelude to battle. War was coming to Ruathym, of that Fyodor was certain, and he would do what he could to help his brothers prepare.

And brothers they were, for the berserkers of Holgerstead had welcomed him into their lodge without question or hesitation. To the young warrior, so far from his beloved homeland—indeed, *exiled* from his homeland for the danger that his out-of-control frenzies posed to his comrades—such acceptance was like water to a parched throat. The Ruathen worked side by side with him, lightening their shared tasks with tales of adventure and rowdy songs.

Wedigar, in particular, spent much time with the young Rashemi, telling him many stories of the distant time when shapeshifting berserkers ruled Ruathym and terrorized the seas beyond. Fyodor noted the grim resolve underlying Wedigar's words and knew instinctively that the storytelling was the First Axe's way of reclaiming the heritage that had so recently been turned against him. It seemed to Fyodor that Wedigar was slowly coming to terms with the knowledge of what he had done while under the nereid's charm. As his memories of that time returned to him, Wedigar began to realize he could not have been responsible for all the mischief that had been worked against his people. This knowledge gave the Northman a measure of patience beyond his nature. He seem resigned to waiting—and preparing—for the strike of their unseen foe.

But there was more to Holgerstead than hard toil and grim tales. When the day's work was done, the men joined in games of chance, bracing swims in mountain rivers made fast and icy by melting snows, and friendly contests of strength and skill. At first Fyodor was hesitant to join in these contests for fear of evoking a berserker frenzy. But Wedigar scoffed at that notion, pointing out that fully threescore of berserker warriors might be enough to hold him down and keep him from harming himself or others. Feeling a little sheepish, Fyodor agreed, and to his delight he found that the feeling of safety Wedigar's assurances gave him seemed to hold the killing rages at bay. It was a joy to hold a good sword again, to practice the art of fighting without the heat of the frenzy driving his arm.

Not even the unexpected arrival of Hrolf's first mate managed to dull Fyodor's pleasure in this newfound brotherhood. Ibn had come the morning before, bearing his share of the goods from the *Elfmaid*'s recent trip to sell in the northern stronghold. The red-bearded mate-turned-merchant kept at his work from dawn until long past dusk, so Fyodor did not have occasion to speak with him. Nor did the man seem eager to have words with Fyodor; he averted his eyes whenever the Rashemi was about or busied himself with his accounts. As the day wore on, such reticence from the usually forthright sailor began to worry the young warrior. Once before Ibn had attacked Liriel; Fyodor wondered whether the man had something to hide, and he began to fear for the safety of his drow friend.

And so he fortified himself with a swig of *jhuild*—for some reason, a bit of the Rashemi firewine seemed to strengthen his connection both to his homeland and the faint gift of Sight that was his heritage—and sought out the first mate.

"Is all well in Ruathym village?" he asked bluntly.

Ibn took the pipe from his mouth and met Fyodor's gaze squarely. "The captain is dead."

Fyodor fell back a step. He had seen Hrolf in battle—surely such a fighter would not give in to death lightly!

"That does not seem possible! How did he die?"

"Drowned," the mate gritted out. "No sort of death for a Northman. For that you can thank them damned sea elves and the female who's so all-fired cozy with 'em!"

"Liriel would do nothing to bring harm to Hrolf," the Rashemi said with complete conviction, and then he returned his stunned thoughts to his original purpose. "Is *she* safe and well?" he demanded.

"Sad to say," the sailor responded, and there was such bitterness in his voice that Fyodor did not doubt the truth of his words.

"I thank you for the news," he said and abruptly turned away to seek out the First Axe. Fyodor was free to come and go as he wished, but still he wanted to inform Wedigar of his plans to leave for Ruathym village at once. Fyodor knew Hrolf had been extremely fond of Liriel, and he suspected the drow returned this affection in equal measure. Although the proud and resourceful girl seemed to have little need of him, Fyodor did not like the idea of her being alone at such a time.

He arrived at Wedigar's cottage to find the First Axe's household engulfed in frantic preparations. Dagmar had come to join the household, to acquaint herself with the ways of his family before being taken as second wife. No one—not Wedigar's grim-faced wife or curious young daughters, not Dagmar, not Wedigar himself—seemed pleased by this. Nonetheless, a feast of celebration was the custom and so preparations were underway.

Wedigar listened to Fyodor's plans and then drew the young warrior aside. "Stay in Holgerstead this one night," he asked. "You cannot reach Ruathym before nightfall, and I feel the need to have a friend such as you beside me."

The Rashemi hesitated for only a moment, then promised to stay for the feast. It was a small thing to do for a friend such as the First Axe had become. And in truth, Liriel probably had less need of his presence than did Wedigar.

Fyodor wished this were not so, but it was his custom to know and speak truth, even to himself.

* * * * *

By midnight, Fyodor found himself almost regretting his decision to stay. The feast was long and raucous, and each person present seemed devoted to the goal of consuming enough ale or mead to satisfy an entire dwarven clan. He himself did not drink—he had little taste for either the bitter ale or the heady, sweet mead. Nor had he ever drunk past the point of reason, not even in the days before his battle frenzies raged out of control. It surprised him that the berserkers of Holgerstead saw no need for such restraint. But then, none of them shared his particular curse. Their battle rages were ruled by choice and ritual. They were in no danger of touching off a killing frenzy through some drunken misunderstanding.

Wedigar especially seemed determined to find temporary escape from his troubles. The First Axe had drunk a considerable amount of ale with his meal and then downed two large goblets of golden mead with no pause for talk and little for breath. He was now snoring comfortably, his bearded cheek resting on the remains of the bread trencher that had held his portion of venison stew. Here and there other warriors and women had nodded off, as well, and many more were beginning to yawn broadly.

A warning flashed in Fyodor's mind, and he snatched up Wedigar's empty goblet and sniffed at the dregs. Sure enough, there was the faint, herbal scent of the sleeping potion Hrolf's men had used on the pirates' remote Moonshae base.

It was then he heard the sounds—a faint scrabbling at the walls that surrounded Holgerstead. The village was based in an ancient stronghold built by long-dead dwarves, and despite the passage of centuries it was still a fastness that defied attack from without. Holgerstead was the last fall-back of Ruathym, a place where the people from other parts of the island might come in times of extreme danger. It would never fall, not unless it were delivered into an enemy's hands. And that, it appeared to Fyodor, was exactly what had happened.

He glanced up at the walls. The sentries were already asleep, sprawled on the walkways or draped limply over the ramparts. No doubt they had been served the tainted mead early on. Fyodor did not know who had dealt this treachery, nor did he have time to ponder the mystery.

Shouting an alarm, the young Rashemi took up his sword and smacked Wedigar with the flat of it. To Fyodor's amazement, the First Axe sat up and regarded the young man woozily. The warrior soon grasped the reality of the coming attack and began to give orders to his fighters.

Fyodor was gratified to note that although Wedigar's voice was slurred, his battle tactics seemed sound enough. The berserkers seemed to have unusual resilience. Most of them threw off the effects of their overindulgence—and even the tainted mead—as easily as a dog might shake water from its coat.

Archers raced up the stairs that led to the walkways atop the outer wall. Women gathered up the young and shooed them into the round stone keeps that lay inside the second wall of defense. In the vast courtyard between the two walls, the tables that had been set up for the feast were upended to form an impromptu shield wall.

Fyodor watched in horror as enormous, scaly hands groped at the top edge of the curtain wall. The first wave of archers had no time to nock arrows; the attackers seized the Ruathen and jerked them from their perches. Arms windmilled briefly as the archers tried to keep their balance, but one by one they toppled and dropped from sight. Faint thuds spoke of their fate on the rocky shore below.

In the courtyard, Northmen fitted arrows and let fly at the shadowy invaders that swarmed up onto the walls. But the arrows merely clicked and fell away harmlessly, deflected by the scaly hide that covered the enormous creatures and glinted a sickly green in the flickering torchlight.

"Sweet Umberlee! What are those things?" demanded Wedigar, his bearded face twisted with consternation.

"Merrow," Fyodor replied grimly. "Sea ogres. I have fought them before."

The First Axe nodded toward the Northmen warriors. "Tell them how."

Without pause the Rashemi turned to the assembled fighters. "Merrow attack in a quick, swarming charge, then fight hand to hand. All of you who have pikes and spears, get behind the tables now! Send a few arrows toward the merrow from behind the shield wall, but otherwise keep yourselves and your weapons out of sight until my signal. All others, take a place behind me."

The Northmen fell into position. Fyodor stood behind the tables so he might see the coming attack. Behind him he heard the chanting that brought on the Ruathens' berserker rages. He himself stared intently at the creatures who descended the stairs toward the courtyard, their webbed feet slapping the ancient stone. When his frenzy came upon him, he wanted to be certain he spent it on the invaders.

Most of the merrow merely batted aside the first storm of arrows. Four or five of them fell, pawing at the shafts that protruded from the soft tissue at the base of a throat, or in an eye—but not enough of them, apparently, to convince the surviving creatures that the fighters behind the shield wall posed much of a threat. One of the sea ogres, a ten-foot creature with three black horns protruding from its forehead, shouted a guttural command. The merrow darted into formation. Leveling their spears and tridents at the swordsmen, they charged.

"They will jump the barrier," Fyodor cautioned the Northmen, speaking fast to time his words with the swift approach of the sea ogres. "Fall back three paces, set your weapons high, brace them well—*now!*"

The hidden warriors snapped up and into position, their pikes and spears angled up for the attack—just as the merrow leaped. The creatures had their eyes upon the swordsmen and axe-wielders beyond, and those few who perceived the new threat could not change their momentum. The ogres fell heavily onto the waiting pikes. The Northmen held on grimly, many of them going down beneath the weight of the impaled sea ogres. Some of the spears broke upon impact, not all found their mark—but the first charge was definitely halted.

Roaring out to Tempus, the rest of the Northmen warriors charged. Axes glinted wickedly in the torchlight as the men felled sea ogres like doomed timber. Here and there in the courtyard some of the merrow faced off in duels against individual swordsmen, but the creatures' speed and strength were overmatched by the berserker frenzy of Holgerstead's fighters.

As Fyodor parried the stabbing attack of a merrow's spear, he felt the familiar heat of the berserker frenzy sweep through him. Suddenly he faced the much taller sea ogre at eye level. The creature's almost comical look of surprise washed slowly over its face; then it rallied and swept the spear up and around in a leisurely arch. An illusion, of course. Always did Fyodor's battle frenzy speed his movements to the point where the world around him seemed to move at a crawl.

The young berserker's hand snapped out and caught the wooden shaft of the merrow's weapon. He stepped aside as he yanked down hard, bringing up his knee in the same instant. The shaft splintered like seasoned kindling. Fyodor still held one end of the shattered weapon. He drove the thing deep into the merrow's gut with such force that his fist followed the shaft, sinking deep into the merrow's body. He released the weapon and plunged his hand farther upward, seeking another hard object: one of the ogre's ribs. His fingers closed on it.

Fyodor used the momentum of the creature's fall to help him tear the rib free. He spun, ducked under the swinging blade of another merrow's hauberk, and then thrust up, burying the macabre weapon deep into the ogre's eye. He tugged at the curved rib, wrenching it down and around as if he were cranking a windlass, in the process thoroughly—and literally—scrambling the merrow's brain. Gray tissue oozed from the creature's nostrils as it plunged face first onto the blood-soaked ground.

With the first threat past, the young berserker looked around for more enemies. The merrow were thickest around Wedigar—in some dim corner of his mind, Fyodor reasoned that the creatures must have been instructed to do away with Holgerstead's leader. He waded in, his black sword slashing a path toward the First Axe.

Wedigar was bleeding from a dozen wounds, some of them deep, and he was weaving on his feet. Yet he fought on, his battle-axe flashing as he fended off the much larger creatures. Fyodor noted that the man did not fight in frenzy. Perhaps the merrow had come upon him too quickly; perhaps his mead-poisoned mind could not summon the needed focus. Whatever the case, Fyodor fell in at Wedigar's back and fought back the merrow that pressed upon his commander and friend.

Screams of warning came from the keep; several Northwomen leaned from the high windows and gestured frantically toward the outer walls. Some of them took up small bows and began to rain arrows into the far reaches of the courtyard.

Fyodor darted a glance over his shoulder. Swarms of hideous, fishlike men were creeping toward the fighters in eerily precise, V-shaped formations. Two of these groups flanked him and began to close in on the beleaguered First Axe and his young protector. Fyodor sensed the solid form at his back falter, then go down on one knee.

Wedigar, the First Axe of Holgerstead, had fallen at last.

A second change swept through Fyodor, something far beyond the fire and ice of his battle frenzy. It was as if a strong wind blew through him, sweeping him toward insentience. The black sword dropped from his hand, and he whirled, lashing out at the two merrow who stood triumphantly over Wedigar, their spears poised for killing thrusts. Enormous claws ripped across the throats of both merrow, and the lifeblood of the creatures washed, like a crimson fountain, over the fallen First Axe.

Fyodor shouted a warning to the others as he pointed toward the new enemy. He was not at all surprised to hear the roar of an enraged bear coming from his throat, or to perceive his gesturing hand as an enormous, black-furred paw. He merely dropped down onto all fours and charged the oncoming fish-men.

The creatures let out clattering shrieks and scattered at once, fleeing from the seemingly rabid black bear that raged toward them. But the Rashemi warrior was faster still, falling upon the fishmen with rending claws and slashing fangs.

A wild shout went up behind him as the Northmen rallied. The uncanny frenzy that claimed Fyodor seemed to touch them as well, speeding their movements and bringing them onward in a valiant rush. For many moments the courtyard was a blur of flailing swords and axes as the Northmen cut down the invaders with relentless glee.

Meanwhile, behind the line of battle, Wedigar stirred, groaned, and wiped the merrow's blood from his eyes. The sight in the courtyard beyond both thrilled and worried him. A new shapeshifter had come to Ruathym; his people would overcome the enemy—although with little credit to him. But the fighter put aside personal pride at once, for as he studied the young Rashemi's unnatural rage, he realized this was no usual *hamfariggen* warrior. Wedigar was not at all certain the battle would stop when the sea creatures had been overcome.

The First Axe dragged himself to his feet and staggered to the thick wooden gate in the outer wall. For several long moments he strained at the bolt; it gave way with a shriek of metal. He tugged until the heavy door swung inward.

The surviving merrow and their sahuagin allies fled at once toward the offered escape. Still in bear form, Fyodor pursued, galloping after them and roaring in inhuman rage. Behind him roiled the Northmen berserkers, intent upon driving their enemies back into the sea.

Wedigar's wife, Alfhilda, came running to him from the keep, her eyes frantic and her skirts flying. Her keen eyes swept over him, noting his sluggish movements and the shivering he could not control. She had been a warrior's daughter before she was a warrior's wife, and she knew well the signs of the numbing illness that came after battle wounds. She shrugged off her cape and wrapped it around her husband's shoulders.

"It is done; it is enough," Alfhilda pleaded. "Come and let me tend your hurts."

"My sword," he grated out.

The woman hesitated only a moment; then she hastened back to fetch the fallen weapon. Wedigar sheathed it, then put one arm around Alfhilda's shoulders, accepting her offered strength. "I must get down to the water's edge," he said, grimacing as a new wave of pain struck him.

Alfhilda had heard the story of the Rashemi's curse, and she followed her husband's reasoning at once. The frenzies of Holgerstead's warriors would cease when the enemy disappeared; Wedigar intended to ensure that Fyodor stopped fighting as well.

Alfhilda's eyes were bright with a pain deeper than Wedigar's as she helped her husband toward the coming battle, and perhaps toward death. Although she was justly proud of her husband's battle prowess, she had seen the young Rashemi fight, and fear chilled her to her soul. But Wedigar had his duty, and she had hers. She would accept her husband's choice and give him what aid she could.

By the time the struggling pair reached the shore, the last of the sahuagin were splashing frantically into the waves. The Ruathen berserkers ceased at once, some of them drooping with exhaustion, others chanting out victory songs. Only Fyodor was not appeased by the disappearance of the sea folk. Still in bear form and snarling with battle lust, he prowled back and forth along the shoreline.

"All of you, back to the fortress!" Wedigar commanded. The men eyed the raging shapeshifter and hesitated, made uncertain by their love and loyalty to their First Axe.

But the Northwoman seized the axe from her husband's belt and brandished it. "Obey the First Axe, or die by a woman's hand," she shouted at them, her eyes blazing.

The men nodded and fell back, shamed into compliance by Alfhilda's devotion and fortitude. Without a backward glance, she followed them into the fortress and threw her weight into helping to close the massive door that would bar her husband from the safety of the fortress.

Wedigar waited, his sword still in his scabbard, until the Rashemi in bear form at last turned away from the sea. The bear's eyes, a bright and incongruous blue in his dark-furred face, burned with killing rage as they settled upon the wounded warrior.

For a long time they stood so. Then a shudder ran through the massive form of the bear, and the fur began to recede, disappearing into the pale-skinned body of a man. In moments Fyodor of Rashemen stood before Holgerstead's First Axe, naked and white with exhaustion, but otherwise unhurt.

He looked at Wedigar with puzzlement, taking in the man's many wounds, the hand poised on the hilt of his sword. Then understanding came, and he nodded slowly.

"You came here to kill me," he whispered.

"Yes."

The young berserker drew in a long, shuddering breath. "For

this, I thank you," he said simply.

Wedigar responded with a grim smile and shrugged off Alfhilda's cloak. He handed it to the young warrior. As Fyodor wrapped it around himself, the First Axe swayed. "I am glad it was not needed," he said in a fading voice. "You are now a true *hamfarrigen*, my friend, and trusted in this as in all other things."

Fyodor caught Wedigar as he fell and slung the unconscious man over his shoulder. Slowly, painfully, he climbed the steep and rocky path that led back to the fortress village.

The door swung open to admit them. Several men rushed forward to take Wedigar from Fyodor's hands, and they carried him into the keep to be tended by the village shaman. Following Alfhilda's calm direction, the other villagers fell to work tending the wounded, building a funeral pyre for the dead, dragging the dead and wounded sea creatures down to the shore to be fed to the sharks—no honorable fire for them.

Garbed in shirt, breeches, and boots donated by some of his berserker brethren, Fyodor worked steadily beside them. His thoughts, however, were with his wounded friend. When Alfhilda came again into the courtyard to bring a report, Fyodor listened as avidly as any Holgersteader to her words.

"The shaman says Wedigar will live. His wounds, however, are many and grievous, and he will not fight for many days. He asks, therefore, that you accept Fyodor of Rashemen as First Axe in his stead, to lead you in battle until such time as he can resume his post. And there is more," she said, lifting a hand to still the rising murmur of astonishment. "Wedigar names Fyodor as the heir to Holgerstead, according to the law and custom of this village, until the day the girl Dagmar bears him a shape-strong warrior son. I accept the customs of this land and the duties given my husband and lord," she concluded softly. "Can you, his sworn men, do otherwise?"

Her face was regal; her eyes defied them to pity her. The men fell silent before the force of Alfhilda's words and the depth of the proud woman's devotion. Then, as one, they drew their weapons and laid them at Fyodor's feet. In solemn unison, they echoed the pledge spoken by the stalwart Northwoman.

"To the First Axe of Holgerstead, all blades be pledged. In peace and in battle, we will follow."

Fyodor stood, silent and stunned, as his berserker brethren pledged fealty. He could not repudiate the charge that Wedigar had laid upon him, but neither could he bear this burden for long.

Although he had not turned on his comrades in his latest and most terrible battle frenzy, the sheer power of it horrified him. He had listened to Wedigar's stories of the shapeshifting warriors, but it had never occurred to him that he himself might take on animal form. It was bad enough that he fought without consent of his will. This utter and complete loss of self was more than he could abide.

The Rashemi knew he would have to travel to Ruathym village the next day and tell Liriel all that had transpired. Unless the drow wizard could cast the rune successfully and soon, Fyodor felt he would have no choice but to seek out Wedigar and beg him to finish the task he was prepared to do at the water's edge. The young berserker could not take his own life; this was strictly forbidden a warrior of Rashemen. Death was a gift that could come only at the hand of a trusted friend, or, perhaps, a swift and treacherous foe.

When the night's grim work at last was done, Fyodor went to the room given him in the warriors' lodge. He stripped off his borrowed clothing and fell gratefully into bed, too tired to care that the faces of slain multitudes would haunt his dreams.

A soft tap at the window roused him from slumber. Despite his exhaustion, Fyodor responded with a warrior's reflexes. He was on his feet at once, his cudgel in hand. He hauled it high overhead as the shutter swung inward.

A pale head poked into the room, and light blue eyes grew wide as they fixed upon the ready weapon in his hands. Fyodor recognized the shaman's daughter, and as he lowered his cudgel, he heaved a sigh of mingled relief and exasperation.

Dagmar crawled in through the low window and sank at once into a deep curtsy. "You saved my new home, Fyodor of Holgerstead, and no doubt my life as well. For this I thank you."

"I accept your thanks," he murmured with a wry smile, "but could they not have waited until morning?"

The woman rose swiftly to full height and met his eyes. "Not as I would wish to express them," she said frankly.

Her meaning was unmistakable. Fyodor fell back a step, and suddenly he remembered he was unclad. He reached for Wedigar's cloak and wrapped it around him.

"The mantle of First Axe suits you well," she said, "but it is not needed just now." With these words she parted the folds of the cloak and laid both palms upon the young man's chest.

Fyodor caught her wrists and put her hands gently away. "You are Wedigar's pledged bride," he said softly.

"And you are his pledged heir. It is expected."

Fyodor dug a hand into his hair and stared helplessly at the girl. He had not imagined anything like this might come with the role he'd accepted! And yet, it seemed to him that the Northwoman's words held little truth. He lifted one eyebrow and fixed a skeptical gaze upon her.

The young woman sighed and then shrugged. "Very well, perhaps it is not the expected custom. But there must be an heir to Holgerstead—a *hamfariggen* warrior who can lead the berserkers in battle. The oracles say I can bear such a son. If you give me a child, I could leave this household and go back to my village with honor. It would be a gift," she said softly, her pale eyes pleading. "To Holgerstead, to all of Ruathym. To me. Even to Wedigar," she concluded with a touch of bitterness.

Fyodor knew a surge of pity for the young woman, for Wedigar was not a man for pretense, and it was clear to all that the First Axe was not happy about the need to take a second wife. And having witnessed Alfhilda's courage and loyalty, Fyodor did not wonder that Wedigar had eyes for no other woman. Not even one as undeniably beautiful as Dagmar.

As if sensing the path Fyodor's thoughts had taken, the young woman stepped away from him and began to tug at the laces that fastened her overtunic. She stripped off gown and blouse quickly, then raked her hands through her braids until her hair fell into long golden waves. The faint light of a crescent moon filtered in through the window, glimmering on her pale hair and white skin. She went to his bed and lay down upon it.

"A gift," she repeated softly.

For a moment the young man was honestly tempted. But an emotion stronger than sympathy, deeper than desire, ruled Fyodor's heart. He reached for his discarded clothing. Dagmar watched with despairing eyes as he dressed and gathered up his belongings.

"But why?" she demanded. "Why do you leave? Are you not like other men, that you do not take pleasures freely offered? Or am I displeasing to you—is that it?"

"You are most beautiful; no one who is truly a man could deny that. But I cannot betray a friend," he responded as he walked to the door.

"But you would not! Wedigar would surely thank you!"

Fyodor paused in the doorway and turned back to face the Northwoman. "I was speaking not of Wedigar, but of Liriel."

Chapter 19

THE PRICE OF POWER

t was nearly dawn when Fyodor caught sight of the roofs of Ruathym village. A rustle in the bushes along the path caught his attention and, before he could draw a weapon, Liriel sprang out onto the path, her dark face joyful. She ran to meet him and threw herself into his arms.

Fyodor was accustomed to such gestures from the impulsive drow. She always drew away quickly, like lighting that flares and retreats. But this time she seemed to be in no hurry to part. Her arms were flung tightly about his neck, and her breath felt warm through the linen of his shirt.

Although he was loath to end the embrace, Fyodor buried his hands in the drow's wild, snow-colored hair and tilted her face up so he could meet her eyes. "There are things I must tell you," he said somberly.

Liriel responded with a smile that warmed his blood and sent it singing urgently through his veins.

"There are those who think, and those who dream," she mocked him softly, "and then there are those who talk too damn much!"

Fyodor's answering smile was slow and incredulous. "It seems we have even more to talk about than I imagined."

"Words can wait," she murmured, and the young man found himself in complete agreement.

Impulsively he swept the dark-elven girl into his arms and carried her off into the forest. To his surprise Liriel did not object. Indeed, she guided his path with whispered directions and sped his step with promises that would have seemed improbable had he not witnessed some of the other wonders of which she was capable. And in the moments when she did not speak, her lips and teeth found keenly sensitive places on his neck and throat and ears that he had not known he possessed. Sometimes gently, sometimes not, she teased him to near madness. Fyodor did not know how far they traveled—a few steps would have seemed as endlessly long to him as a league—but at last Liriel wriggled free of his grasp.

They came to each other at the foot of an ancient oak. For once Fyodor did not think of the vast differences between them or of the unresolved emotions that had haunted him since their last, ill-fated encounter. He cared only that this time there was no fear in Liriel's golden eyes. Their union was like nothing he had ever known or imagined—a fierce and joyful thing that in its own way rivaled the abandon of his berserker rage. But *this* he chose, and with all of his heart.

Much later, Fyodor stroked Liriel's damp curls and watched her as she slept. He himself had no desire to sleep. Never had he felt so alive. For the first time, he allowed himself to admit that he loved this little elf woman, and he even dared to hope she might return his love.

There was also something about this place that quickened Fyodor's fey senses. He knew nothing of wizardly spells and did not pretend to understand the magic that Rashemen's Witches wielded with such fearful authority, but he could feel the natural magic that lingered in certain glades and springs. Never, not even in the Witches' spelltower that overlooked the enchanted Lake Ashane, had he felt such power in a place. His eyes lifted to the soaring branches of the oak tree overhead, and suddenly he understood why Liriel had chosen to bring him to this place.

"Little raven," he said softly. The sleeping drow's eyes flashed open, and she regarded him alertly. "This is Yggsdrasil's Child, is it not?"

She sat up and regarded him with a brilliant smile. "You can feel it, then. That is a good sign."

Fyodor reached out and took her hands. "This I must know: what happened, to make such a change in you?"

The drow did not need to ask what he meant. "I tried to cast the rune and could not. Until then I'd thought of myself as the keeper of your quest and mine. That lesson was hard enough to learn," she added wryly.

Fyodor nodded, recalling how difficult it had been for the drow to expand her dream to include his. "And now?"

"I realized we must be as one if either quest is to succeed. The rune is not mine only. There are things I need of you," she admitted.

"Whatever you need, the same is yours," he promised softly. "And now that you know this, you are ready to cast the rune?"

Liriel did not miss the note of concern in Fyodor's voice. Something had happened to add urgency to their quest. "Tell me," she demanded.

And so he did, leaving out nothing. The drow listened thoughtfully, her dismay mounting as he described the new turn his curse had taken. She had fought Wedigar in the form of a giant hawk; she did not want to know what sort of destruction a shapeshifting Fyodor could leave behind.

"I will cast the rune," she said with more conviction than she felt. She cast a glance up at the sky; already the sunset colors stained the west. "But I will need time to prepare. If the lore books speak true, a trance will come upon me, and I will carve the rune upon the tree unknowing. Will you stand guard?"

"As long as you need," he agreed.

The drow nodded and began the concentration needed for the casting. She sought the power of the ancient oak, the symbolic embodiment of all life, and sank into it. As she went deeper, the days and nights of her rune quest came back to her in vivid detail, each event and sorrow and joy giving shape to the rune she must use. But try as she might, she could not envision the rune in its entirety.

After a time—perhaps a short time, perhaps not—the drow abandoned this attempt. She did not try to shape the rune, but focused instead on the powers she wished to reclaim, and the need to exorcise the errant magic that kept Fyodor from being the warrior he was meant to be. She chanted her goals silently, and the chant grew in intensity as something dark and compelling slipped into her silent voice. The magic of Rashemen, the magic of the drow. Fearful things both, they combined in a way that Liriel did not understand, sweeping her away into a trance that went beyond mere meditation, beyond spellcasting.

No longer ordering her own movements, Liriel watched as if from a high place—as if from all places—as her physical being took the Windwalker amulet from its chain and placed the tiny chisel against the tree. Her hands moved swiftly, surely, but she did not know what marks she made. All she knew for certain was that the faint blue light emanating from her amulet's sheath—the captured magic of the Underdark—faded steadily as she worked. Her conscious thoughts ebbed slowly away, too; this she expected, for in her mind she and her dark-elven magic were inseparable parts of one whole. At last the blue light flickered and died. The empty amulet dropped from Liriel's nerveless hands, and the drow followed it into the darkness.

Elaine Cunningham

*   *   *   *   *

When Liriel awoke, the fat crescent moon was high in the sky, bathing the forest with its silver light. She stirred, winced, and pressed her fingers to her throbbing temples. Within her head raged the violent cacophony of spell-sickness. Long moments passed before the confused girl realized that some of the noise—perhaps most of it—came from without.

The drow lowered her hands from her head and gazed with horror at the scene before her. In the grip of a horrendous battle frenzy, Fyodor fought against opponents that he alone could see. The Rashemi had not gone unscathed, though: his clothes and skin had been torn repeatedly by branches and brambles as he raged through the woods, lunging and slashing again and again.

How long this had gone on Liriel could not know, but her keen eyes caught the bubble of pink-tinged froth that collected in the corner of his faint, unnerving smile. She knew only that she had failed and that Fyodor would die if she could not find a way to stop him.

Instinctively she flung out a hand. To her surprise and relief, drow magic flowed from her fingertips and sent thick streams of spider silk hurtling into the young man's wild path. The sticky strands exploded outward, forming a giant web that stretched from the trunk of Yggsdrasil's Child to a sister oak some twenty feet away.

The amok warrior tore through the web without missing a step.

Now that she knew her Underdark magic was still with her, Liriel reached for a more potent tool. Up came her tiny crossbow. She fired a dart into Fyodor's thigh. He ignored it and parried some nonexistent sword thrust. Again she fired, and again, until her quiver at last was empty. The young warrior bristled with darts and resembled nothing so much as a tall and angry hedgehog.

Yet Fyodor did not fall. He continued to fight shadows—or more likely, Liriel realized with sudden bright certainty, he continued to do battle with all the ghosts who haunted his dreams. And the phantom warriors would kill him, as surely as he had killed them.

Shaking with frustration and fear, the drow leaped into Fyodor's wild path and shrieked at him to stop. To her astonishment, he did just that. The frenzy fell from him like a cloak, and the heavy black sword dropped to the ground as his magically enhanced form shrank abruptly down to its natural size. Fyodor swayed and fell at last into an exhausted—and poisoned—slumber.

Liriel fell to her knees beside him and began to tear out the

darts. He'd already taken enough drow sleeping poison to kill a bug-
bear; she only hoped the berserker rage had absorbed much of it.
To her relief, he continued to breathe—shallow, but steady.

She watched over her friend throughout the remainder of the
night and long into the next day, dosing him repeatedly with antidote until her precious flask was empty. The forest was heavy with
twilight shadows when Fyodor finally awoke.

Nearly giddy with joy and relief, Liriel spilled out the story of
what had happened—to her, and to him, and how he had stopped
only after she'd given up rational hope.

"But I've no idea what any of it means," she concluded.

"I do," Fyodor said softly. "Such things have been done before,
but not in my lifetime or yours."

Liriel waited for him to continue, but his eyes were distant, fixed
upon the old tales and legends that were so much a part of him.

"In ancient times," he began, "there were warriors who gave
pledged service as berserker knights, becoming personal champion
to a powerful *wychlaran*. When this magic was granted, it was taken
as a sign that the Witch was destined for a great task. You did not
fail, little raven," he said earnestly. "The control of my battle frenzies
has indeed been gained—but it is in your hands."

Liriel gazed at him in utter horror. "But I don't want it! I never
wanted that!"

"You sought power," he reminded her. "Now that it is yours, you
may not always be able to choose how and when to wield it. I think,"
he concluded thoughtfully, "that this is ever the way of power."

The drow brushed aside these philosophical musings. "But
where is my choice in all of this?"

"Where was Wedigar's?" Fyodor countered. "Remember how he
was after you freed him from the nereid's charm? He wished to
atone for his acts at once, but when convinced this would not best
serve his people, Wedigar gave up his warrior-bred sense of honor
for the greater good. You, too, seem to be destined to lead," he told
her. "You will have to learn to consider things beyond your own
desires."

Liriel was in no mood for all this talk of nobility and service. All
she'd wanted was her innate drow powers back. She did not seek to
rule, or to lead, or to do any of these troublesome things, and she
did not see why such might be required of her. Nothing in her training had prepared her for this, and she said so.

"Do you wish to leave Ruathym?" he asked her. "Do you wish to

251

be free of me and this burden you did not seek?"

As she considered this, Liriel discovered she did not. "It seems we have both found a place here, and together. When I tried to cast the rune that first time, I got the feeling we have some sort of entwined destiny." She shrugged. "Don't ask me to explain that."

"There is no need," Fyodor responded. "I have sensed that myself, almost from the beginning. Whatever your fate, I accept it, and my part in it."

He spoke these words with an awe that exasperated the drow. She had struggled so hard to accept Fyodor first as a friend, and now as a lover. After all she had endured, she did not want to lose him to her own success!

"Let's get back to the village," she said abruptly.

"At first light," he agreed.

Liriel's heart quickened, but it rapidly became clear Fyodor was concerned only with ensuring them a safe journey. The brief, shining oneness they had shared was gone. She had never thought respect could be a barrier, but she felt the force of Fyodor's new regard for her forcing distance between them. To him, she was no longer just Liriel, but *wychlaran*. Not a female to be cherished, but a power to be revered.

In utter frustration, she turned away. She curled up into a tight ball and wrapped herself in her *piwafwi*, taking little comfort in the renewed sheen of the magical drow cloak. At least, she thought as she drifted toward slumber, Fyodor would no longer be tormented by his dreams. Those ghosts had been exorcised by the power of the rune she'd cast for them both.

But that small freedom seemed pale indeed, when the drow contemplated the servitude to which she had unwittingly condemned her friend. She did not know why this did not bother the freedom-loving Rashemi more than it did. She strongly suspected, however, that a time would come when it would.

Chapter 20

THE COMING STORM

ews of the battle of Holgerstead reached Ascarle with uncanny swiftness, carried as it was by a relay of merrow that moved with brief bursts of incredible speed. One of these merrow—who had drawn the short bone when it and its fellows had cast lots for the task—now stood in the marble council chamber of Ascarle handing over the grim details to the illithid who ruled as Regent and to the black-bearded man who prowled the room like a caged bear.

Vestress received the news with mixed feelings. Some of the berserker warriors had died in battle, which promised to ease the task of conquest, but this gain was overshadowed by the troubling appearance of a new berserker shapeshifter. The illithid took from Rethnor's thoughts the realization that this could mean serious trouble to the invading forces. She also knew the Luskan captain recognized the shapeshifter from the merrow's description, and that he was glad the man had survived. Rethnor wished to use the young warrior as bait to lure the drow wizard into his hands, after which he planned to take his personal vengeance upon the berserker who had taken his hand.

That is unwise, Vestress said coolly, projecting her mental voice into Rethnor's mind. *We see no reason to lower our chances of success by allowing such a fighter to live until the final battle.*

Rethnor glared with ill-concealed wrath at the illithid. The man had yet to reconcile himself with the fact that Vestress could read his thoughts as easily as if they had been inscribed upon parchment. Vestress knew he was growing increasingly restive in Ascarle and the islands above, for the ambitious man would never be content in a place where he himself did not rule. Yet the illithid had a purpose in keeping him in her stronghold—beyond the amusement that the sparring of human and drow brought her. Let the man's frustration build; then let him vent his rage in conquest. This suited Vestress well.

"Bring me Ygraine," Rethnor demanded, snapping out the order with a force that suggested that he must give one or burst. Vestress understood and let it pass.

The illithid also realized at once what Rethnor intended to do, and she approved his plan. So she sent out a mental summons to the slave the man had requested and seated herself on her crystal throne.

After a few moments a tall, pale-haired woman walked into the room, her movements wooden and her blue eyes vacant. When she drew near the crystal throne, Vestress reached out and entwined a lock of the slave's white-gold hair around her purple fingers. It was an odd color, very distinctive—a pale shade of blond that few humans kept past childhood. Rethnor's spy would recognize it and respond to the implied threat.

The illithid tore the hank of hair from the woman's scalp; the enslaved human did not so much as blink. Vestress knotted the lock at each end and handed it to the waiting merrow.

Send this to Ruathym. Give it to Rethnor's spy and demand that the new berserker be slain at once.

The sea ogre bowed low, then hastened to the pool of water at the far end of the illithid's council chamber. The creature splashed in and began the long swim through the tunnel that led out into the open sea beyond Ascarle's walls.

There remains only the matter of the drow wizard, Vestress continued, turning her attention to the restless human. *Unlike you and the drow priestess, we have little faith that Liriel Baenre will respond to the death of her lover. We have, however, found another way of luring her to us. We tell you this,* the illithid informed Rethnor pointedly, *so you will abandon any notion of using her to enact your personal vengeance upon Shakti. The priestess is admittedly of little use to you, but we have plans for her and do not wish her destroyed.*

"As you wish," Rethnor gritted out. The High Captain of Luskan was becoming more than a little tired of taking orders from squid-women and black-elf females, and for once he did not care if Vestress took that information from his thoughts. But he could hardly refuse the illithid, at least not so long as he remained in her stronghold.

You know of my nereids, Vestress continued coolly. If the illithid knew of Rethnor's mutinous thoughts, she did not seem concerned. *One of them crawled back to Ascarle in a sorry state. She brought us some interesting news.*

The illithid glided over to a fountain and leaned over the water. From it emerged a water nymph. It seemed to Rethnor that the creature was hardly beautiful enough to explain her lethal success in charming men. This one was wan and bedraggled, with a woeful face and empty eyes.

Her soul-shawl was taken, stolen through strength and cunning. The shawl holds the essence of the nereid, and she must now obey the person who enslaved her through this theft. Tell the man who did this thing.

"An elf maid, a drow!" wailed the wretched creature. "Let me go to her, I beg you, that I might plead for my shawl's return."

You see? Vestress asked Rethnor. *It is time to test the extent of Liriel Baenre's wizardly skill. A truly powerful wizard could compel a nereid to take her anywhere, even to the elemental plane where the water creatures make their homes. You, however, will bring her here,* the illithid commanded the nymph.

"I cannot, unless she commands it of me! She knows nothing of this place."

Then tell her enough to whet her interest. Go now, bring your mistress to me, and I will see that you get back your shawl!

The nymph turned and splashed eagerly into the water.

"I will leave you, as well," Rethnor said. "My ship is docked at Trisk; we sail for Ruathym at once. There is little time if we are to attack at moondark."

The sea battle is yours to command, conceded the illithid. *Attack at the arranged time, and the armies of Ascarle will await the Luskan forces on the island.*

They would await them, the illithid amended silently, if the drow wizard proved equal to the task before her.

As soon as Rethnor left the room, Vestress leaned over the pool of water that linked her to Ascarle's watery portal. Deep beneath the surface lurked the skeletal face of her ancient adversary, eyes blazing crimson and mouth stretched open in the horrid, keening cry of a banshee.

* * * * *

Liriel was amazed at the speed with which news swept the island. When she and Fyodor returned to Ruathym village the next morning, they found that a ceremony—and the usual feast—awaited them. As the new First Axe of Holgerstead, Fyodor was required to pledge fealty to Aumark Lithyl, First Axe of all Ruathym.

From all over the island people came to give honor to the new battle chieftain and to gaze with curiosity upon the foreign-born berserker who could wield the shapeshifting magic of their ancestors. Many of Holgerstead's berserkers came for the ceremony, along with some of their womenfolk. Liriel was not surprised to see Dagmar among them. The young Northwoman seemed pleased to have an excuse to return to her father's household and, judging from the way Dagmar's blue eyes followed Fyodor's every move, Liriel suspected the woman intended to pursue her chosen plan to remain there.

After the ceremony, Fyodor presented each of his sworn berserker warriors to Liriel in turn, as if she were a ruling matron. What was meant to honor the drow, however, merely filled her with exasperation. His mien was taken directly from the ancient tales he loved to tell: that of a berserker knight pledged to some great lady. Liriel found herself wishing for a way to peel them both off that particular dusty tapestry and return them to the foot of Yggsdrasil's Child.

Liriel noticed, also, that after the initial awkwardness of their greeting, Fyodor seemed glad of Dagmar's presence. And why should he not? mused the drow with a touch of bitterness. Dagmar was a woman, no more, and therefore a welcome respite from the task of keeping a *wychlaran* atop her pedestal.

To the restive drow, the ceremony and the festivities that followed seemed interminable. The feasting lasted for much of the day, accompanied by long songs that told of Northmen valor and conquest. When the afternoon shadows grew long, the Ruathen were far more drunk on memories of ancient glory than they were on the ale and mead. The lesson of Holgerstead had apparently gone home. It amazed Liriel, however, that no one seemed to give much credence to Fyodor's suggestion that the mead drunk at Holgerstead might have been tainted. The possibility that one of their own might turn traitor lay too far off the paths their thoughts were accustomed to treading.

Liriel, of course, thought otherwise and had since the moment Fyodor mentioned that news of Hrolf's death had come to him from Ibn. She had ample reason to know of the first mate's treachery, and she could think of no other reason why Ibn would leave Ruathym village on the day of Hrolf's funeral. Ibn had returned to Ruathym with the people from Holgerstead, and she could feel the heat of his glare through the crowd-filled expanse that separated them. Yet she could think of no one among the increasingly proud and rowdy Northmen who might listen to a word spoken against a warrior of Ruathym.

*   *   *   *   *

It was unlikely that Caladorn, a young nobleman of Waterdeep and one of the secret Lords who ruled that city, could have chosen a worse time to come to Ruathym. He and his two surviving ship-mates came upon the island at a moment when the old tales had lifted the ancestral pride of the people to a fever pitch. The appearance of strangers in the cove was enough to send Northmen into defensive battle with such force and fury that it brought to mind an explosion in an alchemist's workshop. In moments the tiny vessel was surrounded by Ruathen fighting ships, and the prisoners hauled ashore.

Caladorn seldom used his family name. However, the Cassalanter merchant clan was well known in the Northlands, and he used its power to demand an audience with the First Axe.

Aumark Lithyl allowed the young nobleman to tell his story, and the entire crowd swept back to the village center to listen to the man's tale. When at last Caladorn paused for breath, the First Axe turned to the assemblage.

"Of those who sailed on the *Elfmaid's* last voyage, is there anyone who recognizes these men?"

The surviving members of Hrolf's crew stepped forward to study the three mainlanders, but none could place them with certainty. There was little in these thin and bedraggled survivors that recalled the *Cutter's* stalwart seal hunters. But Liriel recognized one of the men by his proud bearing and dark red hair.

"I know that one," she proclaimed, pointing to Caladorn. "He fought Hrolf and nearly matched him—a sight I would not soon forget!"

Aumark turned wintry eyes upon the drow. "This is a council of warriors. Is there one here who can vouch for her words? Fyodor?"

The Rashemi shook his head, regretfully turning away from Liriel's incredulous glare. "I was in the midst of the battle rage; I remember little."

"I will speak for the Raven!"

The crowd parted to allow the speaker to push through to the center. A tall warrior, clad in a scarlet tunic embossed with runes, came to stand beside the drow. Liriel recognized him as the villager she'd saved from the sahuagin's net.

"I am Glammad, First Axe of Hastor. This *dock-alfar* warned our village of a sahuagin attack and fought bravely beside us. To all of Hastor, the Raven is a warrior worthy of honor. Accept her words as you would mine!"

Aumark looked puzzled. "You are known to us all, Glammad, and your honor is beyond question. But you were not on the *Elf-maid* during this battle. Nor does your faith in this elf woman remove all suspicion from these mainlanders. They claim to have been rescued twice by sea elves. Are they in league with those who have done us so much mischief?"

"Look elsewhere for the cause of your troubles," advised Caladorn. "Does it not seem strange to you that the dead sea elves were placed in Ruathen barrels?"

"Your reasoning is unsound," Aumark pointed out. "If the elves believe that men of Ruathym killed their kindred, they would certainly seek revenge."

Murmurs of agreement rippled through the crowd, but Caladorn stood firm. "The dead elves were left in our path for us to find, and the stamp of Ruathym left plainly upon the deed."

"You are accusing us?" Aumark asked with deceptive calm.

"I am warning you," the nobleman replied. "Word of this matter is certain to bring trouble to your shores."

"If Waterdeep attacks, we will be ready," Aumark said stoutly, and the assembled warriors responded with a roar of approval.

Caladorn shook his head. "You mistake my meaning. My family's business concerns are far-reaching. If Waterdeep had plans to attack Ruathym, I would surely have heard of them."

"So you say," broke in a new voice. A burly man with a wild mop of curly, sun-streaked brown hair broke from the crowd and walked with the rolling gait of one not long off a ship's deck toward the young Waterdhavian.

"Wulhof of Ruathym," he said shortly. "My ship put in to home port this morn, after a trip to Caer Callidyrr. Word on the island of Alaron is that a fleet of Waterdhavian ships is headed to the northern Moonshaes. Someone tipped 'em off with news that the Captains' Alliance plans to sweep the smaller islands with a big raid come the new moon. And if *that* was about to happen," he said with a significant glance at Aumark, "*we* would know about it."

"What Wulhof says is true," agreed the First Axe. "Ruathym and Luskan have an alliance by that name, but we have made no such plans." Aumark's blue eyes narrowed and turned cold as they studied Caladorn. "Perhaps this is a ruse by your city, an excuse to attack our merchant ships!"

"Did it not occur to you that the ships now guarding the Moonshaes must have been taken from their normal routes? These are the ships that patrol the northern seas!" Caladorn persisted.

Wulhof let out a bark of humorless laughter. "Don't I know it! A pair of ships flying Waterdeep's colors chased us halfway to the Whalebones! And us not taking so much as a bolt of linen or a keg of honey by piracy!"

"Not this time, leastwise," offered a broadly grinning Northman.

A burst of raucous laughter greeted this jest. When the mirth had faded, Liriel spoke again. "Try to follow what this man is saying: If there is no raid, then why have the eyes of the great sea powers been fixed on the Moonshaes' outlying islands? Isn't it possible the rumors of impending raids are no more than a diversion?"

"I say there *is* a raid," offered Ibn, taking the pipe from his mouth and fixing a venomous glare upon the drow. "It'd be just like Luskan to have a party and not invite us."

The assembled Ruathen responded with mutters of agreement.

"That is not hard to believe," Aumark said with a tight smile. "But if it is so, what are we to do?"

"What good Northman waits for an invite?" roared Wulhof. "I say we set sail for the Moonshaes' Korinn Islands straightaway and join the Luskan raiders. And let our damned 'partners' worry if there's plunder enough left over to make up their share!"

"It could mean battle with Waterdeep," the First Axe pointed out, hoping to deter the rising tide of battle-lust.

"Or, more likely, it could mean war with Luskan," Liriel said, brandishing the ring of the High Captain of Luskan—the ring taken from the hand of the man who had commanded the attack on the *Elfmaid.*

But her warning was lost in the excited roar that followed Aumark's words. The Northmen, who had been denied the glory of combat for too long, hurried off to hone the edges of their swords and axes in preparation for the coming raid—and the possibility of a coming war.

259

*   *   *   *   *

"Stupid, stubborn . . . *men!*" sputtered Liriel as she paced the floor of Fyodor's room. "Idiots who think only with their swords—long *or* short! Even drow males are capable of better. At least they have the sense to watch their backs for the hidden blade. These orc-brained imbeciles are preparing to rush out to sea, leaving their homeland undefended, when it should be plain as moonlight that they are the target of a conspiracy! And rather than listen to someone who understands such things—who was *weaned* on treachery and intrigue—they pay heed to battle-randy sailors. It's beyond belief!"

Fyodor, seated on his narrow cot in Ruathym's warrior barracks, observed the angry drow with an expression of resignation and waited for the storm to pass. Yet he could not deny that there was much wisdom hidden among the ranting words.

"You are sure of this ring? And the sea elf who gave it to you?"

Liriel lifted her pendant of Lloth. "With this I have looked into his mind. Xzorsh is like you—he speaks only truth. I don't think the noble-minded idiot knows *how* to lie, and he's as ridiculously slow as these Northmen to accept the possibility that one of his own might somehow have gotten the knack of it!"

Her exasperated declaration brought several questions to Fyodor's mind, but he was hesitant to ask most of them for fear of setting the volatile drow off in some new direction. One of these questions, however, he could not help but ask. "You have used the symbol of your goddess to look into my mind?"

"No. Lloth will not touch you through me, this I swear!"

The drow's vehement tone and the haunted look in her amber eyes convinced Fyodor not to pursue the matter. "I agree with you that many strange things have happened in Ruathym, but I cannot piece them together."

"Let's start with the raid on Holgerstead," she said. "I suppose you've considered that Ibn might have supplied the tainted mead."

"More than considered," Fyodor agreed somberly. "I have made inquiries among the men of Holgerstead. No one recalls that mead was among the goods Ibn sold."

"Who's to say he needed to sell it? He might just as well have slipped a couple of kegs in among the rest."

"We could check Hrolf's warehouses to see if some is missing," Fyodor suggested.

Liriel responded with a humorless chuckle. "Much good may that do us. Hrolf was not one for keeping records, and he wasn't much of a housekeeper. No one but he knew what was in that place."

The Rashemi sighed and rose from his bed. "You continue to think on it, little raven. I am required to hold council with the other chieftains, but we will speak of these things as soon as we might."

"The heavy burden of power," she said lightly, hoping he might hear the irony—and perceive the truth—in her words. But Fyodor responded only with a somber nod, and they walked together in silence.

After Fyodor left her, Liriel made her way to Hrolf's warehouse and let herself in with the key the pirate had given her. She did not hope to find any answers there, but she was tired and frustrated and in sore need of solitude. So she rummaged about a bit, found a few bolts of cloth, and fluffed them into a bed.

Liriel had no idea how long she'd slept before she was roused by the squeak of the opening door. She was on her feet before the door swung shut behind the three men who had entered the warehouse.

"Thought I'd find you in here," announced a familiar, hate-filled voice.

The drow sighed. This was starting to get tiresome. At least this time Ibn had been thoughtful enough to bring reinforcements. That might add some interest. He was flanked by Harreldson, the sailor who served as cook aboard the *Elfmaid*, and another man whose face was familiar but whose name Liriel had never learned.

"One of us you might catch with your damned elf tricks, but not three. You'll not be getting away this time," Ibn exulted. All three men drew their swords and began to advance on the drow.

"Need help, do you? You prove yourself not only a traitor, but a coward!" she mocked him.

Her accusation stopped the man in his tracks, and a stunned expression crossed his usually stolid face.

"*You* are the traitor of Holgerstead," she continued. "Who else could have supplied the drugged mead? Why else would you have traveled to Holgerstead rather than honor your captain?"

Ibn snorted angrily. "Not that old song again! You've accused me before of getting into the mead, and you know damn well this tale holds no more truth than the last one. You've fooled a lot of folk here, but some of us remember the ways of the Northmen. Elves are not to be trusted, be they black, white, or green! Hrolf died, the damn fool, because he wouldn't see that!"

Something in his words raised a terrible suspicion in Liriel's mind. She knew Ibn's hatred of elves ran deep, but was it possible that he had slain his captain for the "crime" of consorting with elves?

The very thought congealed the drow's anger into a cold and killing rage. Her first impulse was to hurl a fireball at the red-bearded man, one that would leave nothing of him but cinder and ashes. Yet she did not dare. Hrolf had told her of the barrels of smoke powder stored in the enormous room.

"So it was you who killed Hrolf," she hissed as she advanced on the much-larger man. Although he held a weapon and she did not, Ibn instinctively fell back a step before her fury. His bearded face was slack with astonishment.

But he quickly recovered from his surprise and brought his weapon around in a sweeping overhead strike. Liriel dove to one side and rolled clear, hearing as she did the sound of the first mate's sword meeting answering steel. She came up to see Fyodor and Ibn circling each other, blades at the ready. The two other sailors closed in to help; Liriel quickly dispatched these with a pair of thrown knives so she could focus entirely upon the coming duel. Never had she seen Fyodor so angry, not even in the grip of a berserker's frenzy.

"I am Rashemi, and my sword is pledged to the *wychlaran*," he stated. "Once before you attacked my lady; the penalty is death. You would have died that day at sea, had she not asked otherwise."

"Actually, it's three times now, but the last one was hardly worth mentioning," Liriel put in. When Fyodor tossed her a questioning look, she added, "He put a poisonous spider in my bed. How pathetic."

"Give me leave to kill him," he said softly, his blue eyes blazing with wrath.

For a moment Liriel was filled with cold exultation at the prospect of her enemy's death and the absolute power she wielded at this moment over both men. It was an emotion she had seen many times, written on the dark faces of her drow kin, but one she herself had never expected to feel. The realization chilled her deeply. It was as if the touch of Lloth had left icy indentations upon her soul.

"No!" she said with venomous denial, responding as much to

her own thoughts as to Fyodor's request.

The young Rashemi stared at her. "It is a matter of law and of honor. This I must do, if I am to be your champion. Three times this man has attacked you—how can I let him live?"

"Do you think I care for your laws?" she demanded wildly. "I will not send you into battle to kill for me, and perhaps to die. I will not!"

The young man heard the note of rising hysteria in Liriel's voice. He hesitated only a moment, then hauled back his sword and swung it high and hard toward the watchful Ibn. The older man parried the blow. Fyodor stepped in under their joined blades and delivered a single punch to Ibn's gut. With a deep *"Ooph!"* the man dropped his sword and bent double. Fyodor brought the hilt of his blade down hard on Ibn's neck, and the man dropped, senseless, to the warehouse floor.

For a long moment the drow and her champion stared at one another. "War is coming to Ruathym, little raven," he said softly. "A time will come when you must send me into battle. It is my destiny ... and yours."

Liriel spun away from him and walked from the wooden building, her eyes burning with tears she could not shed. It was plain that Fyodor had misread her hesitation, thinking only that she feared to put him in harm's way. That was true enough, as far as it went, and as much truth as she could bear for him to know.

Adding to her confusion was the thought that Hrolf had been slain by a man he trusted. In her homeland many people fell to the treachery of friends, but it pained her to the soul that the openhearted, generous Hrolf would be betrayed in such fashion. It seemed to Liriel that in any way that mattered, this place was little different from Menzoberranzan.

Very well, then. If that were true she knew precisely how to act. As the drow hurried toward the shore, her fingers closed around her holy symbol. She thrust aside the lingering despair that had been her constant companion since the day Lloth had claimed her as priestess. The power was hers; she would use it. She had promised Lloth a battle, a glorious victory. The Spider Queen would have her due, or Liriel would slay every stubborn Ruathen who stood in her way.

But first, she had to convince the battle-mad idiots that they were getting ready to fight the wrong enemy.

Chapter 21
DROW DON'T DREAM

iriel half ran, half slid down the steep bluff that led to the sea. As her anger slipped away, the meaning in Ibn's words shifted and took on new light. She was no longer so certain the man had caused Hrolf's death. In fact, he seemed to have put the blame for it upon the sea elves, and on her as well. At first she had assumed his angry words had no purpose other than to vent his hatred of elven people. Now she suspected he saw them as truth.

And perhaps Ibn was not entirely mistaken. Liriel would not soon forget the image of the hideous fish-man that lurked behind the handsome facade of the sea elf Sittl, or her suspicion that he might be a malenti. Xzorsh had vehemently denied the possibility that his friend might be a mutated sahuagin—had not even so much as acknowledged that such creatures existed—but still Liriel wondered. There was one who might have the answer, or who at the very least could be compelled to seek it.

The drow stopped at the very edge of the water and dug in her bag for a tightly folded square of white silk. She shook out the delicate shawl, letting its fringed length flutter over the water like a banner. According to the lore books, a captured nereid would follow its soul-shawl and plead for its return; Liriel had circumvented this nuisance by commanding the nymph to stay silent and away. But now she had need of the nereid, and her long, high call rang out over the murmur of the waves.

In moments the water nymph came to Liriel's command. The creature retained little of the radiant beauty that had so entranced Wedigar. Even her voice was wan and pale as she begged for her shawl. Pitiless, the drow wrapped the wide silken sash around her own waist and faced down the nereid.

"What do you know of Hrolf the Unruly? A big man, yellow braids, a mustache that came nearly to his chin? Did you cast a charm upon him? Answer truly, or I'll rip these three pieces off the shawl's fringe!"

"No, I have charmed no man since the brown-bearded shapeshifter," the nereid whined. "Is there one you would like me to charm and drown? This Hrolf?"

Liriel's eyes blazed as she tore the threads from the nereid's soul-shawl. The nymph let out a wail of anguish and began to sob into her hands.

"Little raven, what are you doing?"

The drow turned and shielded her eyes with one hand. Fyodor stood atop the bluff, his blue eyes filled with horror as he gazed at the scene below.

"Getting answers," she called up to him. "Listen if you want, and come down if you must, but by all means let me get on with it!"

At once she turned back to the weeping nereid. "Was it you who caused the other men to drown?"

"Some of them," the creature admitted. "Others were lured into the embraces of my sisters. A few, though, were taken in by kelpies."

"Kelpies?"

"Plant creatures. Third-rate sirens," the nereid said with professional disdain. "It was a kelpie, I am told, that captured the sea elves your fisherfolk dragged ashore."

"Xzorsh did not speak of this," Liriel mused.

"As well he would not! It is hardly something to boast of."

"What do these kelpies look like?"

"In water, they appear much as any common seaweed, with long wavering fronds. From time to time they throw off sprouts— small, round things whorled like the shell of a snail. When full grown, kelpies can cast a charm that makes them appear as a woman, a horse, or a sea mount—or whatever other creature the victim is most likely to desire."

Liriel tucked this information away. Most of it was new to her, but she wondered why the seagoing Ruathen did not suspect such creatures were at work. Most likely kelpies were unfamiliar to them, perhaps brought from distant shores. "From where did these kelpies come?" she demanded, hoping the nymph would name Luskan. That was the sort of evidence she needed!

A sly look entered the nereid's eyes. "From a place far beneath the sea. I will take you there," she promised eagerly. "I will show you where they are grown!"

The drow lifted one snowy brow. "Grown?"

"The sprouts are tended, then sown into the sea to grow and to kill. Oh, let us go there!"

But Liriel remembered something she had seen just a few days earlier, and vague suspicion firmed into certainty. She doubted she had to go anywhere with this nereid in order to find the immediate source of the kelpie sprouts.

"You will stay here until I have need of you," the drow commanded.

"But my shawl," the nereid pleaded, her hands extended. "Give it to me, and I will do anything you ask!"

Liriel turned away and climbed the bluff, paying no heed to the nymph's piteous entreaties. Fyodor extended a hand to her and helped her up the last few steep feet of the incline.

"Is such treatment truly a needed thing?" he asked her.

The drow shrugged. She untied the white silk from her waist and stuffed it carelessly into her bag, not caring that this action brought another wail of pain from the evil creature below. But the look on Fyodor's face *did* trouble her. He was clearly upset by Liriel's casual enslavement of the nereid.

"Would you agree that the information provided by a nereid slave was a 'needed thing' if I told you that you, in ignorance of this information, might have killed the wrong man?"

Fyodor frowned. "What do you mean?"

"What if Ibn did not kill Hrolf?"

"He attacked *you*. His death is earned thrice over."

"All right, granted, but I do not believe he killed Hrolf or that he has any part in Ruathym's troubles. The first two times Ibn attacked me, I think he was driven mostly by his hatred of elves and his superstitions about females aboard ship. He didn't want to endanger the other sailors. But today he attacked me because he thought *I* was partly responsible for Hrolf's drowning, because of my involvement with the sea elves. Did you see how surprised he looked when I suggested that he drugged the men of Holgerstead with that wretched mead? I was too angry to see this before," Liriel admitted. "But if this is true, it means there is yet a traitor on Ruathym. We must find him—or her—and not regret the means it takes to do so!"

Fyodor nodded somberly as he took this in. He did not quite agree with the drow's ruthless treatment of the nereid, but he recognized the importance of uncovering the traitor. "Do you know who it is?"

"I think so," Liriel said shortly. "Did it not seem strange to you that Dagmar appeared in Holgerstead the very day of the attack?

With a wagonload of provisions for her 'bride price,' no less?"

"Not really. This is the custom of the land."

"But where could the mead have come from except Hrolf's warehouse? And who else had a key, besides his first mate and me?"

"There might have been many. Hrolf was a man who trusted easily."

"True, but consider this: just before Dagmar left for Holgerstead, she went alone to the warehouse to pick up a few things, apparently as payment for the poor sod who had to take her. Isn't it possible she added a keg or two of mead to sweeten the deal?"

"Possible," Fyodor admitted, "but it does not seem likely. Even if the mead were tainted, even if it came along with Dagmar's bride price, who is to say this was not an accident, but a deliberate act of treason? Dagmar's devotion to her people is beyond question. Why else would she go to Holgerstead as second wife in Wedigar's household?"

Her friend's steadfast defense of the Northwoman was beginning to wear on Liriel's nerves. "Small loss, if she knew the man would be dead long before she was required to bed him," she snapped. "Not that it would be such a hardship. Wedigar is not entirely without appeal, as humans go."

The young man flinched; he could not help but take personally the drow's dubious assessment of human men. "Hardship only in that she does not care for him," Fyodor said stiffly.

Liriel eyes narrowed and turned hard. "But she does care for you, is that what you are saying?"

"I am saying that Dagmar's willingness to go to the bed of a man she hardly knows—be that Wedigar or me—speaks well of her desire to do her duty to Ruathym," he explained. "It is not the way of Northwomen to take such things lightly. I do not see how a woman with such devotion to duty could become traitor."

His words cut Liriel like shards of glass, for despite all her early adventures with this or that drow playmate, she herself hardly took "such things" lightly. Had Fyodor truly so little understanding of what she had gone through before she could accept him as a friend, much less a lover? Fyodor had demanded more of her than she had known was in her to give. To Liriel, a drow of Menzoberranzan, the path that led to such intimacy had been one of painfully won insight, of enormous change and growth. In light of all this, for Fyodor to vaunt the Northwoman's reticence as virtue was past insult!

"As to Dagmar's motives, we shall know them soon enough," Liriel proclaimed wrathfully. "Perhaps you cannot look beyond a woman's pretty face, but by the power of Lloth, I can!" The drow snatched up her obsidian pendant and brandished it purposefully.

A look of horror crossed Fyodor's face. "Do not," he admonished her. "Little raven, have nothing more to do with this goddess!"

An inhuman rage rose in her like a dark, crackling flame. Liriel recognized in it the touch of the Spider Queen, and too late she remembered the cruel rituals required of the drow priestesses who served her. The jealous goddess did not allow her clergy to form close attachments of any kind and was particularly offended by the idea that a priestess might become fond of a mere male. Often were the females of Menzoberranzan required to sacrifice their mates, their lovers, and even their sons to appease the Queen of Spiders. Lloth would not long countenance an alliance with a human male, especially if that male presumed to intrude upon Liriel's devotion and duties. Fyodor did not realize how precarious was the path he trod. Until this moment, neither had Liriel.

"Do not speak ill to me of Lloth," she warned him. "I am pledged as priestess to her. This I did, in exchange for the *Elfmaid*'s magical escape."

Fyodor gasped and reached for her hands. "*That* was the doing of your goddess? Liriel, it is no wonder you wept, knowing to what you had given pledge! Never have I felt such despair in a place, or such evil!"

"Or such power," she added coldly.

"But at what price?" he persisted. "How can good come from evil? I fear for you, little raven, and for what you might become. Already you have taken a slave and accused a good woman of treachery."

His words held enough truth to sting her, and she snatched her hands away. "Have a care how you speak to me," she snarled. "Need I remind you that I could command you to rip out the heart of that 'good woman'?"

A stunned silence met Liriel's words.

For what seemed like a very long time, she and Fyodor merely stood and stared at each other. It was obvious the man was shocked by this outburst, but no more so than Liriel herself. For the first time ever, the young drow heard in her own words the echo of her grandmother's malevolent voice. For a moment, the ancient evil that was Matron Baenre had lived and breathed and found a home in Liriel's heart.

"I didn't mean it," she whispered.

Fyodor nodded, silently accepting her words. But Liriel knew by the sadness in his eyes that he doubted the truth of them—and he knew she doubted it, too.

Impulsively she threw herself into her lover's arms, wishing to recover the closeness they once knew. Fyodor held her lightly, but beneath her seeking hands the muscles of his shoulders and chest and arms were tensed, forbidding. He offered no response to her, and no welcome. Liriel raised questioning eyes to the young man's face.

"My lady, would you command *this* of me, as well?" he asked in a tight voice.

Stunned by this accusation, Liriel fell back from the unwilling embrace. Through the transparent window of Fyodor's eyes, she read both his profound pain and rigid pride, and suddenly she understood the depth of the blow that she had dealt his honor. By the very suggestion that he might do evil at her bequest, she had gone against his dearly held faith in her as *wychlaran*, and in himself as a berserker knight pledged to a worthy lady. And noble and self-less though he might be, his own very personal pride was also deeply wounded. Most painful of all, Liriel saw that Fyodor had come to fear, and to regret, the link that had been forged between them.

With a little cry, she tore herself from him and raced wildly away.

This time, Fyodor did not follow.

* * * * *

After a time alone to compose herself, Liriel returned to Ulf's cottage. She went straight to the garden and to the wooden boxes where she'd seen the odd seaweed Dagmar had tended. She wanted to see if it matched the description given her by the nereid. But there was nothing in the salty water but a few somnolent clams.

Given all that had happened, Liriel could not help but doubt her own memory and the conclusions she had drawn. She hadn't looked all that closely at the sprout she'd nibbled, nor did she truly know whether or not Dagmar had had anything to do with the attack on Holgerstead. Perhaps Fyodor was right—perhaps the power Liriel courted was changing her. Perhaps it was already warping her per-spective and inflaming her desire for petty revenge.

Liriel resented Dagmar for her early condescension and for her attempt to seduce Fyodor. That alone would be enough to send many a drow into an out-of-control fury. So many of her people were blinded by their singleminded lust for vengeance. She wondered if this was the taint left by the worship of Lloth, the ash that remained upon the soul when the flame of power burned low.

The young drow had always taken great pride in her independence of mind. She had chosen and controlled her own destiny to an extent unimagined by most of Menzoberranzan's drow. But it occurred to her now that in her quest to retain her drow powers, she might well have lost much of herself. Where one began and the other left off, she could no longer say.

Finally, too heartsick and exhausted to ponder the matter more, Liriel entered Ulf's cottage and climbed the ladder into the loft. She plunged gratefully into slumber and the oblivion it offered.

＊　＊　＊　＊　＊

Much later that night, a soft, weighty pressure stole the drow's breath and tore her from slumber. Instinctively her fingers closed on the dagger that lay within reach. She lunged upright, slashing out as she rose.

In a haze of lazily drifting duck feathers stood Dagmar, dressed in her nightclothes and holding half of a severed pillowslip in each hand. The woman and the drow stared at each other in stunned astonishment.

"You might have killed me," whispered the Northwoman.

"That was the general idea," Liriel snarled. She rolled off the far side of the bed, putting some space between herself and the much larger human. "What in the Nine Hells do you think you're doing, intruding upon me like this? It might be your father's house, but it's my room! And haven't you the sense not to creep up on a sleeping drow?"

Dagmar shrugged. "I was downstairs, unable to sleep. I heard you call out as if you were in danger."

"And so you rushed to my aid armed with a pillow?" Liriel sneered. "This, from a daughter of warriors!"

The girl's chin lifted. "When I entered the room the first time," she said evenly, "I was relieved to find that you were threatened only by a bad dream. I saw that you did not have a pillow. I brought you one, thinking it might help you sleep better."

"You put it on my face," Liriel pointed out.

"It fell from my hand," Dagmar returned.

Liriel stared at the girl for a long moment. All of her earlier sus-

270

picions returned to her, for she had caught Dagmar in not one lie, but two. Yet the young Northwoman's face was set in strong, certain lines, and there was no hint of duplicity in her pale blue eyes.

The wench was good, Liriel acknowledged with a touch of perverse admiration. She hoped her own performance, as she accepted Dagmar's explanations and sent her on her way, was equally convincing.

Liriel waited until she heard the faint creaking of the roping that supported Dagmar's mattress. She eased on her elven boots and cloaked herself in her *piwafwi*. Silent and invisible, she crept down the ladder into the main room of the cottage, then wriggled out an open window into the night.

The drow made her way swiftly to the barracks where Fyodor slept. She found his room and shook him awake.

Acting on sudden impulse, Liriel crawled under the blankets and nestled into Fyodor's arms. She poured out her story—beginning with her own self-doubts and fearful misgivings. With unfamiliar candor she admitted her fears about the dangers that her reluctant priesthood held for her, and also for him. Fyodor held her as she spoke, and she felt in his physical strength a symbol of the steadfast honor that was like a lifeline to her. She spoke of this, too. Never had the proud and solitary drow poured forth her heart so completely. In its own way, it was a sharing equal to that they had known at the foot of Yggsdrasil's Child.

At length she described the scene that had transpired in her bedchamber, and once again she laid out her accusations.

This time Fyodor listened with a more receptive mind, but he was still slow to accept.

"It might have been as Dagmar said," he ventured. "Perhaps she did not mean to do you harm—perhaps the pillow did slip from her hands."

"She was still holding it after I sliced it in half," Liriel pointed out. "But even if she'd caught it as it fell, there is a more basic question: why did she come into my room in the first place?"

"Perhaps you did call out in your sleep."

" 'There are those who think, and those who dream,' " Liriel quoted softly. "You are forgetting something, something that Dagmar could not possibly know: *drow do not dream.*"

Fyodor was silent as he sorted through all that she had said. "Do what you must to unveil the traitor," he said somberly. "I will help you where I can and try not to question your methods overmuch."

Chapter 22
DEEPER

n the dark hours before morning, the shaman's daughter crept down to the shore and dragged her small boat off the beach. The familiar signal had been left the night before, the strange pattern of pebbles and shells indicating that once again Dagmar was required to meet with one of the creatures who held captive that which was dearest to her heart.

She hadn't rowed far beyond the cove when a pair of slender, webbed hands seized the rim of her boat. Dagmar barely had time to draw in a startled gasp before the creature leaped in and seated himself across from her. The little boat rocked wildly as Dagmar stared at one of the sea elves her nets had recently ensnared. She recovered her wits quickly and dove for the fishing knife at her feet—a thin blade longer than her forearm.

But the elf was faster still. He seized her wrist with one webbed hand and hurled her back onto her seat. "I like this no better than you do," he said with cold disdain. "But there is news from Ascarle. Listen well, so I need not look at you any longer than I must."

"At our last meeting, you promised vengeance against me for ensnaring you!"

"If I acted only to please myself, I would have slain you that day and relished the deed," the sea elf responded. "But the powers of Ascarle wish otherwise. You do your job well enough, and the failure of the raid at Holgerstead is not laid upon you. In other matters, however, you have been too diligent. Leave off the kelpies; there are far too many in these waters. I myself dodged one—and the human she was in the process of drowning—only to be caught by another a few lengths away."

The color drained from Dagmar's face. "We were so close!" she whispered. "The day we caught you, if only we'd cast our nets farther out to sea, Hrolf might yet be alive!"

"A little late for regrets," the elf taunted her. He reached into a sealskin bag and drew forth a small, folded object. "A token from

272

your mistress. Plans have changed; you are not to destroy the drow and deliver her body to the sea. But the new shapeshifter still lives, and your mistress finds this most displeasing."

Dagmar stared at the grisly object in the elf's hand: a blood-stained lock of pale yellow hair, proof that her twin-born sister still lived.

Although all of Ruathym thought Ygraine had been lost in a sudden spring squall, the truth of the matter was that the two sisters had been waylaid by Luskan pirates. The cruel Northmen had cast lots over the girls; Ygraine was chosen as hostage and Dagmar as spy. There was little chance their warrior kindred might rescue the girl, for Ygraine was held captive in a place far beyond the reach of men. Nor was there the possibility that Ygraine, although in captivity, might find her way to an honorable death. Dagmar had been shown a tapestry that held the tormented spirits of slain elves, so she might know what Ygraine's fate would be should she fail to follow orders.

Dagmar's gaze fell on the knife still clenched in one fist, the knife that had sent her betrothed husband—Thorfinn, the future First Axe of Ruathym—to his ignoble death, the knife that would have slain Fyodor of Rashemen and Holgerstead, had he yielded to her that night. There were times when any man, even the greatest of warriors, was vulnerable to the quick thrust of a knife, a time when caressing fingers could count to the spot between the third and fourth rib, force the blade in, and pull the knife down. This and more she was willing to do, to end Ygraine's captivity.

She turned her eyes upon the sea elf seated across from her. Unlike most of her people, she understood that the sea folk bore no special enmity against her people. She had been astonished to learn that this one was part of the plot against Ruathym, and that he was willing to implicate the elves in the island's woes. More, he was willing to work with her to this end, even after she had unwittingly attacked him!

"I know why I must betray my people," she said softly. "But what of you?"

The male responded with a smile of pure malevolence. "Like most of your kind, you are easily deceived by appearances. I am no more elf than you are!"

With these cryptic words, the apparent sea elf dove into the water and disappeared. Dagmar sat silent for a long time and then rowed back toward the shore. Her movements were slow, weighted down by the knowledge that many of her people would soon be dead. At least their deaths would be won in honorable battle, their place in the Northman afterlife assured.

For herself, Dagmar no longer held such hopes. Her soul was in the hands of her tormenters, just as surely as those of the unfortunate sea elves in distant Ascarle, who were locked for eternity in a prison made of wool and silk. But this no longer mattered to her. All that Dagmar valued was held captive, and she would do whatever it took to claim back what was hers.

* * * * *

Unknown to either Dagmar or Sittl, there were two witnesses to the secret meeting. Liriel and Fyodor sat silently nearby, their borrowed rowboat cloaked in a ghost-ship spell that the drow had learned during her days in Ruathym's library.

"Convinced?" she demanded.

Fyodor nodded somberly. "You were right about all. We must go to Aumark with this news at once."

But to his surprise, the drow shook her head. "Not yet. We know Dagmar is playing the traitor, but at whose behest? Luskan, almost certainly, but I have long suspected the city does not act alone. There is another layer to this conspiracy; we must go deeper before we know the true scope of the danger facing Ruathym. I must know about this Ascarle that the sea elf—or rather, the malenti—mentioned."

As she spoke, Liriel remembered words that the nereid had said: the kelpie sprouts were grown in a wondrous place far below the sea. Perhaps it was time to take the nereid up on her offer.

"Judging from what I have read," Liriel began, "the warriors of Luskan do not care much for magic. It seems likely to me that all the creatures of the elemental plane of water are commanded from this Ascarle—including the nereids. I will compel my slave to take me there. I'll scout their forces, do what I can to uncover their plans, and bring back enough proof to force that idiot Aumark to pay heed! But I must go alone."

Fyodor did not like any of this, and he and the drow held long and heated discussion on the matter. Finally Liriel reminded him that he, like Wedigar, must bide his time and accept risks for the greater good—even when they contradicted his own sense of honor and duty.

"I like it not when you quote my own words back at me," Fyodor grumbled.

The drow tossed him a wicked grin, and they rowed in silence toward the shore of Inthar.

* * * * *

The nereid responded to Liriel's questions with great glee. Ascarle, the creature claimed, was a subterranean city full of ancient treasures and wondrous magic. When Liriel asked about sea elves, the nereid nodded eagerly.

"Yes, there are many there, a hundred, perhaps more. The armies of Ascarle capture them as slaves."

Liriel wondered briefly how Xzorsh would respond to this news—and the knowledge that his "friend" had a part in it. "Let's assume I want to go to Ascarle," the drow said. "How would you take me there?"

"You cannot go directly. There is a portal but no mortal may pass. My powers allow me to take you to my home plane, and from there to Ascarle."

Something in the nereid's words struck the drow as familiar. They were very like words spoken not long ago, by a voice from beyond the grave. Liriel's eyes darted to the tower that loomed over the cliffs of Inthar, and her thoughts returned to the strange encounter with the banshee who guarded it.

After giving instructions to the nereid that she was to remain silent and out of sight once they reached Ascarle—or suffer damage to her soul-shawl—Liriel agreed to take the voyage. First, however, she encloaked herself in her *piwafwi*. There was no telling what she might encounter in the undersea stronghold. It did not escape Liriel's notice that the sly nereid seemed a little too eager to take her there.

Liriel had traveled through magical portals many times, but none were quite like this. The moment the nereid took her hand, they were shot through a tunnel of effervescent energy. For a brief, exhilarating moment, Liriel felt as if she were inside a bottle of sparkling wine that had been shaken, then suddenly uncorked.

She emerged, wet and tingling from head to toe, in a marble pool. Colorful fish swam among the water flowers, and a delicate fountain played softly in one corner. The drow looked deep into the water. There, barely visible, was the face of the nereid. She gave a sharp tug on the soul-shawl's fringe by way of reminder, and the nymph disappeared from sight at once.

The drow adjusted her *piwafwi* and climbed over the low marble wall and surveyed the room beyond—a vast, gleaming chamber with a vaulted ceiling. The walls and floor were of inlaid marble, and several pools and fountains sang in a melodic murmur. Dominating the room was a raised platform upon which sat a massive throne of pale purple crystal. The thing brought to mind an image of the Baenre throne. The matron of the First House of Menzoberranzan sat on an intricately carved wonder of black stone, within which writhed the spirits of Baenre victims. Liriel hoped that whatever creature ruled this place was less venal than her dear aunt Triel, the current Matron Mother.

Liriel cast a quick spell to dry herself, for invisibility would be of limited value if she left behind a trail of wet prints. As silent as a shadow, she wandered through the rooms of the vast palace. The entire building was constructed of marble and crystal, decorated with ancient, priceless statues and urns filled with exotic plants. Beyond the palace lay an entire city, the buildings connected by air-filled walkways and tended by vacant-eyed slaves.

With every step, Liriel grew more certain that in this undersea city lived Ruathym's true enemy. Whoever ruled here possessed too much wealth and power for it to be otherwise. No such beings could content themselves in Luskan's shadow. On swift and silent feet she walked through the magic-filled greenhouse where the kelpie sprouts were grown, through storehouses filled with supplies, through armories well stocked with weapons. At last she made her way toward the humbler buildings, assuming these would house the city's soldiers, as well as the slaves of which the nereid spoke.

Liriel was well acquainted with slavery. It was a fact of life in Menzoberranzan. Slaves were the source of most of the drow's battle fodder and supplied nearly all the city's menial labor. In her first meeting with Fyodor she'd learned Rashemi did not enslave each other. He clearly abhorred the very mention of slavery, but she herself had never given much thought to the matter. Some people were drow, some were humans, some were ogres, and some were slaves. It was that simple. But never had Liriel considered the slaves themselves, rather than the useful functions they performed. Here, surrounded by hundreds of listless, nearly lifeless beings, she could do nothing else.

As the drow walked through the cramped and crowded quarters, she noted that all the slaves—sea elves, humans, even some of the merrow that apparently guarded them—were held in tight control. Some sat like animated corpses, with slack faces and vacant eyes, moving only upon the command of one of their sea-ogre guardians. Others, whose spirits had apparently been broken, were shackled only by the deep hopelessness that emptied their eyes and bowed their shoulders. There were, however, a few who still resisted the powers that ruled Ascarle.

Liriel watched as a pair of merrow dragged a struggling sea-elf female down a hall. She followed them into a long corridor lined with cages. Into one of these the merrow tossed the elf, informing her that she would be fetched again when her skills were needed. The drow crept down the hall, taking stock of these hearty prisoners. These were the strongest, those who might be persuaded to turn against their captors when the time came. Suddenly Liriel stopped before one cell, stunned and enlightened.

The young woman pacing the tiny cell was the mirror image of Dagmar: the same strong, beautiful face, the distinctive pale gold hair. Liriel understood at last why the Ruathen woman had turned traitor.

Twin births were not common among the drow, but they did occur from time to time. The link between elven twins was incredibly strong, often enabling one sibling to sense the other's thoughts and to feel the other's pain. And the rivalry between drow twins was ruthless enough to inspire the most ambitious priestess in Menzoberranzan. Rarely did both siblings live to adulthood. Those who did usually pitted themselves against each other in an endless, equally matched struggle. These miniature wars could become so destructive that many drow decided to avoid the bother by destroying such children at birth. As she gazed at Dagmar's twin, however, Liriel wondered how strong that bond might be in cultures such as Ruathym, where all children were cherished, where clan and kindred were valued above all other things.

Abruptly the drow turned and strode back to the palace. She had not yet encountered the leader of this place. This she must do, before she could know the true strength of Ascarle.

Liriel made her way back to the council chamber. Beyond it was a suite of rooms. Judging by their opulence, she guessed they belonged to the shadowy "mistress" of whom the malenti had spoken.

One of these chambers was filled with dozens of scrying devices: small pools, scrying bowls, crystal globes, enspelled gems.

The very air crackled with magic, and the drow hurried through to the room beyond. Here she stopped, more stunned by the sight before her than she had been by the discovery of Dagmar's captured twin.

Stretched out on a large loom was a nearly finished tapestry depicting a coastal village—as one of the creatures of the Abyss might leave it after a few days' dalliance. Dead human warriors lay in moldering piles; sea elves were staked out beneath a blazing sun. Familiar sea elves. Liriel knew those faces, even if she had seen them only in death.

The drow grasped her holy symbol and whispered the words to the spell that had once sought the spirits of the sea elves. There was no misty gray anteroom this time, for Liriel had not far to go. She touched her fingers to the woven image of the elf, felt the mingled despair and hope as the captured spirit responded to her presence.

Liriel snatched her hand away and stared with dismay at the tapestry. Such a thing took powerful magic; this was the work of a mighty and malevolent being.

Her own words rang in her ears—her impetuous promise to free the captured spirits. If she tried to do so, if she tampered with the tapestry in any way, she would surely alert the powers of Ascarle to her presence.

Welcome, Liriel of House Baenre.

The words sounded in Liriel's mind as clearly if they had been engraved there by the finger of Lloth. The drow spun, and her amber eyes widened.

An illithid, one of the most powerful and most feared creatures of the Underdark, glided silently toward her. Liriel did not need to ask how the thing had sensed her presence. An illithid could read thoughts as easily as a drow's eyes could perceive heat patterns.

I am Vestress, Regent Ruler of Ascarle. Your presence here has long been desired.

Liriel flung back her cloak and faced down the powerful creature. "How do you know of me?"

We have need of a wizard, one who possesses considerable command over magic portals. You have proven yourself to be just such a one, the illithid continued. *It is no small thing, to move an entire ship!*

"That was not my doing, but Lloth's," Liriel said bluntly. She saw no reason to prevaricate; the illithid would take the thought from her mind, regardless.

Is it so? You are indeed a priestess of the Spider Queen? A hint of

278

amusement—and speculation—entered the creature's oddly femi-nine voice. *This situation may prove even more diverting than we had hoped.*

"What do you want from me?" the drow demanded, although she was beginning to suspect what the illithid had in mind.

Vestress outlined the plan in detail. As Liriel listened, she kept her mind carefully blank, calling upon the discipline and con-centration she had learned in three decades of magic studies to focus her thoughts entirely upon the illithid's instructions. A moment of doubt, a single stray thread of counterstrategy, and all would be lost.

Finally the drow nodded. "I will do as you say. The banshee will be defeated, the portal opened for the armies of Ascarle."

And in return, we offer you the power you crave, the illithid said slyly. *All the magical treasures of Ascarle will be open to you: the spells and artifacts of a mighty elven people, wonders that form the stuff of legends. This tapestry, which has so taken your fancy, will be yours to do with as you like. And there is one other reward you might consider: a conquered Ruathym must be administered so that the Kraken Society is well served. We agree with your assessment of the human males who rule this island. Order your human champion to do away with the other battle chieftains and establish himself as leader. He will make a most useful puppet—and you will possess a kingdom to rival that of the matrons who forced you from the Underdark, as well as more wizardly might than the father who betrayed you. In time, you could amass power enough to take your revenge and reclaim your place Below. All of this, we offer you.*

"I will think on it," Liriel said in a stunned whisper. She turned and fled the chamber, before the too-perceptive illithid could steal more of her thoughts.

No longer concerned with keeping silent, the drow sped to the council chamber and plunged into the pool. She called the nereid to her and took refuge in the effervescent tunnel that would take her far away from this place.

In moments, Liriel sat alone on the rocky shore near Inthar, hundreds of miles from the wonders and horrors of Ascarle. Yet she could not escape thoughts of the temptations that the canny illithid had laid out before her, temptations made all the more poignant for being torn from the fabric of her own unspoken desires.

* * * * *

Early the next morning, Liriel found Dagmar by the cove, working with several others to mend a torn net. She pulled the young woman away from the other fisherfolk. As they walked along the deserted shore, Liriel told her what she and Fyodor had witnessed, and what she herself had learned in Ascarle.

"You have seen Ygraine. Then you understand why I have done these things," Dagmar whispered. "Even so, I will surely be slain for my treachery. And I would welcome the blade, even if wielded by your hand!"

"Don't tempt me," Liriel said coldly. "Believe me, I have to keep reminding myself that you're of more use to me alive than dead. You're going to go to Aumark and tell him all you know of the coming battle."

Dagmar hesitated, her blue eyes frantic. Liriel thought she knew why.

"Your sister is dead," she said bluntly.

It was a lie, and a cruel one at that, but Liriel was desperate to free Dagmar from her loyalty to her captured twin. The stunned expression on the Northwoman's face assured Liriel she had hit the mark. It did not, however, prepare the drow for what happened next.

Dagmar threw back her head and let out a peal of wild laughter. The veil of pretense dropped from her beautiful face, and Liriel stared up into blue eyes burning with fierce joy.

"So at last I am to come into my own!" the young woman exulted. "Now that Ygraine is dead, I will be the one to bring the *hamfarrigen* magic back to Ruathym!"

As the initial shock of this announcement faded, the drow nodded slowly. There was a certain macabre logic in Dagmar's words, for she was obviously astute enough to realize that Ygraine would never have returned to Ruathym alive. The traitorous Northwoman had been held hostage by her sister's captors—not by the threat of her sister's death, but by Ygraine's continued survival! To a drow of Menzoberranzan, this made perfect sense. There were some things, however, that Liriel did not yet understand.

"Ygraine would have died sooner or later," the drow stated coldly. "You could not have waited for your inheritance?"

Dagmar shrugged. "If I knew for certain that the dutiful fool would soon serve mead in the halls of Tempus, I would have been content to wait upon the pleasure of her captors. But I was shown a tapestry, a magical thing that can hold the spirits of the slain for all time. If I did not do as they bade me, Ygraine's spirit would have been trapped among the threads. Perhaps that would have been sufficient to pass her legacy on to me, perhaps not. It was not a chance I was willing to take."

"Many Ruathen have died," Liriel spat out. "Is your sister's death worth that much to you? What do you stand to gain from this, besides a passel of shapechanging brats?"

Dagmar turned a strange smile upon the drow. "That is how my people think; I would have expected differently from *you*. To the people of Ruathym, a woman's worth is measured by the rank of her husband and the sons she bears him. I would be known for myself!"

Liriel stared at the Northwoman, rendered momentarily speechless by the naked ambition written on Dagmar's face—an ambition that fully matched her own. The drow had the uncanny sensation that she was gazing into a pale mirror.

"What power were you promised?" she asked softly.

"After the conquest of Ruathym, someone must rule," the young woman said bluntly. "Most of the warriors will be slain, the women humiliated, the pride of all the people brought low. The Ruathen will accept someone who provides a measure of hope, who can restore to them their sense of honor. Who better than she who revived the ancient *hamfariggen* magic? And *I* will do it, not a son that some warrior begot upon my body!"

"If that is so, what did you want with Fyodor?" Liriel demanded, for Dagmar's attempted seduction of her friend still rankled deeply with her.

Again, the strange, cold smile. "Had he lain with me, he would have been dead that very night, and the conquest of Ruathym would have been so much the easier."

Liriel nodded. It all made perfect sense. Indeed, the mixture of twisted intrigue and icy calculation was all too familiar to her. Familiar, too, was the desire for power, a desire so strong that any method of achieving the longed-for goal was deemed acceptable. There was an odd kinship between Dagmar and herself that Liriel could not ignore.

"Why do you tell me this?" she demanded. Even to her own ears, her words rang with desperate denial.

Dagmar laughed softly, knowingly. "Is there anyone alive who does not wish to be understood? I tell you because on all this island you alone can understand the things I desire, and the things I have done to get them."

The drow received this explanation in silence. As much as she wished to refute the damning words, she found she could not.

"Besides, who can you tell?" Dagmar continued, her voice ringing with amusement as she pulled her long fish knife from her belt. "Even if you were to live out this day, to whom would you take this tale? Fyodor?" she asked mockingly, and something in her tone froze Liriel in place, her black fingers tightly gripping the hilt of her dagger.

"He had his doubts about me, of course, but he put them aside easily enough," Dagmar said in an arch voice. "You must have been denying the poor man, to send him to me in such a state! I was only too happy to comfort him. After all, he *was* a fine figure of a man."

The woman's cruel emphasis was not lost on Liriel, and the warmth drained from the drow's face. "He is dead," she murmured tonelessly. Grief would come later; she felt numbed to the soul.

"A pleasure deferred," Dagmar mocked. "And now that he is gone, no Ruathen warrior will listen to any word you speak against me!"

"But they *will* listen to *me*," proclaimed a deep voice behind them.

The two females whirled, identical expressions of consternation on their faces. So deep in conversation were they that neither had noted the approach of the red-bearded sailor. Ibn stood a few paces away, his massive arms folded across his chest and angry little puffs of smoke bursting from his pipe.

But Ibn, like most men of Ruathym, had not reckoned with a woman like Dagmar. She darted at him, her long knife leaping toward his heart.

Liriel seized one of the woman's flying braids, dug in her heels, and held on. Dagmar's head snapped back as her attack on Ibn came to an abrupt and unexpected halt. Before the woman's startled curse left her lips, Liriel pivoted on one heel and lifted the other foot in a high, hard kick. Her booted foot connected with Dagmar's kidney, and the woman let out a howl of pure anguish.

The drow kicked out again, this time at the back of Dagmar's legs; the Northwoman's knees buckled and she went down. In three quick steps Liriel circled around to face her foe. On her knees, the much taller Dagmar was not far below the drow's eye level, and Liriel held her pain-glazed stare for a long moment. Then she balled up her fist and drove it into the woman's temple. Dagmar swayed but did not go down—in no small part because Liriel still held her grip on the woman's braid. Holding the Northwoman upright by her own hair, the drow coldly dealt another blow, and then a third. At last Dagmar's eyes rolled up in her head.

It took all of Liriel's self-control to refrain from beating the beautiful face into a bloody mask. She flung the unconscious woman to the ground and turned to face Ibn, ready to fight yet another battle if need be.

But Ibn merely nodded and calmly took the pipe from his mouth. "You should have killed her," he observed.

"I wanted to," Liriel said with fierce candor. "Fyodor would die anew were he to hear me say this, but that felt pretty damned good!"

"Can see how it would," Ibn agreed, scowling at the woman sprawled senseless at his feet. "The elf-loving bitch had it coming to her."

Liriel fell back a step. "I've missed something, haven't I?" she inquired, not at all certain whether Ibn was to be counted a foe or an ally.

"No less than I have," he admitted grudgingly. "Might be that it's time to settle the scores between us and lay things out plainlike."

The drow responded with a cautious nod.

"To my way o' thinking," Ibn began, "Ruathym's troubles came out o' the sea. I had my eye on them sea elves, and you for taking up with 'em. Tried to warn Hrolf, but would he listen? So I've been watching for 'em since the day we came ashore. 'Twas no surprise when the fisherfolk netted those two. But then I saw one of them again, and Dagmar with him. I've been following the wench ever since—followed her up to Holgerstead, though I didn't do much good for the folk there."

"So that's why you went to Holgerstead," Liriel mused. "I'm surprised you didn't suspect she might poison the mead."

Ibn huffed and leveled an angry glare at the drow. "Don't be starting down that path again!" His expression softened somewhat. "She was lying about your friend. The young First Axe was alive and well when I left the village."

Joy filled Liriel's heart, and a smile like instant sunshine burst onto her face. Impulsively she threw her arms around the man in a quick, fierce hug. Before he recovered from the shock of it, she spun away into an ecstatic little dance.

"Here, now," Ibn protested. "There's no call for that. I don't like elves now any more than ever I did. And stop whirling around like a cider-drunk bee when there's work to be done!"

Elaine Cunningham

*   *   *   *   *

Together they sought out Fyodor, for only a warrior could call a Thing. When the village had gathered, Ibn told the council of the meeting he had witnessed between Dagmar and the long-haired sea elf, and of the damning words he had heard her speak to the drow. At Fyodor's insistence, they allowed Liriel to speak. She told them of the three warships that had attacked the *Elfmaid*, and showed them the ring that had been taken from the severed hand of the leader— the ring that marked him as one of the five High Captains of Luskan. Aumark examined the ring and pronounced it genuine, and even admitted that he recognized the man from the drow's description: Rethnor, an ambitious, black-bearded giant of a man who held even less love for Ruathym than most of his fellows.

After a moment's stunned silence, the men began to plan for the coming attack. Liriel was content to listen, for the Ruathen were no strangers to war, and the battle chieftains' strategy was sufficient to meet the threat from Luskan. To the proud Northmen, Luskan was the true enemy, and the strange sea creatures merely tools. Defeat the Luskan ships in sea battle, they believed, and all else would fall into place.

Liriel knew differently, for she herself had pledged to open the door that would allow the powers of Ascarle to invade the island— and that would enable her to free the slaves held captive in the underground stronghold. She could not seek Fyodor's help, for she dared not expose him to the power she would have to channel before the portal could be opened.

And so the drow left the warriors to their plans and made her way down to the cove. Again she called for Xzorsh. When the sea elf came to her summons, she described the submerged city and the forces she had seen within.

"So Ascarle truly exists, and the merrow are based there," the ranger murmured. "You are right; this danger must be eliminated. I will gather as many sea-elven warriors as I can muster—along with some triton volunteers, if such can be persuaded—and advance on the Purple Rocks at once!"

"At least, that's the word you'll send through the Relay," Liriel agreed. "Let the forces of Ascarle prepare for an assault from the sea beyond their city walls. Secretly, you will gather your forces by the shores of Inthar and await my word. I will send you through the portal into the city itself. But take care: if word of this gets to Sittl, all is lost."

Xzorsh still looked doubtful. "Perhaps you misunderstood what he said to the Northwoman."

The drow hissed in exasperation. "If you refuse to listen to reason, perhaps you'll respond to a deal: keep the plan secret, and I will see that you get your magical training!"

Joy flared briefly in the sea elf's eyes; then a rueful smile crossed his face. "All my life I have waited to hear such words. Even so, I would give up this chance gladly to see you proved wrong. Sittl is a friend, and his trust is worth more to me than magic."

Liriel turned away, stung by the elf's wistful words and his willingness to give up his dream rather than betray the values he held dear. Despite all that had happened to the drow and to those she loved, she knew that she herself would not do likewise.

"Do as I say, and prepare for your battle," she snarled, and as she walked away she added in a whisper too soft for the elf to hear, "and leave me to mine."

* * * * *

Before facing her deadly foe—and her even more dangerous ally—Liriel had one task to complete. She had stopped wearing the Windwalker amulet after the night she and Fyodor had spent at the foot of Yggsdrasil's Child, for the artifact's task had been completed even if the quest had not been fully realized. Her only ornament these days was the medallion that proclaimed her priestess of Lloth. Even the pendant that Fyodor had given her, the amber-encased spider, she had tucked away, for she did not wish to tempt the jealous goddess with even so small a competition.

But now she made her way to Ulf's cottage to once again enchant the amulet with stored magic. She admonished the shaman's family to leave her to her privacy, but this was hardly a needed precaution. News of Dagmar's treachery and the girl's subsequent imprisonment had bowed all of Ulf's household under a heavy weight of shame, grief, and helpless frustration. Even Sanja's scolding tongue was stilled as she struggled to accept that Ygraine—the daughter most favored and long presumed dead—lived in horrible captivity, and that the quiet and biddable Dagmar could harbor such deadly ambitions.

Alone in the silence of the loft, Liriel took the Windwalker from its hiding place and opened the book of rune lore to a spell she had used previously to capture the magic of the Underdark in the amulet. Hours passed as she studied anew the difficult spell, adding to it the changes that would store, if temporarily, a very different type of magic. When at last all was ready, Liriel removed the tiny chisel from the sheath. As she chanted the words of the spell, she carefully poured a drop of Fyodor's *jhuild*—the firewine used in the rituals that brought the battle frenzy upon Rashemen's berserkers—into the sheath.

Once before she had considered this spell. In an attempt to save Fyodor from a killing frenzy, Liriel had been willing to empty the Windwalker of her Underdark magic so his berserker wrath might be contained within. But she and Fyodor had fallen under attack before she could cast the spell. When he'd recovered from his battle wounds and learned what she had nearly done, he'd exacted a promise from her that she would never sacrifice her drow powers for him. And there the matter had remained.

Until now. Liriel's quest for power had been answered at the foot of Yggsdrasil's Child, and she no longer needed the Windwalker to hold her innate drow magic. It was hers to command for as long as she might live. But she dared not carry the power of Fyodor's berserker magic with her to her next battle, for fear it might be wrested from her hands.

The spellcasting and the ritual took most of the night, but at last Liriel held the enchanted Windwalker in her hands, taking comfort from the captured power thrumming through the ancient gold. She tucked the amulet back into its hiding place—she could not give it to Fyodor just yet, for fear of alerting him to her purpose—and then she crept silently from the sleeping cottage.

The drow made her way along the shore and then climbed the steep bluff that led to the ruins of Inthar. The ancient keep loomed overhead, secret and forbidding. As Liriel walked through the ruins, she murmured the words of a clerical prayer, one of the most powerful and deadly spells in a priestess's arsenal. It was a prayer seldom granted, for few were the drow who were powerful enough to withstand it. It was a portal of a different sort, one that opened the priestess to the pure power of Lloth.

It was the offer of her body and mind as avatar to the Queen of Chaos.

This was a desperate measure, but Liriel saw no other choice. She had faced the banshee before, and she understood that only two things could defeat its restless spirit: a magic that could dispel evil, or an evil power greater than that of the undead drow. As a priestess of Lloth, she did not dare to dispel evil; all that was left for her to do was to channel it.

And so the young drow sank ever deeper into the source of her darkest power. The Spider Queen looked kindly upon the prayer of her young priestess, for it pleased the goddess to reclaim the spirit of the ancient drow who had, in banshee form, eluded fate for many centuries. Through Liriel, Lloth would wrest the banshee from the portal and spirit it away to its long overdue reward in the Abyss, and the portal would be at last be open.

Yet as the dark power of Lloth gathered and welled up within her, Liriel knew not triumph, but a deep and profound sense of loss.

Chapter 23

THE POWERS OF DARKNESS

 or almost two days Fyodor watched over Liriel as she lay in a deathlike slumber. He did not know what had befallen the drow but suspected she'd been overcome by the banshee they'd encountered before. He'd searched for hours, finally finding the print of Liriel's elven boots on the shore near Inthar and tracking her to the tower where the banshee held sway. He'd found the young drow inside, draped limply, like a discarded garment, over the wall of the fountain, and carried her back to Ulf's cottage. But what had prompted the drow to come alone to this fell place, Fyodor could not say.

He had left her side seldom, despite the urging of the shaman and the scolding of the man's formidable wife. Yes, there were other matters demanding the attention of Holgerstead's First Axe, but the young warrior knew where lay his first loyalty. He was pledged to protect the drow *wychlaran*; he was bound to her with a web woven from the combined magics of the Underdark and Rashemen. But underlying that was something deeper still. And so the joy that flooded his heart when at last Liriel stirred and woke was not, first and foremost, that of a knight for his sworn lady.

The drow's lips formed a request; Fyodor reached for a cup of water and held her head while she drank. She struggled visibly to shake off the deadly lethargy, like a butterfly breaking free of an entangling cocoon. But her eyes, as she focused on her friend's concerned face, were clear and set with purpose.

"How long have I slept? When is moondark?"

Fyodor blinked, astonished anew by the drow's resilience. "Tomorrow night," he said absently. "Little raven, what happened to you?"

The drow brushed aside his questions and pulled herself to a sitting position. "The preparations for battle?"

"All is well. The ships are armed, the men ready."

"Good. The attack will come tomorrow, probably at dusk. I cannot be with you, so you must take this."

Liriel took the Windwalker from beneath her mattress and pressed it into his hand. "Before . . . before you found me, I enspelled the amulet to hold power over your battle rages. Wear this, and command yourself."

"And you?" he asked, his eyes searching hers.

"I am needed elsewhere," she said softly. "Take me back to Inthar, that I might summon the nereid again."

Understanding and dread came to Fyodor in a quick, sweeping wave. "You cannot return to Ascarle after all you have endured! You are not ready!"

"You have no idea what I have endured, and for that you may thank the gods," she said with uncharacteristic fervor. "As to being ready or not, I doubt the battle will wait for me or any other. If you will not help me to Inthar, I'll go alone."

And so the pledged warrior called for food to be brought, and water for washing. He waited until Liriel had readied herself; then he supported her steps until she gained the strength to walk alone.

There were few horses on Ruathym, but as First Axe of Holgerstead, Fyodor could claim any animal in the village stables. He chose two swift mounts, and the companions made their way with all possible haste to Inthar.

When they neared the ruins, Liriel dismounted and walked alone to the very edge of the steep cliff. A strong wind blew in from the sea, whipping her white hair and her glittering cloak behind her as she cupped her hands to her mouth and sent a long, high cry ringing out over the waves. Then she caught at the flying folds of her cape and wrapped them tightly around her. The drow turned back to Fyodor, and for a moment her golden eyes burned into his.

Then she was gone.

Fyodor shook the reins sharply over his horse's neck and urged the skittish beast forward to pace along the very edge of the cliff. He could see no sign of Liriel's passing; she had vanished as completely as a forgotten dream. Yet as the young man's frustrated gaze settled on the sea beyond, he understood what the drow was about.

Slipping quietly from the waves was a small army of sea folk. Fyodor recognized Xzorsh by his short-cropped green hair. Behind the ranger were perhaps a hundred sea elves, and a score or so of strange, silver-green beings, manlike but for the legs that ended in flippers rather than feet. These picked their way carefully among the rocks, heading for the ruins of Inthar.

Fyodor suddenly realized that the banshee's cry had been silenced. The portal the creature had spoken of, through which no living thing could pass, must have somehow been opened. Liriel meant to lead this army into Ascarle and stop the attack before it could come to Ruathym's shores.

Despite the fear in his heart, Fyodor reined his horse about and headed for Ruathym village, where the berserker warriors of Holgerstead awaited his orders. Liriel had her command; he had his.

* * * * *

Liriel dashed the water from her eyes and climbed from the pool in the council chamber. The familiar figure standing before her stunned her into immobility—the round, dark face, the malevolent crimson eyes, the ubiquitous pitchfork. There were many things Liriel missed about her home in Menzoberranzan. Shakti Hunzrin, her former classmate and self-avowed rival, was not one of them.

"At last I have you!" the priestess exulted. She advanced, her hand on the handle of a snake-headed whip. The enspelled reptiles rose from among the folds of her gown, writhing in anticipation.

"So you made high priestess," Liriel commented dryly. "Menzoberranzan must be in a sorry state, that the priestesshood has fallen to such depths."

"Things have changed. I wield powers that you could not begin to imagine," Shakti boasted as she drew near.

Liriel responded with a delicate yawn, patting her fingertips to her lips. As she expected, Shakti was so enraged by this contemptuous gesture that she failed to note Liriel's other hand lifting to grip the obsidian medallion hanging over her heart.

Shrieking with fury, the drow traitor-priestess drew back her arm and lashed forward viciously. But the flailing snake heads came up short, splatting wetly against an invisible wall. All five slid down the unseen barrier—leaving trails of gore as they went—to fall limp at Shakti's feet. The drow stared at the dead snakes for a moment, then lifted incredulous eyes to Liriel's face.

"Blasphemy," she hissed. "You dare to attack a symbol of Lloth with mere wizardry?"

"You dare to speak of Lloth, you who worship Vhaeraun?" returned Liriel coldly as she opened one hand to display the holy medallion. "Oh, I know your tawdry little secret. I know also why you are in this place, and the ambitions that led you here. It is you who do not know *me* for what I am, or you would not have relaxed the mind shields that served you so well in Menzoberranzan!"

Understanding crept over Shakti's stunned face. "You are a priestess of Lloth? The Spider Queen has not abandoned you?"

"Not yet," Liriel replied grimly. "But if I were you, I wouldn't be too quick to give up hope."

"Then I challenge you," the other priestess returned, a weird light entering her crimson eyes. "Let us see once and for all who holds the true favor of Lloth!"

Liriel shrugged. She stood, arms crossed, while the Hunzrin priestess chanted a fervent prayer, pleading for some sign of the goddess's presence and favor. It was a common enough spell, one cast nightly in the temples of the great houses and the chapel of the clerical school, Arach-Tinilith. From time to time Lloth rewarded her faithful with a sign of favor, such as a skittering rush of spiders, the creation of a magic item, the appearance of an otherworldly handmaiden such as a yochlol and, rarely, a visitation by an avatar. On rare occasions, warring priestesses used the spell to face off in a duel. If Lloth ignored the contest, both priestesses were summarily put to death. But if one priestess was favored, she was accounted the winner and could demand death, dethronement, or worse for her vanquished rival.

Never once in her greedy and ambitious life had Shakti desired anything so much as she craved this victory. She poured forth all her strength, all the force of her pent-up hatred and rage, into the clerical spell. Fueling her anger was the utter absence of concern—indeed, the seeming lack of interest—on Liriel's beautiful face. Ever had it been so. What Shakti desired passionately had meant little to the Baenre princess, who seemed to take for granted that all things would go as she willed them. It would not be so this time, Shakti exulted as she felt the surge of dark power growing within.

And yet . . .

Shakti's chanting voice fell silent as the summoned manifestation of Lloth took shape before her. Her prayer had been rewarded with the rarest, most powerful manifestation of Lloth's power: the creation of an avatar. Yet the young priestess did not count herself the victor. The form the Spider Queen had chosen to take was that of Shakti's most hated rival. Lloth herself gazed at Shakti through Liriel Baenre's golden eyes.

Liriel raised hands that crackled with dark energy and pointed them at the stunned priestess. A wave of power surged forward and engulfed Shakti. There was a sharp, quick burst of light and sound, and then an arid silence, like that left behind after lightning's strike. A wisp of sulphurous steam rose from the place where the lesser priestess had stood.

Well done, applauded a voice in Liriel's mind.

The drow turned slowly, still thrumming with the waning power of Lloth, and faced Vestress.

Shakti is dead? the illithid inquired.

"Returned to the Abyss," Liriel said in a voice that was not yet entirely her own. "She may well make her way home from there, for the priestesses of Lloth are adept at traveling the lower planes. Yet she is lost to you, illithid!"

Vestress shrugged, a gesture ill-suited to her misshapen form. *The loss is not so great. You will rule Ruathym for a time, amass what power you need, and then return to the Underdark. I have lost one drow and gained another; it is a fair exchange.*

Liriel did not comment. "The tapestry," she demanded.

Ah, yes. You are full of contradictions, drow. I find your obsession with freeing the enslaved sea elves most curious, especially considering the shawl you wear at your waist, Vestress said slyly.

With a shrug, Liriel acknowledged the hit. She wielded the power of Lloth; she wore the token of an enslaved nereid. The illithid was taunting her, pointing out that Liriel's methods were little different from those used by Vestress herself.

So be it.

The first, immobilizing blast of power took Vestress by surprise. Before the illithid could rally, before she could summon her own strength of mind and magic, the icy hand of Lloth closed around her.

The illithid's blank white eyes focused on the drow, and with the coarse and common power of physical sight Vestress at last perceived what her mental powers had failed to tell her: for the first time in centuries, Vestress had underestimated an opponent. She accepted her failure and waited for the killing strike to come.

But this was not the way of Lloth, or the vengeful creature who channeled the dark goddess's power.

"You will stay here in Ascarle," Liriel Baenre proclaimed in a voice that resounded with power. "We may yet have need of the information network you control. But you will stand here until the end of this day, beyond the reach of sword or spell, and watch the destruction of your army and the end of your plans for conquest."

And thus it was. Unable to move, unable to strike, Vestress watched helplessly as the first of the sea-elven invaders emerged from the magical portal.

Chapter 24
THE BATTLE FOR RUATHYM

zorsh pulled up short at the sight of the strange squid-faced creature and the grim expression on the face of his drow friend.

Liriel pointed to a doorway on the far side of the chamber. "The tapestry you seek is in a room beyond that one. Do not fear the illithid—she cannot harm you. Good luck."

The sea elf nodded. He waited until all his forces had poured through the portal and Liriel had slipped back into the pool to return to Ruathym. Xzorsh had hoped she would fight beside him, but he realized that a deeper loyalty commanded the drow's heart. It was not in him to envy another, but he hoped Fyodor of Rashemen treasured what the gods had given him.

Xzorsh retrieved the tapestry and then turned his full attention to the coming battle. It was difficult to ignore the wonders around him. All his life he had heard tales of lost Ascarle, and a part of him longed to explore the legend, to search for the lost treasures left by elves who had raised the crystal walls and imbued the city with such magic that he could feel it, even now.

But the sea elf turned and strode purposefully from the room of marble and magic, leading his forces toward Ascarle's slaves. When the slaves were free, and armed, he would turn them against the merrow who had captured and enslaved them. This evil must be routed from the seas, for the good of all peace-loving sea folk.

The sea elves and their triton allies crept down the winding halls. The city was eerily silent, and their webbed feet made soft patting noises on the marble floors as they made their way toward the slave quarters. Weapons at the ready, they edged into the buildings and moved cautiously into the long halls that led past rows of caged prisoners.

At first all went well. There were a few somnolent guards, but these were easily overcome by thrusts from the tritons' three-pronged weapons. As the tritons stood watch, the sea elves set to work, with metal picks and small, keen saws, on the door locks and chains. Quickly they freed one room of slaves after another. Hope entered the eyes of even the most wretched of these, and they fell in behind their rescuers, gathering up weapons as they went from the bodies of the fallen sea ogres.

A whisper of air moving over wings was the only warning of the coming attack. The invaders spun. Sweeping toward them from the far end of the corridor was a swarm of fearful creatures, swift and silent as manta rays but hideous beyond description. Some of the elves managed to throw themselves to the ground; others were seized in stony talons and carried away, struggling like mice in the claws of enormous owls.

"Kapoacinth!" shouted Xzorsh, warning those behind him. His forces carried no weapons that could defend against gargoyles— creatures of animated stone. "Flee this place! To the portal!"

But from the corridors beyond came the clatter of weaponry and the triumphant, guttural shouts of many merrow. The sea elves had been caught in an ambush between two deadly forces.

The elven ranger darted a glance up and down the corridors. Most of the slaves had been freed and were joining their rescuers in desperate battle. Only a few prisoners remained, but the entrance to that corridor was blocked by a trio of nine-foot sea ogres.

Xzorsh drew his knife and raced toward the enormous creatures. Grinning horribly, they raised their spears and charged forward to meet the ridiculous challenge. With his free hand, the sea elf tore the drow's throwing spiders from his belt and hurled them, first one, then the other, at the advancing merrow. The ranger's aim was true, and two of the sea ogres went down at once, pawing frantically at the animated steel that burrowed deep into scale and flesh. Without missing a step, Xzorsh gutted the third merrow as he raced past.

There was a ring of keys on a hook; these he took and quickly unlocked one door after another. These prisoners did not have to be told what to do; with eyes bright with battle-lust they charged toward the creatures that had enslaved them. Only once did Xzorsh pause, startled by the eerily familiar face of a tall Northwoman. But he set her free and pressed an ogre's knife into her hands. She thanked him with a grim nod and strode purposefully toward the battle.

The door of the last cage was already open, but the sea elf slumped within did not stir. Thinking the elf had been wounded, Xzorsh went in and placed a hand on his shoulder. With a lightning-fast stroke, the elf slashed a knife across the hand meant to support and comfort him.

The ranger leaped back, staring with dismay into the leering face of his partner and friend.

"You should have believed the drow," Sittl said. He lunged again as he came to his feet, his dripping blade leaping for the ranger's throat.

Xzorsh parried the strike. "I did believe her, as I believed you until your own words proved you a liar."

"Unlikely," sneered the malenti. "I made no mistake that a trusting fool such as you might notice."

"The dead child, the one found aboard the ship," the ranger returned coldly. "You told me she was yours in order to gain my sympathy and thus cover a lapse in your facade. But I found the child's true father; he fights at my side."

"I don't see anyone with you at the moment."

With this taunt, Sittl advanced in a flurry of slashing blows. Xzorsh held him off, but his wounded hand was numb and his grip made slippery by his own blood. In moments, Sittl knocked the weapon from Xzorsh's hand. A wide smirk spread across the malenti's elflike face. "You do not know how many times I have longed for this moment," he exulted.

The triumphant smile disappeared as his head was jerked sharply back to strike the metal bar of the cage with a sharp thud. White hands deftly wrapped Sittl's long, plaited hair around his neck. Holding the braid in both hands, the Northwoman leaned back hard, throwing the force of her weight behind the impromptu garrote. Although Sittl's webbed hands tore at his treacherous braid, he could not dislodge it from his throat. His eyes bulged, and his tongue protruded, wagging in a grotesque and silent counterpoint to the Northwoman's furious battle cry.

Merciful Xzorsh picked up his knife and ended the creature's life in one quick stroke. Then he and the Northwoman began to fight their way back toward their overwhelmed and retreating forces.

* * * * *

Rethnor raised his eyeglass and gazed with satisfaction at the battle raging before him. The darkening sky was bright with flaming arrows and the leaping flames of burning ships. Somehow Ruathym had seen beyond the rumors of a raid and had mustered an impressive sea force to meet the invasion. Even so, a fleet of thirty Luskan warships could more than match the motley flotilla that came to meet them.

Nearly as destructive as the fire, and almost invisible in the gathering darkness, were the two water elementals that surged and retreated, dealing swift blows to the Ruathen vessels and then disappearing into the waves. The water wraith, Iskor, was doing her work well. Rethnor smiled broadly as a dragon ship was capsized by the force and fury of an elemental's attack.

Then, before his astonished gaze, the sea stirred wildly, and an enormous serpentine creature rose from the waves and *of* the waves. The gargantuan water snake spoke in a roar audible even through the distance that separated Rethnor from the battle. The elementals responded at once. Acting in concert, the creatures lifted a Luskan warship from the water, upended it, and drove it prow-first into the sea. Rethnor waited, breath abated, for the ship to bob to the surface.

It did not.

And neither did the elementals reappear. The watery sea serpent, however, advanced upon the nearest of Rethnor's ships. It dove over the ship and circled around, looping it twice, three times, in its enormous coils. When the ship was utterly engulfed, the creature began to squeeze; in moments the wooden ship splintered with a boom like that of summer thunder. The creature sank into the waves, drawing the ruined ship toward whatever watery hell had spawned its captor.

Rethnor cursed bitterly. Such horrors could only mean the drow wizard was still alive, and more powerful than before. He trained his eyeglass toward the shore, drawn by a light shining high above on the rocky cliffs. There, blazing against the night sky, was a tiny, familiar figure limned with light and magic. The wizard floated in the air, her dark hands outstretched like the talons of a striking hawk.

Well, there was one way to bring the thrice-damned elf wench to heel. The High Captain swept his eyeglass over the remaining warships. On one of these raged a battle too fierce to be natural: the berserkers of Holgerstead spent their fury against a hundred of Luskan's finest fighters. And fighting beside the wild, yellow-braided warriors was a ferocious, dark-haired youth whom Rethnor knew only too well.

A grim smile spread across the High Captain's bearded face,

and he signaled the helmsman to pull in close to the beleaguered warship. He would have his revenge, but first he would see what price the elf wench might be willing to pay for the young man's life.

* * * * *

Liriel floated high over the ruins of Inthar, her keen elven eyes taking in the battle raging below. To her surprise, her very presence seemed to have a rallying effect on some of the fighters. On a nearby ship, a scarlet-clad warrior pointed to her and shouted to his men that the Raven had taken flight, the better to guide the souls of their enemies into death. The drow recognized the voice of Glammad, First Axe of Hastor. Once she had saved his life from the sahuagin; twice he had spoken for her. Liriel was more than happy to even the score. She sent a stream of fireballs hurtling toward the warships that pressed in on either side of the ships from Hastor. The men cheered her wildly as the Luskan fighting ships exploded into smoldering kindling.

The drow did not pause to savor this triumph. With wizardly spells she had summoned a water weird, a creature from the elemental plane that could seize control of water elementals. At her command, the serpentine creature had turned the elementals against one Luskan ship, then destroyed another. But the effort of keeping such a creature on this plane was draining; Liriel could feel herself slipping down toward the stony cliff. She quickly dispelled the water weird, on the condition that it take the other creatures back to the elemental plane with it. The sea serpent eagerly agreed and fled back to its watery home.

But that did not solve the source of this problem: somewhere nearby was a creature powerful enough to command the beings of the elemental plane. Liriel had to seek out and destroy that creature. She unknotted the white shawl from her waist and shouted a command to the nereid who cringed in the water below. The creature emerged, gesturing wildly toward the shore nearby.

Liriel looked, her amber eyes widening with surprise. Dancing along the shore and, like some delighted child, clapping her glassy hands at each new destruction was the strangest creature the drow had yet seen. Although shaped like a woman, the beautiful thing encased a bubbling fountain within her glossy, transparent skin. Liriel had read about water wraiths—they were flighty, capricious creatures, often acting as messengers for the gods—but none of

298

these sources gave any hint as to how such creatures could be fought.

Inspiration came to the drow in the form of a remembered party trick, one of the mischievous cantrips that Menzoberranzan's dark elves loved to cast to tease and taunt each other.

"Take my regards to Umberlee," the drow murmured wrathfully. She cast a small spell and drew in a long, deep breath. Cupping her hands to her lips, Liriel sent a single note, as pure and high-pitched as that of an elven flute, soaring out over the waves.

The water wraith looked up, her beautiful, glassy face contorted with surprise and pain. Her form began to shudder as the magically enhanced sound resonated through her. The bubbles within roiled frantically, building up in force and speed. Finally the creature exploded in a spray of water and glassy fragments.

Liriel's keening song ended in a burst of wild laughter. Even to her own ears, the sound held a touch of hysteria. She was nearing the limits of her power, and the battle was nowhere near its end.

Even as the thought formed, the sound of clashing blades rang through the ancient stone keep below her. A handful of battered sea elves staggered out of the tower, only to fall under the surging charge of wave after wave of well-armed merrow.

Liriel knew a moment's despair. The battle for Ascarle had been lost; the invaders had broken through. The sea ogres swept down the hillside toward nearby Ruathym village, where no warriors awaited them. The drow had seen the destruction ogres could accomplish, had heard stories of how they treated the women and young ones who fell into their taloned hands. To prevent such a thing, she would do whatever needed to be done.

Liriel's shaking fingers fumbled for her obsidian pendant, and she steeled her will and numbed her soul to accept what she must once again become.

*   *   *   *   *

Fyodor swung out high, his sword blocking the downward sweep of a Luskar battle-axe. With his free hand he punched forward and spattered the warrior's nose across his bearded face. The enormous man let out an incongruous whimper and then fell face first to the deck.

The young berserker stepped over the fallen man and looked around for his next fight. Beneath his tunic the Windwalker amulet seemed to burn with cold fire against his skin—painful, yes, but the drow's magic held true. For the first time in many months, Fyodor was in full control of his fighting power. Yet he took no joy in battle, nor did he exult in the deaths of those who fell before his black sword. It was a necessary thing, to protect the land that had sheltered him and Liriel and to lead the berserker brothers who trusted in his strong arm and quick wits.

The young man nimbly sidestepped an onrushing warrior. The Northman's enormous broadsword plunged deep into the ship's mast and stayed there, quivering slightly. Fyodor backhanded the weaponless warrior and sent him sprawling. The man spit teeth, lurched to his feet, and came in again. Suppressing a sigh, Fyodor seized the hilt of the impaled sword and pulled it back toward him in a curving arc. With a swordsmith's sure instincts, he released the weapon a moment before it would have shattered. The sword sprang back into place with an audible twang—at the precise moment that its owner stepped into its path. The flat of the sword caught the man at waist level. His feet flew up, his arms went wide, and his head hit hard as he measured his length on the ship's deck. This time, he stayed down.

Next Fyodor ran to the aid of a Holgerstead berserker whose axe was hard pressed by four Luskar swordsmen. He fell in at his brother's back, parrying a sword strike as he tapped the man's hip in a prearranged signal. Once, twice more Fyodor parried the Northman who engaged his blade, taking care that the strikes were loud enough to ring above the clamor of battle. Then he lunged, running the Northman through and heaving him off the blade with one quick movement. In the next breath, Fyodor spun, swinging his black sword with all the force of his Rashemi might and magic.

As he did, the Holgersteader went down on one knee. Fyodor's blade whistled over his brother's head—and through the necks of all three men who had faced him. There was no time for any of the Northmen to raise a parrying sword, no arm with the strength to stop such a blow. Three heads tumbled to the deck, still wearing the triumphant leers of men who had been sure of their prey.

The Holgersteader lunged upward, arms spread wide, catching the headless bodies as they fell and then hurling them into the paths of two approaching fighters. The Luskar warriors instinctively veered away from the horror; the berserker coolly advanced upon the unnerved men, his dripping axe held high.

Seeing that matters here were well in hand, Fyodor turned his attention to the battle beyond the Holgerstead ship. Another warship approached them at ramming speed. Standing in the bow, his black-bearded face suffused with an unholy glee, was someone Fyodor knew. The faces of the slain had fled from his dreams, but for good or ill, the memory of each of his battles was his again. He remembered fighting this man, remembered severing the man's sword hand. Yet the man gripped his sword with obvious anticipation, and his eyes burned into Fyodor's as the warship closed the distance between them.

The young First Axe shouted an alarm, sending Holgerstead archers to the port rail to meet the new attack. Fyodor had no doubt that he would meet this man in battle before the fighting was through.

At that moment a thunderous explosion sent waves rocking out to sea with a force that defied the sea's natural rhythm. Fyodor grabbed for a handhold and turned his gaze toward the shore. What had been two Luskar warships now littered the sea as bits of smoking flotsam. For a moment he knew mingled joy and relief; this could only be Liriel's work. She had returned, triumphant, from Ascarle!

But as his eyes followed the trail of shining magic, they lifted to the skies above Inthar and to the tiny, gallant figure that floated there. Before his disbelieving and horrified gaze, Liriel took on size and power, much as a berserker did at the onset of a fury. But never in his life had Fyodor sensed such a cloud of evil as that which surrounded the drow, crackling with dark energy and malevolent delight.

At that moment, Fyodor knew that confrontation between him and Liriel, so long in coming and so painfully denied by them both, was at hand. How she would choose, he could not begin to say.

* * * * *

The Northwoman burst from the watery portal like a breaching dolphin and hurled herself, knife leading, at the back of the merrow who had preceded her. She clung to the creature as it leaped, howling, over the wall of the little pool. The sea ogre whirled, swatting frantically at the woman who clung like a burr just beyond the reach of its black-taloned hands. She stabbed again, driving the knife in viciously. The merrow slipped in its own blood and fell to the stone floor.

Elaine Cunningham

Xzorsh climbed from the water, astonished at the woman's fury. Her cold blue eyes settled upon him, and she seized his wrist, hurling the much slighter elf into the path of a merrow who was turning, an aggrieved expression on its hideous face, to see why its comrade had tripped and jostled it.

Xzorsh reacted with an elf's quick reflexes. He brought up his knife and braced his elbow against his side, letting the force of the Northwoman's swing drive the knife home. The astonished merrow wheezed as the blade went in, sending a burst of foul breath over the sea elf. Xzorsh yanked the knife free and sidestepped the falling ogre.

"Who are you?" he demanded of the woman in a wondering tone.

"Ygraine, oldest daughter of Ulf the shaman," the girl gritted out. "I will not see those creatures enslave my village as they did me. Will your sea people fight?"

"They will, with you to inspire them," the sea elf said with deep admiration, ready to yield his command to one whose passion and commitment outstripped even his. He motioned for her to wait, and together they helped the rest of the freed slaves from the portal. When the last of them had emerged, Ygraine of Ruathym led the charge down the hillside toward the village. Her fierce, keening battle cries roused and rallied the women waiting below.

They poured out of their cottages to meet the attacking sea ogres. Few of them owned swords or knew the art of fighting, but all had chopped kindling and knew the handling of an axe; all had slaughtered hogs with the coming of autumn and could wield a butcher's knife with swift authority; all had turned the soil with pitchforks, and speared fish with lightning-fast thrusts. These homely tools came into play now as Ruathym's women remembered their warrior heritage.

With a fierce intensity that would have given pause to many of their battle-seasoned menfolk, the women fell upon the invaders. And at their sides fought the sea elves. The Northwomen did not seem to remember or care that they had accounted the elves enemies earlier that same day.

The sound of pounding on the door of a familiar wooden building drew Xzorsh's attention. The sea elf ran to the prison that had once held him and his treacherous friend. He recognized the voice within and quickly threw back the bolt that kept Caladorn of Waterdeep imprisoned. The tall fighter pried a sword from the fist of a fallen merrow and leaped into the fray. Behind him, reluctantly at first but with growing fervor, the two surviving seal hunters fought their way deeper into the frenzied, terrifying, exhilarating melee that swept through the village like a wave of death.

And in the frenzy, no one noticed that the disgraced daughter of Ulf crept from the prison and made her way to the fisherfolk's cove.

* * * * *

When at last no more elves emerged from the tower, Liriel began to chant the words to a spell that would close the portal for all time. It was a difficult spell, made more taxing by the impatient, insistent power that coursed through her in a dark and pulsing tide. The Lady of Chaos had little love for the orderly discipline of wizardly magic.

But Liriel pressed on, summoning all the power she could call her own, channeling it into one final, desperate spell. At last the ancient tower began to shake. Cracks rippled upward from the base, and the keep that had withstood the centuries collapsed into a pile of dust and rubble.

Liriel coughed, choking on the clouds of roiling dust, and instinctively moved farther out to sea. She felt her innate levitation magic slip away, and she recognized, dimly, that there was nothing between her and the jagged rocks below but the power of a capricious goddess.

The girl's hand lifted, without act of will, and spat dark fire at a Luskar ship. The oiled canvas of the sail turned into a sheet of flame. Nearby a small Ruathen ship tossed wildly, rocked by the hands of a score of vengeful nereids. Pulses of energy coursed from Liriel's outstretched fingers into the sea near the beleaguered ship, heating the water around it to an instant boil. The screams of the scalded nymphs could be heard even over the sounds of battle and the crackle of burning ships.

But to Liriel's ears, the only sound was the wild, exultant laughter that rang through her benumbed mind. Her defenses down, her strength spent, the young drow was utterly open to the power that held her in its demented hands. She felt with horrifying clarity each death, and Lloth's delight in it.

She had promised the Spider Queen a victory, but the chaotic goddess seemed to have lost sight of this goal amid the wondrous carnage of the moment. It did not seem to matter to the blood-drunk

Elaine Cunningham

Lloth whether the slain were invaders or defenders, merrow or sea elves. There was no purpose to the killing, and no apparent end.

Liriel knew the depths of her own folly and bitterly regretted the course she had taken. Fyodor had warned her that there was a price for power; she should have realized that Lloth's would have to be paid in blood.

* * * * *

Despite the force of the battle rage that coursed through him, Fyodor could not take his eyes from the drow who floated above the haunted ruins. Never had she appeared so beautiful . . . or so deadly. She was no longer just Liriel, but a conduit for sheer, evil power. Many times he had seen her channel magic that seemed a burden too heavy for one so seemingly frail. This time, he knew with the surety of Sight, that unless he could stop her, Liriel would be consumed by the dark flame.

"Think, think," he admonished himself fiercely. He searched his storehouse of Rashemi tales and legends for inspiration, his frenzy-enhanced mind flashing from one possibility to the next. None told him how to challenge an elven goddess.

In desperation, Fyodor reached for the Windwalker, the ancient amulet that had linked him with the drow from the beginning. With it, Liriel had lent him the ability to control his berserker magic—and perhaps, to press its limits to untried heights.

With grim determination the young man sought a berserker's ultimate power, the *hamfarir*, which would send his spirit forth to do battle in the shape of some mighty animal.

The wind of the shapeshifting rage had seemed a small thing compared to the change that now swept through him. Fyodor's spirit tore free of his physical form with a sensation that went far beyond pain. Leaving his body behind on the embattled ship, Fyodor willed himself into the form of a giant raven and sped forward to snatch Liriel from the hands of her goddess.

Chapter 25
AS ONE

he sweep of wind from enormous wings buffeted the exhausted drow. Instinctively she raised her hands to attack as a creature the size of a small dragon closed in upon her—a looming blackness that blotted out the stars.

At the last moment, the bird veered away, its wing feathers brushing her face with a gentleness that was oddly familiar. It seemed to anticipate the drow's attack; Liriel's bolt of killing magic sizzled harmlessly into the night sky. She struggled to focus on the bird. It was a raven, with eyes the color of a winter sky. In some distant part of her mind, Liriel remembered the time that Wedigar had fallen upon her and Fyodor, clad in the form of a giant hawk. That hawk's eyes had been gray—like Wedigar's. At last she understood the nature of the avian beast.

So also did the power that gripped her. Rage, fierce and possessive and all-consuming, rose in Liriel like flame. As the giant raven circled around for another pass, the young drow priestess felt the inexorable demand of her goddess for the sacrifice required of all who walked the pathways of Lloth. Before Liriel could protest, the killing flame crackled ready at her fingertips. She watched, helpless and despairing, as Fyodor came steadily toward his death.

But the words of the shaman, spoken not long before, cut through the fog that clouded the drow's benumbed thoughts. "Our dealings with the gods are more honest. We name a bargain. If the god doesn't hold up his end of the deal, we call it off and go our own way. Why should we hold mortals to higher standards than gods?"

"Victory," Liriel murmured, taking strength from Ulf's remembered words. "Queen of Spiders, I promised you a victory; in return, you demand the death of one who above all others could help ensure it!"

With her last vestige of physical strength, the young drow tore the obsidian pendant from her neck and hurled the hated thing toward the sea. The fire magic that danced ready at her fingertips sped after it, flashing down into the sea and sending a geyser of salty steam jetting into the night sky.

"I have fulfilled my pledge to you, Mother Lloth," she whispered. "I am priestess no longer. From this moment until the time of my death, I will have nothing more to do with you. This I swear, by all the power I call my own."

Suddenly cut off from the evil power that had both sustained and tormented her, Liriel began to plummet toward the rock-strewn coast. Giant claws closed around her with startling gentleness; utterly spent, the drow allowed the blue-eyed raven to bear her away.

*   *   *   *   *

Despite the tumult of battle, Rethnor noted the mysterious fall of his berserker nemesis. As his warriors engaged the Holgerstead fighters, he stalked up to the dark-haired youth. This was not the battle he had craved, but it would have to do. Rethnor was not one to let an opportunity pass. The Luskar captain raised his sword high, preparing to cut down the defenseless fighter in a single stroke.

A woman's furious shriek startled him into immobility. Rethnor barely had time to swing his sword into defensive position before a familiar, pale-haired girl hurled herself toward him, armed only with a knife such as might be used to gut and clean a large fish. Rethnor instinctively parried the strike.

"Ygraine?" he muttered, staring with consternation at the illithid's slave.

"Dagmar," the girl spat.

The Luskar smiled grimly. He knew of this wench. Although he did not often fight women, it would give him pleasure to cut her down. Her cold ambition, her willingness to kill even her own sister to appease her ambitions, was enough to sicken even the hardened High Captain.

But Dagmar did not yield to death so easily. With a fury that defied even his expert swordsmanship, the Northwoman pressed Rethnor back toward the rail.

"You have failed—all is lost!" she shrieked at him. "Ygraine lives; I am disgraced! You have commanded this from the start. Take me away from this place, promise me a place of power in your land, or die now at my hand!"

As she spoke, one of the Holgerstead berserkers tossed away his sword and strode toward the embattled girl. Before Rethnor's disbelieving eyes, the man's face shifted, becoming fierce and furred. In moments an enormous wolf stood in the berserker's place, blue eyes gleaming and lips curled back in a feral snarl.

The clatter of weapons echoed here and there as other Holgersteaders changed and joined the pack. Rethnor backed away slowly as the Wolves of the Waves, the legendary defenders of Ruathym, began to close in with deadly intent.

Dagmar saw the horror in her opponent's face and whirled to face the new threat. A wild joy filled her eyes as she beheld the ever-tightening circle of shapeshifters.

"She is dead at last," Dagmar said in a wondering tone. "Ygraine must have fallen in battle, and the prophecy is mine to fulfill!"

"Not so, Sister."

A second feminine voice rang out over the ship as Dagmar's twin clambered over the rail.

"The battle for Ruathym village is won," Ygraine said. She walked across the deck, her hands outstretched to her twin. "Our homeland is safe, the ancient glory restored to our warriors. Between you and me, nothing lies beyond the power of forgiveness. Come home with me, my sister!"

The truth of the situation struck Dagmar with the force of one of the drow's fireballs. It was Ygraine who had rekindled the shapeshifting magic! It was ever, *always* Ygraine! It was she who had received the power of the prophecy, the deepest love of their parents, the troth of the future First Axe. In all things, Ygraine had been chosen above Dagmar—even the pirates of Luskan had chosen Ygraine when they needed one sister to hold captive!

"How I hate you," Dagmar said in a low, burning voice.

Ygraine flinched, but she continued to walk slowly toward the furious girl. "Come with me, Sister. Perhaps the healers can ease your mind and your heart, and restore you to your kindred. I will speak for you before the Thing and ask that this be done."

"How many of your cast-offs must I accept? I will die before I take refuge in your secondhand honor!" Dagmar shrieked as she raised her weapon for a killing lunge.

"That you will," the other woman said softly, "and soon, unless you put down the knife. The Wolves of the Waves cannot long be held back."

Dagmar looked down, and for the first time she noticed that the shape-changed warriors were closing not on Rethnor, but on her. Indeed, there was no sign of the Luskar captain. He had disappeared, along with her last chance of becoming something more than Ygraine's pale shadow.

The low growls of the advancing wolves sent a tremor through the half-mad girl; a moment more, and they would be upon her. Dagmar lifted her eyes, seized her sister's beseeching gaze, and held it fast. Then she lifted her knife and thrust it deep into her own heart. A cry of anguish burst from Ygraine, and she leaped forward to catch her sister as she fell.

And with her last bit of strength, Dagmar spit in her sister's despairing face.

* * * * *

In the water below, Rethnor swam for his ship with strong, steady strokes. The battle was lost, and with it his ambitions of conquest, his lust for vengeance. The failed attack on Ruathym would carry a heavy price. There would be Nine Hells to pay at home, as well as increased pressure from Waterdeep and the Lords' Alliance. But Rethnor had weathered worse. He was fairly confident of his ability to hold on to his power as High Captain of Luskan, perhaps even his position as an agent of the Kraken Society.

In the future, however, he would know enough to steer clear of dark elves and illithids. His failures and humiliation at the hands of these strange females grated upon Rethnor's pride. But at least his forces had dealt a devastating blow to the island. He was confident the conquest of Ruathym would come in time, even though this night's battle had been lost.

* * * * *

The giant raven circled low over the ruins of Inthar, coming down to a sheltered nook and gently dropping the exhausted drow. Liriel struggled to her feet, wishing to throw her arms around the creature's glossy neck. To her horror, the avian apparition began to fade away. There was a deep contentment in the raven's human eyes, and an expression of selfless love that would haunt the drow until all her centuries of life had been spent. There was no time given her to speak, to so much as lift a hand in farewell, before the raven disappeared.

Liriel's anguished cry echoed through the haunted ruins. She, too, had heard the Ruathen stories of the *hamfarir,* and she knew only too well what this meant. Fyodor was gone—perhaps slain by some coward as his abandoned body lay defenseless in battle, or perhaps his wandering spirit had not been able to find its way back in time.

Always Liriel had known that her journey would not come without great cost, but this was the one price she had not been prepared to pay.

* * * * *

His task completed, his heart at peace, Fyodor's spirit left the drow in safety and soared back to the ship where lay his body. For a moment he floated above the Holgerstead ship, aware of the battle raging below and the triumph of shapeshifting might that had come over his berserker brethren. But he could do nothing to join them. The immense effort of the *hamfarir* had taken its toll.

The young Rashemi felt a call that was somehow familiar, a pull too powerful to be denied. He knew a moment's regret for the grieving drow, but then he was beyond all such considerations. Fyodor yielded himself to the summons, and at long last the wandering warrior felt his spirit unite with the magic that was both his heritage and his curse.

Chapter 26
SONG OF THE SKALDS

n the aftermath of battle, the surviving Ruathen began to understand the extent—and the cost—of their victory. The forces that had been arrayed against them had been turned aside, the invaders either destroyed or forced to flee. And the shapeshifting magic had returned in force to the fighters of Holgerstead. The ancient glories of their ancestors seemed once again within reach. This gave hope to the survivors even as they went about the grim business of tallying their losses and mourning their dead. The songs of the skalds would be long indeed, but at least they would tell tales of heroism and glory.

As the drow had expected, Fyodor was among those brought lifeless from the ships. For reasons she could not understand, Liriel could not bear to consign him to the funeral pyre. Taking his cold hands in hers, she summoned a gate that would take them both to the foot of Yggsdrasil's Child.

As she knelt beside the body of her dearest friend, memories of her drow upbringing crept into Liriel's mind, bringing with them a temptation beyond any she had ever known. It was her habit to yield promptly to impulse, but the enormity of this thought stole her breath: a powerful cleric of any faith could resurrect the dead. She could petition Lloth for one last clerical spell—one powerful enough to restore Fyodor to her!

And why not? she asked herself passionately. What was the evil of Lloth, compared to the good that was left undone by this man's having been snatched from life too soon? All that Fyodor had done for Ruathym, all he might do for his beloved homeland—did this not outweigh the cost of one more prayer to the goddess of the drow?

Yet even as she formed the thought, Liriel knew what Fyodor would have wanted her to do. He had died to snatch her from Lloth's hand; she would not dishonor that, or him. And to her surprise, Liriel realized the pledge she herself had made possessed a value of its own.

"Honor," she said softly, understanding the legacy Fyodor had left her. This she had, and her memories, and the Windwalker. She would keep the amulet as a tangible reminder of her promise to never again seek power through evil, no matter how worthy the end.

The Windwalker still hung about Fyodor's neck. Liriel gently undid the chain and clasped the amulet in one hand. To her astonishment, the amulet thrummed with power. The berserker magic she stored within was still strong!

Strong enough, perhaps, to lure a wandering spirit into its enchanted depths?

Hardly daring to hope, the drow twisted open the amulet and released the captured magic—and perhaps something even more precious. Her eyes darted toward the darkening sky and to the sliver of new moon that rose above the clearing. Instinctively she rose and began to dance, knowing as she did that such was a prayer to a goddess of a very different kind.

* * * * *

Fyodor awakened slowly, unaccountably stiff until he recalled the battle he had endured and the dangerous shapeshifting journey he had taken. He remembered nothing of what had happened after that. He blinked painfully, trying to find some focus.

A faint light drew his eyes, and a slow smile crossed his face. In the clearing before him, Liriel danced in the moonlight. The silvery radiance of Eilistraee clung to her like a shining cloak, and the aura of evil that had surrounded her during the battle was utterly gone.

"Little raven," he called softly.

The drow stopped dancing at once, and the fey silver light fled from her like a startled fawn. Only her eyes glowed—strangely, intensely—as she advanced upon the Rashemi warrior. From one outstretched hand dangled the Windwalker.

"Return to the village," she said softly, but her voice held the force of command. "There you will find a circle of skalds, singing the stories of Ruathym's heroic dead. Summon your berserker frenzy and silence them!"

For a long moment Fyodor stared at the drow, fearing mightily that she had lost her wits—and perhaps her soul—under the strain of her Lloth-granted power. Then he saw the joy shining in her eyes, and it dawned on him that he need not obey her command.

At long last, they were both truly free.

EPILOGUE

tay with us and make your home on Ruathym," urged Aumark Lithyl as he stood at water's edge with the Rashemi and the drow. "There is a place of honor here for you both."

Days had passed since the battle's end, and life on the island had fallen back into its familiar routine. Fyodor's gaze swept the now-familiar landscape, taking in the village beyond the cove and the hills that cast long green shadows over both. In this wild and warlike land he had truly found a home, and he discovered to his surprise that the leavetaking did not come easily.

"Wedigar is nearly well, and he can choose his successor from any number of shapestrong heirs. He has released me from my pledge; I am honor-bound to return to Rashemen," he replied simply.

Aumark nodded, accepting the young warrior's duty. "And what of you?" the First Axe asked, turning to Liriel. "You have heard that Glammad has offered to yield the ruling of Hastor to the Raven. In ancient times, this village was led by rune-casters; it seems that all of Ruathym is eager to return to her former glories."

"Thank you, no," the drow said without hesitation or regret. "I have pledges of my own to keep. A cleric must be found who can unravel the tapestry and release the spirits of the elves and men entangled within. I must also seek tutors for a certain sea elf. Xzorsh shows genuine talent for the art of magic, but I lack the patience or the skill to teach him myself. It is one thing to do, another thing altogether to teach," she muttered with a touch of exasperation. "I know now why so many of *my* tutors quit in despair!"

Fyodor passed a hand over his lips to hide his sudden smirk, for he was certain there was more to the story than Liriel's words suggested. He could not imagine the fiery drow had been the most biddable of students.

"We must go now," he said, placing a hand on Liriel's shoulder.

She nodded and stepped lightly along the plank that rose to the deck of the waiting ship. The Ruathen crew took her presence among them in stride; the three Waterdhavian men aboard, however—the lordly young man known as Caladorn and the two seal hunters—eyed the dark elf with a mixture of dread and foreboding.

Fyodor noted this with a touch of resignation as he followed Liriel onto the ship. The measure of acceptance she had won here on Ruathym had not come easily; surely she knew life elsewhere would be an endless struggle. He wondered why the drow was so determined to leave, but he dared not hope her answer would be the one he most longed to hear.

That night, in the cabin they shared, he asked why she had refused the opportunity to rule in Ruathym.

"I have seen what power can do, and I want no part of it," Liriel said at once, snuggling into his arms like a contented cat. "I am content to be a wizard and to seek adventure. I have no ambition—and no desire—to rule anywhere. And I *will* not!" she vowed fervently.

But Fyodor believed otherwise. He had long suspected the girl was destined for a role of great power—he considered his brief, magical servitude as evidence of this. But, being wise beyond his years, he kept his opinions on the matter to himself. And holding Liriel's needs above his own dreams, he hid his deep disappointment at her answer.

"And after Waterdeep, what then? Will you return to Skullport and take a place among the chosen of Eilistraee?" he asked.

The drow recoiled as if he had struck her. "I had thought to go with you to Rashemen," she said with quiet dignity. "Or is there another who awaits you there?"

Joy flooded the young man's heart. He quickly claimed Liriel's hand and raised her fingers to his lips. "Of course I want you with me! But I know what faces you in the world and would not ask you to walk this path unless you came to it yourself. But no matter where you might have chosen to go, for so long as I live, there would be no other for me," he swore.

"Nor for me," the drow repeated. As the implication of this sunk in, her face took on an almost comic look of dismay. "One male," she muttered distractedly. "By all the gods—it isn't natural. It just isn't *done!*"

Fyodor burst out laughing; he simply couldn't help it. "I will do my best to stave off boredom," he promised her in a droll tone. "And it may comfort you to know that humans do not live so very long."

"How long is that?"

He shrugged. "Sixty, perhaps seventy years."

"That's all? Well, at least that's some consolation," Liriel said tartly, sending him an arch, sidelong glance. "It's well to know there's a reasonable end in sight!"

Fyodor chuckled, reading the truth of the matter in her golden eyes and deft hands. Apparently Liriel had come to terms with her sentence of monogamy. At the very least, she seemed determined to make the best of matters.

Much later he held the sleeping drow in his arms and thought of the journey that lay ahead. A struggle awaited them both, for dark elves were known—and hated—in his rugged homeland. His hard-pressed kinsmen would be appalled by the elf woman whom Fyodor's destiny, and his heart, had chosen for him. The hazards that lay before him and Liriel were many and real, the joys only those that they could find together, or in each other.

And yet Fyodor did not doubt that these would be enough to content them both. As to Liriel's prospects, he chided himself for dismissing them so soon. The elven girl was resilient, resourceful, and possessed of a quirky charm that spoke to hearts other than his.

"How long will it be," he murmured in jest, "before you rule among Rashemen's Witches?"

As if in response, Liriel's lips curved in a knowing smile.

For a moment, Fyodor thought his words had awakened the ever-alert elf. Yet as he studied her repose, the truth of the matter came to him slowly, and filled him with a contentment beyond words.

What thoughts sweetened her sleep, Fyodor could not say, but this much he knew: the drow had learned at last what it was to dream.